Survivors and Bandits

CHERNO JOURNO

Copyright © 2013 PDS Publishing Pty Ltd

The moral right of the author has been asserted.

Published in the United States and Australia by PDS Publishing, an imprint of the PDS group.

www.chernojourno.com

National Library Of Australia

Cataloguing-in-Publication data:

Journo, Cherno, 1977-

Survivors and Bandits / Cherno Journo

9780646593562 (pbk)

ISBN: 0646593560
ISBN-13: 978-0646593562

DEDICATION

This book is dedicated to Caz, Eva and Luca.

Most writers feel lucky to have one muse,

I'm blessed with three.

CONTENTS

SPECIAL EDITION CONTENT

ACKNOWLEDGMENTS

The creation of any book is a mammoth effort on the part of many to create a work that gets attributed to just one.

First and foremost I want to acknowledge the fans of Cherno Journo. The people I've interviewed, the players I've met, even the ones that have killed me. Due to the joys of social media, I've been lucky to have and interact with fans from all around the world. This book is for you, because without you there would be nothing.

Special mention must go out to Alex, Janik and Helmut. They have helped the Cherno Journo grow from a small idea to the founder of the Chernarus Free Press. Thanks guys.

Special mention must also go to the DayZ Development team lead by Dean (Rocket) Hall. Thanks for creating the world that has led to so many great moments and stories.

On a personal level I want to thank my long suffering editor Caroline. If anyone else saw the amount of work and effort that she put into fixing my early drafts, they would immediately demand she receive a co-writer credit. Trust me when I say she's a miracle worker to make me look good.

Most importantly I want to thank my wife and children for their love and support. You give me the strength and courage to go on writing when all I want to do is run away from that evil cursor that blinks at me daily.

SPECIAL THANKS

These special people are all funders or otherwise friends of the original Indiegogo crowd funding campaign.

Thanks goes out to each of them for their faith and support.

Alex Roudenko
Ben V. (CF Donuts) & Donut Zombies
BarbaricMustard
Cameron C.
Cole "Prof.K" Rockman
Conner P.
Dylan Mangan
Dr Faust
Derpington Steele
Endrid
Ivanlad
Janik F
JoSchaap
Josh Madden
Kevin MacLeod
Kristian Thom
Lachlan Castles – xNeon
Liam Carolan
Mandalore
Mafia Snitch
Mark Vanagas
Moochie
Puggles
Ryan
Steve T.
The Diva
Wahby
Wesley Schadan
WiseGuy

CHAPTER ONE

THE SINKING SHIP

Captain Nestorenko looked out over the coastline of Chernarus through his binoculars. It was all quiet and as expected there were no lights on anywhere. He knew this coast well - somewhere in that foreboding dark there should be two lighthouses providing beacons of safety to passing ships. Instead all he saw was a long endless blackness that was only broken by the outlines of trees, silhouetted by a backdrop of flickering stars.

The ship's First Officer Shutov was worried at being so close to the shore "Captain, this is foolhardy. We can no longer trust the GPS to ensure our position is safe"

Nestorenko nodded – Shutov was right – it was risky to traverse this area without the aid of lighthouses. But Nestorenko did because he had to see the coast for himself – he had to see if the reports about Chernarus were true. Now that he was here he realized it was a pointless endeavor.

The reports started coming in two months ago, garbled and panicked transmissions on the civilian frequencies. They spoke of ordinary citizens who suddenly turned into seemingly mindless creatures, they were called the 'infected', but the disease was never named. Mothers would turn on their own children, tearing them to shreds without hesitation, consumed by a ravenous desire to feed on the flesh of the living. The deeply religious called it Armageddon - the beginning of the end - when the dead would walk the earth.

Only the Captain should have received the reports but on such a small ship, word got around fast. At first there were jokes - no one believed that the living dead could really exist. Then the reports became more pressing, the stories so fantastic they had to be true. The Russian army had been sent in. They'd secured key locations and airports with the United States providing military help. Even in this post-Cold-War Russia it seemed fantastical that the Americans would send their troops in.

Then the troops were attacked by the infected. Unlike a traditional fighting force, the infected could not be reasoned with. They had no moral qualms, no supply lines to disrupt, their attacks were relentless and continuous until the troops were overrun. Over time, every established point was lost. The last reports were desperate and pleading 'Whatever you do, don't come to Chernarus.' That was a month ago. No further radio transmissions had been received since.

Regardless of the warnings, he still changed course for Chernarus, a flagrant misuse of his command. He brought with him a merchant ship that had forty souls on board and should have been returning to port. Chernarus was the land of the Captain's youth - he grew up just outside a small town called Zelenogorsk. He worked the docks of Elektrozavodsk until he was old enough to work on a ship. His parents were still here on their small farm. He had to come back, like visiting a terminally ill relative for the last time before they passed. He had to see Chernarus one last time.

"Shutov you're right. There's nothing here," said the Captain as he looked out over the coastline.

"Then let us be away from this coast. It was a foolish venture to come here," replied Shutov.

"And where would you have us go now?" challenged the Captain, "we've had no further radio transmission, haven't seen or heard any other ships, the world has been dead for a month. Which port will be different from Chernarus?"

"Then we stay at sea. Our provisions are good, although fuel is running low. We could last another month before needing to go ashore."

"But you're just putting off the inevitable. Sooner or later we need to face what's out there."

"Then I vote for later," replied Shutov.

The ship suddenly juddered and they heard the unmistakable sound of steel tearing, that pierced the otherwise silent night. Bedlam erupted as the ship groaned in pain. From the bow, a crewman pointed to the tear as the ship began to list.

"We've hit some rocks under the water, the tear is too great," called out the crewman.

"Captain?" Shutov asked as he watched the bewildered Captain try to stand upright while the boat leaned over, "Captain, we must abandon ship!" Shutov's words sounded less like pleading and rather like barking an order.

Nestorenko looked over at his second in command, his face expressed how defeated he felt. What was waiting on the shore for him, for the entire crew, was certain death. Almost imperceptibly he nodded, and Shutov fired into action.

Over the ship's PA system he addressed the crew. "Abandon ship. This is not a drill. The ship is sinking fast, take the survival patrol packs and swim to shore. Disregard the boats we are close to shore..." *too close* he wanted to say, "so swimming is possible. We are sinking fast. Every man to shore."

He looked out the bridge at the panicking crew jumping over the side. The smart ones waited, getting their bearings, finding a landmark to swim towards. The weak just jumped in and hoped for the best.

The bridge emptied out quickly until only Shutov and Nestorenko remained. He looked over at the Captain who was at the ship's safe, unlocking it. *What important papers could he need now?* Shutov pondered.

"Captain, shall we sweep the ship before departing?"

The Captain didn't respond and instead removed a M1911 pistol from the safe. Shutov was surprised that the Captain was thinking of weapons as he watched him load a magazine into the gun. *Yes, we would need control on the beaches and a weapon would be handy,* he mused, impressed by the Captain's foresight.

"What have I done?" asked the Captain.

"Sir?" replied Shutov, bemused.

"Are the men off the ship?"

"We need to check to be certain, but it appears so."

"And they are swimming to the shore, to the infected coastline of Chernarus."

"Yes sir, that is where you brought us."

"So I ask you again - what have I done?"

"Sir I'm confused, we need to check the ship and swim to shore."

The Captain snapped back the pistol loading a bullet into the chamber. He raised the gun and pointed it at Shutov.

"Stop kissing my God damn arse and answer the question. What have I done?"

"You fucked up! You brought us here to this God forsaken place and most likely killed us all," Shutov yelled back, unable to control his rage.

The Captain was taken aback by Shutov's outburst.

"Thank you Shutov for being honest this one time," said the Captain.

Shutov was momentarily confused until the Captain put the pistol to the side of his head and pulled the trigger. In the small room the gunshot and its accompanying echo was deafening. As the ringing faded from his ears, Shutov looked over the dead Captain. He had been weak, his weakness brought them too close to shore and his weakness had him check-out early. He didn't feel pity for the Captain but instead his mind became clear – he knew with the Captain gone he must lead the men once they reached the shore. He must command them.

These weren't disciplined men, sure some were ex-military, but they were also merchant seamen. Most were running away from lives that didn't want them. To lead this rabble he would need to control them. And to control them he would need a gun, that gun. He pried the M1911 from the dead Captain's hand and wiped off a small smear of blood onto the dead Captain's shirt. He looked in the safe and took out a second magazine, pocketing it.

At the bridge's exit he took one look back at the Captain, his brain matter slowly oozing down the wall beside his limp body. "Coward," he uttered and walked out. Captain Nestorenko would be the first victim from the MV Rocket, a mocking name for such a slow and lumbering work ship. He may have been the first of the crew to die but certainly he wouldn't be the last.

Shutov looked down the ship's corridors, there could be more people inside. Technically he was now the Captain and therefore it was his responsibility to sweep the ship. Under maritime law he could be prosecuted for failing to do so... he spat onto the ship. *What law? Only the law of the jungle matters now,* he thought as he jumped into the cold black sea. Being First Officer, Shutov had seen all the reports, heard the radio transmissions first hand. He understood that he was swimming towards a future fraught with danger, facing an enemy unimaginable.

CHAPTER TWO

THE BOY

They called him 'The Boy'. The nickname was apt as he was only fifteen. To get on the ship he lied about his age and although they may have suspected he wasn't eighteen, they didn't probe. This was his first job, his first outing and although big and strong for his age, he couldn't hide his youth or innocence. The others joked with him, mocked him, some kidded that he might make a nice wife on those long journeys – at least he hoped they were kidding.

Even at shore they called him The Boy. At the seaside brothel they'd stopped at in the last port he was mocked by the crew. The girls were kinder, they called him cute and one grabbed his crotch. He remembered how hard that got him – how quickly his erection had come on. But he didn't have enough money to pay and the others, his so called crewmates, wouldn't lend him any. When he asked about owing her or paying next time he was in port the girl laughed at him and suddenly the erection was gone.

Dejected, he left and walked the streets – in hindsight he was lucky not to have been robbed and murdered. Being a naive country boy, he wasn't aware of the dangers that existed in a city late at night. He didn't understand the perils of trusting people who would do him harm just for the paltry sum of money he carried. Even his plan for the ship was naive. He figured that he would travel on the ship until he found a country that was interesting and then he'd just jump off and stay. Oblivious to the need for things like visas and immigration clearance, The Boy thought the plan sounded reasonable – and what adventures he would have.

Those adventures seemed to be short lived as he huddled, cold and wet, on the shore of Chernarus. The First Officer had announced that they should jump and swim to shore and that's just what he did. It had seemed close, but he wasn't a very strong swimmer and the currents had pushed him down along the coast. After a while his arms became heavy and each stroke weighed them down further. He heard the waves crashing on the sand and he knew the beach was close. Pushing on, he swallowed water until actual waves formed, dunking him underneath the water with every crash. He knew then that he was close to the shore.

The sand scrubbed his baby smooth face as he was suddenly thrown on the shore. Coughing up sea water, he dragged himself further up the sand and flipped over, staring up at the sky. The sky was cloudless and the stars were bright – without any electrical lights or buildings to blanket them. It reminded him of home. He stared for a long while - as his breath slowed and his brain began to function again. There was the northern star. Using that and his watch, he could find north. Being a country boy had its advantages it seemed. His back was sore – something was digging into it. The patrol pack – he still had it on. They were designed to provide assistance in an emergency – everything he needed would be inside.

Greedily, The Boy opened his pack, certain he would find water, canned food, a compass and a map - all the survival essentials. Looking inside, all he found was a torch, painkillers and a bandage. *How could anyone survive with this useless bunch of junk? Where was the gun? Or at least a hunting knife?*

Lying in the sand he cursed his bad luck - what sadist decided this would be useful in a survival situation? Fortunately he was near a town, even though there were no lights on, he could see the shadows of tall buildings in the distance. All he needed to do was walk in that direction, and he had a torch, so it wasn't like he was going to break a leg fumbling in the dark.

He rested for a while in the sand, double-checked his provisions and tested the torch. Waterproof - of course it was waterproof - this is a boat survival kit. Satisfied everything was in order, he rose and brushed the sand off his soggy clothes. Walking away from the beach, he listened to the sounds of crashing waves and his almost silent footsteps on soft grass. Not wanting to waste battery life, he kept the torch off as he made his way from the beach towards the buildings' shadows. His footsteps changed sound as he arrived at something hard. Kneeling down, he patted the surface which felt like bitumen. He turned on the torch to be sure - he was right – he'd arrived at a road. Sweeping the road with his torch he saw an unused road flare which he grabbed. The road went north and south but north was where the buildings and ...

"Urrrrrrrrr," softly in the distance he heard the moan. It was faint and he wasn't completely sure he'd heard it. He turned on the torch and shined it in the direction of the sound. "Hugrhuhhhhhhhhhhh," the moaning was a little louder, definitely coming from up the road.

"Hello?" he called out.

"Ugurghhhhh," the moaning sounded back. The Boy walked down the road calling out with the moaning response that came closer with each step. *One of the crew must have washed up ahead and was hurt,* he thought.

He could hear a sound – a scraping along the bitumen. He stopped walking so that the only sound was now the scraping. Looking down the road he saw a person crawling along the road. *Oh shit he's hurt really bad,* The Boy thought as he rushed to the person, the light of the torch swinging wildly with every step. Looking down at the person on the road his first thought was that whoever he was, he was not from the ship. Then the smell hit him - rot and the decay of human flesh. Whatever had broken this poor person's legs had turned gangrenous – just like the lame sheep they had to put down last year. The Boy looked around; there were no buildings or cars nearby. How long had this poor person been crawling along the road for help?

The injured man crawled closer and his face looked like it was caked in dried blood, especially around the mouth. But it was dark and even under the torchlight The Boy didn't really believe it was blood, it was dark brown and could have been dirt. The man couldn't speak, he just kept groaning and crawling towards the light.

The Boy stood looking around. There was nothing he could do for this poor man alone, but maybe with someone else helping, they could carry him to help. He waved the torch around but it wasn't that bright, so people wouldn't see it from far away. He dropped the still lit torch and the man crawled towards it grabbing it with both hands.

Then he remembered the flare he had just found. The Boy took it out of his patrol pack and looked it over. *This was better; people would see this from far away.* Stepping away from the crawling man to the middle of the road, he cracked the flare.

Suddenly the whole area was illuminated in a bright red light. He waved the flare over his head a couple of times before dropping it at his feet. *That would get their attention.* Proud of himself, he stepped back from the red flare and looked around for people.

Behind him he didn't notice the injured man crawling towards him. Although technically he wasn't crawling to The Boy as he was more interested in the red flare, The Boy was just between him and it. The Boy heard the man crawling towards him.

"It's okay, help will be coming soon," he said as even now in the distance he could see shadows running towards them. He felt the man grab his leg as he watched the shadows run towards him, it looked like three men had seen his flare.

The grip around his ankle tightened and then without warning he was suddenly experiencing pain. He looked down to see that the man had bitten him - like a rabid dog. Instinctively he kicked the man off his leg and stepped back. But the man now had a taste for blood and was no longer interested in the flare as he crawled back towards The Boy.

The Boy called out to the running men, "hey this guy's really sick. He just bit me so don't go near him." The running men had no intention of helping and they ran straight at The Boy, toppling him over. In the red light of the flare he could see their eyes were solely white, no pupils or iris within. And that *was* definitely blood on their chins and around their mouths.

They bit into him at his arm and stomach. He felt their hands tearing at his chest, pulling the flesh apart to get at the organs inside. The Boy remembered there was talk on the ship about an infection in Chernarus, but being new, nobody really spoke to him about it. On the ship they called him a noob and being a noob, he had to learn things for himself because no one would tell him. As he bled to death with these three monsters ripping and gnawing at his flesh his last thought was of the lame sheep he had put down last year, how its soft brown eyes looked up at him as he swung the axe above his head.

CHAPTER THREE

THE BUTCHER

Although he wasn't a qualified chef - and what the fuck was that anyway - Jeremy Kristiakov was still the ship's cook. He was instead a trained butcher, and for a ship full of men who wanted meat all the time, this was a useful trade. They would have a whole cow delivered on board and The Butcher, as they liked to call him, could make that cow last for weeks. He would strip it bare - every useful cut served as meat and turning the not-so-useful parts into sausages or mince.

Still, he was just the cook, low on the totem pole of the ship's hierarchy. He was also soaked through, shivering on the wet beach - he longed for the warmth of the kitchen. In summer they stayed away in droves but at sea in the bowels of winter, the warmth of the kitchen was what everyone flocked to.

Looking around it was dark – so dark. Being a city person, Jeremy hadn't known a dark like that which was presently surrounding him. Even his torch cut a meager swath of light that barely extended 8 feet in front of him. There were many stars above him and although he didn't know how to read them, they did look impressive. He had been walking along the beach for a while but had not come across any other people, hadn't passed a building. It was just sand and the occasional ship's debris that had washed to shore.

Absentmindedly, he picked up a jagged part of steel, most likely derived from the ship's hull. It ended at a sinister point and could possibly make a useful weapon for any wild animals – although deep down he knew wild animals wouldn't be his problem.

One thing about being the ship's cook is you're often ignored whilst people are eating around you. And when people ate they usually talked, or, more appropriately, gossiped. They may joke about their wives and how much the women gossip but the gossip swapped by the men on a ship would put any sewing circle to shame. Information and rumor was the currency on board when you've been out to sea for a while, and the galley is usually where such trade occurs.

He'd heard the snippets of conversation, the hushed mutterings and the shared looks the senior members of the crew gave each other. This place they were sailing near had been... damaged, scarred? The word he heard a lot was 'infected', especially from Doc with whom the Captain had spent a lot of time talking, away from other crew members.

From what he gathered, some sort of virus or infection had decimated the population. Those that were alive were primitive; they didn't possess normal human functions. They feasted on blood and each other, although to Jeremy that sounded like rumor, the military had been overrun and had abandoned the area a while ago. No one knew if other areas had been infected as well, if the whole world had gone to shit. For weeks, long range communications had been silent, satellite and radio had ceased to receive anything. Either they were shut down or they were blocked to stop information getting out, as the tin foil hat wearers on board kept spouting.

All he knew was that some bad shit had gone down on this miserable part of the Russian coastline where he was now washed up with nothing more than a Band-Aid, flashlight and some pills. He'd seen enough shit to know it was better to have a weapon and not need it than not to have a weapon and need it. He thought about all the mistakes he'd made to get him to this point. People talked about karma and but he'd always laughed it off. He'd done a lot of bad shit and gotten away with most of it – for him it had always seemed that karma had turned a blind eye.

Now he was thinking maybe karma just stored it all up and gave it all back as one major 'fuck you.' He had a feeling this situation was karma butt fucking him back, and the prick wouldn't even give him a reach around. His instincts told him this shit was about to get a whole lot worse and he trusted those instincts unquestionably. He tested the sharp point of the steel shard and felt ready to give back as good as he got.

CHAPTER FOUR

THE DUNCE

It wasn't a nice name but it beat Dopey which was what they had formerly called him at school. And it was an apt name for the simple fact that he just wasn't that bright. Sure he was a nice guy, he followed the rules and did what he was told - he just happened to be dumb. Show him how to do a task and he'll follow it, ask him to reason out why, or to come up with a better way, and you'd get the same response from a lump of cheese. The Dunce just did what he was told, he didn't care about the how or the why. As far as he was concerned that was unnecessary information.

When they told him to jump off the ship and swim, that's just what he did. He didn't ask why, he didn't ask where to – he just swam until he hit the beach. And now he just sat here waiting for someone else to come along and tell him what to do next.

He didn't even grab one of the patrol packs before jumping into the water, so he didn't have a torch to see anything around him. He wasn't afraid though – many of the crew assumed he was like a child because he was naive and slow. But he was no child - he was just dumb.

It was cold on the beach and dark, so dark. The dark bothered him so he sat on the sand tracing patterns with his fingers. Some of them were letters, which together made words and some of those words he knew. Like his name. Rory. His parents had helped him in that regard, nice and short, two of the letters the same. For The Dunce, it was easy to remember. His last name was long, it had too many letters and was long forgotten. Since everyone on the boat called him The Dunce, it didn't matter anyway.

His reverie was broken by the sound of someone coming along the beach. It sounded like a person hopping along, slow but methodical, and definitely coming towards him. He stood up, uselessly waved his hands, too stupid to realize that no one could see that far away.

"Over here," he called out. Now that got a response, a low moan echoed back and he called out again. "I'm over here," this time the returned moan was louder and definitely coming towards him. Its pitch and tone increased, like it was becoming more aggressive.

And then the smell hit him, like old meat that his mother always said you shouldn't eat. This person really needed a bath and in that slow brain of his a warning light began to flash.

"Who is that? You smell," The Dunce asked, but the hopper just groaned in response. And then it ran, straight to him. He'd encountered enough bullies to know if someone ran towards you and you didn't know why, it was best to run away - fast. So that's what he did.

Away from the groaner and along the beach he ran. But the groaner followed him and he could hear others joining him. The joiners all groaned as they chased after him. Now he was back at school with a gang of children chasing him, pens in hand ready to write bad words on his forehead.

He knew he could run fast but this gang, these naughty boys who wanted to hurt him, were keeping up with him. And now it sounded like there were at least four of them back there. It was too dark to see but he could differentiate the groans behind him. In school his saving grace was always his stamina. Most bullies just got bored and gave up after a while. But these bullies just kept chasing, matching him step for step.

Ahead he saw a small building. Since he couldn't outrun them maybe he could hide in there. He ran to the building, through the open door and slammed hard against the wall opposite. Pushing back off the wall he spun around and shoved the door shut. It was flimsy and there was no lock. Seconds later the things were outside, thumping against it. He didn't have long before they were inside.

He looked around the ground for something to brace against the door but all he saw were old tin cans and used soda cans. Someone had holed up here for a while and there was blood on the floor, but no body. And then he saw it, lying on the floor near the dried up dark brown blood stain.

An axe. It must have belonged to whoever had previously hidden in here, but now it was his. He picked it up feeling the weight and heft – it was strong. Not strong enough to brace the now splintering door, but maybe strong enough to scare them away. He swung it a couple of times, getting used to it as a baseball player might get used to a bat before stepping out to the plate. Then the door broke and four of them stood there at the only entrance/exit looking at him. They were long dead, one so injured that he was unable to stand and instead crawled inside.

It was too dark to see the detail on their faces but as they shambled into the confined room the smell overpowered him. Now he could place it - it was the smell of death. These weren't people, these were monsters, the bringers of death. He swung the axe one more time as they moved towards him – batter up.

CHAPTER FIVE

THE HIPPOCRATIC OATH
FOR HYPOCRITES

Doc was certain that he would be the last person off the ship. The cowards had all lept off at the first sign of trouble and left him with his patient, a crew member who had been struck down with malaria on this trip and was currently shivering in the ship's poor excuse for an infirmary. Doc had spent the last hour looking around the ship for a life raft to go with the stretcher since the patient was unable to swim. In the bridge he did find the Captain with a bullet hole in his head – you didn't need to be a doctor to know that was fatal.

The ship was drifting at a 45 degree angle which made his searching much more difficult. As he moved through the ship he was overwhelmed with how empty it seemed as it drifted along the coast in the dead of night. His patient was unconscious, strapped onto the bed to prevent falling in high seas, which meant he had no issue with the current angle.

With the search proving fruitless and his patient stable, he had nothing else to do. Savoring the moment he stood on the deck and watched the stars. It was peaceful.

For a moment.

Then the ship juddered and rocked as it hit sand, slowing down. He heard the sounds of rocks scraping the side of the hull and the ship lurched to a sudden halt. The speed with which it happened caused Doc to lose his footing and he knocked his head against a rail. The impact would leave a mark that he wouldn't see until morning, although the pain was instantaneous.

Rubbing his forehead he looked out at the coast. The ship had beached at a peninsula somewhere on the coast. He could see the outlines of nearby rocks but that was all. His head throbbed not only from the bump but from the ungodly noise that was coming from the bowls of the ship. The engine lurched and whined, screaming for mercy with the propeller jammed in a rock, forcing it to screech as the motor tried to dislodge it.

Thankfully, something in the engine blew and it cut off, granting Doc blessed silence. It was so dark that he would need to wait it out here until dawn. The wait would give him time to form a plan and find some way of getting the patient off the boat.

He could see the shore; it was just a small jump to land. *Would it be so bad to just jump off?* He had been abandoned so why should he risk his own life to look after this sick person who would inevitably die anyway? Even with a stretcher, getting him off the boat would be risky. Doc could break a leg and then what – he'd be no use to anyone.

He pondered going to shore, looking for help and maybe some supplies, and then coming back for the patient. There might be a town right near him or he might have a long hike ahead. And if he made it there would he really come back and would there be anyone to come back to? The patient was very sick and would most likely die without the right medication – medication Doc just didn't have on board. He couldn't just leave him here to die a slow and painful death – but he couldn't just euthanize him either. *Why was this suddenly my problem? The Captain had checked out so why can't I?*

Doc had always been selfish, always looked out for number one. When he was younger he worked hard, and did his best. But age and life had beaten him down and now he just coasted by, did what was needed and took care of himself first.

Perhaps that's why he punished himself by working the ship – running from his problems like most on the ship did. He wanted to run now – and he could find many reasons why he should. Survival was key and this patient was already proving to be dead weight. He'd had many conversations with the Captain so he had a pretty good idea what was waiting for him in Chernarus. Dragging a fevered malaria ridden patient through a town already swarming with the infected didn't seem like a very good plan – unless your plan was to be lunch. But then again, he couldn't just leave him without any chance of survival.

Looking out at the shore that was so close and yet felt so far away, he knew he was going to be in for a long night. And if he was honest with himself he already knew what the outcome would be – it was always the same for him. Self over others – but because he was selfish he needed the night to reason it out and come up with an excuse. He knew that inevitability he would abandon the patient - he just needed the night to make himself feel better about it.

CHAPTER SIX

FOOTSTEPS ON CONCRETE
ARE NEVER GOOD

The shivering had almost stopped. Janik's hands were starting to get warm and his clothes were almost dry. It was quiet and his eyelids started to push down on his eyes. He didn't want to sleep but it felt like he didn't have much say in the matter. *Maybe just a quick nap then, five minutes or so, a power snooze to recharge the batteries.*

Then he heard it - footsteps on concrete. He'd already seen one of those things kill Ruben. They'd both washed up together, but Ruben had made the mistake of running on concrete, while Janik walked slowly, staying on the soft grass. The infected went to town with his body, ripping and feasting away at it. Janik watched from the distance, unable and unwilling to help.

The sounds were louder and definitely coming towards him – urgent, fast footsteps on the hard concrete outside. His breathing stopped and his heart started pounding. All his senses were heightened as he listened to the sounds.

There were more pounding footsteps chasing the first set - a group running behind the first man. Janik listened, straining, turning his head towards the sounds. *Yes, they were outside this building.* Janik was hiding under a window. If he wanted to, he could just look up and see.

But he didn't want to. He wanted to sleep. He wanted this to all be over, a bad dream perhaps. And if he couldn't wake up from it he'd go to sleep and escape that way. He didn't want to be here. Anywhere but here, hiding in a warehouse with those things outside. Walking around, groaning, looking, no not looking, hunting. Yes, hunting - and he was the prey.

Being prey came with the territory if you were unfortunate enough to have been born much smaller than your peers. Janik was born short and in his world, size really did matter. If you were small you were weak – he wanted to be like Joe Pesci in Goodfellas, small and angry, kicking ass and not taking shit from anyone. Instead, he was more like Pee Wee Herman – small, skinny, and getting his ass kicked all the time.

So the concept of being prey wasn't new to him, but getting killed and eaten if he was caught certainly was. At least he'd had years of hiding and dodging under his belt. He knew how to be quiet, stay off noisy surfaces and avoid roads and footpaths – unlike that clumsy oaf outside, pounding the concrete as he ran, drawing the attention of all those things around.

Maybe that wasn't so bad. It might give him a chance to run. But to where? What was out there that wasn't in here? He should wait until morning when he could get an idea of the lay of the land. Work out a path, a destination. The truth was he'd rather stay and hide than run and fight – waiting until morning was just a lie he told himself.

I should look out of the window. They won't see me since it's so dark. He was up one flight and felt reasonably safe. As he looked out the window his vision was obscured by both the dark and the built up grime on the window. He could make out shapes, one large shape chased by four smaller ones. The large shape ran into a small shed, slamming the door shut behind him. Janik had already been in there before. It had only one way in or out so he'd left it and instead went into this larger warehouse. The warehouse had two exits which suited him - he always looked for more than one way out of every hiding place.

He watched the things pound on the door. The door was weak and broke easily. And then they were inside. The poor guy inside was a goner for sure. He heard the groans and an inhuman scream tear into the night's silence. Subconsciously Janik did the sign of the cross – no one deserved to die like that. He could hear the crunch of bones and soft splotchy sound, like a wet mop slapping down onto a concrete floor.

Then it was quiet. Janik realized he was still holding his breath. He loudly exhaled. From the shed he heard a similar exhale and the heavy panting as someone tried to catch their breath. Wait, those things didn't breathe, they groaned but it was like air pushed through vocal chords, a long monotonous groan with no real pitch or tone.

In the doorway of the shed he saw the outline of a man with the axe held up high. He remembered seeing the axe but at the time he didn't think anything of it – further proof to him that he was a coward. This man was obviously a warrior, a fighter. What Janik saw as debris he saw as a weapon and used it to take four of them down. One part of Janik wanted to signal to him, call him inside for safety. But the other part, the part that had been calling the shots for most of his life, vetoed that idea. *What if he kills you? What if he attracts more of those things inside? Best to leave him be. You stay down, you stay quiet, you stay alive.* End of that internal discussion.

Janik slinked down from the window and sat up against the wall. He heard the sound of the man running along the concrete. *Stupid fool doesn't realize he'll attract more of them,* his cowardly conscience reminded him. *Axe or no axe he keeps that noise up he won't see the sun rise tomorrow and if you follow him you will share that fate.* Janik buried his head in his arms and finally let sleep overcome him.

CHAPTER SEVEN

THE FIRST MURDER

Helmut had just found a shotgun with some ammunition so his luck was still holding out. He'd already managed to avoid being killed twice that night and that was only through sheer luck. His friend Freddie wasn't so lucky.

They'd found each other at the docks and Freddie thought the people shambling around were other survivors. Helmut thought differently and held back. The way they walked was what tipped him off – they had no purpose or reason, they were just roaming and groaning. And their heads were strange - they hung off their necks like a piece of meat. They killed Freddie and chased after Helmut – but he was lucky as they lost their line of sight on him around a building.

When he'd lost them he rested against a wall while another one had just walked right by him. It was only two feet away but it didn't pay him any attention. He stood still, held his breath and just watched out of the corner of his eyes as it shuffled past him. Helmut assumed the dark was what saved him that time – two times lucky.

And now he was armed. He had a double-barrel shotgun with 6 slugs. He gathered the gun and ammo up and walked towards the beach, away from the rest of the buildings. The monsters seemed to stay around buildings so he hoped the beach was clear. Helmut didn't know much about guns but he loaded up the shotgun shells and looked for a safety catch - there didn't seem to be any. He assumed that meant the gun was now loaded and ready to fire.

What was it his dad always said about assumptions? It makes an ass out of you and me. He should be sure it was working before he *needed* it to be working. But not here of course. He could hear them walking around and it seemed like a bad idea to make a big noise in the middle of town. Better to wait until he was far away from everything and test the gun then. To Helmut, that sounded like a plan.

A plan that was about to be upended as he heard the sounds of running footsteps come towards him. He unslung the shotgun and trained it towards the sound. *Is he friendly?* Helmut thought as he listened to the running.

He could see the outline of the runner but Helmut was pretty certain the runner couldn't see him. With his back to a wall and the shotgun ready, he felt fairly safe as the runner approached. There was a gate near him and he assumed that's what the runner was heading towards.

As he approached, Helmut recognized the runner. *Oh shit it's the fucking Dunce and he's got a bunch of them on his tail.* Helmut's mind raced through his options. He could do nothing. He could help. He could kill The Dunce. Hell, they might feed on his body and that would give him an opportunity to get out. *Fuck who are you man?* He berated himself, *three hours of this shit and you're already turning cold blooded.*

He couldn't do that to the guy. Sure he was a simpleton but that didn't mean he deserved to be killed in cold blood. "Hey Dunce! This way," he called out. It took The Dunce a moment to register that someone was there.

"Helmut help me, please help," he pleaded.

"Sure man sure. But not here, let's lead them out to the beach," replied Helmut.

Helmut ran and the Dunce followed, quickly catching up to him. They both ran side by side towards the beach, a large number of the infected following them.

"Around this building. Let's see if we can lose some of them," Helmut yelled. They circled a building and when they returned to the start it sounded like there were less of them chasing. Helmut filed that away 'under useful shit to know' as they continued towards the beach.

They felt the sand underfoot as they ran. "Helmut they don't stop. I run and run but they don't stop," The Dunce explained.

"I know man. We're going to have to stop and fight them soon. I have a gun, you have an axe so we should be okay."

"I don't want to kill no more people."

"They're not people man. They're monsters, it's okay to kill monsters."

"It's okay?" The Dunce queried.

"Yeah man, it's okay. So don't feel bad about killing them." It was hard for Helmut to tell in the dark but The Dunce did look relieved. "But let's run a little more. I'm sure this gun will be loud and I don't want to draw more of them here."

They continued to run along the beach when ahead they saw a torch waving towards them. Helmut and The Dunce ran faster towards the torch as the distance between them and the infected increased. As they got closer to the torch waver, Helmut heard a voice.

"This way over here," The Butcher called out. The Butcher was up the roof of a small shack, he pointed to the ladder on the side. "Climb up. They won't reach us up here."

Helmut and the Dunce climbed up the ladder and once they were on top of the shack, The Butcher pulled the ladder up, laying it flat behind them.

The infected ran to the shack and then ran around it. They slowed down and roamed around looking for the two missing men. On the roof their former prey watched them below, The Butcher holding his fingers to his lips to indicate they should keep quiet.

"They're not leaving," Helmut whispered.

The men watched and Helmut was right. The infected moved away for a moment but then came back to the shack, back to the last place they saw the men.

"It's like they know," The Butcher pondered.

"What are they?" Helmut asked.

"Bad news, that's what they are," The Butcher answered.

"Monsters," Rory offered.

"Yes that too," The Butcher replied, "you know how to use that?" indicating Helmut's shotgun, "you want me to take that? I'm a pretty good shot."

"I'd just as soon hold on to it for now if you know what I mean," Helmut answered.

"Of course. Just offering to help."

They went back to watching the infected. Sensing movement to his side, Helmut turned to see The Butcher licking his lips before he swung the sharp metal shard and jammed it into Helmut's neck. Helmut's hands dropped the gun as he futilely raised them to try to stop the torrent of blood that poured from the gash in his neck.

"You should have just given me the gun," The Butcher chastised, as he grabbed the shotgun and fished around Helmut's pockets for the shells.

Beside him Helmut watched the Dunce's confused face as the scene unfolded, too fast for his slow-witted brain to comprehend. Helmut tried to say kill him but it just came out as a bloody gurgle.

Loaded up, the Butcher pushed Helmut off the shack to the waiting infected below. They swarmed onto Helmut and began to tear at his body. While they were distracted, The Butcher lowered the ladder on to the other side and started to climb down.

"You better run dummy because it won't be long before they finish with him," he said as he climbed down the ladder.

The Dunce turned his head from the running Butcher to Helmut and back again. He does this too many times for it to be comical and Helmut could almost see the thought process running around the Dunce's head.

"Run!" Helmut gurgled out and mercifully, that was clear enough for the Dunce to understand. He climbed down the ladder and ran after The Butcher as Helmut's vision was filed with an infected standing over him. Its eyes were a murky white and the blood dripped off its chin onto Helmut's face. It opened its mouth to show blood-stained teeth before chomping down onto Helmut's cheek, tearing the flesh from his face.

CHAPTER EIGHT

THE CYCLE OF WAR

Vuk looked around at the rag tag group huddled in the large cold empty shed. The MV Rocket's first officer Shutov - who Vuk always thought was a prick - had so far done a good job of keeping them alive. Only one of them was dead and it was that fool Vasily's fault for trying to run off when he should have stayed put.

When they had first grouped together at the beach it was chaotic, people screaming, no one wanted to believe what was happening. Shutov had tried to group them, create some sort of order but all everyone focused on were the two dead crew members and the infected feasting on their bodies.

The rising panic was understandable as others called for Shutov to shoot the infected. Vuk knew you needed to give panic a moment - let it say what it needed to say - and then move on. Vasily didn't, and instead he ran, afraid there would be more infected. So Shutov shot him in the back after giving him fair warning. Vuk had seen this play before in prison and in the war. It was an effective, if not very subtle, way of keeping order.

Shutov was setting himself up as the alpha male, king of the yard and that was just fine with everyone, including Vuk. He'd already been through this in the Serbian war previously, seen his wife and daughter raped and killed in front of him. He'd seen men play soccer with the decapitated heads of their enemies, so it was safe to say he'd seen some shit before. At fifty five years of age he no longer wanted to lead, he just wanted to get through this. Although right now it looked like the odds of just surviving were low, Shutov was slowly pushing them up into their favor.

There were now nine of them in the shed. Vuk knew the two men guarding both entrances with hatchets well - Harrison and Kai. They were strong, stupid bullies who stuck together like flies on shit. Huddled in one corner was The Butcher and The Dunce, a strange pair who were deep in conversation, although The Butcher was doing all the talking and The Dunce was just nodding and listening. Lying down and trying to get some rest were Alejandro, Luther and Sam.

Shutov was coordinating the group and although Vuk didn't know for sure, it certainly seemed like Shutov was using some form of military training in his decision making. Vuk watched as he tapped Kai on the shoulder and then pointed at Vuk to take over. Vuk nodded, rose and stretched out the kinks before taking the axe and guarding the door.

The sky outside was glowing red from all the road flares they'd laid down. The flares formed a pointed arrow to the shed in the hope of encouraging other survivors. So far it had worked, bringing in The Butcher and The Dunce. Unfortunately, it was also effective at attracting infected as the pile of dead at each entrance could attest. Nobody wanted to touch them for fear of catching whatever had created them, so they had been roughly kicked aside at each entrance forming a macabre barrier.

Vuk looked out onto the beach looking for Yuri, another one of the *old men* of the ship. Vuk and Yuri had spent many a night playing cards, swapping stories and generally bonding over Vodka or Rakia - depending on who was buying. They had both jumped into the ocean together but it seemed Yuri was not as strong a swimmer as Vuk. Vuk was swimming directly to the shore when he turned and saw Yuri was being pulled by a current. He called out to not fight it, let the current take him and once it had lost its potency to then swim to the shore. Yuri nodded and gave Vuk a thumbs up, before turning on his back and floating away. Vuk hoped that wouldn't be the last time he saw his old friend.

The flares' lights were fading, almost in sync with the increasing sunlight as the dawn sun was preparing to burst over the horizon. Shutov patted Vuk on the shoulder, it felt like a hollow gesture to Vuk, as he looked out the entrance to the lightening sky. "Dawn is coming... we can use the light to find equipment," said Shutov, as they both looked up at the lightening sky. "You have been in war before, this is correct Vuk?"

Vuk nodded, "it was a long time ago, but yes, I have fought in enough wars for any lifetime."

"I'm afraid my friend it looks like another battle is ahead of us. How is your aim?"

"It has been a while but I'm sure it will come back."

"Good, then I can count on you?" to Vuk that sounded less like a question and more like a demand.

"I have lived too long and seen too much to die at the hands of these things. So yes Sir, you can count on me." He threw that 'Sir' in and Shutov smiled when he heard it. Yes, the young were easy to read and Vuk would feed this man's ego if it kept him alive.

"Good, this is good," he gave Vuk another hearty slap on the back and walked off to the next survivor, ready to make the same pitch. The Big Dog was going to pee on every tree before another dog got the opportunity to.

Whilst Shutov kept recruiting his army, Vuk looked out in the distance and saw a lone survivor running towards the flares. He had a large number of infected chasing him.

"Sir we have a man incoming with a lot of them behind him," Vuk called out. The others all lept up and congregated at the entrances, calling out to the runner.

The runner saw them and smiled - salvation was so close that he didn't notice the rubble pile until it was too late for him to safely leap it. He tried to jump it anyway and his back foot caught on a protruding washing machine tripping him up. He fell, tumbling over himself and scraping his leg on the hard concrete. Momentarily dazed he looked up at the screaming men in the shed not less than 400 meters from him.

He rose up, getting ready to continue towards them, when he was blitzed and knocked back down by the first infected. The pain in his legs was instant and excruciating; he looked down at the sharp white point of a bone protruding out of his thigh. Then they swarmed. Mercifully, he blacked out to die in relative peace.

At the shed they all watched in silence, like gawkers at an accident site. Shutov broke the silence, "does anyone know who that was?"

"I do sir," The Butcher responded, "that was breakfast," and he laughed. Some nervous laughter followed, but not nearly as heartily as The Butcher's laughter at his own joke.

Vuk looked away from The Butcher and back at the poor man being torn to shreds. Yes, if he stayed close to people like Shutov and The Butcher, he may survive, but at what cost?

CHAPTER NINE

THE LAST MAN ON EARTH

The thing about going insane is that it doesn't happen all at once. You don't wake up one morning and decide to do some crazy shit – it takes time. In Joe's case it was about three weeks and was so gradual that increasingly he was never really sure what was real and what he'd imagined. He started doing stuff that a week ago would seem strange – like talking aloud to himself. It was just such a long time since he'd heard another voice - the demon's groans didn't count - that he wanted to hear one, even if it was his own. Then he started answering the questions he pondered aloud, only it was not his voice he answered with. This was soon followed by praying - lots of praying. He prayed for salvation, for a way out, for a purpose to his now meaningless life that was solely based on the daily struggle to survive.

Before the event, Joe was a farmer. His father was a farmer and his father's father was a farmer. The only choice Joe ever got about farming was whether to plant wheat or corn. Since farmers don't need to go to school he was taken out at ten and put to work on the land. His life was all mapped out, next year he was going to marry the Mozhayev girl and take over his parents' farm. She was a nice girl, pleasant to look at and had a kindness to her that Joe had learnt to adore. She would be a good mother and Joe felt at peace with his dictated world.

Then one night she was at his door – but it wasn't her. She had blood on her face and her eyes were crazed. Joe tried everything, he locked her in a room, tied her up, fed her real food. But she spat it all out and wouldn't stop trying to attack him any chance she could. In the end it broke his heart to put a bullet through her brain. Her corpse was the only one he burnt and although it wasn't in that exact moment that he snapped, it was definitely then that cracks began to form.

It was a week later while Joe was praying in the Mogilevka church that God had finally answered his prayers. Not with a sign but with actual words spoken from the icon of Madonna and the baby that sat behind the altar. His mission was now clear – this was the end of days as written in the Bible. As prophesied, the dead had risen and it was now his duty to eradicate them from the earth before he too could ascend to heaven.

He hadn't kept count of how many demons he had killed but the pile of corpses in Chernogorsk showed it was a lot. There were corpses all over the place except for the church – he would not have those demonic beings defiling this holy place. He opened the church door, climbed the tower and rang the bells – the noise would attract them from far and wide. Saying a quick prayer as he cleaned his gun he then genuflected before leaving the church, kissing the icon of the Madonna and baby on his way out.

Down the street Joe walked towards an old factory with a high smoke tower that had a platform at its tip. This was his preferred sniping position. From here he could see all around and the military at one point had set up a forward operations base here. Below him there were medical tents and some military tents that still held the weapons they'd discarded when they abandoned this area. Joe ignored the weapons there and instilled his faith in God and his trusty CZ550. It was easy to use, easy to clean and ammo was plentiful so for his holy mission, it was the best tool.

As he climbed the ladder up to the high tower, he was once again filled with an overwhelming revelation that he was getting closer to God. He knew that once he had completed his mission and exterminated all the demon spawn from the land, he would finally ascend into heaven as the last man on earth. He will have returned the earth to the plants and creatures as it was in the beginning and now take his rightful place at the right hand of God.

The thought filled him with comfort and he whispered "Amen," as blew the dust off the first magazine before loading it into the rifle. "Thy will be done," he uttered as he crossed himself before lining up the first demon in the sights and squeezing the trigger.

CHAPTER TEN

A BAD MORNING TO BE HUNG OVER

Robert woke up on the floor of his cabin – a blanket covered him as his face rested in a pile of vomit that he hoped was his. It was not unusual for him to wake up like this, but through the fog of his brain there seemed to be a part of him that was saying this time something was wrong.

He grabbed a clean part of the blanket and wiped his face but kept it over his head. *Just one more minute of blissful dark,* he pleaded to himself. He enjoyed that minute listening to the woodpecker pounding the inside of his skull. Another distant message tried getting through his brain and he smacked his forehead a couple of times to help it along. *What is it? What's wrong?*

And then it came to him. Silence. There was too much silence. Being the ship's mechanic, Robert was relegated to sleeping in a room near the engine room, one where he could hastily attend to any emergencies. But right now his engine, the one that he cared for and maintained as a gardener would their garden, was quiet. She was never quiet, even in port there was always a soft hum as the generator ran to maintain power to the ship. He threw the blanket off his face and light streamed in through the round sun roof, blinding him. He blinked and rubbed his eyes, trying to push back the demon light, but he was unable to. In the end he adjusted to it just as he had adjusted to the throbbing behind his temple.

Wait! Why do I have a sunroof? At first he thought he'd ended up in someone else's cabin. He was drunk last night but surely not that drunk. He looked around and confirmed it was his cabin, noting some of his meager possessions on the floor beside him, next to the door. *Why is there a door on the floor?* And then it burst through the fog in his brain like a train coming out of a tunnel – the ship was on its side. That sunroof was his porthole and this door used to be on the opposite wall. *Well technically it is still on the wall - it's just the wall that has moved.* It was too early and he was too hungover to get technical with himself.

Robert opened the door and fell into the corridor. He meant to climb down but the whole coordination thing wasn't 100 percent yet, and the ship's weird angle wasn't helping. Fortunately, the ship was designed for rough seas so it had many handholds and railings that he could use to get up to the deck. Each head knock and shin bang was another notch closer to sobriety as he opened the final door and fell outside into the sunlight.

He landed hard with a thud and the immediate torrent of swearwords he yelled woke Doc from his fitful slumber. Doc had decided at some point during the night that moving the patient was too risky and he would instead leave him behind. The finality of that decision provided him with enough mental clarity to snatch some form of sleep that Robert's entrance had just disrupted.

"Doc what the fuck is going on?" Robert queried as he rubbed his tormented head.

"The ship appears to have hit a rock and listed. The crew abandoned ship thinking it would sink but it has instead run aground here," Doc replied.

"Where are we?"

"Somewhere in Chernarus but all I can see are trees so I have no idea where."

"And what about Arnold? Is he okay?"

Arnold was the malaria patient and also Robert's bunkmate, in many ways a little brother to Robert – although he'd never admit that publicly. To Robert it seemed that the Captain assigned roommates based on how likely they were to clash with each other. Robert and Arnold were chalk and cheese but somehow still pretty close. Arnold was a hoarder; Robert didn't keep anything he didn't immediately need. Arnold took pride in his appearance; Robert wore the same jeans until other members of the crew demanded he wash them or be thrown overboard. Arnold liked to collect trinkets from the different ports they visited; while Robert stayed on the ship and used the respite from Arnold to read. It was on one of Arnold's touristy adventures in Turkey he found the evil eye necklace and caught a bad case of malaria. Yet despite all their differences, or perhaps because of them, Robert had a big brotherly concern for Arnold. Also he was worried that if Arnold died it would be up to him to sort through all the crap in their quarters.

"Robert you need to understand that Arnold is very sick. There is nothing I can do for him on-board and the move might kill him."

"What are you saying?" probed Robert.

"We have to get off this ship and I don't think it would be prudent to take Arnold with us."

"How can you say that? You're a Doctor."

"Yes, and a realist. I don't think you're fully informed about what's waiting for us out there."

Doc filled Robert in on all he knew about the infection and Chernarus. The information wasn't complete and to Robert it seemed like Doc was taking the piss - until he looked at the grave expression on his face. Like others on board, he saw Doc conversing intensely with the Captain in the galley. He had heard the rumors but put them down to bullshit or hearsay. But now hearing it from Doc, with that expression, Robert knew it was real – Chernarus was now hell on earth and they may well be walking right into it.

"I get all that Doc but we can't leave him here to die."

"Robert if we carry him then it will take us longer to cover ground. We'll get tired more often, need to carry more provisions."

"So it takes longer. We are not leaving Arnold behind."

"You're not being rational," Doc pleaded.

"I'm being very rational. We are stranded on a part of the Russian coast that is infected with the living dead. The military and citizens have failed to contain the infection and have instead chosen to abandon the land to them. We need to somehow get through that mess whilst carrying a very sick Arnold and find some sort of way out of here."

"Exactly. It's hopeless," sighed Doc.

"I didn't say it was hopeless. It's a tough situation but it's not fucking hopeless. We're on a boat. There's food and water here, we should be able to carry enough for a couple of days. There's the stretcher we used to carry Arnold onboard, which we'll now use to carry him off. We'll go slow, carry him for an hour at a time, rest for fifteen minutes and then carry him again.

"You're right – it will be slow, but it's possible - and we might find a working car out there that we can put him in. There have got to be other people here, other survivors from the boat or even people who lived here and couldn't get out. We meet up with them, we pool our resources and we all survive. It's as simple and as complicated as that."

Doc shook his head, "that's a fool hearted plan. You'll find it tough carrying him by yourself because I'll have no part of it. I want to live. Dragging Arnold across the country with the infected out there is not the best way for me to achieve that."

"Then let me introduce you to plan B. And you're right I will find it tough dragging Arnold along by myself but I'll have the soothing sounds of the ship's fog horn to keep me motivated."

"I don't get it," Doc asked confused.

"The fog horn. That really loud, really fucking loud, horn that the ship has - I'll place something heavy on the button so it continually sounds until the ships batteries are drained. Which, if I shut the power off from everything else, should be at least a couple of days."

"Why would you do that?"

"Because after I overpower you and tie you to one of those trees out there I'm hoping that the horn will attract whatever is out there right to you and away from me as I drag Arnold through the forest. You'll definitely live but probably not for as long as under plan A and death won't be as nice as starvation or dehydration." Robert let the words sink in before he asked, "so any thoughts on the two plans?"

Reluctantly Doc responded, "I think plan A is a winner."

"Glad you see it that way. Now let's go get that stretcher."

CHAPTER ELEVEN

THE LONE WOLF

Duke took stock of his surroundings as the pre-dawn light peeked over the horizon. Ahead of him he could see a small military encampment, barbed wire all around with makeshift sniper posts at each of the four corners. During the night he'd heard the sounds of survivors and infected clashing and saw one poor bastard go down near a road flare. Having been a party to all the rumors on the ship he had a pretty good idea what was going on and he wanted no part of it.

Duke was the only American on-board, even though the ship's crew list looked like the United Nations. This suited Duke just fine as he avoided most of the other crew mates and did his own thing in his down time. He took that same attitude when landing on the beach. Around him he saw other survivors group up and head towards the town while Duke purposely avoided them, ignoring their calls and going the other way.

Survival was Duke's guiding principle - for a long time he'd stopped living his life and just survived it. As an orphan with no subsequent family or children of his own, he travelled the world eking out an existence. He'd done good things and he'd done not so good things, but he felt that overall, he was a decent person. He had dealt with shit that would have broken a lesser man and he knew that if he wanted to survive this new world he would need some sort of a weapon. The camp in front of him looked like a very good chance of providing him with one.

Duke had nicknamed the infected 'Zeds', a term he'd read once and was short for the Z in Zombies. He wasn't sure if they were living or dead but he'd seen what they did to the living and that was zombie-like enough for him. The Zeds were all shuffling around inside the camp, trapped by the makeshift barbed wire fence. Outside there was no movement, just ruined cars and bodies that were long dead. Slowly he crawled on his belly towards a disused Humvee that was near the road. The shuffle of his elbows made a slight noise and he intently watched the Zeds for their reaction. Thankfully, there was none, and he safely made it to the Humvee. Looking inside he didn't find anything of use.

Damn it, I have to go in. He looked over the camp. It had been abandoned long ago and sealed up, the main walkway entrance closed off with wire. But to the side he could see a gap in the barbed wire where there were sandbags instead, this must have been where the people who closed it down got out from. Crawling over to the sandbags, he listened out for the tell-tale groan of Zeds nearby. They were mercifully silent. He inched over the sandbags and into the camp.

There was a tent directly in front of him and he crawled over to it. Looking through the window he could see that there was no one inside. He made his way inside but couldn't find anything of use. All he found were some old army cots, disused medical supplies and other junk. The place had been cleaned out, any weapons or useful equipment removed, and only items too large to carry or with no value had been left behind. After an hour of crawling around the other tents, Duke found it was the same story with each of them. They'd cleaned the place out and his plan was officially a bust.

He was about to make his way out when he remembered the sniper posts, maybe they would have something. He didn't like the idea of climbing up there and being exposed but he'd be stupid not to at least check them out. Checking that the area was clear, he crawled over to the first sniper post and began to climb up.

Inside he'd found the jackpot – if you were into recycling. Tin cans next to soda cans, although there was one still full can of Coke and some chemlights. He took both and began to walk down the ladder.

He froze at the bottom rung as there was one Zed right underneath the sniper post. Duke focused on the dried blood mixed with hair underneath the dead soldier's helmet as the Zed groaned and swayed, sensing he was there even though it had its back to Duke. He stood like a statue on the ladder and then slowly stepped down to the next rung. "Urggghhh," the Zed responded and began to turn.

Run, he thought as the Zed saw him and lashed out, missing Duke by seconds, instead hitting the rung. The groan and Duke's footsteps drew in the other Zeds and they all began to run towards him. Duke knew the tents would be no help and instead ran to the next sniper post that was on the short side of the camp rectangle. He hoped to hell they couldn't climb ladders as he made his way up.

They had congregated down at the bottom of the sniper post and thankfully it seemed that ladders were too complicated for them. Instead they stood at the base of the ladder looking up, arms outstretched like evil versions of Oliver Twist wanting 'more'. It appeared to Duke their motor skills were too limited to climb, but now he was stuck.

He looked around this sniper post and at least found some more useful items. He took a hunting knife, a green smoke grenade and threw out one of the empty tin cans in frustration. *Damn useless junk,* he thought as he listened to it bounce along the concrete floor. One of the Zeds moved towards the can, lashing at it a couple of times and then returned back to the sniper post. *They are attracted to sound,* he thought as he threw the second tin can to test the theory. This time two Zeds went over to investigate where the can landed before returning to the sniper post.

Let's see what they think of this little show, he thought as he pulled the pin on the smoke grenade and tossed it far away from him. It hit the ground and spun, spewing out green smoke with a loud hiss. The Zeds went batshit crazy and ran straight to the smoke grenade kicking and grabbing at it like pigeons fighting over the last scrap of bread.

Duke used this moment of distraction to climb down and check for weapons in the other two sniper posts. In the third sniper post he found a Makarov PM without any ammunition, it was a decent enough gun but Duke wanted something with more firepower, and if he was honest with himself, he didn't trust any weapon that wasn't American made. *One last sniper post - one last chance,* he thought as he climbed up the ladder.

As his head cleared the final rung, the rising sun glinted off the steel of an assault rifle resting against the far wall. She was a thing of beauty, an American made M16A2. This gun he knew, having fired off plenty of rounds when he was a teenager back in Oregon, and it was a great all-rounder. He scooped it, up along with the two magazines of STANAG rounds, and examined the gun. Without having fieldstripped it, he could see it was in good shape, but probably needed a good clean out. He also grabbed the empty water canteen and placed that in his patrol pack. Duke loaded a magazine and slung it over his shoulder before climbing down the ladder and crawling towards the nearby exit.

Once outside the camp he immediately ran for the nearest tree line wanting to get away from the camp and Zeds before more were drawn towards it. He followed the trees up the rise of the hill in order to get a better look around, wishing he had some form of binoculars so he could see in the distance.

Down the hill he could see a large town with a large industrial area and docklands. Although hard to make out at this distance, he could see the slow movement of more Zeds. The town looked like a good next stop - there were lots of buildings for him to look through and it would be easy to avoid the Zeds.

He looked over the town, planning some sort of route through it, when he heard the first shot fired. It sounded like a sniper rifle and the boom echoed off the hills behind him. Then he heard another shot, and a third - all coming from the same direction. "Fuck that. Shit is going down over there," he exclaimed as he turned and ran up the hill away from the town.

CHAPTER TWELVE

CHERNO GOES CRAZY

Duke was right about shit going down in Chernogorsk that morning. Shutov had continually tried to quell the rising panic that rushed over his men but this became more difficult with each additional shot that rang out across the town. This wasn't helped by the ringing of the church bells. What had been - up until then - an orderly unit, was very quickly breaking apart, with the men speaking over the top of each other in increasingly panicked tones.

They were looting the general store when the first shots sounded. Prior to their arrival the store had been almost picked clean but there were still enough supplies to provide the men with some hope. The loot had been gathered and placed in a pile in the middle of the store. It consisted mostly of canned food and water but they'd also found a map and compass, which Shutov was studying, when the sound from the first shot had reverberated throughout the store.

Vuk was at the store entrance looking out to determine the direction from which the firing emanated. "I think it's coming from that way," he said as he indicated to the west.

Shutov tried to keep the men calm. "It could just be another survivor. There's no need to panic," but to him it seemed too orderly and too consistent to be another survivor just firing at infected.

"Vuk, take The Butcher with you and get eyes on the shooter. If he's from the ship then get him to stop before he draws in every infected around."

The Butcher nodded, popping open the double-barreled shotgun to check that it was loaded.

"Do we really need that?" asked Vuk.

"Hey, you want to go out there with only your dick in hand? Be my guest, axe boy. Me, I'm taking Vera with me." He smiled as he popped the shotgun closed and he walked out of the store.

Vuk and The Butcher moved methodically along the edge of the road, hugging buildings and fences where possible to keep a low profile. Most of the infected they passed weren't interested in them – instead they were drawn to the sounds of the shots or the ringing of the church bell. As they rounded a red brick building, Vuk saw a figure standing at the top of the smoke stack. His heart lept into his throat as the figure had a sniper rifle trained right in his direction. Assuming he was done for, Vuk closed his eyes and waited for the shot which rang out, almost immediately. Realizing he was not hit, he opened his eyes to see an infected lying fifteen meters in front of him, the fresh bullet hole gaping open in his forehead. Vuk scrambled back around the corner to The Butcher.

"He's around this corner at the top of the smoke stack," he whispered to the Butcher.

"Can you tell who it is?" the Butcher asked.

"No. It's too far and he's in shadow."

"Then we'll cut across the road and keep making our way down this street."

"That's suicide. He just got a headshot off from that far away. Whatever he's shooting with, it's long range and he's very accurate. He'll shoot us before he hears our voices."

"So what then?"

"Fuck, give me a moment, I just had a rifle pointed at me."

They both leaned against the wall as Vuk looked around. Another shot rang out, causing them both to jump. Vuk looked back east, shielding his eyes from the sun.

"The sun. We use the sun. If we go back and two blocks over, we should be able to keep the sun on our backs as we make our way over."

"And that helps us how?"

"The sun is low and strong. It's almost blinding. If we keep it on our backs he won't be able to see us moving, which means we can get close while he's virtually blinded. You can't shoot what you can't see."

The Butcher nodded impressed, "okay, we'll do it that way."

Vuk indicated towards the shotgun, "don't fire that thing unless you need to. I don't want to scare him until we find out why he's shooting."

Using Vuk's plan and keeping the sun to their backs they made it over towards the entrance gates of the building the shooter was perched on top of. The Butcher was about to open the gates when Vuk grabbed his hand and inspected the gate. "It's old and rusted, so wait for a shot before you open it," he whispered. They didn't have to wait long; the shot's echo masked the squeak of the rusted gate as The Butcher opened it.

Before them was a helicopter landing pad with a red cross and some military tents. It appeared that at some point this had been a staging area for medical evacuations or treatment. There were bodies nearby still in body bags which made no impact on masking the smell. Vuk and The Butcher surveyed the area from the shadow of the wall, noting the ladder that led all the way up to the top of the smoke stack.

Vuk pointed to the furthest tent, "You get in there where you can see him but he can't see you. I think he's just shooting infected but if not, it's better that he only sees one of us."

"Works for me," and with that The Butcher started to creep over to the furthest tent. His shotgun was trained on the figure thirty meters up the smoke stack.

"Don't bother with the shotgun," Vuk whispered, "the pellets will never reach that far up if you do fire."

"Maybe he doesn't know that," The Butcher replied.

Once The Butcher was in place, Vuk stashed the axe inside a tent and moved out on to the helipad, his arms held high and palms out to demonstrate that he was unarmed. He called out, "you there shooting. Down here."

Joe wiped the sweat off his forehead as the rising sun beat down on him. His ears were ringing from the sounds of the shots and once again he cursed himself for not getting ear plugs, although he wasn't sure if he'd still be able to find any. He could hear some other sounds but with the ringing he couldn't be sure.

"You up there, I'm down here at the helipad."

It was a voice. The demons had gained the power of speech. Joe put it down to hallucinations and looked for another demon to wipe off the scarred earth.

"Can you hear me?" the voice was louder and more insistent. Joe moved around and looked down. The sun was bright on this side and Joe had to shield his eyes but he could see something down at the helipad. There was a black figure standing there, all in shadow. The figure was waving both arms at him. Joe smiled in elation. It was Jesus. He had come down to personally take Joe up to heaven – the mission was complete.

"Jesus! My Lord I am ready," Joe called back.

"I'm not Jesus, my name is Vuk. I'm from a boat that was shipwrecked last night. There are other survivors, and we mean you no harm."

"You're not Jesus?" Joe asked forlorn.

"No I'm a survivor. Like you."

Joe studied the figure that was in shadow. What trickery was this? There were no boats. There were no survivors. There was only Joe and the demons, he knew he was the last man on Earth because God had told him so. But if this was not a man and he was not one of the demons then... and then it came to Joe. A revelation. This was not Christ, it was the Anti-Christ. Satan himself had come to tempt Joe and take him away from his mission as he had tempted Christ in the desert. That's why the figure was in shadow. That's why he had no face. Joe watched Satan intently as he unloaded the last magazine and reached into the pile for a new magazine.

From his vantage point Vuk saw the man move, saw him load another magazine into the rifle. He started to back away towards the wall, arms still up. "Hey I'm not sure what you're thinking but it's true. We can help each other. It doesn't have to be like this."

From up high Joe responded, "I cast thee out Beelzebub. You and your demon spawn."

Vuk scanned around as he saw the rifle rise and train on him There was no cover but he ran and dived anyway hoping for a miracle which, ironically, was also what Joe was hoping for.

The first shot whizzed past Vuk's feet to the place he was standing seconds ago. Vuk rose up and ran towards the smoke stack, hoping the angle would help. It did as the second shot was too wide. Joe stood up and looked down the stack trying to find Vuk when his body was abruptly riddled by AKM bullets. He stumbled back with each hit before toppling over the rail and falling to certain death. Vuk heard the sickening sound of Joe's spine crack as he landed neck first, ten meters away from him.

Vuk turned to where the shots had come from and saw The Butcher walk towards him with an AKM in hand. Vuk was at first relieved that Joe didn't have someone else with him but that relief quickly dissipated as The Butcher kept the rifle trained on him. The AKM looked formidable in his hands, similar to the well-known AK-47 it was an upgraded version, holding larger caliber bullets and had a clearer iron sight. That clearer iron sight was pointed directly at Vuk.

Vuk had good cause to be worried as The Butcher was at this moment debating whether or not to pull the trigger and also kill Vuk. The Butcher knew it was an irrational thought. He felt his breath quickening and his blood pressure was up, he was learning that he liked to kill. He looked around, there was no one to see, no police force to lock him up, he could just pull the trigger and kill this man right here and now without any consequences. He took a deep breath in – that kind of power was heady. Finally the rational part of his brain got a word in. There is no benefit in killing him right now, so wait until there is. You have a better chance of surviving with him alive than not – when that changes, pull the trigger.

The Butcher called out, "Is he dead?" Vuk nodded, not taking his eyes off the gun trained right at him. The Butcher nodded in response and lowered the AKM, at which point Vuk let out a long held breath. Recognition passed between the two of them – they both knew how close Vuk just came to dying and it had nothing to do with Joe shooting at him. Vuk decided there and then the only way he was going to get through this was to make himself indispensible.

"I see you upgraded," said Vuk.

"Yeah, her name is Grace and she had no trouble reaching up there. You can have Vera if you want, I left that bitch back there," said The Butcher as he took the CZ550 off Joe's corpse, not thinking of offering it to Vuk. "This is for Shutov."

The Butcher slung the rifle over his shoulder as he rifled through Joe's corpse. Vuk was repulsed with the ease with which The Butcher killed and subsequently looted Joe, as he walked towards the tent to collect Vera.

CHAPTER THIRTEEN

RINGING THE DINNER BELL

The distant sounds of gunfire reinforced Janik's decision that he'd made about leaving Cherno. Although he was dog-tired he couldn't sleep for long. Instead spent the rest of the night circumnavigating the town by staying along the coast. Janik felt that if he was going to survive this he would need to stay away from major towns, but he was too cowardly to make it alone. He'd need help but not back in that town - that town Cherno was fucking dangerous.

He was following the coast eastwards when he came across a small group of farmhouses, which he was about to ignore when he saw it - a bicycle resting on the side of a house, it was light green, looked a little worse for wear, but usable. The problem was that there were four of those things walking around there. Under normal circumstances Janik was very much a 'no reward is worth the risk' type of guy, avoiding anything that had danger attached. But these were definitely not normal circumstances and he was actually contemplating going up there and taking that bicycle – even though it would put his life at risk.

It was the dull ache in his belly and the parched taste in his mouth that pushed him over the edge, to risk going for the bike. His patrol pack was empty and he had no idea how far it would be to the next town. Getting closer, he peeked around the farm shed he was learning against – between him and the bike was an ocean of concrete. "Dammit," he cursed, as he looked for another way around, but there wasn't one. He knew that if he ran across the concrete he'd draw all four infected straight to him.

Dejected, he went inside the shed to get out of sight and come up with a new plan when he saw it - just lying there on the ground – a tin of sardines and a can of Pepsi. Not even thinking about expiry dates or rationing, he cracked them both open, and greedily consumed them. He looked around for more food but apart from some wood and a jerry can, there was nothing else.

He crept out the back of the shed and decided to move towards the barn that was near it. Slowly, he dropped down and crawled across the concrete and through the barn's entrance. He rose - looking over a hay bale he froze. One of the infected was there. Its legs must have been broken as it crawled along the floor using only its arms to move forward. At the sight of Janik it gave an unholy groan and moved towards him.

Janik ran up one of the stairs to the hay loft of the barn as the crawling infected moved towards him. Outside, he could hear the pounding of footsteps on the concrete as the other infected responded to the groan and ran towards him. Panicked, he searched for a way out, but Janik was trapped and there were more coming inside. He climbed up the stairs to the higher hayloft and looked out of the circular window. "Help! Help!" he called out but only the infected groaned in response.

Janik was not alone up here, on the ground next to him was a dead body. The dirt-covered denim overalls showed that he had been a farmer - this was most likely his barn. His head was a dried mess of blood and brains, with the top left side spread out against the wall behind him. In his hands was the instrument of his doom – the Lee Enfield rifle he'd apparently used to shoot himself. Janik looked at the gore and shrieked, to which the infected downstairs responded with inhuman groans as they made their way towards him.

Janik tried to pry the rifle out of the dead farmer's hand but long term rigor mortis made that difficult. He pulled at the fingers of the left hand until he heard them all break and the top of the rifle was released. The infected were walking up the stairs as Janik began snapping fingers on the farmer's right hand. The index finger around the trigger proved especially difficult but Janik finally snapped it, and the rifle was his.

Janik's hands shook as he held the rifle with his breathing coming in quick, desperate pants. He lined up the first infected in the iron sites and pulled the trigger. The bullet went wide, missing it and striking the wall behind. Janik wiped his sweaty hands on his shirt and took a deep breath, holding it in, as he lined up the next shot. He aimed for the center mass of the infected and when he was sure, he gently pulled the trigger, finding a surreal calm in the moment.

The infected dropped to the floor and Janik's world went silent as his ears shutdown from the noise of the rifle. He smacked at his ear with his palm, creating a popping sound, but otherwise the world was still silent and more were coming up the stairs. He lined up the next one and pulled the trigger. It joined its buddy on the floor. Sounds slowly returned to Janik's world as he shot the third and fourth infected, killing both instantly.

He slid down the wall to a sitting position - keeping the rifle ever trained at the door in case more entered. His breathing slowly returned to normal but his eyes and the rifle didn't move from pointing at the entrance. Janik was in shock, he'd never done anything like that before. His body had moved of its own accord and now his brain was catching up and trying to come to terms with it.

Eventually Janik looked away from the entrance as reason and logic returned to his world. He'd just killed four of those things - did that make him a murderer? He didn't know what they were but he didn't think they were human so he guessed he was okay. *They were people, they could have been this poor bastard's family,* he mused as he looked over the dead farmer. *It's you or them, so make it them,* his brain responded, and Janik felt the guilt dissipate. He rifled through the pockets of the dead farmer, finding a map with Russian notations he couldn't understand, and a compass. Taking both of them, he studied the map, using the compass and the coastline to determine where he was.

He could see that there was another large town nearby, Elektrozavodsk, which he would avoid. Avoid people, avoid big towns and get inland - that was his new plan. With the Lee Enfield and the deaths of four infected, Janik felt a new found bravery, maybe he could make it on his own. The map showed there were plenty of other small towns inland that he could hole up in. Remembering the bicycle outside, Janik smiled as he bounded down the steps, forgetting all about the one infected with broken legs that was still crawling around down there.

The sudden groan reminded him, but all too late as it struck out and hit Janik, causing him to trip and fall off the last couple of steps. He landed hard and the wrong way on his ankle as debilitating pain shot up from his twisted ankle. He shuffled away from the infected trying to get a shot as it crawled towards him. Arriving at the end of the barn he had nowhere to go, and realized it was now or never. He fired and fortunately hit it right in the head. There was no blood splatter but a black fluid oozed out of the hole as the infected's head hit the ground, hard.

Janik tried to stand but the pain in his ankle was intense and he couldn't get more than a step before needing to lie back down. Cursing himself for being so stupid he began to hop towards the bicycle. He might not be able to walk on that leg but he hoped he was still able to ride. Using the wall to steady himself, he swung the injured leg over the bicycle. Pushing down on the pedal made his ankle hurt but it was manageable which fortunately meant he could ride. He rode down the hill but it was slow going and painful. Janik found he was able to stay on the bicycle by using his good leg to pedal and support him when he stopped.

Janik rode towards Elektro, his plan of staying away from people and large coastal towns now forsaken. He needed to find another survivor to help him if he was going to last out here. He just hoped Elektro was safe because Cherno sure as hell wasn't.

CHAPTER FOURTEEN

EUTHANASIA

Robert was comforted by the sound of the ship's foghorn blaring in the distance. Although initially it was just an idea he threw out there to scare Doc, on reflection, it seemed like a good way to draw the infected towards the boat and away from them. He had written on the side of the boat the date and direction they had departed in case any other survivors came across it. Their packs were loaded with food and water canteens, the weight of which, coupled with carrying Arnold on a stretcher, made travel hard going. Doc was definitely out of shape, constantly asking for breaks more often than Robert would have wanted, but he obliged. He needed to keep Doc onside after his threat at the ship, and right now compliance was easier than conflict.

Having left at first light they followed the coast north and had made it to an inlet that went inland. Along the way they had seen nothing but trees. There were no signs of civilization along this part of the coast, and Robert was beginning to doubt if this was the right direction to take. Arnold had become increasingly worse, beads of perspiration reappeared on his forehead no matter how often Robert wiped them away. He'd also taken to muttering in his sleep. Doc constantly reinforced that if they didn't get medication soon, Arnold would die. Robert wasn't sure if this was a diagnosis based on medical training or Doc's own survival instinct, but he took heed anyway as they followed the inlet inland.

With the sun directly overhead they moved into the cool shade of a pine tree to stop for lunch. The lukewarm water in the canteen was still surprisingly refreshing and Robert drew a large sip. Doc slurped down the water, splashing some on his chin, which irritated Robert as he snatched the canteen away from him.

"Go easy on that. We only have two more and no idea how far it is to any other water source," he said as he tipped a small amount of water into Arnold's mouth before handing the canteen back to Doc.

"You rest here for half an hour. I'm going to scout ahead and see if there's a mountain range or some high ground where I can get the lay of the land," he moved away before stopping and turning back to Doc.

"Give me your pack."

Doc handed it over asking, "why?"

"Insurance," Robert replied, taking out some tinned food and water and giving it back to Doc, "what's left won't last you very long so my best advice is to stay here rather than run off." Doc nodded as Robert slung his pack over his front and walked off. He took a rebellious long swig of water as he watched Robert disappear into the distance.

Arnold's muttering was beginning to really get on Doc's nerves as he pondered a way out of this shitty situation. Right now he needed Robert but it was frustrating that Robert couldn't see that Arnold was just dead weight. Arnold was going to die, of that Doc was certain. The medication he needed was highly specialized, and they were not likely to find it on some piss poor part of the Russian coast. And even if it was there, by the time they got to it, Arnold would most likely have perished. He'd tried explaining this to Robert as they walked, but the man's stubbornness knew no bounds.

As a doctor he was used to making tough decisions and this was one of those. No matter what Robert said, they both knew that carrying Arnold through the woods was jeopardizing their own survival. Robert just refused to acknowledge it out of some stubborn loyalty to his roommate. Deep down Doc felt that Robert would have done the same for any one of the crew, Robert was just that kind of guy.

If only Arnold died right now, that would save them a lot of trouble. It would almost be a mercy. The man was very weak. He probably wouldn't struggle that much if his airways were blocked. Sure, an autopsy would show the true cause of death but that was unlikely to occur out here. Robert would suspect, of course, but suspicion is not the same as knowledge, and he could suspect all he liked.

The thought burrowed deep into Doc's brain. If he was going to do this then he needed to do it now, while Robert was away. He was unlikely to get another chance and it was a much more peaceful way to die than what was otherwise ahead for the poor man. Doc wiped the perspiration off his hands and ruffled his hair a few times, trying to come to grips with what he was about to do.

And then he heard it. It was faint but distinct, the sound of an outboard motor. All thoughts of murder were replaced with hope. There was a boat, he would be found and saved. He left Arnold alive under the tree and rushed to the shore, waving down the boat. In the distance a black shadow came towards him, the motor's droning bringing sweet music to his ears.

Robert waved back from the PBX, grinning from ear to ear. The PBX was a very lucky find, just sitting there at the inlet's edge. For a fleeting moment he thought maybe it was someone else's boat and they might be back soon. Taking it was theft but Robert justified that he needed it to save Arnold's life - so he took it. Perhaps later on he could return it once Arnold was better, but for now it was their best chance of moving Arnold.

He pulled it up at the shore next to Doc with a proud look on his face. Doc was amazed, "Where did you find this?"

"It was just parked on the coast a bit further up. Let's get Arnold on and get out of here, it's only got half a tank and I have no idea if we'll find more fuel." They tenderly loaded Arnold and the stretcher onto the boat, part of the stretcher hanging out the front. Doc squeezed on board, his legs crammed underneath the stretcher and although uncomfortable he was in, so they pulled away.

They travelled back along the inlet towards the ocean, wind in their hair and the fine mist of sea spray cooling them underneath the harsh midday sun. For a moment they both felt good, at peace with their situation. Doc reflected on the variety of large yachts and boats he'd been on in his life and how pale those experiences were compared to this one. It was amazing how quickly the little things began to matter and Doc couldn't help but smile. Then he remembered how close he'd come to murdering Arnold and although outwards his smile didn't change, to Doc it suddenly felt really forced. Things weren't better yet - this was a small drop of okay in an ocean of fucked-up that they still needed to swim through.

CHAPTER FIFTEEN

SANCTUARY

Janik wasn't sure why they had picked this place to hole up in. Sure the church was in good shape but it had only one entrance, which would be a problem if they were ever overrun by the infected. Janik didn't feel it was his place to complain though, he was just glad to have found the Survivors as his situation was looking bleak until then. Although he missed his bike he didn't really feel like he could say no when they asked to use it.

He rubbed his ankle, it was bandaged up and he didn't feel any pain. That was due to the miracle of morphine that one of the Survivors had injected him with. He could now walk on the leg and didn't feel a thing, although he had no idea how long that morphine would last - he hoped forever.

They were all from the ship, and almost all of them were armed. Some with pistols, some with axes and the lucky few with shotguns or rifles. Nobody walked around without a weapon by their side. It was an NRA wet dream - no one debated the right to bear arms, they all just did.

Alfie had recounted to Janik how they'd all washed up at the Elektro docks, caught in the same current. Not everyone made it that night as the Survivors came to grips with their predicament. Fortunately they had found some axes and very quickly turned the tide on the infected. While Janik was cowering in a shed in Cherno, these men had worked together to get everyone armed. They'd traded up from axes to pistol, pistol to rifles and scavenged what supplies they could in the town. Sure they'd lost some good men along the way, but Janik was enthralled to hear how they'd worked together to survive so far.

Janik examined them as the story was told, the men finding catharsis by recounting the tale. Some of them had the same hollowed-out look that Janik saw in his own reflection, the look of a survivor who had secretly wished he hadn't survived. And this was only after a day – what would they be like in a week, and how many of them would make it that long?

Everyone was amicable, sharing what they found and ensuring there was enough food and water to go around. They were coming and going with no real leader and no order to it. He saw this as weakness and noticed that some of the others were already hoarding food and ammunition. *Yeah this little hippy commune wouldn't last very long*, Janik thought as he made the decision to grab what he could and get out as soon as his bike had been returned.

Janik had swapped his Lee Enfield rifle for Alfie's crossbow. Alfie had acted as though he'd won the lottery but Janik valued silence over firepower, and was happy with the trade. He speculated about how long trading would last before people decided it was just easier to take, rather than to trade. What would happen when ammo got scarce? He didn't have a lot of faith in himself and therefore not a lot of faith in humanity. He wanted to be well on his way before things really became desperate.

Mitch and Pablo had just returned with a large boar over their shoulders. The others all cheered, Janik silently cursing them at their stupidity for making all that unnecessary noise. *These fools ready did need a leader*, he thought, as he watched them break up a church pew for firewood to roast the boar. He had to admit it did look tasty but creating a fire indoors didn't seem to be the brightest idea. *Maybe you should put your hand up to lead them,* but Janik berated himself for the thought. He would have liked to do it but he really didn't have that leadership quality. People just didn't believe him when he spoke because he didn't believe in himself. This was life or death for these people and Janik knew he wasn't the one to lead them.

Instead, he planned to skulk away in the night and find his own little hole to hide in and ride out the shit-storm. By himself - that's how he'd survived so far and that's how he would continue. His mind tactfully ignored the whole broken-ankle-and-the-need-for-morphine-provided-by-someone-else-thing. Janik would provide what help he could, so long as it didn't get in the way of his survival. So he'd decided to stay with them for as long as he benefited - when that changed, he was off.

The smoke was starting to get thick in the church. "We need to get this smoke out," he told no one in particular and, in return, no one paid him any attention. Janik looked up at the roof and took note of the high stained glass windows. They were too high for an infected to get in but high enough to let the smoke out. "These windows up here, we should break them to let the smoke out."

Some of the others looked around but they didn't react so Janik grabbed some rocks and began to throw them at the windows. He felt a slight twang of guilt as he threw the rock but soon he wouldn't care less about stuff like that as things became more desperate.

Others joined in and soon there was a blessed rush of fresh air as the smoke went out. Some Survivors patted Janik and slapped his shoulder, impressed by his thinking. Janik allowed himself to feel joy in the moment – it felt good to be useful and it seemed a long time since he had been that. The boar crackled along on the spit and Yuri, who always ignored him on the ship, sat down next to Janik to plan a raid tomorrow.

As he sat on the floor eating boar around the campfire, the talk of tactics and the infected died down and everyone just ate while watching the fire. It felt normal, and for now, that feeling, was a scarce and highly valuable commodity.

CHAPTER SIXTEEN

XAVIER

When Xavier had first washed up on the shore he was alone, with only the sounds of the ocean to comfort him. He did see further away a red flare and watched helplessly as The Boy was attacked and killed by infected. Afraid it would happen to him, Xavier stayed motionless on the beach, watching for any signs of help. After hours there wasn't anyone else, and he figured he had been separated from the rest. The only shape he was able to make out was the Air Traffic Control tower in the distance. Slowly he made his way there, crawling past some of the infected, and spent the remainder of the night and early dawn hiding out inside.

As light appeared, Xavier used the binoculars he'd found to search the surrounds. The airfield had the remnants of a large battle - dead soldiers and burnt-out cars littered the runway. There were the remains of barricades that had been set up and in the distance Xavier could see a forward-operating base with four sniper posts. It was here that he first caught sight of Duke, and while watching him, Xavier become increasingly impressed with his behavior. He watched Duke from afar as he'd used the smoke grenade to distract the infected; he watched as Duke, who was armed with the M16, still turned away from Chernogorsk at the sounds of shooting.

Duke seemed to want to avoid any other human contact which right now suited Xavier, who had no weapon. Instead he stalked him, following him from the airfield as Duke went off into the forest. Duke stayed in the cover of trees, avoided open fields and often stopped to listen to the sounds around him.

Xavier had no idea what was going on but he knew the infected were trouble and Duke seemed to know how to handle them. It wasn't much of a plan but for now he figured that stalking Duke would be better than sitting in an ATC tower for a rescue that was never likely to come. All he'd found in the ATC tower were some binoculars and a map. He wasn't quite sure how to read it, but it looked like Duke was heading north out of Balota following the dirt road at his right, but being careful to stay off it. The large mountain at the left could be Windy Mountain which meant if Duke continued along this road he would come to two towns.

Xavier watched Duke as he approached a cluster of what looked like farm buildings. When he was close Duke sat under a pine tree for a while and surveyed the infected as they roamed around the buildings. Watching him through the binoculars Xavier assumed Duke was debating whether to go down or avoid it. Duke opened his pack, took a swig of water and then went back to watching the buildings. Finally, Duke seemed to have come to a decision and packed up his gear before circumnavigating the barns. From Xavier's vantage point, it seemed like that was the smart call as there were ten infected at his count. Maybe if he had a partner Duke might have risked going in, but being alone he played it smart and avoided it.

Xavier felt that Duke was well suited to this situation, as though he'd been born for it. He handled his gun well, seemed to have a basic understanding of survival and orienteering, and played it safe. Xavier on the other hand was the opposite, having hailed from Marseilles and lived all his life in the city, he was now well out of his element traipsing through the forest. Xavier had decided he'd watch and learn, following Duke from a distance until an opportune moment struck. He didn't exactly have a plan for what to do in that moment but the key was to get a weapon and right now that was proving to be extremely difficult.

Duke approached the next large town, which if Xavier was reading the map right was Zelenogorsk, since Duke had stayed along the trees and avoided Drozhino. Once again, Duke stopped at the top of the hill and watched the infected roaming around the town. It was spread out but at the southern entrance there was a general store. From high up Duke could see through the glass that it hadn't been picked clean, there was still stuff inside. The store's car park was littered with burnt out and abandoned cars, bordered by a concrete wall on two sides. From his vantage point up in the hill, Xavier could see that the store still had items littered on the ground and assumed that's what Duke was hesitating about. Go in and raid the store or go around and avoid it?

Duke watched the roaming infected before cutting back along the road and around the field to his left. There were houses with infected between Duke and the store and it seemed that he was going to take the long way around to avoid them. Xavier saw a barn nearby and decided to take a position inside. From inside the barn he could see out the doors across the field to the store. He watched as Duke circumnavigated the field and avoided the houses as he moved towards the concrete wall.

Duke walked along the field he kept looking around, not at the infected but far off into the tree lines. The day and craziness of this situation had made him very paranoid and he couldn't shake the feeling that he was being watched. At the wall Duke kept low and walked slowly along it, trying, where possible, to stay in its shadow. Of course there were infected everywhere but they didn't seem to watch, they were more like animals than people. His instincts told him that someone else was watching him and he knew to trust those instincts.

Leaning against the wall he looked around wondering where they could be? There were trees everywhere and any one of them could be hiding someone. He took a sip of water, shook his head, hoping that would somehow also shake off the feeling of being watched. It didn't. Instead, he continued along the wall towards the general store. He needed gear to survive and right now the store was the only option for miles.

The wall ended and from there he could see the back of the store. He could also see there were three infected roaming around the back entrance. To Duke it looked like they continued to roam around where had once lived or been infected. Here in the town, the infected were wearing worker clothes and Russian civilian gear, whereas the first ones he encountered at the camp were all wearing military uniforms. They must also be able to see, as they avoided the piles of debris on the ground. They also ignored each other and walked around vacantly, staring off into the distance. That probably meant he should avoid high population centers as higher populations meant more infected – but right now he needed those supplies.

Crawling along the concrete towards the back entrance of the store, he kept an ever-watchful eye on the infected as they roamed nearby. He felt a shudder run down his spine as the reality of the situation overwhelmed him for a moment and he stopped. *Fuck. This shit is real, this is actually happening.* He allowed the moment to pass as he looked into the scratched whites of the nearby infected's eyes. He couldn't put his finger on what it was that was getting to him about the eyes, until he realized that they never blinked. The infected was close enough for Duke to notice its eyeballs were dried up and scratched by millions of particles of dust. Looking out from them must be like looking out from behind the worst cataracts in history.

The infected was looking right in his direction. Duke slowly moved his hand back and forth. It groaned but ignored him as though it didn't quite see the movement. He then waved his hand quickly, and the infected's demeanor instantly changed. It roared aggressively and started making its way towards Duke. He grabbed a nearby tin can and tossed it away from him. The infected followed the movement of the can in the air and ran towards the place where it landed. Duke nodded, storing this new found information as he continued to crawl into the store.

Xavier watched from the barn, also taking note of what Duke had just learned. *Fast movement and sounds attract them. Being close isn't a problem so long as you're slow and quiet.* Duke crawled his way to the back of the store which was concealed from Xavier's angle, so he dropped the binoculars – to come face to face with a crawling infected not three meters away from him. Xavier had been standing still for so long watching Duke that the infected hadn't noticed him. It looked like it used to be a teenage boy but its lower half had been torn off and it was now dragging a train of entrails as it crawled toward Xavier.

Unable to stem his rising panic, Xavier backed away slowly before turning to run. Another infected was walking around the back entrance so that exit was out of the question. Instead Xavier went up to the hay loft, hoping that the infected wouldn't be able to crawl up the stairs. He scurried around but found nothing to defend himself with, so if the infected could come up the stairs then Xavier was a goner.

At the same time the infected was crawling into the barn, Duke slowly walked into the back of the store. With one hand he pushed open the door, wincing at the quiet squeak it made as it opened. It was comparatively dark in the back of the store but still light enough for Duke to ascertain there was no one in this storage room. A fine layer of dust was kicked up as he walked down the back of the store towards the front entrance. The dust danced around in the high beams of sunlight that pierced through the high ventilation shutters. Duke walked through to the front of the store where the light streamed through the large display windows.

Outside the windows, Duke could see the infected roaming but they appeared to be ignoring him. He began to gather up any pertinent supplies, placing them in a larger Alice pack that he found at the back of the store. Although he still hadn't found a map, he now had a compass and matches, so survival in the woods was looking more feasible. He could hunt game but without anything to gut and skin it with, that would be redundant, so he gathered as much food and soda cans as he could carry. Satisfied with his haul, he looked out the glass windows as he slung the Alice pack on his back.

Across the field there was a commotion and movement. It seemed a person was running from the infected and heading straight towards town. Every infected he passed was drawn to the sound and motion and his followers increased. *Shit! If that fool does that in town he'll have the whole lot on him in no time,* Duke cursed as he trained his M16A2 at the door. He watched the figure running straight towards the store. Duke realized he was heading straight towards him and recognized the man as being Xavier, the Frenchy from the ship. *That's already a dead man running, so if he comes in here I'm putting him down myself.* He flicked off the safety and trained the gun right at the door.

Xavier had fucked up, plain and simple. He learnt the hard way that possessing the knowledge that you should stay quiet and low means jackshit when you panic. Back at the barn the crawling infected was unable to climb up the stairs but its rustling and moans had attracted the other walkers. Xavier panicked when the walker came into the barn. He didn't want to be trapped in the hay loft with the walker, even though it hadn't seen him. In that moment it seemed logical to run - so he did - right out of the barn. The flash of movement caused both infected to become aggressive and give chase. As they were between him and the trees, Xavier ran instead down the field – that was mistake number two.

His running visage across the field drew the attention of all the infected roaming around nearby houses, so they also gave chase. Xavier looked behind him to see three more angry bloodstained monsters behind him and his mind became a white ball of panic. Reason checked out on a two week holiday and fear moved in and made itself at home. He ran faster, harder, his lungs burning and a pain forming at his side. He wiped away at the tears blurring his vision and focused on the general store. It was sanctuary, he would be safe there.

As he got closer he could make out Duke inside the store, his gun primed and focused on the entrance. Xavier felt a moment of relief until he heard Duke's voice. "You bring those things in here you French fuck and you're dead! Get the fuck away from me!"

"Help!" was his meek response.

"Your problem. You deal with it!"

Xavier's world fell apart and he contemplated just stopping and letting the infected finish him off there and then. He would become a macabre sacrifice that would hopefully riddle Duke with guilt. But the will to live prevailed so he ran past the store, past boarded up houses, down the road looking for somewhere to hide. Nothing else was open, there was nowhere to hide. Then he saw the dome of the church.

The church wouldn't be locked that was some kind of rule or something, Xavier thought as he ran towards it. Of course when he got there it was locked, and he reminded himself that the rules don't apply anymore. Xavier couldn't see anywhere else to go so he turned around and doubled back to the store, trying to use the houses between the store and church to break the chasing infected's line of sight.

Duke watched from the window as Xavier ran past with the infected following. Silently he was relieved that Xavier had listened because he wasn't sure whether he would have shot him if he had come in. Relief was quickly replaced by the guilt - crushing and immediate. He'd essentially condemned the man to death. Sure he hadn't pulled the trigger but he hadn't helped him either. He had a rifle, they could have fortified the store. Together they he could have taken out the infected. Instead he threatened Xavier with death and then ensured it would be very soon. What did that make him? *A survivor,* his mind responded, but his mind wasn't very convincing. Duke thought it was too late to do anything - but he was about to get a reprieve.

Xavier burst into the back of the store slamming against the far wall. He shut the door behind him and pulled down an empty wire shelf, creating a small barricade at the door. At his feet he found a revolver and two speed loaders. Xavier had never fired a gun before but he'd watched plenty of movies so he scooped up the gun and bullets and loaded it. From the main part of the store he heard Duke call out, "Frenchy is that you?"

"Who the fuck is back there!" Duke called out more insistent this time. Then the pounding on the door started as the Zeds tried to get in.

"You fuck - you left me to die," Xavier yelled back.

"I'm sorry," was all Duke could say.

Xavier tried to process that, but the pounding interrupted any thoughts. The shelf was getting pushed back as the Zeds were about to break through the barricade. Xavier turned his shaking hand to the door and backed away from it. An infected knocked through the door, shoving aside the barricade as Xavier fired. He didn't see where the bullet went but it didn't hit him.

"Was that you firing?" Duke called out.

"Yeah! They're coming through the back," Xavier responded.

"Then get in here! We can cover both entrances from here." Xavier turned and ran into the main part of the store, holding his revolver in front of him. As he walked through the entrance into the main store, he saw Duke with the M16A2 pointed right at him. Xavier froze, this was the first time he'd ever had a gun pointed at him. "Move!" Duke called out, breaking Xavier's reverie as he moved out of the entrance and next to Duke.

Xavier copied Duke and pointed the revolver at the entrance. Duke noted the shaking hand, "don't shoot that unless you need to. I have 30 rounds in this mag which should be enough to deal with them." He pressed the butt of the gun against his shoulder and exhaled as he waited for the first infected to pop out from the back of the store.

Xavier lowered the revolver. He wouldn't do it right now but he resolved to save at least one bullet for the back of Duke's head. Not now though, as Duke was his best chance for survival. Later, when things were safe - when Duke trusted Xavier - that's when he would get his revenge for being left for dead.

CHAPTER SEVENTEEN

KILL OR BE KILLED

Shutov felt like they'd had a good day in Cherno but observing his men, he noted their demeanor told a different story. Many of them weren't used to hearing the gun shots that had been ringing out all day. Emanating firstly from that religious nutter shooting from the tower. Then, later on, different rifle shots rang from out-of-town before, finally, their own shots in Cherno. The men had already learnt not to shoot infected that were located in town, but sometimes it was unavoidable, and every time a shot was fired, the men panicked. Every shot led to a barrage of questions and analysis.

"Who's firing in Cherno?"

"Where did the shots come from?"

"What gun was that?"

"Who do we know who had one like that?"

Despite the rising panic, they'd had a good day - no one had died, and it seemed everyone was well kitted up. They had food, water, basic survival gear, and some of them even found camouflage clothing. Sure, there were a few sheep among the wolves, but overall, he was pleased with the men he had and didn't want to lose them.

They were now bunkered down in a small apartment building across the road from a hospital. Vuk had picked the location - it was easily defensible with men able to observe from the roof and only one entrance to guard.

Shutov was becoming increasingly impressed with Vuk – he had good instincts coupled with military training and he understood the need for rank and control. Vuk had also found the military documents that Shutov would look over tonight. He hoped they would contain information about what was happening in Chernarus.

Shutov had put The Butcher and Sam on the roof to take first watch. The Butcher was a concern to Shutov - he coveted his AKM which he refused to relinquish when others needed a gun. The man was intent on survival and Shutov was sure he was using them until he didn't need them anymore. He didn't really trust The Butcher so he made sure that The Butcher always had another man nearby. The Butcher was a killer, cold blooded and without remorse, so right now Shutov would rather have him nearby that out in the unknown.

He walked up the stairs, nodding to the men as he passed them. Some nodded back but many kept their eyes down, focused on themselves. Shutov felt that if he didn't do something soon he was going to lose some of them. They already looked defeated and it had only been two days. If they continued to be beaten down by this situation then by the end of the week they'd all be dead.

Vuk was seated near the ladder that led to the roof, eating some baked beans from a can. Shutov sat down next to him, resting the CZ550 on his lap. The fool from the tower had carved the word *Salvation* in the wooden grip and Shutov had taken to unconsciously tracing the letters with his trigger finger.

Vuk noticed this and indicated towards the word, "salvation is what these men need sir. We're in an unprecedented situation here and all this shooting, it's..." Vuk trailed off looking for the right word.

"I know Vuk, but what am I supposed to do? Sometimes killing is necessary. You yourself were nearly killed," replied Shutov.

"I understand that Sir, but that man was delusional, he thought I was Jesus."

"These are crazy times filled with crazy people. Would you have preferred The Butcher didn't kill him?"

"Of course not. I still want to live, I'm just concerned about the cost. We could have tried to talk him down, tried to communicate with him. The Butcher didn't do any of that - he just fired - and now a man is dead."

Their conversation drew in the other men who sat at the stairs and listened to them. "It was killed or be killed," Shutov responded, "the man was well armed and shooting at you. Who knows how many others he may have killed if he wasn't killed?" Some murmurs of assent came from the men on the stairs.

"The Butcher did the right thing," said Luther, "the man was dangerous up there."

Vuk looked over to Luther. The man was a worm, he was one of the weak that attached himself to Shutov like a newborn on the teat.

"We could have talked him down," said Vuk. Luther shook his head and went back to rifling through his pack. Vuk turned to Shutov.

"We lost a very good opportunity to gain intelligence about this situation. Those papers I gave you are weeks old, his knowledge was up-to-date. Who knows what information was lost when he died?"

"I don't think you would have had a chance to ask a lot of questions with bullets flying at your face, do you?"

"In this case I think you're right. But what will we do when we see the next survivor?" Vuk queried.

Shutov thought over a response until finally he exhaled, shaking his head, "I don't know. The only people I trust right now are the men in this building. I would die for them and they would die for me. What if we bring someone else in and they steal from us?"

"What if one of us steals from another?"

"Then he will be executed," replied Shutov and some of the men cheered, fists pounding the stairs.

"Death? For something as simple," he held up his meal, "as a can of beans?"

"Vuk look at our food situation. We have enough for two or three days maximum. A can of beans may mean the difference between life and death."

"So then we should ration the food out, no man should eat well while another man goes hungry," Vuk offered up his beans to the men around him but they refused and waved it away.

"Are you setting up rules now?"

"In a way we all should. You've just said stealing equals death and I think we should also ensure no man hoards the food whilst another man starves."

The men nodded and Shutov followed with his own nod.

"Agreed. Let it be known we share everything, food, water, ammunition – everything. But only with the men before me."

"What will we do if we see another man not of this group?" asked Vuk.

"Like you Vuk, I want to live. How can I trust someone I don't know? And even if I could trust them, every extra man is another mouth to feed, another person to arm up. Can we really afford to further spread thin our supplies?"

"No!" some of the men responded.

"We can't," Vuk also replied, "so if we see someone else, then we let them pass."

"Why the sudden concern about others?"

"Because tomorrow we move to Elektro. And just as we have found sanctuary here there may be others there. I've been on the other side in Serbia, scared, running alone, afraid of groups of men with guns. I want it to be clear - we leave others alone - we don't assist them but we don't harm them either."

"We could let them pass, form a truce of sorts," Vuk nodded but Shutov continued on, "but then what? Perhaps the one man we let pass returns with ten others. Or perhaps he's alone and follows us from afar, waiting until we are asleep to kill and rob us."

"You can't be certain of that."

"No. All I'm certain of is that these are desperate times and in desperate times, men are unpredictable and dangerous. If we are to be safe then we must be suspicious of all others, I'd rather be paranoid and wrong, than trusting and dead."

"So what should we do then?" Vuk asked.

From the ladder upstairs came The Butcher's cold response, "we kill on sight."

Some of the men nodded and Vuk shook his head, "it can't be like this. Not again."

Shutov rested his hand on Vuk's knee, "Vuk I agree it's not pleasant-"

"Not pleasant! You speak of killing men for petty crimes they may or may not commit."

"And you speak of laws in a lawless land. There are no rules out there, no police force to rely on, no judge to sentence a man. I speak of survival - that's all. But you are right that we should all be committed to this. We will vote on this. After all, we're not savages."

"You could have fooled me," Vuk retorted.

"You misunderstand. What we're proposing is savage. To kill men so as not to be killed by them. But we don't do this out of animal instinct, or a homicidal desire," *not all of us* Shutov thought, glancing up at The Butcher, "we do this solely to survive. Any person we kill may have valuable loot that may help one of our men survive another day. He may have food, water, weapons or ammunition - therefore we kill him so that one of us may live. But only if we all agree to this. So a show of hands for those who agree. Will it be kill or be killed?" Immediately two hands appeared down the hatch to the roof.

Some of the other men raised their hands quickly and the few sheep were slower but eventually the eyes of the others forced them up. Only Vuk kept his hands down as he buried his face in them, trying to erase the moment. He pulled his hands away and looked around at the others, some encouraging him to raise his hand.

"What you speak of is banditry. Murdering others for the gun on their back and the beans in their pockets," said Vuk.

"I speak of survival," Shutov replied.

"We could survive without killing others, but, as you say, it would be more dangerous. So let us be clear that we are agreeing to banditry. If anyone takes issue with that then lower your hand now," Vuk hoped one would lower his hand because alone he had no chance.

Vuk and Shutov looked around but all hands stayed raised. Vuk pondered on this. If he left them he'd most likely be killed by Shutov. If Shutov was prepared to kill men for the food in their packs, what would he do to Vuk if he betrayed him and left? As distasteful as it was to him if he didn't agree, then he'd probably have an 'accident' and die anyway.

"Then I will be a bandit with you my brothers, not because I want to but because I need to, and together we will survive," and with that Vuk reluctantly raised his hand. A small cheer erupted from the men and they congratulated each other as a small amount of camaraderie returned.

"Very good my brothers. Rest well tonight because tomorrow we move to Elektro," a hurrah resounded as the men dispersed to find somewhere to sleep.

"God help any Survivors we see tomorrow," Vuk whispered but it was still loud enough for Shutov to hear. Shutov ran his trigger finger across the carved word *Salvation* on his rifle, this time consciously.

"I think we can both agree God forsook this place a long time ago," he slung the rifle on his shoulder and walked down the stairs, not waiting for a response.

Vuk looked up the ladder at The Butcher's smiling face staring down at him. The Butcher nodded before moving away from the hatch and returning to the darkness. Using his finger Vuk scooped the last of the beans out of the tin and tossed it aside. *He's right - the Devil rules here,* Vuk thought as he pulled his shirt up over his eyes and tried to get some sleep.

CHAPTER EIGHTEEN

ARNOLD IS SAVED

They disembarked from the PBX boat at the docks of the first town they saw. Arnold had gotten worse. His skin had taken on an orange tinge and his side was distended, causing him to groan in pain any time Doc examined it. This town was swollen, with infected so Robert left Doc and Arnold in a warehouse near the docks as he went solo, to look for a hospital.

The town was split between an industrial area to the north near the water, and a residential area further south and inland. As he looked through the northern part of the town, he spent most of the time on his belly, crawling past groaning infected whilst hunting for supplies. He'd found food, water, clothes and lots of dead bodies clutching guns, but no hospital. By the state of decomposition, these people had been dead for a long time, but for some reason they weren't infected. Robert took lots of mental notes, the occasional drink, and a map and compass as he continued on his search for medication.

Running along a field he saw a sign posted on the road that indicated the town's name was Berezino. Looking at the map and tracing back his route he could see the inlet where he'd found the PBX, the peninsula where the ship had been beached and the docks where they had left the PBX. He took out a pen and marked some of the locations that he'd return to - especially the military area that had been set up near a football field - as he planned a route south.

In his morning of scouting the northern part of Berezino, Robert had learnt to dodge the infected and understand that their sense of hearing was far better than their sense of sight. So long as you were low and quiet you could crawl almost right beside one and they wouldn't notice you. It also seemed their olfactory senses were not working – or else overpowered by their own stench - as they didn't seem to smell Robert either. He didn't know about their sense of touch, and he hoped to never discover whether they still possessed their sense of taste.

He was carrying a Remington 870 shotgun which he'd chosen over some pretty impressive looking rifles at the military tents. Robert figured that any contact with the infected would be up close and he liked the stopping power that a shotgun provided over the range of a sniper rifle. He had 24 slugs and fortunately, so far, hadn't needed to fire one.

Crossing the field he passed a crudely constructed observation post that had three infected roaming around it. Robert decided to avoid any risk, circumnavigated it and continued across the field to the large buildings in the distance, hoping one of them was a hospital. He came upon a general store that had a burnt-out Humvee and a pile of body bags at its rear entrance. Avoiding the infected, he made his way inside the store looking for something to eat.

There he found cans of beans, cans of pasta and a larger Alice pack which he took, ditching his ship-issued patrol pack. He filled the backpack with as much food and drink as he could carry and found another map, which he also took along with a hunting knife and matches. The pack was heavy with food and loot as he walked out the front of the store and crawled across the road. He moved low and kept to the building's shadows as he turned the corner to see the big red cross painted on the side of a tall building. This was a makeshift hospital with camouflage netting and tents set up outside the main building. *Bingo*, he thought as he made his way around the back, avoiding the front and the infected wandering around there.

He looked through the tents but they had been picked clean of weapons, although he found a medical supply box on the ground outside one. Inside the box were epi-pens, morphine auto-injectors, bandages and blood bags. They weren't on the list of medications Doc told him to look out for but he decided to take one of each just in case. With the back of the hospital a dead end, he slowly made his way to the front.

The front was a wall of glass but inside he could see similar medical boxes on the floor. He made his way to the front door and found that the double doors had been chained shut. He violently rattled the doors, but since he hadn't suddenly developed super-human powers, it was futile as the doors remained locked tight. He tapped on the glass window with the tip of his Remington, two or three shots and the glass would break. He looked around at all the walkers that roamed nearby and further away and decided he wasn't going to do that alone. He needed help, he'd need Doc. *If he was still there,* he couldn't stop the thought from forming as he sensed Doc would abandon them at the first opportunity he could.

He started to make his way back to Doc when the flame decal caught his eye. Leaned up against a pile of wreckage was a Kawasaki motorbike, bright red with a flame decal on the fuel tank. He assumed the owner was the dead youngish looking man nearby. A quick rummage of his pockets recovered the motorbike keys and confirmed his assumption. The bike's fuel was low but it started first go and seemed to be in good shape. Robert revved the engine and the infected came from everywhere, the sound attracting them like ants to a sugar pot. He pushed back the kickstand, put the bike in gear and took off down the road, a train of infected chasing him.

The speed of the motorbike made short work of outrunning the chasing infected, they lost sight and interest once the noise of the bike faded away. Robert arrived back at the docks and was relieved to find Doc still sitting with

Arnold, drip feeding him water. Doc was just as relieved to discover it was Robert making that noise and even managed a smile as he rode the motorbike into the warehouse.

Robert parked the bike and closed the warehouse door. He lifted the heavy Alice pack off his shoulder and handed Doc some food and soda, "I found a hospital in town with a medical box outside. This was all that was inside it." He indicated the medical haul he laid at Doc's feet. "Is that any help for Arnold?"

Doc looked it over picking up a blood bag and reading the label, "O negative."

"That useful?" Robert asked.

"It's the universal donor so it can be used for anyone. But it's not refrigerated and we don't know how old it is so it may cause more harm than good. The rest of this stuff looks like combat hospital provisions. It'll get someone patched up and moving again, but it's no help for the treatment of malaria."

"So we have to go back. There were more boxes inside but the place was locked. I think there's a way in but I'll need help."

"We have to be quick about it. Arnold's getting worse by the minute."

"Then we'll take the bike but we need to make a quick fuel stop and get you a gun."

Doc was shocked, "a gun!"

"You said so yourself Doc, this is a war zone. And you don't go into a war zone unarmed."

After a quick side trip back to the military tents, Robert returned to the front of the hospital, this time with Doc. They left Arnold as comfortable as possible in the shed and at the military tents, Robert found Doc a silenced M9 pistol. Doc got a crash course in gun safety as Robert set up some tin cans as a crude firing range. Doc's first shot was wide but the silenced nature of the gun didn't attract any infected. The next two still missed and Robert decided they should conserve ammo and avoid wasting any more shots.

"Just point it at the chest and keep pulling the trigger until they fall down," was the final instruction Doc was given as they stood outside the hospital.

They'd left the bike at the back of the general store and had moved quietly across to the hospital, Doc learning about avoiding the infected from Robert.

Later on, the intellectual side of Doc's brain would try to comprehend the physiological reasons for the sense of hearing becoming more dominant than that of sight. For now, survival was all he thought about. Being so close to the infected unnerved him, and it was not something he could get used to.

Outside the hospital he pointed a shaky pistol at nearby infected, willing them to walk away as Robert pumped the shotgun and fired at the glass window. The boom shattered the peaceful silence of the countryside, and was immediately followed by a second shot. Doc looked around at the infected all running towards the noise. Panicked, he called out, "they're coming, get that fucking window open."

A third shot broke the glass and it shattered at the base of the window. "Inside, now!" Robert yelled at Doc as he took stock of the infected running towards them. "Get to the back and look through those boxes. I'll take care of them."

Robert went behind a check-in counter and trained the Remington at the broken glass entrance waiting. He breathed hard desperately trying to catch his breath with rapid pants that did nothing as the first infected entered. The sound of Doc rummaging through boxes behind him disappeared and his mind went blank as he focused on the infected. Looking down the iron sights he waited until one was close and squeezed the trigger. He didn't hear the shot fire but suddenly the infected's face was gone, replaced by a blackened cavity oozing out dark brown bile.

He sensed Doc was saying something behind him but his mind shut it out as he focused on the entrance waiting for the next infected to rush in. It was just as quickly disposed of as four more came through the glass. Robert fired off three more shots before the shotgun fired dry – out of ammo.

Suddenly the sounds and groans of the infected returned as he kicked the last one away trying to reload the Remington. The infected struck at his side and Doc noticed blood seeping out of the wound as Robert reloaded the gun and put a round into its chest. The infected dropped and Robert made short work of the final four that came through the glass.

The hospital was suddenly quiet - but for the sounds of their breathing - and Robert turned to face Doc, "did you find the medicine?"

"No, nothing. I have some antibiotics that might keep him alive for a bit longer but they won't cure him."

"So all of this has been for nothing," Robert looked over the bodies at the entrance.

"You're bleeding, so let's get that sorted first before we worry about Arnold." Robert looked down the wound at his side as Doc patched it up with a bandage.

"Oh shit. Does that mean I'm going to turn into one of them?"

"I don't know. I've taken some more useful supplies but let's get out of here before more of them arrive. We'll give Arnold these antibiotics, at least it will buy him some more time," replied Doc.

They returned to the motorbike at the general store. The shock was wearing off as Robert's mind returned to almost normal function. "We'll come back at dusk. As the glass is now open we won't need to make any noise which should give you enough time to find the right medication," Doc nodded as he hopped on the bike and they returned to the shed.

But they didn't return that night, instead they spent the night burying Arnold out in a field. When they'd returned from the failed hospital run, Arnold was dead. Silently, Doc was relieved as realistically this now increased their chance of survival. Robert said nothing, instead he beat his hands against the tin walls in fury until they were bloody. He looked around for a shovel and cried for the entire duration it took him to dig Arnold's grave. Doc watched from under a tree as Robert insisted on doing it himself.

As Robert shoveled down the last of the dirt over Arnold's body, the cloud-cover cleared and a bright full moon lit up the field. Doc asked, "should we leave a marker of some sorts?"

"No," Robert replied, as he patted the dirt one last time with his hands. He tossed the shovel aside and walked back to the shed. In essence, Arnold was now saved – he was spared from ever knowing a world that had been eclipsed by the infection.

CHAPTER NINETEEN

THE CLASH

It was a peaceful and serene start to a day that would ultimately result in the violent end to some of the survivors of the MV Rocket. Inside the church the fire had died down during the night, its embers retained a final glow that competed against the brilliant rising sun to light the room. The Survivors rubbed the last vestiges of sleep out of their eyes, which Janik noted with disdain also included the two sentries who were supposed to have kept watch.

Fortunately, the night had been incident free and Janik was relieved to note that his bike had been returned and was now resting along the wall. He gathered up his meager possessions and loaded them onto his backpack as he prepared to leave.

"Janik, you shouldn't go out alone," Yuri berated him.

"The bike only holds one and I want to scout out the area. See how far it is to the next town," Janik replied. He hadn't told anyone that he had a map so he needed somewhere private to look it over and plan his departure. Yuri wasn't convinced but Janik held up the crossbow, "I'll be fine. A couple of hours max and I'll be back before midday. It'll give me a chance to look for some good places for us to raid in the afternoon." Placated, Yuri relented as Janik hopped on the bike and went on his way.

A different kind of protest was echoed at the Bandit camp as they prepared to move out. Alejandro had just returned from the nighttime scouting mission in Elektro, reporting back that it seemed like all of the Survivors were holed up in the church. As they looked over the map, Vuk proposed that they leave them be in the church and instead raid the area east of them near the water. The map showed many buildings and they were sure to find something of benefit around there.

The Butcher had a different idea and proposed that it would be better to blitz them whilst they were unaware and take them all down in the church. "It is one thing to kill on sight. It's another to hunt and murder a man for sport," Vuk retorted.

"This is not sport, this is survival," The Butcher replied.

"No, it's murder. They pose no threat to us."

Shutov interjected, "you are both wrong." He turned to Vuk, "if they are not with us then they are a threat," and to The Butcher, "but Vuk is also right. There is no reason to hunt them. We'll leave them be if they stay west. More importantly, Alejandro noted there was a bus in Elektro that looked operable."

"Why do we need a bus?" Harrison asked.

Shutov showed them the military papers he'd been reviewing all night, "because this tells me there is a better prize up north and the bus will provide the best way for us all to get there."

Vuk was happy with this plan, so long as it avoided conflict he could live with it. He turned to Alejandro, "what do we need to get the bus operating?"

"There's some work required - I saw a tire was flat. I'm not sure about the engine but its cover was up so I suspect it had given the previous owner trouble. We'll most likely need fuel."

Shutov called forward Sam, a small man who has surprisingly large arms. "Sam you worked under Robert on the boat."

"Yes, I made that drunk look good," Sam responded.

"Do you think you can fix the bus?"

"I've done years of MOS repairs in the Air Force, I think I can fix your little bus. But I'll need tools, and by the sound of it, some spare parts."

Shutov turned to the others, "then men, we have a goal for today. We get Sam what he needs to get that bus working by nightfall," they begin to disperse, gathering their things when Shutov continued, "but make no mistake. If we see one of the Survivors we kill them on sight. Forget about your previous life on the boat, they are not who they used to be and neither are we. I don't want anyone knowing our plans." The men nodded and continued preparing to move out. Shutov looked over at Vuk.

"I'll kill but I won't hunt," Vuk responded to his look.

Shutov nodded in agreement, "that's all the commitment I need from you to keep us safe."

Lucas was seated up in the firehouse of Elektro looking out over the fields, enjoying the serenity, that is if you ignored the infected roaming around. He was watching them through the aimpoint sight of an M14 rifle he'd found in the firehouse. Although he was disappointed it didn't have a zoom sight, it was still a nice weapon to have and Lucas was practicing killing infected with it.

Lucas had hunted with his father from a very young age and it was these outings that cemented their relationship. His father was sparse with words but loved Lucas, and teaching him to hunt was the best way he knew how to express that love. Lucas understood that his father was shell-shocked, having been discharged from the Army for failing in his sniper duties. At family gatherings when his Uncles got too drunk, they would mock his father for not being able to take the shot, but Lucas thought he understood why. His father enjoyed the thrill of the hunt, the tracking, observing of prey, testing wind conditions, lining up the shot, waiting for that moment. He was fine with hunting animals and shooting paper targets but the first time his father needed to pull the trigger to kill a man he couldn't, and for that he was discharged from the Swedish Army.

For Lucas, this meant he received military training in effective sniping whenever he hunted with his father. The first time he took down a prize buck, his father was so proud he relayed the story to the entire village. Lucas was only ten at the time. That night his father hardly touched the venison but looked at Lucas with pride, constantly smiling. From then on Lucas was hooked, much to the disdain of his girlfriend who believed hunting was barbaric and cruel.

He was now applying that training to the infected, who were in many ways like animals. They didn't hide behind cover, they didn't notice anything that wasn't in their immediate vicinity and they were singled-minded about their prey. With ammo too precious to waste, he lined them up, watched their paths, followed the movement, and when ready, he took the shot. Lucas kept the safety on so the rifle wouldn't fire, but he longed to flick it off and shoot for real. He turned away from the field to face the Survivors he was supposed to be providing overwatch for, as they looted the store.

Lucas was like Janik in his assessment that many of the Survivors were undisciplined and that this would be their undoing. Unlike Janik, Lucas wanted to help them, to teach them what he knew. So when the general store raid was planned, he volunteered to go overwatch and keep the raiders safe. He received a lot of blank looks but took the time to explain the benefits of having an overwatch.

Lucas felt decisions were being made without any real forethought - like planning to loot the store without any effective cover. Without someone watching over them, the men in the store wouldn't know they were in danger until it was too late. As Lucas watched them inside the store, he wished he'd had another overwatch at the second firehouse near to the power plant. That would provide cover from the south. But for now, it was just him.

Janik rode far away from the raiding parties and had taken to the shade underneath a pine tree to study the map. He was on the top of a hill and could see in the distance the silhouette of Lucas on the top of the firehouse. He returned to studying the map and was so focused on it that he didn't notice the Bandits until they were near the fuel station. There were four of them, all of whom Janik recognized from the ship: Kai; Alejandro; Rory; and Harrison. Janik was surprised that Rory was amongst them. Both Harrison and Kai had mocked him on the ship, having knighted him with the unfortunate nickname of The Dunce. *I guess desperate times make for strange bedfellows,* Janik mused, as he stepped further back into the tree's shadow to ensure he was hidden.

He watched the men scout around the fuel station. They were carrying jerry cans and attempting to fill them at the pumps which, judging by the fact that Harrison threw his on the ground, wasn't very successful. Janik noted that they were all armed, although Rory was only carrying an axe. It was the way Rory carried the axe that triggered the memory for Janik – this was the man he saw kill four infected the first night. *Good for you,* Janik smiled, and was about to call out to them when his reverie was broken by the snapping of a branch behind him.

Frozen with fear, he strained to listen as the snapping was followed by footsteps, again reminding him of the first night when he heard Rory on the concrete. Although he was in the forest, the bearer of the footsteps made no effort to conceal his movement as he marched through the trees. Janik carefully turned his head and peered through the branches of the pine tree. Further up the hill, another six Bandits from the ship walked along, and to Janik they looked prepared for war.

They were all armed, some had assault rifles, AK-74s and some had shotguns. The men were spread out in two by two formation with men covering the front and rear. Janik figured that these were the men that were shooting yesterday in Cherno and whatever their plans were in

Elektro, it didn't look like they were friendly.

Vuk had stopped at the tree line 50 meters from where he'd unknowingly just passed Janik. He took out binoculars and scanned the buildings down below them. Shutov and Alejandro also looked through binoculars, with Alejandro pointing out key buildings he had discovered the night before. Vuk paid little attention to their discussion, instead focusing on the movement down in the town. From his vantage point he could see infected moving around, which he had expected. Thankfully, he didn't see any Survivors, and back down the road he could see the second team of Bandits following the road. They'd left the fuel station behind them and were passing a farming shed, about to arrive at the outskirts of Elektro.

Although Shutov hadn't said anything about the plan to Vuk, it looked to him that the four men were the decoy - or bait – depending on your perspective. They were all expendable, and walking along the road would definitely draw the attention of anyone watching. This second team had been tasked with fuel gathering and infected elimination, but having lived through fuel scarcity before, Vuk knew the first places to dry up would be fuel stations. He recalled back in Serbia people would hoard fuel so their best bet for gas would be out of other vehicles or from storage tanks beside buildings and factories.

Having just come up empty at the fuel station, the four men turned to task number two and began shooting infected on sight. *Definitely bait,* Vuk mused, as the sounds of their shots rang out across the town.

Shutov's plan was working as their shots did draw all the infected nearby from the buildings towards the second team. Vuk was right in his assessment that the second team were all expendable, this was why Shutov had chosen them. His plan worked in drawing infected away from the buildings the first team were heading towards. They moved from the tree line and crossed the field and heading into Elektro. Vuk hoped that the shooting only attracted the infected and that the Survivors had already moved on.

From the top of the firehouse Lucas couldn't hear the shots but he saw the movement across the field. The men were too far to make out, but by their movement and the fact they were carrying guns, Lucas was sure they weren't infected. Since he had no idea what the other Survivors were doing, he just assumed he was watching some of them move to raid a different location. Again he cursed the fact that they didn't have radios to communicate with, as he went back to lining up infected for practice kills.

Mitch wished he was back at his house right now and not for the obvious reason of safety. Back at his house, if you made dinner, you didn't have to wash up. To Mitch it seemed unfair - since he'd killed the boar, he shouldn't also have to make a meal out of it. Without refrigeration the meat wouldn't last very long and with nothing else to do that morning he'd followed Yuri's suggestion to use the remainder for cold cuts. And now he was delivering them - his last stop was Lucas at the firehouse. As he walked over he grumbled to himself that since he made the lunches, he shouldn't also have to deliver them.

He climbed up the ladder panting, sweat dripping off his face onto the rungs. He had never been worried about being slightly overweight before, but after spending the morning roaming Elektro, his lack of fitness was catching up with him. At least Lucas showed the right amount of gratitude as he thankfully took the food from Mitch. Mitch took the moment up high to rest, his largish belly contracting with each breath.

"Busy morning?" Lucas sputtered the words out of a full mouth.

"Just playing delivery boy and you're my last stop," replied Mitch.

"Did the guys over at the factories take theirs with them?" Lucas indicated behind him to where he saw the men crossing the field.

"There's no one out that way. We've got the guys at the store and the rest are at the church consolidating supplies."

Lucas swallowed his bite and spun Mitch around standing him up. He pointed and Mitch followed his line of sight, just able to visualize men at the edge of the field as they arrived at the town.

"Then who the hell are those guys?"

"They're not us," Mitch said.

The Butcher caught the movement on top of the firehouse in his peripheral vision. From this distance he couldn't make out details but there were definitely two men standing at the top of the firehouse, their silhouettes stark against the blue sky background.

"Sir, I have two contacts in the distance," he told Shutov, pointing. Shutov took out his binoculars and looked to where The Butcher pointed.

He saw the men standing up and they were definitely looking his way. The fat one turned and climbed down the ladder. "So much for stealth," he said aloud as he turned to Vuk, "send the second team out to cover us from that direction. Everyone else stay on task, we need these vehicle parts if we're going to get out of here."

Mitch cursed his bad luck at having been downgraded from delivery boy to messenger. He walked towards the men they had just seen, the hot sun not helping his sweating. The field between the firehouse and the others was too dangerous - he could see it was crawling with infected and there was no cover. So he had to take the long way around, following the houses and crawling from cover to cover, which turned a 10 minute walk into a 40 minute crawl.

As he followed the side of a dirt road, Mitch saw that there was a person in the distance, seated on the steps of a boarded-up house. The person hadn't seen Mitch as he crawled closer, passing an infected. Once he was well clear of the walker, Mitch felt safe enough to rise to a kneeling position and waved to get the other man's attention. Rory rose up, leaving the axe that he was holding, and waved back, beckoning Mitch towards them.

From his sniping position Lucas saw only Mitch waving. Whoever he was waving at was obscured by the boarded-up house and the tree beside it. He looked down the M14 sight - although it didn't magnify his view it did help him focus. Subconsciously, he flicked off the weapon's safety.

Rory called out to Kai and Harrison who were hidden out of view at the side of the house, "it's Mitch from the ship."

"Good work Dunce," Kai responded, "Keep calling him over here."

"It's Mitch, not one of the monsters. You don't need the guns."

Kai and Harrison ignored him and kept their guns trained at the road that Mitch would eventually walk along. In a low hush Kai barked back to Rory, "don't worry about us, you just get that fool over here."

Mitch thought he could see Rory talking but he couldn't see to whom and didn't pay it any mind. He was more concerned that there may be other infected around and Rory was from the ship, so Mitch felt safe.

Lucas kept looking down the sight, cursing the damn tree. He thought he saw movement but the leaves obscured it. Regardless, Mitch was definitely walking towards someone.

As Mitch rounded the house he came face to face with Kai and Harrison - both pointing double-barreled shotguns at him. "Hey, hey calm down. What's with the guns?" Mitch asked as he backed away, "I'm friendly," he pleaded.

"Then why are you strapped?" Kai asked, as the barrel of his shotgun pointed to the pistol in Mitch's hand.

"Infected management. But if you want, I'll put it down," Mitch answered.

Lucas watched as Mitch lowered his pistol, leaving it on the road and stepping away from it. Mitch was speaking to someone, obscured from Lucas by the house, and gesturing back towards the firehouse. Lucas watched Mitch step back, frantically holding his palms out, when suddenly, his chest burst open into a spray of blood. Mitch fell back and landed hard on the road, as Lucas tried to comprehend what had just happened.

"Friendly that, bitch!" Kai mocked, as the smoke wafted out of the tip of his gun.

"Why you gone and done that for?" Rory asked, running over to Mitch to try and help him. He put his hands on the wound, tried to stop it bleeding, as Mitch opened his eyes and looked at Rory.

"Why?" Mitch asked.

"I didn't know they would. I'm sorry," Rory replied, the last thing Mitch heard before he died.

"Come on Dunce, let's get back to the others," Harrison commanded.

At a factory building, Shutov and the others all stopped, having heard thee gun shot that echoed across the town. Similarly in the store, the Survivors had stopped and listened, waiting for another shot.

Lucas watched through the rifle sight as Rory kneeled next to Mitch. He could take the shot but something felt off, so he hesitated. It didn't look like Rory was hurting Mitch and he didn't have a weapon. Rory gestured back to someone else behind the house. *Take the shot you coward,* Lucas berated himself, *he may not have pulled the trigger but he was complicit in Mitch's murder.*

"I'm not going back," Rory answered, "you're bad men."

"Bad to the bone baby," Kai joked.

"Give me my axe," Rory asked.

"So, you're not with us anymore?" queried Harrison.

"No. Give me my axe and I'll go."

"This is our axe now."

"But you have guns. I need a weapon. I can't go off without a weapon."

"Oh we wouldn't think of letting you go off... without a weapon," replied Kai.

Rory looked down at the pistol near Mitch's dead body.

"Don't even think about it Dunce. You'd probably point it the wrong way and shoot yourself," Kai mocked as Rory looked up at him and then back at the pistol, "get up and step back from the gun."

Lucas watched Rory rise and step back, his palms held out - just like Mitch's were moments ago. Rory stepped back, trying desperately to shuffle away from an unseen assailant. From down low behind him Lucas heard Yuri's voice. "Lucas what's happened? Who's firing?"

"Mitch is dead," Lucas replied.

"What?"

"Someone just shot him. I have eyes on one guy but I think he has friends. Get the others and get back to the church."

"What are you going to do?" Yuri asked.

Lucas watched as Kai walked out from behind the house and stalked Rory with the shotgun. He lined Kai up in his sights, "what my father couldn't," and with that, he pulled the trigger.

Harrison watched as Kai was flung to the side by the impact of the bullet. Rory turned and ran as Harrison watched the blood spurt from a second bullet that hit Kai on his side. He backed away from Kai, certain he was dead, and searched in the direction from where the shots came.

Vuk and Shutov both watched the puffs of smoke as the shots were fired from the top of the firehouse. From their angle on the second story of the TEC building they couldn't see where the shots landed, but through the binoculars they confirmed that whoever was on the top of the tower was now firing.

Shutov lowered his binoculars and turned to Vuk, "can you tell what gun it is?"

Vuk shook his head, "it's definitely a rifle, high powered and shooting at where the second team were set up."

"You still think they could be friendly?"

Vuk lowered his binoculars, "Those aren't friendly actions. From now on we are weapons hot."

Shutov heartily slapped him on the back as he called down to the rest of the men, looting the factory below them.

"You heard him men. They are firing at us. It's kill or be killed, now go get them."

Lucas continued to scan the buildings from where Kai appeared. The adrenaline flowed freely though his veins as he swung the sight around, scanning for any movement. He saw Harrison running across the main road and attempted to line up a shot. Harrison was running too fast and was back behind cover before Lucas could get an angle.

Lucas watched the wall that Harrison had ducked behind, waiting for him to appear on the other side where it ended at the train tracks. *If he crosses those tracks he's a dead man,* Lucas mused, as he scanned the area for Harrison.

Suddenly, movement from further away caught Lucas' eye. From the TEC building in the distance he observed a large group of men fan out and head towards him. They were too far away for Lucas to have an effective shot, and they kept cover between them and the firehouse. Lucas' sight jumped from one man to another but there were too many and he couldn't get a bead on one.

Instead, Lucas rose and turned to the church calling out, "Yuri! Yuri!"

Yuri ran out, "what's going on? Who did you shoot at?"

"The guy who killed Mitch. But he has friends, I can see more of them coming towards you. You've got to get the fuck out of there right now!"

"What! Why? We can try to talk with them," pleaded Yuri.

"That's what Mitch was trying to do before they murdered him. These guys are armed and they're not here to talk. Get everyone together and get the fuck out. Head into the trees and go North, I'll catch up with you later."

"What are you going to do?"

"I'm going to buy you some time so don't waste it talking to me," replied Lucas as he turned away from Yuri and back to the men.

They spread out and weaved in between buildings and shipping containers at the docks. Lucas lined one up and fired. As he expected, the man was too far away for the bullet to be effective as it fell short. Fortunately, the sound travelled further and caused the man to stop and look around. Lucas took the other DMR magazine out of his pack placed it on the ground in front of him. If he was conservative with his fire he should be able to slow them down as they tried to hide from him. He might even get lucky and hit a couple of them.

Shutov tried to circle around to the firehouse but every shot made him pause as he tried to ascertain where it landed. Some of them were uncomfortably close as he kept moving along the docks. The men were panicked, they fired indiscriminately at infected rather than avoiding them. In the crowded city, every shot that killed one infected attracted another three with its noise. If they made it out of here alive he would have to lay down some ground rules about ammo conservation, because at that moment, the infected weren't the threat - the sniper on the tower was.

Vuk broke off the other way from Shutov and sprinted across the train tracks. He had watched the sniper from behind cover and timed his run across the tracks at the moment the sniper faced away. They could still get him if they continued to spread out, they had the advantage of numbers, since the sniper couldn't look all ways at once.

Vuk continued down the road and noticed that there were two dead bodies up ahead. He slowed down as he got closer, looked around for infected and tried to ensure there was always cover between him and the firehouse.

As he got closer to the bodies he heard sobbing. He looked past them to see Rory cowering against the wall of house opposite. "Rory what's wrong."

"My axe. I need my axe," he pointed to the axe on the steps near Vuk.

"What happened here Rory?"

"He killed him. He just shot him," Vuk looked down at the bodies of Mitch and Kai.

"Why? Why did Mitch kill Kai?"

"It wasn't Mitch. Mitch had no gun," Rory pointed at the pistol lying on the road in between Mitch and Kai's bodies. "Mitch put the gun down like Kai said. And then Kai shot him."

"Why? Why would he do that if Mitch was unarmed?"

"Kai said Mitch was a bad man. But Kai was the bad man. He tried to shoot me and then he fell down, dead."

"Why would he shoot you?"

"Because I don't want to be around bad men. I told him that, but he wouldn't give me my axe. Please just give me my axe. I'll go. I won't tell anyone."

Vuk assessed the situation. He looked past the house and across the field to the firehouse. To him, it looked like a clear shot to Kai's body from there, and slowly he pieced together what he thought had happened.

Vuk picked up the axe and tossed it to Rory. It landed near Rory's feet and he scooped it up. "Wait there. When I tell you, Rory, run. Run into the trees and stay away from other people. Don't trust anyone. We're all bad men here Rory. Do you understand?" Rory nodded, holding the axe close.

Vuk watched Lucas and when he saw Lucas turn away towards he church he told Rory to run. Rory didn't hesitate and bolted straight across the open field towards the trees. Vuk alternated between watching Rory run towards the trees and Lucas facing the church – silently willing Lucas to keep his back turned away from Rory. He heard Lucas fire one shot followed almost immediately by another.

Lucas watched as the last of the Survivors, Kiam, ran down the road into the woods. Kiam was being chased by two infected with another five further back. Lucas lined up the closest infected and was about to shoot it, when another infected ran out from the side of the building and knocked Kiam down.

"Fuck!" Lucas called out as he watched the infected begin to feast on him. He shot one infected and it went down, landing on top of Kiam. The other infected pushed his brethren off Kiam and continued to feast on him as the five stragglers got closer.

Lucas assessed the situation - there was nothing he could do for Kiam. He couldn't even put him out of his misery as the infected blocked any shot.

"Sorry Kiam," Lucas whispered as he turned and focused back on the Bandits heading towards him. He had lost sight of many of them and looked at their last known positions for any movement.

Shutov lay prone behind a bush from where he could see the top of the firehouse. He watched Lucas look around, scanning the area with his rifle. He lay his CZ550 on the ground and looked down the scope, but Lucas kept moving so he was unable to get a shot. Infected walked nearby, ignoring Shutov for now, but he knew once he fired they'd all converge straight on him. This meant he got one shot - so he had to make it count.

Lucas kept scanning, looking for a target. He looked back at where he first killed Kai and thought he saw movement. He steadied the rifle against his shoulder and looked down the scope, holding his breath to keep still.

Shutov smiled as Lucas stopped moving and he was able to line him up down the sight. He also held his breath as he squeezed the trigger.

A sudden movement to his left caused Lucas to swing the rifle around, following it with his head. It was just a rabbit and he almost laughed when he felt, rather than heard, the bullet whiz past his head. Lucas dropped to the ground and lay as flat as he could.

Shutov stood up, "fuck!" he cursed, unsure if he had hit Lucas. The infected rushed over to him as he observed the firehouse tower - there was no movement but he couldn't be sure. He ran back towards the factories to lose the infected that chased after him.

Vuk was also watching the firehouse tower but all he could see from this angle was the rifle poked out over the edge. He recognized the sound of the CZ550, having had it fire so close to him previously, so he assumed Shutov took a shot. The rifle was still, *maybe Shutov got him*.

Lucas patted himself all over. He didn't feel hurt but he'd heard that shock can deaden the senses. His hand came back clean – he wasn't bleeding. He crawled away from the edge and towards the ladder, taking the rifle with him, *it's time to get the fuck outta here*.

Vuk saw the rifle retract behind the tower, glad that Shutov had missed whoever was up there. He watched the tower but there was no movement. From this angle he could see the ladder up to the tower, and since he hadn't observed anyone climbing down, he knew someone was still up there.

Lucas took the magazine out of the M14 and counted the remaining bullets - there were only three. He slammed the magazine back into the rifle and patted it. "Sorry baby, I gotta leave you behind," he said as he laid it on the ground.

Lucas pushed it back out so that part of the rifle was exposed over the edge again.

Vuk watched as the rifle poked back out of the edge of the tower. It turned towards the shore and then fired. *Strange,* Vuk mused, *since the rifle is lying flat the bullet will be just shooting far off into the air.* He saw the rifle pointed far over his head and it fired another round, again high and into the air followed by a third high shot to his right. Then the rifle was still and Vuk looked behind him, attempting to locate a possible target. In the distance there were just trees, nothing worth shooting at. When he turned back to the tower he saw Lucas climb down the ladder. Vuk nodded, impressed, *clever boy.*

Shutov also watched the rifle, having cursed himself for missing. From his angle he couldn't see Lucas climb down the ladder but did see the rifle poked over the edge, and so like everyone else, he assumed Lucas was still up there.

Vuk watched as Lucas jumped off the ladder and ran away, disappearing over the hill. Vuk scanned the surrounding area but there was no one else around, so Lucas' escape stayed his secret.

It took another 20 minutes of no further shots before Vuk 'bravely' volunteered to climb the ladder and see what had happened. By this time they had all angles of the firehouse covered and no one had seen the rifle move for a long time.

As Shutov watched Vuk climb up the ladder, he secretly hoped his shot was successful and it had just taken the prick a while to die.

At the top of the tower Vuk grabbed the M14 and held it up high as he called down, "he's not here. Just the gun."

"Fuck!" Shutov cursed.

From up high Vuk, saw Alejandro and Sam converged on the bus which had broken down on the road near the church. Vuk recalled that this was the same church Alejandro said the Survivors were holed up in. Then he realized that Shutov also knew this, knew the bus was near the church, knew that it was always going to end in blood. Vuk shook his head, *the bastard played me like a fool.* Although there wasn't any ammo, Vuk still took the M14 and stashed it in his pack.

Down on the ground the Butcher skulked over to Shutov. "It looks like they all got away, they must have headed North into the woods. Should we chase them?"

"Why would we do that? For the beans in their packs?" Shutov chastised The Butcher.

"But they have guns, they killed Kai."

Shutov walked away from The Butcher towards the bus, "let them have their pathetic guns and their little victory. We have the bus," he turned to Sam, "get working on that bus right now. Alejandro I want you to set up a perimeter. I want people in every direction covering Sam until he gets this bus up and running." Alejandro nodded and started to assign the others roles.

"What's so special about this bus?" The Butcher asked.

"Nothing. It's just a bus. Where it can take us, now that's special."

"Why? Where are we going?"

Shutov held up a map.

"The Northwest airfield, that's where our salvation lies. Believe me when I say this war has just begun and if we cross path with the Survivors again, none of them will leave alive."

CHAPTER TWENTY

TIMOR DID A BAD BAD THING

Timor looked down at the small hair elastic that he twiddled in his hand. A long blond hair was caught up in one end of the metal stud that holds the elastic together. Timor rubbed it between his fingers, luxuriating in its feel, reminiscing about the girl to whom the hair had once been attached. Now the hair caught in the elastic was all that remained of the girl. Timor wished he'd got her name.

He reflected back on that night. That fateful night so soon after the chaos had erupted. It was when people were still in their homes and farmers opened their doors with welcome arms to any military. The girl was so young and so innocent that Timor and his squad knew there and then that she would be theirs. Her parents were easy to dispatch, and being on an isolated farm, there was no help to answer her cries. They did some very, very bad things to her that night before finally putting her out of her misery in the morning.

Timor breathed deeply in, savoring the memory. He didn't know at the time what drove him to take the elastic band out of her hair. Nor can he understand now what drives him to leave it on his wrist. Maybe because she was the first, maybe because that night the group of men he travelled with were forever united by that one act. Instead of an allegiance to a government that most likely was gone, or loyalty to a uniform that was now stained and in tatters, they pledged allegiance to each other. They looked into the darkness of each man and found a shade of black they could all live with – and now they were kindred spirits. She was not the last but she was the one that bound them together. So maybe keeping this small piece of her was a way of honoring that night – that glorious night.

The season was starting to turn and the nights were getting colder. Soon they would need to sleep indoors again, but for now, outside was still a viable option. The problem with indoors were the infected, for some reason they stayed close to the towns and houses.

Timor mused over the nickname the Americans gave for the infected. Zed. Short for the Z in Zombie, it was smart of them to turn infected into monsters. Technically they weren't dead, they were living humans that, thanks to the infection with no name, now roamed in a feral state. Although Zed was just a name, it did work - it helped not to think of them as once living, breathing people. Better to refer to them as the monsters that once lived in fiction, the zombies of our collective nightmares.

The woods were still not completely safe, at least once a day they'd come across a Zed that needed to be dispatched, but these moments were sporadic and each was usually alone. This was one positive attribute that came out from the Chernarus population being so small.

Of course, both the Russian and US military injecting soldiers in an effort to contain the outbreak did increase the population, and therefore eventually the Zeds, but overall it was manageable. He couldn't imagine what his home town of Moscow would look like, the swarms of Zeds that must be roaming around there. It was best not to think about it. Moscow was very far away and they were stuck here.

At least it wasn't too bad outside. The rain had stopped so the ground was dry and they had tents set up deep in the woods. The rules of survival in this new world had to be learnt each day and failure usually resulted in death. Their group of eight had now been whittled away to four, men toughened by the circumstances and ready to survive at all costs.

The number seemed right. The group was now manageable and it was easier to travel in this tight squad. They may have been born of different mothers but the last month had made them brothers, at least until circumstances said otherwise. Timor had no illusions about the tenuous grasp of loyalty they held for each other. If slaughtering the other three of his brothers was required to escape from this hell, then the only question that would run through his mind was which gun to use.

He stared into the campfire that was surrounded by a makeshift stonewall to block any of its light from a distance. Timor was on watch in three hours' time and should have been sleeping, but right now, sleep evaded him. He was exhausted beyond belief but Timor could never really rest. It had fallen on him to lead this group although technically the snoring Pavel was a higher rank. Pavel was weak so Timor felt forced to step in and lead or they would have been dead long ago. Timor sighed, he just wanted to survive this but now he was burdened with three other lives to worry about.

Every day was a struggle. A struggle for food, for bullets, to scavenge fuel for their car, find wood and stones for a fire. Timor took a sip of water and spat it out, reminded of the taste of fuel from siphoning a car earlier that day. It was becoming increasingly wasteful to drive around in a vehicle; although working cars were plentiful, the fuel to run them was not. Any gas stations or military fuel depots they came across had long been cleaned out. So now they resorted to siphoning fuel from the abandoned cars scattered all over. Soon that source would also dry up and they'd be on foot again, suffering their own little oil crisis. Timor laughed, it seemed the hippies would win this one once the processed fossil fuels ran out.

Tomorrow they would move their camouflaged UAZ car off the side of the road and go into Mogilevka on foot. It had been a while since they'd had to raid a town, having effectively lived off ambushed cars for a long time. But there were no cars on the roads anymore, they hadn't seen another living person for weeks, and so now they were forced to raid towns again. Mogilevka looked quiet, but Timor wanted the full day's light for the raid. They learnt early on to take time and be sure to clear each building. It was a lesson learnt the hard way in Dolina when Sergov was attacked.

Sergov was gathering supplies in a house when it had happened. They had all assumed the town was clear - the infected roaming around had been taken care of, and scouts were posted to warn of any more approaching. The men were relaxed, weapons lowered, safeties on, and the task of gathering supplies had started. Sergov had broken into an ordinary looking house, like he'd done many times before. This one had taken a while to get into because the owner had barricaded the door quite well.

Once inside, the stench of death almost knocked him down. By now, everyone was used to this; it was a sight and smell they'd seen repeatedly - over and over again. Usually a family had been barricaded inside a house, they felt safe, they relaxed. Then the food started to get low, the water was all drunk, and panic started to set in. After a while of this, the hopelessness of the situation sunk in and most of the time the occupants took the easy way out. Usually it was the father who shot everyone before turning the gun on himself.

The scene was always the same. The poor bastard would have the corpses of his child or children in his lap before turning the gun on himself. Surprisingly, they always did it before the food had completely run out, so there was always something left to find.

The house that Sergov had just entered was different. Here there was only one dead body lying on the ground with no other bodies in the vicinity. It was possible the other bodies could be in other rooms, but usually they were all found dead in the same room. The only time he had seen bodies in different rooms was also the only time he'd found a house with absolutely no food inside.

In that house Sergov found a pile of human bones, both adult and child, piled into the corner of a bedroom. They had been picked clean with even the marrow sucked out. Only the decomposing heads had been left untouched, sitting on the fireplace mantle, staring back at the unfortunate bastard who had shot himself in his armchair. That scene still haunted Sergov's dreams and so he was glad that this time it was just a single dead farmer lying in the kitchen.

He grabbed the remaining bullets from the farmer's pistol but left the pistol behind. It was a rusted old Makarov PM that would most likely seize when fired. Sergov searched the kitchen cupboards but apart from cleaning products and plates, they were bare. Had Sergov been more observant he would have noticed the family picture on the wall. The picture that displayed a wife and child who weren't accounted for when he first entered the house. But the hunger in Sergov's belly was all he focused on so when he opened the walk-in pantry he was hoping to find some food.

What he found was the daughter huddled up in the corner. She looked dead until her eyes sprung open and she leapt up at Sergov. He had seen this before, once the infected are confined in a small space, they stopped moving - somehow they understand the need to conserve energy. All that stored up energy came upon him in one pounce and she was on him, a crazed 7 year old tearing into his flesh with her nails and teeth.

Sergov threw her off him and she slammed into the rear wall of the pantry, the girl was just skin and bones and therefore as light as a feather. She didn't even acknowledge the impact as she turned and rushed back to him. With his own Makarov he shot her in the head, a messy shot that hit the top right of her temple and split it into two. She went down but the noise of the shot drew all the other soldiers into the room.

Timor was one of the last ones into the room and by then it was chaos. The others were all pointing guns at Sergov and telling him to drop his pistol. Sergov's eyes were wild, he was panicked and screaming that he was okay, he didn't feel sick, the girl must not have drawn blood. But there was a clear gash on his neck, with blood dripping down to the floor. Everyone, including Sergov, knew what that meant. But this was early days, when rules were not established, when they were still learning as they went along. Now, they would have just shot Sergov without hesitation, if he hadn't already done it himself. But back then in that room, there was screaming and chaos.

Timor stepped forward and commanded everyone to shut up. He ordered the men to all lower their guns and stop pointing them at Sergov. Reluctantly, the men did so and the tension stepped down a notch. Then Timor asked Sergov to give him his gun. Timor promised they would tie Sergov up, wait it out and see if he would turn. On that promise, Sergov hesitantly handed over his pistol to Timor who immediately shot him in the head with it.

Timor took another sip of water as the memory washed over him. It was a hard lesson learnt that day and now they spent a long time clearing any town they came across. Everyone raided in pairs, each door was opened and cleared. Even after they thought the town was safe, certain all of the infected had been cleared from it, they would still split off and search again to be sure. It was slow going, but since following this doctrine, there hadn't been a repeat of the Sergov situation. It also meant that they had to stick to smaller towns as a small group of men could never clear and hold a large town. To them, the large towns were still considered death traps - at least until their supplies started to dwindle once more and desperation forced them to reconsider.

CHAPTER TWENTY ONE

KEEP THE DARK AWAY

Rory's head was pounding, the veins in his forehead were strained against the skin, desperate to burst open. His breathing was labored and in gasps, his feet ached, his face was all scratched up from the brush he'd been running through. His sweaty hands held onto the treated wood of his axe which was right now his most valuable possession in the world - it was also his only possession since Vuk had told him to run hours ago.

Rory had no idea where he was, there was woods all around him. He encountered two separate monsters and killed both in his hours of running. Then when he'd came across one he'd already killed hours before, he stopped, done with running. The sight of his failure, the reminder of his stupidity, lying there in the grass was too much for him. He gave up to exhaustion and failure the tears welling up in his eyes.

Now he rested on a rock looking at the dead monster. He'd been running around in circle for hours and was back here again. He couldn't do it anymore, couldn't walk, let alone run, another step. He needed to rest, his mouth was cotton dry no matter how much he smacked his tongue against it to produce saliva. In his chest his heart was pounding so hard against his ribcage Rory was sure it would burst out like he'd seen in the movies. He wished he'd had his patrol pack, inside there were some beans and water at least. The light was almost gone, with only a dead monster in front of him to keep him company.

It was already getting cold and Rory thought it would be a good idea to start a fire. He used the axe to chop at a tree branch, breaking it up into smaller pieces. He wasn't sure exactly how to get a fire going but he figured this was a good start.

After a while there was a nice pile of sticks surrounded by rocks to keep the fire from jumping. His breathing had slowed down and things were starting to feel normal again. Sure he'd be a bit cold tonight and definitely hungry, but he'd have a fire and that would keep the dark away.

Rory had always been afraid of the dark, and unlike most adults, he never grew out of it. To him it made sense to be afraid of not being able to see, but he knew if he told anyone he would be laughed at. Instead he'd always made sure there was some light around when he was sleeping, even if it was just the moonlight from his porthole or if it was a cloudy night, the light from his watch. Normally that was enough to give him comfort but tonight he wanted a real light – a light from the fire.

Rory's mother insisted that his fear of the dark was irrational – that it was something he should just snap out of. So he hid it even from her, and Rory never hid anything from his mother. *But Mummy,* he thought, *you're wrong. There are monsters in the world - they are real.* He looked over at the dead monster as he got the wood ready.

And then he remembered matches, he'd need matches or a lighter to get the fire started. Rory fumbled through all his pockets but he had no matches. *They were right to call me The Dunce because I am stupid,* Rory thought as he chastised himself. Futilely he searched all his pockets again just in case he missed the matches the first time, but there were none. Rory sat back down on the rock wondering what he should do now.

In the movies people start a fire by rubbing two sticks together, I should try that. Rory grabbed two small sticks and rubbed them together. Faster and faster. There was some smoke. Excited by the prospect he rubbed them together even harder. Snap. The sticks broke. Rory threw the broken sticks on the ground in frustration. Now what. He needed fire, looking over at the dead monster near him reminded him of how important light would be. Light pushes back the dark, holds off the monsters.

The monster was of course a person once, the best ones always were. By the look of his clothes he was a hunter - although there was no gun on his shoulder, he had a woodland cap and camouflage clothes. Slowly an idea swam around his brain. Perhaps he would have matches. Not the monster of course, monsters don't make fire. But the person might, the person that was once inside him. He might have taken matches with him when he went hunting, they still might be on him.

Rory wondered if he could just search the monster's pockets. Would just touching him turn him into a monster, could it do that? And was the monster really dead? Maybe it was just lying there pretending, waiting for him to get closer before it jumped up and ate him. Rory's mind raced. On one hand he needed to check the pockets but on the other it was really dangerous. Too dangerous perhaps.

He inched closer to the monster, his axe out in front of him. Closer and closer, the axe stretched out ahead. He got even closer to the monster, close enough that the axe could reach it. He prodded it with the axe. Nothing. He prodded it again harder. Nothing. *But maybe it's waiting, knows that's just an axe, and is waiting for my hand*. Rory wouldn't fall for that trick. He'd need to be sure the monster was dead. Needed to be 100% percent certain before he's put his hand anywhere near it.

He prodded even harder, the axe digging into the clothes and ample belly of the monster. A black bile oozed out and Rory knew it was still alive. Monsters have black blood everyone knows that. *Ha ha, you can't trick me*, he thought as he lifted the axe over his head.

Not being very bright Rory had always been relegated to manual labor, but he did not mind hard labor, it was simple and easy to understand: carry this from here to there; hit this until it breaks; load those things onto that truck. These were instructions he could understand.

All that hard work also made him strong, really strong. So when he swung the axe down hard at the monster's neck it went clean through the first time. The head rolled towards Rory and he instinctively kicked it away. The black bile oozed out of the neck running into the ground. Rory knew you shouldn't touch blood, that it could make you sick, and that was doubly true for monster blood. He watched it ooze and waited until it stopped, like when a chicken has its head cut off. Satisfied the flow had stopped, he lowered the axe.

Nothing could live without a head, not even a monster, Rory was certain of that. He very carefully started rifling through the pockets, being extra certain not to touch skin or the black bile. In one pocket, he found a granola bar which he greedily ate. But there had to be matches, the hunter would definitely have had matches. And then in the inside vest pocket he found it, it wasn't matches but it was even better. A silver plated lighter. Rory shook it near his ear and heard the sloshing of the lighter fluid inside. He flicked the cover off and spun the wheel, it lit first time. Rory kissed it, he was safe, and there would be no dark tonight.

He gave the monster's body one last check to make sure he hadn't missed anything, but that was all it had, a bit of food and a lighter, not much, but Rory was ecstatic. In no time he had the fire roaring and sat next to it, tonight he'd be safe and in the morning he'd keep moving, like Vuk told him to.

CHAPTER TWENTY TWO

PANIC

It set in fast – the panic – rushing over them as the Survivors ran for their lives. Yuri had no idea what had happened back at the firehouse but he ran along with the others because that was what Lucas told him to do. There were others, either from the ship or already here, that attacked the group and killed Mitch. So they ran from them, up the hill and away from Elektro, with only what they could carry.

In the panic people had become lost, there were five of them running out from the church but Yuri only counted four.

"Where is Kiam?" he asked the others.

"No idea. He was behind you wasn't he Alfie?"

"I thought he was over to the left. Didn't he go left?"

"He was definitely behind you Alfie."

"I thought I was last?" queried Alfie.

"No you fool, Kiam was the last one out," Yuri responded.

"What about Lucas, did he make it?"

"He was covering our escape. I don't know if he got out."

The group slowed down their running and stopped to look back. They were all out of breath, some doubled-over gasping for air. From up on the hill they could see Elektro in the distance. There was movement in the town but it was hard to make out.

"Did anyone grab the binoculars?"

"I did," responded Alfie as he rummaged through his

pack. He took them out and handed them to Yuri. Yuri peered through them - although they magnified the scene down at the Church it was still too far for him to make out details.

"What do you see?" asked Alfie.

"People, there are lots of people down there. I can't tell who they are."

"Let me see."

Yuri handed the binoculars back to Alfie. He cleaned them off and looked through them down into town. "They seem to be setting up a perimeter around the church. I see two guards   north, two more south and another where Lucas was."

"Why are they doing that?"

"Looks to me like they're bunkering down for the night. I see someone at the bus so maybe they're trying to get that up and running."

"Why?"

"Beats me. That's the only useful thing there and since they're not staying in the church but guarding outside I'm guessing they're protecting the guy working on the bus." Alfie lowered the binoculars and turned to Yuri, "so Yuri what should we do?"

"We need to regroup. This seems like a good spot to hole up for now. I propose we stay here and watch the others to see what they're planning. We should also keep scouting for Lucas and any of the others. I count us to be three short, not including Mitch."

"What happened to Mitch?"

"I didn't see it but Lucas said these men killed him, murdered him in cold blood," Yuri said.

"Was that why Lucas started shooting? Did he get any of them?"

"I don't know," Yuri replied, "it got pretty crazy back there. Lucas said to run so we ran."

"And now we're here."

"Yep. Stuck up on this hill."

Alfie opened his pack and started to empty out its

contents. "We need to do an inventory count. Find out what we managed to grab on our way out of there." The others joined in and emptied out their bags. Between them they had a meager bunch of possessions and weapons, some food, some water, soda cans, hunting knife, shotguns and pistols. Alfie and Yuri looked it over.

"This won't last us very long," said Yuri.

"Agreed," Alfie replied, "I would have preferred some sort of rifle but Lucas was the only one with a sniper. Fortunately we do have a map and if that's Elektro then I place us up here at this AO6 whatever hill."

"Dobryy hill. That's Cyrillic for Dobryy."

"Really? How the fuck do you get a D from that?"

"It Ukrainian. Dobryy means good."

"Okay fine, then we're on Good Hill. You can see there are two towns nearby. This one," he pointed on the map and looked up at Yuri for help.

"Pusta. That's Pusta."

"Pusta, and this one on the coast, Kambobivo."

"Kamyshovo," Yuri corrected.

"Kamyshovo. We're going to need to raid one of those to get more supplies. Does anyone have an opinion on which one?"

"The inland one, Pusta. I say we go there," Pablo responded.

"Why?" Yuri asked.

"To me it seems that inland is safer. There are lots of infected on the coast and remember they were once people. If it were me and I was trying to get away I'd get to the coast as well. That's why I think we should go inland. There's a better chance of not meeting other people or the infected, and still finding gear and equipment, especially food."

"Makes sense," Alfie nodded, "Anyone disagree?"

They all shook their heads.

"Okay then it's settled. We head to Pusta," the others started to gather up their things, "Woah, woah, hold up! We need to wait until it's dark. It will be safer to travel when they can't see us. So we stay here for now, watch the Bandits and search around for our missing Survivors. We'll wait for darkness before moving off. They'll be night-blind from their fires and less likely to see us moving up in the hills."

Yuri nodded, agreeing. "Pablo. Joseph. You two gather this stuff up and share it around. I want it shared evenly so if we lose someone they can still eat and drink until they find us again. Once that's done, spread out and cover the sides. I don't want anyone - living or infected - sneaking up on us. I'll cover the back and Alfie you watch them in town. How many bullets do you have in that Lee Enfield?"

"8," Alfie replied.

"Damn. Hopefully that will be enough. Don't shoot unless it's necessary."

"Roger that."

Alfie lifted up the binoculars and turned back to watching the Bandits in Elektro.

"What's so special about that bus?" he muttered to himself.

CHAPTER TWENTY THREE

LIVE BY THE SWORD

With a cough and a splutter, the motorbike's engine abruptly stopped and it coasted to a halt along the road. The engine - although still in good condition - could no longer continue to run on only the fumes emanating from the empty fuel tank. Robert dropped the kickstand and climbed off the bike. Doc, his passenger, followed suit. "God dammit! It looks like we're back on foot," Robert cursed. Doc nodded, stretching his muscles as Robert turned and kicked the motorbike, knocking it down. "Fucking piece of shit," Robert yelled as he kicked it some more.

Doc left him to vent his frustrations on the bike. All morning Robert had been swearing and screaming as they searched the abandoned cars for fuel. Occasionally they'd strike it lucky and find some but it was slow going and they'd barely made any ground. Although only a medical Doctor, it didn't require the skills of a psychiatrist to tell that Robert was taking out his own anger at Arnold's death on anything and anyone around him. Doc had tried to stay out of Robert's way all day after copping a verbal tirade the last time he suggested that kicking their only form of transportation wouldn't be wise.

After most of the day slowly travelling, they now found themselves stranded with a motorbike, an empty jerry can, and no cars visible from which they might salvage any fuel. Doc dropped his pack and sat under the shade of a tree as he watched Robert beat on the motorbike.

Doc opened his canteen and took a sip of water, looking up and down the road. The coastal road had been pretty clear of other cars and barricades. Sure there was the occasional burnt out car or makeshift barricade in a town, but they posed no problem. The infected though, they were a different story.

The motorbike made it easy to navigate the roads, to move through the numerous accidents that had occurred, and go off-road in fields when necessary. But it also exposed them to the elements, including the opportunity to be pulled off by the infected. And it was loud. Every time they rode near one of the shambling infected it would suddenly turn towards them and run. They always outran them but one accidental crash, a blown tire, or some other mishap that stopped them at the wrong time would mean they would be swarmed. Fortunately, this time the bike ran out of fuel on an almost deserted road, north and south seemed clear of any infected. The forest was to their right but it seemed judicious to both of them to stay on the road, where at least they could see vast distances in either direction.

Robert stomped up to Doc and slammed down his pack hard on the ground, bringing Doc out of his reverie. He withdrew his canteen and gulped the water down, his face shiny with sweat from his attack on the bike, "You ready to go?" he asked Doc, who nodded in response.

"Where are we going?"

"I don't know," Robert answered as he took a map out of his pack. He spread it out on the ground in front of them and Doc looked over his shoulder to the map.

"I think we're around here," he pointed to an area on the map along the coast, "I'm thinking that lighthouse we can see in the distance is Krutoy Cap." Robert pointed to the lighthouse on the map. "So from here we have two options. We can stay on this road along the coast and head into Kamyshovo. Or we can go inland to this town Tulga. Inland is probably riskier as we may get lost but Tulga is closer than Kamyshovo, and if we went along the coast I'd like to check out the lighthouse along the way, so that would add even more time."

"Why bother with either town? We should be staying away from the infected where possible."

"Because our supplies are getting low and unless we find a stocked up Unibomber shack in the middle of nowhere, the towns provide our best chance to get any food or drink."

"We can reduce rations and spread out what we have for longer," Doc implored.

"We can, but eventually we'll need to get more supplies and at that point, be it either tomorrow or next week, we'll have to go into a town. There's no point in putting it off and going in hungry and weak later on when we can hit it hard and fast now. So the question isn't when, it's where. Where should we raid next?"

"Then let's stay on the coast. I don't want to be stumbling around in the woods unnecessarily and get lost."

"Alright," Robert affirmed as he folded the map away, "then Kamyshovo it is. We better get a move on, we won't have much light and I want to be inside before dark."

Robert and Doc shouldered their packs and walked down the road. Robert scratched at his patched up arm where he was hit by an infected yesterday. Doc noticed this.

"Is it hurting? I should have another look at it."

"It's fine."

"And you don't feel any... different?"

"You mean hungry for human flesh type different?" Robert joked, "nope not yet, our food situation isn't that dire."

"You shouldn't be making light of it Robert. If you do turn into one of the infected there won't be many options for me."

"I understand that, but so far so good, and I'd prefer if you didn't jinx it by talking about it. Right now I feel fine and if that changes you'll be the first to know."

"I have no idea of what the incubation period is and how

this infection spreads. From the reports we received on the ship, it appears that bodily fluids spread it, like saliva and blood. The incubation period was listed as between a day and a week so you're still well within that period."

"If I start acting funny you know what to do."

"Knowing and doing are not the same thing."

"Well Doc, you'd better grow some balls if the shit hits the fan, otherwise we'll be walking around together looking for the next poor bastard to munch on. And I for one don't plan to spend eternity like that.""

CHAPTER TWENTY FOUR

BUNKER DOWN AND DIE

Duke double-checked the barricade on the door again. It felt strong and looked like it would hold for the night. Beside him, Xavier was ripping up sheets and blankets, using them to cover the windows of the small farm house. Regrettably, they didn't have enough wood or nails to barricade the windows as well, so Duke suggested they block them to stop any light coming in.

The room was slowly becoming dark as the light faded from the setting sun and the windows were blocked off. Xavier's arms ached as he tied up the last blanket and gaffer-taped it to the window. He was not used to all this physical exercise and it was starting to show. With the window blocked off and the door barricaded, they both slumped to the floor, enjoying the dark and quiet. This was a new sensation for Xavier, the sensation of just being thankful to be alive. But after the night and day he just had, being alive was now a lot to be thankful for.

It hadn't even been 24 hours since the Zelenogorsk supermarket, but it felt like a week. Xavier closed his eyes and reflected back on how they got out. He didn't want to re-live the previous day but his brain had decided it was not enough to have lived through it once, now it was going to make him suffer again.

They had barely made it out of the supermarket. Duke was becoming increasingly agitated at the Zeds as they kept pouring in, each shot from his M16A2 would take one down but also acted as a call to others. The thing about the infected is that they are fearless; they don't care if they see others killed in front of them. They don't care if they've been shot. They don't feel pain. Nothing can stop them except for a bullet to the brain, and Duke had just run out of bullets.

Xavier thought they were done for when he heard Duke's assault rifle click dry. Duke kept calm, he grabbed the revolver from Xavier's hand, popped it open and checked, 5 shots left. "Alright Frenchy, we're getting out of here!" was all he said as he grabbed a supermarket shelf and threw it through the store window. The glass shattered and Duke kicked at the largest remaining attached pieces until there was a large enough area for them to both get through.

"Follow me," Duke said as they jumped out of the window and into the supermarket car park. Duke got low and crouched between the houses of Zelenogorsk, keeping quiet and low where possible. It took time, and there were a couple of close calls, but they managed to circumvent the town and escape unharmed.

Once in the woods and relatively safe, they stopped to catch their breath. Although it was impossible, Xavier felt like he hadn't exhaled since they'd left the supermarket, afraid that even the slightest sound of air being expelled would attract a Zed. Duke unslung the rifle from his shoulder and popped out the empty magazine. He grabbed a new magazine of STANAG ammunition - his last one - and inserted it into the rifle.

"Fuck that was tense!" said Duke.

"Shit they just don't stop do they?"

"I've never seen anything like it. They're relentless," Duke responded, "I don't know what the fuck's happened out here but this shit is crazy and we need to bug out."

"Where should we go?"

"No idea," Duke said, "for now we need to bunker down somewhere safe. It's nearly dark and I don't know if that's good or bad with these things." Duke looked around, "there's a farmhouse up ahead. Let's hide out in there tonight."

Duke started off towards the house in the distance.

"Can I have my gun back?" Xavier asked.

"Shit yeah Frenchy, of course."

"Xavier. My name's Xavier, not Frenchy."

"Sure Xavier. I'm Duke," Duke held out his empty hand.

"The gun please," said Xavier as he ignored Duke's hand.

"Look, I said I was sorry about the supermarket. This has been some crazy shit and you were running with those things behind you. I panicked, said some shit I shouldn't have and I'm sorry. We must be square now after what we went through."

"The gun please. I really don't want to ask again," Xavier held out his hand.

Duke removed the gun from under his shirt and slammed it into Xavier's open palm, "There's your fucking gun if that's all you want."

"I hope you don't expect a thanks. We'll stick together tonight, watch each other's back so we can get some rest but tomorrow I'm going my own way. You go yours."

"Fair enough Frenchy," Duke continued on toward the farmhouse.

"Xavier. I said my name's Xavier," Duke didn't acknowledge Xavier as he stomped away.

Xavier sat in the cool darkness of the house, remembering the exchange. He now wished he could have taken it all back, wished he knew what was the right thing to say to Duke. Although a smaller abode than the farm house they bunkered in last night it somehow felt safer. He barely saw the outline of Duke across the room but he could hear him breathing.

Already Xavier had started to listen less and hear more, learning which sounds to ignore and which sounds to pay attention to. He could hear Duke shuffling around in his pack, the clinking of metal against metal. Xavier listened as Duke stood up and moved towards the kitchen, heard the strike of a match, the light from which cut into the pitch black and silence in one strike. For a moment the kitchen was lit up then the match lowered to the stove and a small blue flame appeared.

"Cup of Joe?" Duke asked.

"You think that's a good idea," Xavier derided.

"It might not be your fancy latte shit but it'll still get you buzzing."

"I meant the light from the stove. After last night you want to bring them in again?"

"We blocked the windows this time, the door's barricaded. We're locked down tight in here. We'll be fine."

Xavier looked around and agreed, yes tonight they should be safe.

"So, I hope you like your coffee black and shitty because that's all we got," Duke said.

Xavier laughed, "after last night black and shitty sounds fine."

Duke smiled and turned his attention back to the boiling water. He stared at the water as it just started to bubble and boil, the hissing drew him back into the memory of the previous night.

They were in a larger farmhouse last night but the kitchen was almost the same. One of the windows had been broken, most likely from a raider who was now long gone and had taken everything useful with him. When Duke walked into the kitchen a cursory glance showed him it had been picked clean. Cupboards were open, a sour odor came from the open fridge which Duke kicked closed, and a test of the stove showed it was empty of fuel.

With the sun outside setting, Duke dropped his pack on the ground and moved into the next room.

"I'm going to check the other rooms," he told Xavier on his way out. Xavier nodded and dropped his own pack on the ground. He started to empty out his pack, unloading food for the night, and didn't think anything of the map as he placed it on the ground. He was futilely looking through the drawers for anything useful when Duke returned to the room and was drawn straight to the map.

"Is that a map?" Duke asked excitedly.

"Yeah, I found it at the airport." Xavier responded.

"Why didn't you say you had a fucking map?"

"You didn't ask."

"Ha-dee-fucking-ha. Do you know where we are?"

"Possibly." Xavier spread the map out on the kitchen table.

"That town was Zelenogorsk. See the roads coming in match, and here are the power lines." Duke nodded. "I think that puts us a little north at this farmhouse." Xavier pointed to a place on the map.

"I assume you're taking this with you tomorrow?"

"Yep."

"Then let me take first watch. I want to study it and plan a route while you sleep."

"I don't think so."

"You think I'm going to run off with it while you're sleeping?" Duke asked.

"I'm not that tired but I am hungry. You give me one of those tins of food and I'll let you look over it while I'm eating. You can have a couple of hours with it but I'm not sleeping until that's back in my pack."

"Fine. You can cuddle it to sleep tonight after I've made a plan of where to go next."

Xavier nodded and Duke turned on his torch to take a closer look at the map. "Fuck I'd love a pen and paper so I could copy parts of it. This Chernarus place is huge."

"I'll look around and see if I can find something."

Duke didn't hear him as he focused on the map while Xavier moved into the lounge room. It was quiet in there and sparsely furnished. With the sun almost gone the room is dark, but in a nice way. Xavier gave up looking for a pen and instead sat on the armchair. It was old and musty smelling and one of the springs dug into his side but right now it felt like heaven and Xavier sunk into it. He stared out the window as the sun dipped behind a hill, and felt his breath slowing. Without thinking, his eyelids closed and his body shut down, not even giving him the option to decide to sleep.

Xavier woke with a start. The room was now completely dark and he panicked, feeling around for his revolver that had slipped out of his hand and was now on the floor. He lept out of the chair and listened, but there was no sound coming from the other room. *Duke. The map. They're gone. Dammit you idiot now you're really fucked.* The thoughts raced through his mind as he fumbled in the dark to where the door should be and pushed it open. He pulled back on the hammer of his revolver and held it in front of him as he slowly crept into the kitchen.

There on the kitchen table was Duke, torch in hand lighting up the room as he studied the map. Duke looked up from the map at Xavier as he entered the room, gun pointed at him.

"Nice nap Frenchy?"

Xavier looked around before lowering the gun and yawning, "why'd you let me sleep?"

"You were out like a light. There was nothing for you to do so I left you alone."

"But..."

"But what? The map's still here, I'm still here and you got some much needed rest so what's the problem? There's some food on the counter. Grab that and come over here. I think I might have a plan for our next move."

"You mean your next move," Xavier corrected as he moved towards the tinned food on the counter.

"Maybe after you've heard it you might want to come along."

And that was when it happened. Duke was too focused on the map and copying details onto a nearby writing pad. Xavier was too busy fetching dinner to look out of the window. Neither thought that Duke's torch was that bright - that it would act as a beacon to the roaming Zeds nearby.

From the nearby broken window an inhuman hissing started. Duke instinctively raised the torch from the map to the sound at the window and lit up the face of military Zed. The whites of his eyes soaked up the light from the torch as his mouth opened to expel a long loud groan.

"Fuck!" Duke screamed out.

The Zed responded by trying to climb through the already broken window. The sharp broken shards of glass cut its already scarred face but it seemed to feel nothing as it continued to climb through. Xavier just gawked at it, a spoon of cold tinned pasta hovering near his gaping mouth.

Duke grabbed his rifle from beside the table and lined up the Zed's temple. He squeezed the trigger and the Zed was flung back outside as its head split open from the bullet impact. Another one appeared at the window and was quickly dispatched by Duke.

"Frenchy grab your shit," he screamed out, "we're getting the fuck out of here."

"Where did it come from?"

The door to the kitchen rattled and Duke ran up and braced himself against it. "There are more outside. I don't know how they found us but we need to bug out now." Xavier scooped up the last of their supplies and put the pack on his shoulders. Duke leaned up against the door, fighting against the horde trying to get inside. "Grab my pack and put the map away. This door isn't going to hold much longer." Xavier put Duke's pack on his front and exhaled from the added weight.

"You right with that?"

"I'll be fine," Xavier responded.

"You better be, because we're going to have to move fast. Grab the torch, you're going to have to spot them for me."

"What does that mean?"

"I'm going to step away from the door and they're going to rush in. You keep the torch on the door and I'll get as many as I can, but we're going to have to push through and get out of here. You got it?"

Xavier nodded, shining the torch at the door. Duke popped open the magazine and checked his rounds. "I haven't got many rounds left and this is my last magazine, so when I say run, we run. Keep the torch in their eyes, I think that'll blind them enough for us to get past. Ready?"

Xavier nodded again. Duke pulled away from the door and it burst open. Duke moved back from them, lining up Zeds in his iron sights. BAM! BAM! He dropped two, but another two immediately filled the doorway. Duke lined them up and fired again, taking both down.

"Okay, run."

He blind-fired into the doorway as he charged towards it. The Zeds were driven back by the bullet impact and the shock of the light in their eyes. Duke and Xavier pushed past them and made it outside to find a large horde waiting for them.

"Fuck me, it's worse than I thought! This way Frenchy," Duke sprinted to the right and Xavier followed, shining the torch ahead. Duke ran across the road and towards the trees with both the Zeds and Xavier following.

"Drop the torch."

"What?"

"Throw it away from us and hopefully they will follow that."

Xavier flung the torch to his left and down the road. The sound of metal on asphalt and the light drew the attention of the closet Zeds.

"Good, it worked," whispered Duke.

"Now what?"

"Keep running. We aint out of it yet."

They ran along the road away from the torch. Some of the walkers were drawn towards their footsteps and chased after them but the majority followed the torch. Duke looked back and saw the shapes running down the road at them.

"Fuck I can't see shit out here."

"You told me to throw the torch away."

"Quick get down," Duke dragged Xavier down an embankment along the side of the road. He held him down and covered Xavier's mouth with his hand, staring into his eyes. Duke held a finger to his own lips and when Xavier nodded that he understood, Duke took the hand away from his mouth. He pointed up along the road - a few feet away from them three Zeds ran along the road. Duke could make out the details on their faces and one looked directly at them. It then looked the other way and Duke exhaled. He covered his eyes to show Xavier they can't see. Xavier nodded getting the message.

They stayed still as the Zeds moved down along the road. Duke held up his hands and patted the ground, indicating they should wait here. He pointed to his watch and circled his finger over one rotation. Xavier nodded, getting the message. They should wait for one hour.

Duke scrutinized for any movement up the road while Xavier surveyed down the road. Neither dared to move from the awkward positions they lay in as they waited out the hour.

They made it through the night alive, but silent. Once it was light enough to see they continued on, trying to find a landmark and regain their bearings. What they did find was a small isolated house at the end of a dirt road. They travelled along the small dirt road that led from the house, but it didn't seem to have any landmarks or mountains, all they could see was a tall radio tower far off in the distance.

With no idea of where they were, and exhausted from the lack of sleep and running, Duke decided it might be best to turn around and spend the next night at the house. It took them some time to fortify the doors and block out the windows, but fortunately, the previous owner had left some gas in the propane tank and instant coffee in the cupboard.

Duke handed Xavier the steaming black liquid in a mug.

"Black and shitty, as requested."

"Merci," Xavier took the cup, "so how long should we stay here?"

"I don't know. At least for tonight. You take first watch and wake me in four hours. We'll move at dawn and try to work out where we are. I have no idea which way we ran last night so we could be anywhere near Zelenogorsk."

Xavier took a sip from the mug and winced, "it's horrible."

"Drink up, who knows when you'll be able to get another coffee."

CHAPTER TWENTY FIVE

STALKING THE BANDITS

During the clash at Elektro, Janik spent the entire time watching from the hills. From his vantage point he could see what was happening but unlike Lucas, he did not see Mitch's murder. He just heard the gun shots and later on saw The Dunce running up into the hills with blood on his hands. From Janik's perspective it that the Dunce had killed Mitch.

He watched as Lucas shot at them from the fire station and panicked for a moment when it looked like Lucas was aiming straight at him. Janik observed as things settled down after Lucas' last shots and the Bandits took over the church.

Janik surveyed them as they focused on the bus, covering the buildings around the church. As dusk approached they spread out on sentry duty, settling in for the night. The whole time he watched, his mind kept telling him to take the bike and run, get out while he could, but another part said to watch and see if he could learn anything.

Janik was impressed with Shutov and his Bandit crew. They seemed much more organized than the Survivors, and were focused on the task at hand. *Maybe you should go up and say hello,* Janik's mind mocked him. *Maybe they'll give you a big sloppy kiss and say Janik we're so glad you're here, now we can feel safe again.* Janik watched them work. *Would it really be so bad to join up with these guys? Surely, he'd have something to offer them that they needed. But do you really want to be like them? Even if they would accept you, would you really accept them?* Janik's mind swung back and forth between both options as he watched the sun dip and the day get darker.

With the sun lowering, Janik started to feel brave, he decided that he should get closer to the Bandits and then choose what to do. Not wanting to be burdened, he unloaded his pack and stashed it along with the bike in a nearby house. Taking only the crossbow and three bolts, he slowly made his way towards the church.

The setting sun acted as a beacon for Janik, blinding him but also casting long shadows that he could creep and hide in. He skulked through the streets of Elektro, walking slowly and lightly so as not to disturb any of the roaming infected. As Janik made his way closer to the church, he questioned why he wanted to go into the lion's den, so to speak. Was he there to give himself up, to join them, or for something else? For some reason he felt compelled to get closer. To take a chance when he would have previously stayed safe.

As he got closer to the church he noticed one man patrolling the roof of the fire station. This was the same roof that Lucas was on previously, but no sign of him remained. Janik wondered if Lucas was dead. Were the others dead? Did any of them make it out alive? Maybe this was what drew him towards danger, the need to know, the desire to understand. Janik recognized the man on the roof as being Harrison, who loved giving Janik shit because of his size. He searched around for the others that he previously saw Harrison come into town with, but there appeared to be no one else, other than the wandering infected.

Janik leaned around a street corner, and looked right into the eyes of an undead. This one was still, its head moved around slightly as it listened for any sounds. Ever so slowly and quietly, Janik raised the crossbow. The movement was slow, so slow it was almost imperceptible but the crossbow was now pointed towards the infected in front of him. Janik pulled back on the bolt and caressed the trigger with his finger. He looked down the sight to see the infected's head fill it as it turned to face him. Janik paused for a moment, stared into its eyes, looked for some semblance of a soul or intelligence. There was nothing there but a milky whiteness. It opened its mouth ready to groan when, with a rustle through the air, the bolt flew out of the crossbow and buried into his eye socket.

The infected dropped, his mouth still open from the groan that never made it out of his lips. Janik looked around but the sound hadn't attracted any attention. He crept over to the body and grabbed onto the bolt lodged deep into the eye socket. It was jammed in tight and took him a couple of hard pulls before he yanked it out. He wiped the black ooze off the bolt onto the undead's clothes and loaded it back into the crossbow.

Janik looked across the road towards the firehouse. It was almost night and the shadow from the tall building cast the car park into near darkness. Harrison was patrolling around the roof but he continually rubbed his eyes as the light from the setting sun contrasted against the darkness of town. Janik scoped out how to get to the firehouse.

In the car park there were some debris, an upright oil drum, a low barricade, some discarded wooden pallets – none of it large enough for him to hide behind. Near the open gate there was a small guard house. If Janik could get there it would provide him with good cover until it was completely dark. Between Janik and the guardhouse was a street that if he walked across would expose him for too long to anyone looking down that direction.

Fortunately for Janik, the street was not completely empty. Near him on the road were two burnt out cars jammed together - the remains of a car accident long gone and never to be cleared away. Although they didn't form a very good barricade for any vehicles trying to pass, their presence provided Janik some cover from Harrison if he happened to look in that direction. Janik lay on his belly and crawled across the road. His arms were pockmarked from the asphalt digging in to them as he crawled. Janik cursed the fact that he still didn't have a jacket.

Having made it safely across to the other side, he crawled towards the open gate. Janik watched Harrison on the roof, waited for him to turn and face the other direction. As soon as Harrison was facing the other way Janik quickly scooted across on tiptoe, his feet provided the lightest touch to the ground and making almost no sound. Janik moved into the guard station where he now had a clear view of the fire station roof. Between him and the roof was the scattered debris, but it would be dark soon and Janik planned to move across then.

Janik sat on the floor of the guardhouse, peering over the edge of the window to the firehouse roof. It was now almost night outside, and in the darkness, Janik was well hidden and felt safe. Comforted by that thought, he took a sip of water and studied Harrison as he paced. His movements were erratic, and he muttered to himself, although Janik was too far away to hear what he said.

What he did hear were the loud footsteps of a man approaching. Janik scampered against the wall, trying to make himself as small as possible. He listened as the footsteps got closer. *Dumbass you've been spotted*, Janik thought as he looked around for a way out.

He realized that he wasn't thinking when he entered the small guard station. It had only one entrance and although the person approaching was probably not infected, he would most likely be dangerous. *You stupid fool,* Janik chastised himself and he raised the crossbow and pointed it towards the only entrance. If anyone did enter, Janik would only have one chance to shoot him.

"About time. I can't see shit out here," Janik heard Harrison call out from the roof.

"Hey someone's got to be last, may as well be you," the second man responded. Janik strained to listen. The man had stopped walking somewhere in the car park and Janik heard the sound of wood hitting metal.

Suddenly he was squinting as the whole area became lit up. Janik panicked and crawled further back under the window, worried he would be seen by the sudden burst of light.

"That better Princess?" the man called out. Janik recognized the voice - it was The Butcher.

"Much. At least I can see now. How much longer does Shutov want me up here for?"

"I don't know. He's pretty intent of having Sam fix that bus tonight so we can roll out to the airfield tomorrow."

"Fuck, so it could be all night?"

"Looks like it. And don't be sneaking any sleep up there either. You're covering the whole North East."

Janik looked over the window's edge and saw that the drum he hadn't paid much attention to previously was now alight, with wood from the pallets sticking out of it. The drum light created an eerie glow that spread out and flicked along the walls. It had also now lit up the entire car park. Janik watched as The Butcher left the car park and walked back towards the church.

Janik looked back across at the fire station roof but it was in darkness as the light from the drum didn't reach that far. He tried to squint and block out the light but couldn't see any better, which meant he couldn't tell where Harrison was and which direction he was facing. *Fuck!* Janik thought as he realized he was now trapped inside the guardhouse, unable to see Harrison and unable to move without Harrison seeing him.

CHAPTER TWENTY SIX

FIRE AND ICE

Yuri and the crew of Survivors had packed up their equipment and were moving along the tree lines towards Pusta. Having watched the Bandits for hours, Alfie felt sure that they intended to stay in town and were not making any plans to move that night. For them, this meant their best chance to travel was while it was dark, since they would be sure where the Bandits were for at least the next couple of hours.

Since it was a cloudless night and the moon was out, they had decided to travel without using torches until they were over the other side of the hill. This did make movement much slower in the dark but they all agreed it was the safest way. Yuri was concerned that they still had not seen Lucas, Janik or Kiam the entire afternoon and wanted to leave them a note stating where they were going. The idea was discussed but it was agreed that it would be unlikely that anyone would find it and they couldn't be sure that if someone did it, wouldn't be a Bandit.

Yuri hoped that maybe they were already at Pusta. It wasn't that farfetched, as it was the closest inland town and no one had seen Lucas or Janik running along the coast that morning. They could, of course, had travelled south towards Chernogorsk, but Yuri kept hold of the hope that they would be found in Pusta.

As he walked, he noticed in the distance a campfire burning. He grabbed Joseph and pointed towards the fire in the distance. "You see that?" Yuri whispered. Joseph followed his finger and nodded. "Get the others," Yuri said, as he watched the fire ahead. Soon all the men stood near him, watching the fire. Alfie looked at it through the binoculars and observed one man lying on the ground near the fire.

"I can't see who it is?" Alfie explained.

"Could it be the missing men?" Yuri asked.

"It could be. Or it could be a scout. It could be a trap. We don't know."

"So do we approach?" Joseph asked.

"No, too dangerous."

"But if it's the missing men, it could be Janik or Lucas there. We should at least be sure," Yuri said, "I'll go. I'll make sure."

"You'll have to approach quietly. There might be others in the darkness keeping watch."

Yuri nodded, "let me have your rifle." Alfie swapped the Lee Enfield in his hand for Yuri's pistol. "You all stay here, if you see anyone approach besides me, then be careful. If it's the others then I'll come back, but I'll whistle as I approach so listen out for it."

"Good luck Yuri," Alfie slapped him on the shoulder.

"I'll be fine," Yuri answered as he checked the time. "Half an hour. If I'm not back in half an hour then something's wrong."

Alfie nodded as he watched Yuri creep off towards the fire. Yuri walked slowly, gently pressing down with each step to avoid snapping branches. He held the Lee Enfield out in front of him, looking and listening for any signs of others around him.

As he got closer to the fire, he could hear the crackling and snapping of the wood as it burnt, smelt the smoke as it wafted over his head. Yuri looked towards the fire and saw a second man lying on the ground. One was covered in rugs and the other seemed to be lying flat. There was something amiss about the flat man and when Yuri got closer he saw what it was – the man had no head. *Shit what happened here?* Yuri wondered as he circled around to get a better look at the sleeping man's face.

The sleeping man had a jacket over part of his head to keep the cold off, which forced Yuri to continue inching around. He kept the rifle pointed directly at the man as he circled around.

Finally he was able to see the face and Yuri gasped when he recognized Rory, The Dunce. *Jesus what's he doing here?* Yuri looked around but it appeared that Rory was all alone and fast asleep. Yuri watched him and noticed that Rory only had an axe and the clothes on his back. *Christ he'll stave out here. We need to help him...* the thought was interrupted by gunshots emanating from the town behind them.

Rory's eyes burst open and he looked down the barrel of Yuri's rifle not ten feet away from his face. His eyes were wide and he sat up, looking around like a caged animal. Too late, Yuri realized he still had the gun pointed at Rory and lowered it. As soon as he saw the gun lower, Rory lept up and ran off into the darkness carrying his axe.

"Dunce, wait! I didn't mean to scare you," Yuri called out but not too loudly as the shooting continued in the town down the hill.

"Fuck!" he chastised himself as he looked around for Rory but he was already gone. From the left there was the crashing of branches as the other Survivors charged through the brush, weapons out looking around the campsite.

"Yuri what the hell happened? We heard shooting," Alfie asked as he scanned the campsite.

"It was The Dunce, but he got scared when he heard the shooting and ran off."

"Which way?" Joseph asked.

"Down the hill towards Elektro."

"We can't chase him down there."

"So what was he doing out here then?" Pablo asked.

"Maybe he was a scout, or some sort of lookout?" Alfie responded.

Yuri wasn't convinced, "really? The Dunce? Would you put him on lookout?"

"Maybe not. But you tell me what he's doing out here all alone with a fire lighting up the night. And when he sees you he runs off back into town. I don't see any tents around here, just the dead infected. Did he have any weapons on him?"

"Just an axe. He didn't even have a pack."

"So he's out here with just an axe and a fire. If he's not one of them then why would he do that?" Alfie asked.

"Fuck I don't know," Yuri replied.

"Neither do I," Alfie offered, "but we've got to assume the worst. Which means Pusta is compromised."

"Why have we got to assume that?"

"Because there's nothing else around here. Pusta's north, Elektro is south. We know they're in Elektro and if the Dunce tells them he saw us here then they'll assume we're heading to Pusta. There's no other reason for us to be walking around up here so I say Pusta's out."

"But what about the others, they might be there?" Yuri asked.

"And if we could warn them we would. Look, I don't want to stand around here all night arguing. We should double back and go to the other town on the coast."

"Kamyshovo?"

"Yeah Kamyshovo. With torches off it'll be slower but when we get there we'll camp down for the night. It's not much of a plan but it sure beats waiting around here. Are we all good with that?"

The other Survivors all nodded.

"Then let's roll. Leave the fire burning. Hopefully they'll see it and head North."

CHAPTER TWENTY SEVEN

SURVIVOR PARANOIA

Moments before Yuri had come upon the Dunce sleeping by the campfire, Janik had his own problems with fire back at Elektro. Janik thought through his options while hiding in the guard station. The probable outcomes weren't great.

He could wait it out until morning. The problem with that was, as it got light he'd be more exposed moving through the town. He could just step out and announce his position but then he couldn't be sure they wouldn't kill him so that wasn't an option. If he could somehow smother the fire and put it out, then he could then use the cover of darkness to escape. The problem with that was the fire going out would draw a lot of attention and possibly others to this location.

None of these possibilities were any good. The only idea that had a reasonable chance of success was to kill Harrison quietly, and sneak off. The problem with that was that he couldn't see Harrison and therefore couldn't kill him. While he rummaged through the drawers of the guardhouse, Janik found some roadside flares and the plan was updated. Janik contemplated using them to light up the roof and then take the shot. Of course the bright red flares would definitely grab everyone's attention, so he wouldn't have long to kill Harrison and sneak away.

Janik turned the flare over in his hand trying to think of another way. His mind was in a loop. All it kept saying was, *pop the flare. Do it already.* It was stuck on that idea and wouldn't let another one in. Reluctantly, he cracked the flare and tossed it onto the roof.

The effect was immediate. The roof lit up bright red and Harrison was easily visible again, as he stood confused at the suddenly-lit flare landing near him. Janik stepped out of the guardhouse and raised the crossbow, Harrison lined up in his sights. Harrison noticed the movement below and called out "Who's there?" He tried to use his hand to shield the flare's brightness but all Harrison could see was a figure standing there. He walked closer to the building's edge to get a better look.

Janik looked down the sight as Harrison approached. *He's lined up, it's an easy shot, just pull the trigger already.* His finger rested on the crossbow trigger but he couldn't do it, couldn't squeeze and end this man's life.

"Who is that?" Harrison asked, his eyes now adjusted to the brightness which allowed him a better look at Janik.

"Drop the gun," Janik called out. He hadn't spoken for a long while and his voice cracked as he barked out the command so it sounded more like a yelp.

"Shorty? Is that you Janik?"

"I said drop the gun."

"You've made it. Great. Come join us we got plenty of food."

"I'm not going to ask again. Drop – the – gun," Janik ordered as he moved closer.

Harrison's eyes had now adjusted and he could see Janik down below, the crossbow pointed at him.

"Hold on now. There's no need for this shit," he unslung the AK-74 and put it down on the roof. "There, it's down. Now let's just talk."

"Kick it off the roof to me."

"Fuck you. I'm not kicking it off."

"I said kick it off."

"And I said fuck you!"

"Don't make me do this."

"Do what? Kill me? I already lost a friend today because of you pricks. He didn't get given a chance."

"I know nothing about that. I'm just asking you to give me the gun."

"You want to kill me then kill me. But I'm not giving you the gun to do it with."

Janik looked down the sight with Harrison lined up. Harrison stared back defiant and Janik raised his arm to wipe some perspiration off his forehead. The small moment's distraction was all Harrison needed. He dropped down prone and grabbed the AK-74.

He started blind-firing off the roof towards Janik. The bullets went wild and missed him but Janik wasn't taking any chances. He kicked over the flaming barrel and ran off into the darkness. Harrison looked over the edge and saw the car park was empty.

"Come back shorty. I thought we were negotiating," he yelled out as he fired into the darkness.

Shutov, Alejandro and The Butcher turned the corner and ran into the car park.

"What's happening? Who are you shooting at?" demanded Shutov.

"One of them was just here. He ran off into the darkness," Harrison answered.

The Butcher smiled, "I told you they'd be back. Let me go after him. Which way did he go?"

"I didn't see. I think up into the hills but I'm not sure."

"So he could still be around here?" Shutov queried.

"Dunno."

"Are there others or was he alone?"

"I just saw him, but that doesn't mean there aren't others around."

"There are too many unknowns. Butcher, you stay here. I want every man guarding the bus and church."

"Let me go after him. I'll find out what he knows," The Butcher said.

"No!" Shutov commanded, "for all we know this was a

distraction and they're already at the bus right now. I want every man awake and guarding the perimeter. Alejandro, scout around and see if you can find them. But do it quietly and if you see anything come back here and report, don't engage."

"If they're out there I'll find them," Alejandro said, brimming with confidence.

"I have faith in you brother. Now, go and scare out these rats from their little hidey hole."

Alejandro scurried off into the darkness. Shutov looked up at Harrison.

"You! Stop wasting ammo firing at shadows and keep a lookout. If you see anything call out and we'll come running," Harrison nodded, "Butcher - you're with me, we're checking the bus and then the perimeter."

Without waiting for a response, Shutov walked out of the car park. The Butcher looked back into the darkness one more time before he turned and followed Shutov.

Janik ran hard and fast, letting the darkness swallow him. His face was already sore from when he tripped and fell. He looked back but the firehouse was lost in the shadows and he allowed himself a moment to pause. His mind caught up with him and reprimanded him. *See you are a coward. Now look what you did. They know who you are and they'll be coming after you.* Janik looked around but apart from his own gasping, it was quiet.

He looked up the hill and noticed in the distance a flickering light like a campfire. The light disappeared and reappeared as though something was blocking it. Janik rubbed the sweat off his forehead and off his eyebrows and he tried to determine what was happening. And then he saw it.

There was a campfire but it was being intermittently blocked by the shadow of a man running towards him. Janik hunted around for somewhere to hide but he was out in an open field, there was nowhere to go and nothing to hide behind.

The figure kept running towards him and Janik realized it was carrying an axe. He raised the crossbow and pointed it at him.

"Stop right there whoever you are," Janik shouted.

"Janik?" the figure asked.

"Rory?"

"Janik is it you?" Rory stopped running 8 feet away from him and walked towards him.

"Stop right there Rory."

"We got to move. There are men with guns at the fire."

Janik looked past Rory to the campfire.

"Who? What men?"

"It was Yuri. He pointed a gun at me."

"Yuri's up there," Rory nodded, "why did he point a gun at you? Is it because you're with them?"

"I'm not with them. I'm alone. I was sleeping."

"I've seen you with them before. Kai, Harrison, Alejandro at the fuel station. You were working together."

"Kai's dead."

"You killed him?"

"No! They tried to kill me, but Vuk let me go."

"Vuk's with them too?"

"And Shutov. He's the boss man - like on the ship."

Janik let all this all sink in, "Why did you kill Mitch?"

"I didn't kill Mitch, Kai did."

"Then why do you have blood on you?"

"I tried to help him but the bleeding wouldn't stop."

"Then why did they kill Mitch?"

"I don't know, they're bad men. Vuk said to run, so I ran."

"Look Rory, I don't have time for this shit. I need to find Yuri and the others. I might believe you but I can't be sure. The bad men are in town so you don't want to go that way. I'm going to the camp and I don't want you following me. So you run that way," he pointed west, "and keep running until you find somewhere safe."

"Why can't I go with you?"

"Because I don't trust you, that's why. You want to live - you go west. You want to die - take another direction. If I see you behind me I'm going to shoot you."

"I thought we were friends."

"That was before all of this. There are no friends now, only people who haven't killed you yet."

And with that, Janik moved off north towards the campfire. Rory looked around and contemplated his next move. He took a couple of steps along Janik's path before he shook his head and moved west, the direction Janik pointed.

CHAPTER TWENTY EIGHT

THE STANDOFF

It was cold inside the house but Robert didn't notice it. He was used to the cold so tonight felt like a balmy spring night to him. Although it took them most of the afternoon to get here, Kamyshovo ended up being a good choice. There were only two roads in and out and the infected management was not too difficult.

They picked a house at the crossroads where they could see down both roads, and therefore anyone approaching. The house was small with only two rooms and one way in, but it was easy for them to barricade and they had even found a few blankets to keep them warm. Doc had wrapped himself up in a blanket as he kept watch.

Doc was on first watch while Robert slept and when they changed over, Doc reported that nothing of note had occurred on his watch. The infected roamed around outside but they seemed unaware or uninterested in their presence and kept wandering.

At the start of his shift Robert watched the infected, looking for patterns in their movement. To him they seemed to just walk, shuffle, or shamble, depending on the level of decay in their bodies or the damage that had been done to them. After watching them for some time, Robert couldn't see any patterns in their movement. The only thing he picked up on was that they seemed near-blind at night, but without a fire to test the theory he couldn't be certain.

The sky was clear of any clouds and Robert found that he could see clearly once his eyes adjusted. The nearby infected didn't seem to notice him standing at the window. Some walked right past looking into the window but paid him no mind. Admittedly, he stood very still, the Remington shotgun rested on his shoulder, so he figured his stillness had something to do with it. He was learning more about this world every day and just hoped that it wouldn't be in vain if he ended up one of them.

After an hour of staring into the night, Robert began to get bored. This was another thing they would need to get used to, looking out for the infected day and night, remaining vigilant during a dull and silent night. It could take just one moment of lost concentration for a fatal error to occur, and this state of continued hyper-vigilance was something Robert wasn't used to.

The lighthouse had been a bust. They had found nothing worthwhile there and since it was automated, everything had been long since shut down. Robert hoped for some notes or intelligence about what had happened - ship movements in a log, or maybe some military maps. What they found were cobwebs and a generator that had been drained of fuel.

Robert studied his own map, using the light from his watch to see. From here it seemed their best bet would be to travel along the coast to Elektrozavodsk. It was a big town and if there were any survivors from either the ship or the infection then the odds were high that they would be there. Robert looked out the window down the road when he noticed lights in the distance.

For that moment he stood still, the map hanging down his side, as he tried to focus on the road ahead. *Could it really be lights down the road.* It was hard to be certain as they were so far away and there were a lot of cars and debris on the road. The lights got closer and Robert could make out details. There were two beams cutting a definite path of light, they swept the surrounds, and searched the trees and any cars they happened upon.

Ever so quietly Robert checked his Remington - it was loaded. He flicked the underside mounted torch on and off to test it. *Yep, still working.* Robert moved into the second room where Doc was sleeping.

"Doc wake up," he whispered loudly.

"I can't sleep with those things groaning outside," Doc replied sleepily.

"Well slap yourself awake anyway. We got company."

"What kind of company?" Doc asked as he sprung upright.

"Two people coming down the road."

"Great, let's go out and meet them."

"I'd rather not. We have no idea who they are or what their intentions are."

"They could be from the ship."

"And if they are then we'll know them. I just don't want them to see us until we know who they are. If we recognize them then we'll announce our position but if not, we stay quiet until they leave."

Doc went to the window and looked out.

"Oh I see them down there, but there are more than two."

"Shit, you're right!"

Behind the two figures holding torches Robert identified another two holding guns. They kept the guns pointed in the direction of the torch beams.

"This is bad," Robert muttered.

"Why, they can't see us?"

"Yeah, but they don't exactly look friendly. The rear guard are carrying guns and definitely looking for someone."

"You think it's us?"

"Doubt it."

"Do you recognize any of them?"

"Can't say I do," Robert replied, "We better get out of sight, there are no curtains on this window and if they shine a torch at it we're fucked."

Robert and Doc ducked down behind the window and peeked over the sill to watch the approaching men. The men had turned off their torches and moved from walking on the road to walking along the beach. Robert watched them as they disappeared behind a warehouse at the docks.

"Can you see them?"

Doc got up and moved to the other room and looked out the window. His view was blocked by the fence outside and he couldn't see past it.

"Nada. Damn fence is in the way," Doc replied.

"Shit! I don't like this. Do you think they've gone inside that warehouse?"

"They could have just gone past it and kept walking."

"Fuck, we have to go out there."

"You just said to stay here."

"I don't want them to know about us but we need to find out who they are. We can't lose them."

"What would it matter?"

"Because they're the first uninfected people we've seen in two days. They might know stuff, they might have food or water. Hell they're travelling at night, maybe they learnt that's the best way to do it. If we are going to survive we're going to have to work with others."

"But they could be bad people."

"You're right - so let's get closer and then make that call. Leave all this shit here, we can come back for it. Just grab the 9mm and all the ammo."

Doc grabbed the pistol and pocketed two spare clips. Robert pushed the barricaded furniture away from the door.

"We stay low and quiet. We should move around to the other side of the warehouse and see if they're inside or have gone past. Be prepared for anything, but don't shoot unless you have to. Got it?"

"Yep, I got it."

"Good," Robert opened the door, "Let's go."

Yuri and Alfie held their guns out as Pablo and Joseph used the torches to spot. The travel had been slow going until they were well out of sight of Elektro, but with the torches and an empty road it had been much faster. Yuri had the feeling that they were being watched, but since he couldn't see anyone, he ignored it. Still he couldn't shake the sense that up in the mountains somewhere there was another person watching them.

The feeling returned when they got closer to Kamyshovo. Rather than risk going into town in the dark they had decided to stop in a warehouse at the docks. Along the beach they could see there were no obstacles and so Yuri had the torches shut off to conserve power. Also, he preferred the dark to keep any prying eyes away.

Arriving at the dock area they found two infected roaming around the front of the warehouse. The four men lay still in the sand watching them - with no need to rush they agreed to wait until the infected moved away. It took some time before the two infected walked towards the beach further away from them and, more importantly, away from the warehouse.

With the undead having moved on, Yuri was about to rise when Alfie grabbed him by the shirt and pulled him back down. Annoyed, Yuri turned to Alfie but Alfie was not looking at him. Instead he was staring into the distance where along the other side of the warehouse two figures were creeping along the wall.

Both men were walking low with the lead man holding an ominous looking shotgun while the second carried a pistol with a silencer attached. Yuri pointed them out to Joseph and Pablo and all four men watched. The two strangers sneaked towards the warehouse entrance - the lead man stopped at the large sliding doors and peeked inside.

"I could feel we were being watched," Yuri whispered.

"You think they're looking for us?" queried Alfie.

"I'm certain of it."

"What should we do?"

"We stay here and wait for them to move on."

Robert looked inside the warehouse but it was dark and he couldn't tell if people were inside.

"Do you see them?" Doc whispered.

"Too dark, can't be sure," Robert replied.

"What should we do?"

"I'm sure they came this way. Can you see anyone down the road?"

Doc searched around. Up ahead were buildings and debris - but no people. He looked down south along the beach. Nothing there except for four shadows near the water's edge. Doc stared at the shadows trying to make out shapes.

"I think I see them."

"Where?" Robert looked around.

"Over there on the beach. See the shadows against the moon's reflection off the water. I think that's them lying down on the sand."

Robert followed the sand line with his eyes and saw the shapes Doc was referring to. To him they just looked like shadows, until one moved slightly - a head turned to face the others.

"You're right, and they're looking right at us."

"We've been made," Alfie whispered.

"They can't see us," Joseph responded.

"Then why are they looking this way?" Alfie asked.

Yuri watched as the men hastily moved inside the warehouse, slamming the door shut behind them.

"Alfie's right, they've spotted us," Yuri asserted.

"Oh shit we're fucked!" exclaimed Pablo, "What are we going to do?"

"What are we going to do?" pleaded Doc.

Robert had the Remington shotgun's under-barrel-light turned on and searched around the warehouse. Apart from some disused machinery and car parts, it was empty.

"It's not that bad," placated Robert.

"Of course it is – there are four armed men outside there."

"If they wanted to kill us they would have-" Robert was cut off by the groan of an infected that was crawling along the floor near him. He swung the shotgun light towards it just as it was about to reach out and grab him. Without hesitation Robert fired at the infected, turning its head into a wet pile of mush on the concrete floor.

"Shot!" Pablo called out.

"We hear it," Alfie responded.

"Are they shooting at us?"

"I'm not waiting to find out," Alfie raised his Lee Enfield and fired at the door.

The bullet went through the sheet metal wall and whizzed past Doc, a little too close for comfort.

"Fuck, they're shooting at us!"

"You don't know that. Maybe they have problems with the infected out there as well."

Another bullet pierced the sheet metal and Doc dropped to the ground, panicked.

"You were saying?"

Robert looked around but there was only one way in or out.

"This cat and mouse game has to stop."

Robert walked towards the door and slid it open until it was wide enough for a man to walk through. He stood near the entrance.

Yuri watched as the door opened.

"They're getting ready to fire back. If you see a shape at the door, shoot it," Yuri ordered. The men all pointed their guns towards the now open door. They saw the light arcing across the entranceway but couldn't see anybody.

From the warehouse Robert called out, "stop shooting at us. We weren't shooting at you, we had infected in here."

The men all looked at each other but no one lowered their gun.

"Can you hear me?" Robert called out.

"Yeah we hear you!" Alfie yelled back.

"Alfie! Is that you Alfie?"

Alfie looked at the other men wondering what he should say. Yuri shook his head no.

"C'mon Alfie I'd know that scouser accent anywhere. It's me, Robert."

"Robert, what are you doing in there?" Yuri asked.

"Trying to survive this shit storm, same as you."

"Are you hunting us? Are you with them?" asked Alfie.

"With who?"

"The Bandits. The men who attacked us this morning."

"Look I have no idea what's going on. I'm here with Doc and we didn't attack you. In fact you're the first uninfected we've seen since the ship ran aground," Robert yelled back.

"I don't believe him," Yuri whispered, "I've had this feeling for a while that we were being watched. I think it was him and his partner tracking us from the camp."

Doc still lay on the floor watching Robert.

"What's happening?" he whispered to Robert.

"I don't know. They seem to be talking."

"We don't believe you," Yuri called out from the beach, "Why are you in this town?"

"Because our bike ran out of fuel up the road and this was the closest place we could get to before dark," Robert replied and then under his breath whispered, "Oh shit."

"What is it?" Doc asked.

"They're spreading out. Looks like they're getting ready to rush us," Robert whispered back.

"We're going to die. They're going to kill us. They don't believe you," Doc whined.

"Shut up," Robert whispered back, "If they wanted to kill us they would have already. They're scared, just like us. Somebody's got to take the first step."

"What do you mean?"

"Alfie, call your men back. I'm coming out. Unarmed."

"What!" Doc called out.

Robert unloaded the Remington and pushed it out of the door and away from him and the warehouse.

"See, there's my shotty. Now shine your torches at the door," The door stayed in darkness, "come on, we saw you use them down the road. Shine them at the door so you can see me."

The door was suddenly lit up.

"Thanks. Now I'm going to step into the light. I'm unarmed. I'm going to lift up my shirt and show you there are no hidden guns. Now the thing is - I want to live, so for fuck sake don't shoot me. I've got nothing to do with anything that has happened to you. I'm just like you, a poor bastard trying to survive. Are we clear on that?"

"You have no guns?" Yuri called back.

"I'm going to show you I have no guns on me. Can you guarantee my safety."

"What about your friend inside?" Yuri asked.

"He'll do the same thing." answered Robert.

"Like hell I will. You want to go out there and get shot then be my guest. I'm staying here."

"You what?" Robert barked.

"I'm staying here. Alive."

"It's Doc from the ship," Robert yelled to the men on the beach, "But he's too much of a pussy to come out."

"Fuck you," Doc sneered at him.

"No, fuck you man," Robert spat back, "you're going to get me killed with that cowardly attitude."

"No I'm not. Stepping out into the open where there are guys with guns who've just shot at us, that's what will get you killed. I'm trying to stay alive."

Robert turned back to face outside. "He won't come out, he's afraid you'll kill him. We'll deal with him later on, for now, I'm stepping out."

Robert stepped out of the shadows and into the torch light with his arms up, "you see me?"

"Yeah we see you," Pablo responded.

"Okay, I'm going to lift up my shirt slowly and show you I'm not hiding anything. Are we cool with that?"

"Do it," Alfie called out, "but no funny stuff and real slow like."

Robert slowly lowered his hand and grabbed the edge of his shirt. He slowly pulled it up to show that there was nothing concealed in his pants waistband. Satisfied they'd got a good look he started to slowly turn, the other hand still high up in the air. Once he had completed a full rotation he let go of the shirt and raised that hand up as he walked towards the light.

"So are we cool?"

"You always were a crazy bastard," Alfie couldn't hide the smile in his voice.

"Hey you've played enough poker with me to know I can't bluff for shit, you scouser prick."

"Don't think I still won't shoot you."

"Come here you silly bastard."

Alfie got up, leaving the Lee Enfield behind. He walked out to Robert and they hugged. The other men all lowered their guns and got up.

"Fuck that was tense," Robert exhaled, "I hope one of your pricks has spare underwear cause I shit-stained these ones after stepping into the light."

"Mate how did you know we wouldn't shoot you?" Alfie queried.

"I didn't. I just fucking hoped you wouldn't," admitted Robert as he walked back towards his Remington and picked it up off the ground.

"So you've been travelling with Doc all this time," Yuri asked.

"Yep. Take a look." Robert shined the flashlight into the warehouse floor where Doc was lying on the ground, pointing a shaking pistol at the doorway.

"Hello Doc. You look like the one who needs medical attention," Alfie mocked. They all laughed at the joke while Doc rose up.

"Now he's everyone's problem. Aint that right Doc?"

Doc slowly nodded as he looked around at his new compatriots, the pistol still shaking in his hand.

CHAPTER TWENTY NINE

THE PARTY BUS

There was still a chill in the air as the sun slowly broke over the horizon. The men who were on watch were glad for the impending warmth as they rubbed tired eyes and looked around at the slowly lightening streets. The remnants from last night's guard duty were scattered around them. Bodies of the infected, many had been killed with an axe or other blunt object to maintain silence and conserve ammo.

Shutov walked out from the church hiding his tiredness behind a smile and some water – although he would have gladly traded the water for coffee. He had spent half the night patrolling the perimeter with The Butcher, certain of an attack that didn't happen. Between being on edge and listening to The Butcher's complaining, Shutov didn't have a very good night – although it would have been worse had an attack occurred.

Already the strain of leadership was taking its toll on Shutov. The responsibility for these men's lives was different now than it was previously. Sure, he has always been in command, had positions of power, management roles. But this was different. If he made a mistake here it wasn't like people could just find another job. If he fucked up in this world people would die – there was no coming back from that. No social security or welfare to fall back on – dead was dead, and that included him.

This was why he spent the night running events over in his mind, hunting for a reason for Janik to be at the firehouse last night. It made sense for the Survivors to use Janik as a scout, he was small, fast and smart. But if his being at the firehouse was to distract them then where was the attack? Did they scare it off? Were there men hiding in the trees waiting to attack them in the daylight? Was there an ambush set up further along the road?

And what of the camp fire. Alejandro found the fire while looking for Janik but it being there didn't make sense. The fire was lit but there was no sign of life around it, no tents, no packs, nothing. Only a dead and decapitated infected and a granola bar wrapper. Neither he nor Alejandro could make sense of it. The actions of the Survivors last night perturbed him and this kept him awake most of the night.

He slapped his face and rubbed the growing stubble. *Good that would keep me warm,* he thought as he walked over to Sam. Sam looked as tired as Shutov felt. He had spent the entire night working on the bus, trying to get it running.

"Tell me you have good news Sam. Tell me my bus lives," Shutov probed, patting him on the back.

"The keys are in the ignition. Turn her over and let's see," Sam replied, opening the door. Shutov climbed into the bus and sat in the driver's seat. He blew on his hands and made a sign of the cross, before turning the key and starting the engine.

The motor whined and a black cloud of carbon monoxide spluttered out of the exhaust. Shutov pumped the gas and willed the engine to start. It whined louder, then the whine turned into a low roar and the engine started. Shutov could feel the vibration through the steering wheel as the engine powered up. He pressed hard on the accelerator and the engine roared even louder in response. Shutov cheered and some of the men standing around to watch joined in.

He left the motor running, jumped off the seat and out of the bus. He walked over to Sam, who was tuning the engine, and slapped him heartily on the back.

"My boy you are a miracle worker. This is good, a good start to the day," he turned to the others, "alright men, grab something to eat and load up onto the bus. We move out in one hour."

"There is one problem Sir," Sam interjected.

"Don't give me problems, give me solutions."

Vuk stepped forward, "the problem has nothing to do with Sam, it's gas. There's enough in the tank for maybe one or two kilometers but that's all we could salvage from nearby cars. We're going to have to find more gas along the way and it won't be at fuel stations."

"So where then?" Shutov asked.

"Same place we found this fuel. Abandoned cars, factories, generators, farm houses. We can either spend today searching for gas and fill up the bus in one, go or we drive off and stop along the way, siphoning where we can."

"Then we move out today. Stop along the way."

"It's riskier," Vuk retorted, "we could run out of gas in the middle of nowhere."

"Every day we wait gives the Survivors more time to set up an ambush or plan an attack on us here."

"Surely you don't think they're still coming for us. They're trying to get by, like we are, they're not interested in us."

"Then why was Janik sneaking around last night? Why did they set up camp just up the hill? Where did the sniper who killed Kai go?" pressed Shutov.

"It matters not, I have his gun," replied Vuk.

"That one, yes. But what if he has others? What if there's a crosshair on us right now?" Vuk and the others looked around slightly nervous, "Vuk you may be right and they may be long gone, but would you risk your life, my life, and everyone else's life on it?" Vuk shook his head. "Then let's move out. We'll find fuel along the way."

Vuk nodded and moved to the church, along with the other men, and gathered up their supplies.

CHAPTER THIRTY

RUNNING SCARED

Shutov couldn't have been any further from the truth when he implied that Lucas was possibly looking at him through a sniper scope. Lucas had no extra rifle, in fact he had nothing else with him when he'd left that firehouse almost 24 hours ago. To Lucas it had felt much longer, he'd been running almost the whole time - not only from potential pursuers but also from his own thoughts.

He didn't exactly feel guilty about killing Kai - he had just watched him murder Mitch in cold blood - but Lucas didn't feel right about it either. Kai was the first man he'd ever killed and Lucas kept replaying the moment over in his mind. From a hunting point of view it was a great kill; the first shot hit the central body mass and knocked him down, the second - most likely finished him off. But this wasn't a prize elk, or a grizzly bear, it had been a human being. Lucas wasn't particularly religious but he did believe in a soul or spirit and he sure as hell snuffed Kai's out without hesitation.

Is this what the next kill would feel like? Would it be easier or harder? Hell, would there even be a next kill? Could I do it again? The same thoughts keep circling around Lucas' mind as he re-lived the kill over and over.

Lucas was lost in the woods without a weapon or a map after running all day. As the sun set, he climbed up into a tree and tried to sleep, but the fear of falling or being discovered made that impossible. As soon as it became light enough to see, he gave up on any pretense of sleeping, and climbed down to continue on his journey.

Fortunately after all the travel within the woods Lucas had finally found a road. It was a sealed road and he could see abandoned cars and a dam further north. *Great, the cars will surely have something useful,* Lucas mused, as he approached them. There were some bags strapped to the roofs, but there were also suitcases strewn all around, with clothes and other items scattered everywhere.

As Lucas got closer to the cars, he saw the dead infected lying on the road. It was hard to tell when they had been killed but it looked like it had been a while ago. Lucas started to pick through the clothes on the ground but all that was left were women's and children's clothing. *Looks like someone else has been through here,* he determined. He found other items, like DVDs and portable computers, crunched underfoot. But no guns, no ammunition and no food. Whoever had been through here had taken everything useful and moved on.

Lucas looked at a small white hatchback that didn't have any damage. The doors were all open and the contents strewn around. As he walked towards it he noticed the fuel cap was open. Lucas sniffed at the opening - there was only a very faint odor of fuel. He looked at the other cars, they all also have their fuel caps open.

Inside the car he noticed movement. Concerned, Lucas stepped back and circled around, edging closely as the movement became more frantic. In the driver's seat was a moving infected strapped into the seatbelt. There was a large piece of its shoulder missing with only a bite mark left behind. *Looks like he got done while still strapped in.* The infected was frantically wiggling and snapped at Lucas but its lower jaw had been broken off and some bile still dripped from its face as it turned to Lucas and tried to reach out. The arms were also gone, only stumps left just below the shoulder. Both wounds had been sealed with a black bile and the shirt sleeves still hung loose. *Looks like this was done after he turned.*

As Lucas continued to circle around taking in the macabre tableaux, he noticed something on the hood of the car. As he got closer, it looked to him like the driver's arms had been cut off and laid in a pattern on the hood. Lucas circled around completely and took it all in.

Both arms had been cut at the elbow to form four pieces. These pieces had been arranged to form two letters on the white hood. Three arm pieces made the letter **H** while the last arm piece and the missing jaw created an **i**. Lucas spun around looking in all directions to see if someone was watching him. He scrutinized the cars and how they had been arranged on the road. At first it looked haphazard but in fact they had been arranged in such a manner as to create a very effective road block. Lucas looked around and absorbed more of the details. The road was between two hills with lots of tree coverage, the perfect place for a sniper to be set up. He looked closer at the road and pushed aside one of the suitcases. It was covering a bloodstain on the road, a human blood stain. He noticed the dam nearby, the water level was high but he could see the hulks of cars in there, most likely pushed in after being stripped clean.

"Oh shit, this is an ambush point!" Lucas exclaimed, as he ran up towards a hill, half expecting a hail of bullets to come raining down on him.

Lucas ran. The panic that had earlier subsided was back and was now pounding at both his heart and his skull. *You fool, how could you have not realized it?* His head wildly looked around, searching every pine tree under which he imagined a sniper was waiting with him in his sights. He ran scrambling up the hill, confused at the lack of shots, but too panicked to really think about it. *Just get away from the road. You'll be safe in deep of the woods.* The same thought spun around his mind as he ran. He kept running towards a thick bundle of pine trees - if he got there he would be safe.

100m.

80m.

50m.

30m. *Oh shit it'll be now. They're just playing with me.*
10m.

And then he dove into the bunch of pine trees and lay on the ground. The only sounds were his panting and the rustle of the leaves. Otherwise, nothing. No shots. No hail of bullets. No one screaming at him to "stop."

Lucas just lay there for a long time, breathing and staring at the sky. He was sure that he would be dead by now and so Lucas was luxuriating in life again, enjoyed the sensation of grass under his hands and the wind in his hair. He was also confused. That was definitely an ambush site but it seemed like it was abandoned. He crept through the pine trees and looked around.

Lucas was further up the hill but he could still see the ambush point at the road. From this vantage point he could also see three houses further north along the road. Maybe he would be able to get supplies there. There did seem to be some movement down at the houses but being so far away he couldn't tell what it was. Lucas' hunting instincts took over. He knew if he moved too close they might see him, so he stayed back and watched for now. It could just be infected or it could be the people who set up the ambush – but until he knew which, Lucas had no plans of moving from the safety under the cover of his trees.

CHAPTER THIRTY ONE

THE AMBUSH

Lucas didn't realize it yet but he was watching Timor and the other Russians prepare to raid the town of Mogilevka. They had stashed their UAZ and any superfluous gear further up the dirt road. As planned the night before, they were going to walk into town to ensure the sound of their vehicle didn't give them away to any survivors or infected.

Oleg had a map spread out on the hood of a car that had been long ago burnt out. He was a massive man - a former Olympic weightlifter, who in a feat of brute strength once ripped an infected's head - with the spinal cord still attached - clean off its body. Oleg then wrapped tape around its snapping mouth and kept it as a good luck charm on his belt. It took the infected another week to finally expire, or so they thought as its eyes had stopped moving. No one was prepared to take the tape off to be certain so Oleg crushed its skull under his gigantic boot.

Oleg was usually the point man on raid, his weapon of choice was a sharpened scythe. Between his long arms and the additional reach from the scythe, Oleg was able to dispatch most infected with a single decapitating swing before they could even reach him. Every town Oleg had traveled through he had left a calling card of decapitated infected in his wake.

Timor and Pavel looked over the map and planned a route through the town. Mogilevka was a decent sized town with lots of houses and a church. The church would most likely be their most profitable location if the town had not already been raided – there was something about the world going to shit that brought a lot of people back to church. Timor pointed to the point on the map where Grigory had set up.

"Grigory is here, north west of the town. He's been there since dawn so if there's anything amiss he will have spotted it. We'll take the long way around and rendezvous with him first and find out what he's seen," Timor moved his hand to the western edge of Mogilevka.

"This is where the church is. Oleg and I will go in there first and clear it out. If we find it's ripe for the picking then we'll assume the rest of the town is too, and signal for you two to come down. The go signal is this," Timor held two hands above his head in a cross, "if anything is wrong I'll come out and take off my cap. You see that, then make sure Grigory is ready for shit to go down."

"Did he take the AS-50? I saw the SVD in the truck," Pavel asked.

"Yep. Ever since we took down that Humvee, Russian hardware isn't good enough for our Grigory. If we are a go, then you and Grigory take the southern part of town, Oleg and I will take the north. Same drill as last time. We kill the infected silently where possible, prioritize food and ammunition, once a building is cleared carve an X in the door."

Oleg looked up from the map, "Are we on radio silence?"

"It's a smallish town I think we can keep radios off and conserve power. If you see a working generator then mark it down and we can come back with electronics tonight and charge everything up. The sun should be setting at 18:00 so we meet back here at 16:00. If we can't see each other at 16:00 then turn your radios on and we'll find out what the holdup is. Any questions?"

"Resistance?" Pavel asked.

"Doubt it. We've driven through a couple of times and I haven't seen any signs of life, but stay on your toes. You never know..." Timor trailed off, his thought interrupted. He looked up from the map and listened.

Oleg turned to the direction of the same sound. He nodded to Timor. In the distance the roar of a bus could be faintly heard.

"Sounds like a bus coming from the south," Oleg said.

"Looks like we might not have to go into town after all men," Timor snapped off the safety on his AKM.

"What of Grigory? He's too far away."

"We'll do it with the three of us but only on my go. Don't shoot your load too early men, they don't know we're here. It'll be the same as last time, just without sniper support."

Oleg and Pavel checked their weapons before they split off and double timed it down the road towards the approaching bus.

Lucas watched the men as they poured over the map. Their precision in movement and head bobs when speaking pretty much indicated to him that they weren't infected. They were too far away for him to identify so he remained still, and watched them. Lucas also heard the approaching bus and observed the men's demeanor change at once. As they split off and moved down towards the sound, Lucas was sure that whatever they had planned for it, it wasn't a welcome wagon. Again he cursed himself for not having a weapon as he moved along the hill to get a better vantage of the ambush point.

As Sam turned the corner he saw the wrecked cars in front of him. The cars had blocked the road and so he was forced to stop. Shutov moved up to the front of the bus.

"What is it?"

"Accident ahead. We should be able to clear it off and the cars might have fuel as well," Sam replied, as the bus came to a complete stop. He pulled a lever and the doors opened up. Shutov turned to face the men.

"Butcher, Vuk, I want you two collecting fuel. Alejandro, Harrison and Sam get those fucking cars off the road, but not before checking for anything useful. I want it done in ten minutes, so get moving!"

The men climbed off the bus, stretched, yawned, glad to get a bit of movement. Vuk looked around as The Butcher unloaded two jerry cans with hoses and handed one to Vuk. Vuk waved it away as he indicated the closest car.

"Don't waste your time, there's no fuel left," Vuk explained.

"You have X ray vision now?" The Butcher taunted.

"Nope, just eyes that see. How about you?" Vuk responded. Shutov moved over to them.

"The fuel caps Butcher, you can see they're already popped open," Shutov answered on Vuk's behalf.

Not one to be outdone, Vuk continued on, "and all the open bags scattered around. Someone else has already been here." Vuk looked down at the blood stain on the ground and then around at the hills.

Oleg and Timor watched them from behind tree cover. They were close enough to hear what was being discussed.

"The old man's working it out. There are only seven of them, we can take them," Oleg whispered.

"I don't want to kill them."

"Look at the bus and all those guns, imagine what's on there."

"Don't look at the things Oleg, look at the people," Timor chastised, "look at them. They're well fed, clean, they're not Russian or American. How did they get here and where have they come from? Do they have a boat? A way off this shit hole? I want information, not just loot." He singled out Shutov. "That one is obviously the leader. If he moves away from the others then we kill the rest and take him with us. But not until I say so," Oleg nodded and returned to watching the bandits.

From his vantage point Lucas could see the Bandits had no idea the Russians were hiding nearby. Lucas contemplated warning them but calling out would also put his life at risk – something he wasn't prepared to do for the men who murdered Mitch. Lucas was able to hear what they were saying and assumed the Russians were too.

Vuk asked Shutov for the map.

"Why, what is it?" Shutov queried as he handed it over.

"I don't like this place. Something feels wrong about it. I think we should go back."

"We're not going back, we're going to the airfield."

"Sir look around you. These blood stains are human, look at all the cars in the water, do you think they were all drunk drivers? And the hills and trees all around us, they make good cover. I strongly suggest we move out of here, right now," Vuk explained as he constantly looked around. Shutov followed Vuk's eye line as it dawned on him.

"Men, back on the bus - right now!" Shutov commanded. The men that were struggling to move the cars were thankful for the reprieve and hurried back onto the bus. Sam started the laborious process of turning the bus around.

"They're getting away," Oleg implored.

"Let them," Timor responded, "I know where they're going and I know where we can get them. We will do it properly with a new ambush."

As the bus drove away, Lucas watched the Bandits leave unscathed and was confused. *The Russians had the chance to take the bandits down but didn't. Why?* He watched the Russians run down the road back past their original meeting point before they disappeared down the road. Once he was sure they were safely out of sight, Lucas stood up and went to follow them.

CHAPTER THIRTY TWO

SINS OF THE PAST

Grigory had already started to feel the sweat run down his sides as he surveyed the town. His trusty AS-50 lay on the grass next to him as he looked down at the town through his binoculars. Mogilevka was dead, so to speak, with only the infected roaming around. Grigory saw the church door was closed - a good sign that it hadn't been breached.

He checked his watch again. *The others should be here soon.* He looked around the area at the church, searching for any signs of civilization. There were no toilet troughs, no piles of disused garbage out the front, and no fortifications in sight. The church and town looked like many others they had seen, abandoned by the civilian population and taken over by the infected.

Grigory lowered the binoculars and looked around. He was pretty exposed laying in the field but there wasn't anyone around and this location did give him the best vantage point in the town. He turned back to the church and wondered if there was a priest still alive inside - someone that could forgive him for all his sins. It was of course unlikely, as the only priests they had seen since the outbreak had all been turned, so it seemed God wasn't selective about who was infected.

Many churches were now just hives of infected - almost without fail they would open the door to a swarm of infected waiting inside. It was still a comparatively small risk to take for the reward of all the provisions they would definitely find once the church was cleared. It seemed like many towns had the same story repeated. Word of the infection spread and the population suddenly turned to God. They went to the church, the priest was so overjoyed by the increased numbers he took everyone in. There was no thought of hot zones, nor concerns about screening people, it just became a free-for-all. Many of them brought food, water and guns, with the intention of trying to live out the infection. But there was always one. One selfish bastard who had been bitten, scratched or in some other way infected. Someone who thought that being in the church and praying would somehow magically ward off the infection.

At some point this fool would turn, and take down more with him. Since it was the early days of infection, people weren't sure what was happening. They may have tried to have restrain him, rather than shot him. Or they may have shot him but he came back because it wasn't a head shot. Eventually one became two, two became four, and before you knew it, they abandoned the church and locked the infected inside. That was if they made it out at all. If someone turned during the night while everyone else was asleep, they usually managed to take out the entire church in the ensuing panic and cover of darkness. These ones were the hardest to clean out, they took the longest time but also gave the best chance of finding food and water.

So since it was unlikely there was a living priest inside to absolve him of his sins Grigory was pretty certain he was going straight to hell. In the last months, he had amassed more sins than during his entire 24 years prior. Rape, murder, theft, - there were multiple ticks in each box. *How did I get to be like this?* Grigory pondered as he looked over the church. There wasn't one answer, one defining moment he could point to. It was just a collection of sins that got bigger and easier to repeat. Kill one man and it was easier to kill two next time. Rape one woman and it was easier to rape her daughter next. Back home Grigory was considered a feminist - he stood up for women's rights. Now he was out here raping the women he used to stand up for. How had he plunged so far?

Grigory tried to push back the memories, but the church and thoughts of redemption brought all his sins to the surface. How many men had he killed? And for what purpose? What value was placed on these men's lives? The sad thing was Grigory couldn't remember how many, the number was too high - the reasons were too numerous, and they all felt justified at the time. As though it could be right to kill a man just for the gun on his back. There was something about being in a group. It was like the worst characteristic in each man fed on the worst characteristic in the man next to him. And before you knew it the group committed actions that no man would commit alone.

Also, for Grigory, shooting a man from 300 meters away somehow didn't make it real. But these were real people, with real families and real problems. All were just trying to survive the catastrophe that they had no part in causing but which had irrevocably changed their lives. There were multiple ways Grigory could have interacted with each man he killed. *Why didn't we work together? Why didn't we all take over a town and fortify it, plant crops, dig wells, ride out the infection and wait for a cure? It could have been a Utopia among all of this death, so why didn't we do it?* Grigory watched a butterfly land on a flower near him. He had been so still that the butterfly didn't feel threatened by him. *Greed, that's why. And laziness. It's easier to steal than it is to build and create.*

Were there communities like the one Grigory imagined still out there? They hadn't been that far north so maybe there was still a chance. Maybe people up north had more of a warning and managed to close off a town. If they found such a sanctuary would they be welcomed in? After all, they are deserters from the Russian army. They were rapists and murderers. *Yeah I can just imagine them opening their arms wide and welcoming us into their homes.* Nope, this was his lot in life - to scrape out an existence and wait to die from either the infected or starvation, or be killed by other raiders.

"Hello," a cheery voice spoke from behind Grigory. He dropped the binoculars and turned around to come face to face with The Dunce standing behind him, holding his axe over his shoulder. Grigory was so lost in his own thoughts he hadn't heard him approach.

"Errrr... Hello?" Grigory stammered out.

"I'm Rory. Are you a bad man?" asked Rory innocently.

Grigory looked over the large man standing in front of him holding the axe. There was something about him that seemed noble, as though nothing could touch him. Grigory didn't feel that Rory was a threat but he played it safe anyway.

"I don't know Rory. I don't think I'm a bad man but I've done some bad things," Grigory was surprised at how easily the confession came out.

"You don't look like a bad man," Rory responded.

Grigory tried to smile but it felt forced. He looked around but there wasn't anyone else nearby.

"Where did you come from Rory?"

"I was on a boat but it was sinking so the Captain said to jump off."

"What about the others? Were there others from the boat?"

"Yes lots - but they were bad men so I ran away."

"So you're here alone?" Grigory asked as he surreptitiously felt for his pistol in its holster.

"Yes," there was a pause as they looked into each other's eyes. Grigory moved his hand away from the pistol. "Do you have any food?" Rory asked.

"I have some dried salted beef," Grigory answered.

"May I have some please? I'm awful hungry."

Grigory reached into his jacket past the pistol and took out the beef wrapped in a linen cloth. He handed the entire cloth to Rory.

"Here, have all of it."

"Oh wow, thank you!" Rory said as he lustily devoured all of the beef.

"How about some water?" Grigory asked as he handed over his water canteen.

Rory nodded and gulped down the water, almost draining the canteen in one go.

"See, you aren't a bad man," Rory said as he licked his lips.

Grigory answered softly, "I'm trying Rory. I'm trying."

CHAPTER THIRTY THREE

TRUST YOUR INSTINCTS

The Survivors were in good cheer as they trekked through the woods. Both Robert and Yuri had been trading stories about their adventures over the past two days with the others joining in to provide color. Both men were gifted storytellers and their recounts gave the others a chance to feel normal - if only for a moment.

They were walking towards Staroye where they hoped to find more supplies. Robert referred to it as Crappee after seeing how it is written in Cyrillic. Every time the group lagged behind, Robert gave the same one-liner to keep them motivated. "Come-on assholes, who wants to be the first to take a dump in Crappee?"

They were slowly moving up a hill as they followed the dirt road. Due to the incline of the hill their movement was slow going with Doc consistently complaining that they should get a car. Yuri attempted to distract them from the hard climb "So what do you miss most of all Pablo?" he asked.

"Women. Beautiful women," was Pablo's response.

"You must be kidding mate. It's only been three days, how could you miss women already?" asked Alfie.

"What can I say, I'm a lover," Pablo grinned.

"Come off it mate. We've spent longer that three days on the boat without any women around," interjected Alfie.

"Ah yes, but there was always The Boy," Pablo joked and they all joined in laughing.

"Did The Boy make it? Jesus what was his name?" Robert asked.

"No idea. Haven't seen him."

"And Vuk, has anyone seen Vuk? I lost him in the ocean," Yuri asked the men. They all shook their heads and were silent as they continued the climb, each man lost in his own thoughts.

"Alright Mr. Cheery, since you fucked that one up, tell me what you miss the most," Yuri probed Robert.

"It's quite appropriate considering the destination," Robert let the words hang in the air.

"So what is it?"

"Toilet paper. Beautiful, soft, thick toilet paper. I've found guns, watches, food, maps, compasses but do you think I could find even one roll of toilet paper? Hell I'd even take the scratch-your-ass-single-ply at this point, but no, not a single roll anywhere. I'm sick of wiping my ass with leaves. You got to pick out soft green ones, then you got to make sure there are no bugs or dirt on them, and no matter how well I bunch them up either the stalks scratch my ass or they break and I get shit on my finger."

"So let me get this straight. The world's gone to pot, we're stuck in a God forsaken Russian hell hole with the living dead all around us, and the thing you want most of all is fucking toilet paper?" Alfie asked incredulous.

"Hey I was married once, so I'm used to going months without sex," Robert cheekily replied and got a rip-roaring laugh from all the men. They had now crested the hill and started down the other side.

"Alright Yuri, your turn. What do you miss?"

Yuri pondered on his answer. "Sleep. I miss sleep."

"Come off it mate, I've heard you snoring the last couple of nights," said Alfie.

"I may have been asleep but it has not been sleep. Not like from before. You may sleep because you are dog tired, because your body needs it. But it's not peaceful, it's not restful, and God forbid if you actually have a dream. So yes, sleep, sleep is what I miss most of all."

Others nodded in agreement and returned to their own thoughts. As the road wound around a corner they saw in the distance a man sitting in the middle of the road with a bicycle upright behind him.

"I know I aint had much sleep as well, but tell me that really isn't some bloke just sitting up there in the middle of the road."

They all saw him and immediately became tense. Robert jumped into action as he raised his shotgun and pumped it.

"Spread out, keep guns on him but get to cover," the others moved out following Robert's orders.

The man on the road realized they were fanning out and stood up, holding his hands up in the air.

"I'm not a threat," he called out.

"Janik? Is that you Janik?"

"Yuri, you've made it!"

"Stand down everyone, it's Janik," Yuri called out.

The others all lowered their weapons as Yuri rushed up to Janik and bear-hugged him, spinning the small man around. Robert was more hesitant to approach and stood back, his Remington lowered but still ready. He scanned the trees that surrounded them, trying to see if anyone else was there. The woods were too dense and he couldn't see anything. Pablo and Joseph both bro hugged Janik and patted him on the back.

"Where have you been?" Yuri asked.

"It's been a crazy day," answered Janik.

"What about the others? Lucas and Kiam. Have you seen them?"

"No I've been solo the past day. I got back to Elektro after scouting around to find Shutov, and the Bandits had taken over. Luckily they didn't see me and I managed to sneak away. I saw the camp fire up in the hills and thought I could see a group walking across a field. I wasn't sure who it was so I trailed them for a bit but lost them in the woods-"

Yuri interrupted, "That was us. I knew I could feel someone watching me."

"Anyway I lost you and so I went back for my pack and bike. I stayed in a farm house that night which is where I found a map. Looking it over I figured you were either heading to Kamyshovo or Msta. I rode up to Msta first but there were no signs of you there. So I was riding down to Kamyshovo when I heard you all coming up the hill – you were pretty bloody loud. I didn't want to get shot accidently or call out in case there were others around so I figured I would be non-threatening, just sitting and waiting."

Robert took out his map and looked it over.

"You're telling me you've covered all this ground in the last couple of hours."

"Yeah, the bike is pretty good on and off road."

Pablo opened his pack. "What about food or water? Do you need any?"

"Nah I'm good. Grabbed some supplies while I was in Msta thanks to Alfie's crossbow, I'm getting pretty good with it."

"You're welcome to it Janik. You can have silence, I'm all about raw stopping power," said Alfie as he patted his Lee Enfield.

Robert stepped closer to Janik, "What did you see back in Elektro?"

"They locked down the town pretty tight, especially around the church. Some of the men were collecting gas and I heard talk about getting the bus running."

"The busted up one outside the church?" asked Alfie.

"Yeah that one. I heard talk that Sam was working on it."

"If it's fixable then he'll be able to do it. What else?" said Robert.

"They wanted to use the bus to get to an airfield."

Robert looked over his map, there were three airfields marked on it. "Which airfield?"

"I didn't hear. But whatever is there has got Shutov excited. He was pushing Sam to get the bus fixed all through the night."

"Anything else?"

"No that was it. I didn't stay around long."

Yuri patted Janik, "huzzah my friend, you did well."

"Yes Janik, it's good information. If we stay away from the airfields we should be able to avoid the Bandits. This intelligence might just save all of our lives," added Robert.

"I guess being small has its advantages, and sneaking around is something that I'm used to."

"Why do we want to avoid them?" Doc asked, "they are our colleagues from the ship. We all worked together before, why can't we do that again now?"

"They murdered Mitch," Yuri growled.

"You don't know that."

"Lucas saw him get shot, he told me himself."

Doc turned to Yuri, "I'm not denying that Mitch was killed but you said he was murdered. How do you know that? Were you there?" Yuri didn't respond, "how do you know the killing wasn't an accident? Or that Mitch didn't attack first and was killed in self-defense."

Robert interrupted, "this is Mitch we're talking about. The chubby funny guy from the boat. Why would he attack anyone?"

"You're the one assuming Shutov and his band of Bandits are bad news. Sam worked under you two days ago and now you assume if he sees you he'll try to kill you."

"That's different. Shutov's always been a prick. I wouldn't put it past him to enjoy having his own private army and do anything to keep that. If you ask me I reckon he killed the Captain."

"That was an apparent suicide," Doc answered.

"How do you know? Were you there?"

"You saw the body too."

"What I saw was our Captain on the bridge with a hole in his head and no gun around. If he killed himself then where did the gun go? To me it looks like Shutov killed him so that he could give the orders from then onwards. Everyone knows he was gunning for the Captain's job, maybe he brought retirement on early."

"I don't buy it," said Doc.

"I'm not trying to sell it. The point is, we can't trust him, the only people we can trust are each other. Now I really don't give a fuck what Shutov and his group have planned, so long as they stay the fuck away from us. I want us all to get through this and the best way we can do that is to work together and be careful, and that means avoiding any Bandits."

The others nodded in agreement but Doc shook his head, "This is wrong. They have a bus, guns, food. They're our best chance of survival."

"No, they are their own best chance of survival. To survive we need to get our own shit together and not rely on anyone else," Robert replied. He turned away from Doc, to him the conversation was now over, and returned to studying his map.

"Janik we were making our way over to Crappee..."

"Staroye," Yuri corrected.

"Sorry, Staroye," Robert pointed to it on the map, "I think it would be good if you went ahead and acted as a scout. Ride in, check out the town and the surrounding area. Make sure it's safe for us."

"Sure."

"Don't just say 'sure' Janik. It's a dangerous task. You'll be out there alone and we don't have any radios so you can't contact us if you get into trouble."

"I said yes. Look, I understand the risk but you're right. It would be better to have someone scout ahead, and I'm the best person to do it - with my bike of course," he patted the bike seat.

"Great. We'll meet you here just south of town. If you do encounter any other people or camps just mark them on your map. Don't approach them. If the town looks clear don't risk going in. Wait for us but check the cars on the roads, we could definitely do with a working vehicle."

"Got it. Don't worry, you can count on me."

"Yes we can Janik, yes we can," Robert smiled and Janik couldn't help but smile back.

CHAPTER THIRTY FOUR

THE UNEASY ALLIANCE

Xavier awoke with a start and groped around for his revolver. It was hot and very dark. He looked around, confused, but couldn't make anything out. *Where am I? What's happening?* His groggy brain fumbled out these two thoughts over and over. Xavier threw the blankets off him and stood up.

Hearing movement, Duke entered the room. His eyes had adjusted to the dim light for a while and unlike Xavier he could see pretty clearly.

"Morning Frenchy. The last of the coffee's brewed if you want it."

Remembering the foul taste from last night Xavier groaned and waved his hand away. "Don't call that monstrosity coffee ever again American."

"Your loss," and to emphasize the point, Duke took a long swig from his own mug and snapped his lips in appreciation, "ahhh tasty."

"What time is it?" asked Xavier.

"About mid-morning," Duke answered, holding up his wrist and showing his busted watch. "Unfortunately this baby wasn't water proof."

Xavier gathered his gear together, "can you pull down the blankets and give me some light?"

"I wouldn't recommend that," Duke said, "take a peek outside."

Xavier moved to a window and pulled back part of the tape, peering through the gap he had created. Outside he saw Zeds roaming around the house, almost as though they were patrolling it.

"Sacrebleu! How many are there out there?" asked Xavier as he closed the gap.

"I counted five."

"What happened while I was asleep?"

"Nothing. Nothing at all. That's the weird part they just came around during the morning."

"Maybe they can smell us, or hear us."

"Maybe, but they don't seem to be trying to get in, not like the last house," Duke peered through a curtain gap, "take a look at them. What do you see?"

Xavier looked through the gap again. The closest one was a female Zed, her long brown hair was tangled and matted with dirt and blood. She wore a torn night dress that exposed her greying flesh underneath. Near her were two teenage boys, identical twins. They both had similar haircuts but were wearing different clothes, also torn pajamas. Further away near the well there was a young girl, 5 years old, in a Dora The Explorer night gown with Cyrillic writing.

"What am I supposed to see?" Xavier asked.

"Look at their clothes Frenchy. They're wearing pajamas and nightgowns, like they were attacked while sleeping."

"So?"

"So, there are no other houses around here, that's why we picked this place. I think that's a family, mum and her three kids, the dad's around the other side."

"Okay so it's a tragedy. What does that matter?"

"You don't get it, this is their house," Duke took a picture off a mantle and handed it to Xavier, "that's them, in better condition of course."

Xavier looked at the photo. It was of the infected he saw outside, standing at a beach smiling.

"So they're roaming around their own house," Xavier mused.

"That's exactly what they're doing. Like it means something to them."

"Okay, but what does it mean to us?" Xavier queried.

"It means we shouldn't stay in houses any more. It's too risky, we could get attacked going in or coming out."

"But where were they yesterday?"

"I don't know. We had a clean run in but they must have been nearby. Maybe they're the opposite of whatever nocturnal is. They might have been resting and we just didn't see them, I don't fucking know. The point is, houses and towns aren't safe. They mean something to these things, so I think we should stay in the woods."

"We?"

"Yeah we. I've been thinking about that too and I think we should stick together for now."

"Are you forgetting the supermarket?"

"No I'm not forgetting the supermarket, but I wish you would."

"You left me for dead!"

"Yes and I have fucking apologized for that too many times now. I checked the attic and it looks like the boys were into camping. I found a small two-man hiking tent and some camping supplies, including these babies," Duke pulled out two small hand held hatchets from his pack, "this is how we're going to clean up our little problem outside."

"I don't know."

"What the hatchets are silent, and we'll save on ammo."

"I meant about us sticking together."

"What's there to think about? It's the smartest option. How are you going to sleep at night without someone standing guard? How are you going to raid a town without me watching your back and you watching mine?"

"It makes sense but..."

"What! What is it?"

"Nothing."

"No, what is it?"

"It's nothing, I'd just prefer to be alone."

"Then why did you follow me?"

"I never followed you."

"Fuck off! You did. How else would you have ended up in the same town as me? Look at the map. There were a hundred ways you could have gone but you ended up in this one little town at the same time I was there and you want me to believe it was just a coincidence. I could feel someone was watching me but I never saw you, obviously I was right."

"I was lost that's all."

"You followed me because you wanted help. Let me help you."

"Oh like the supermarket?"

"Fuck you man I-"

Xavier interrupted him, he pulled out his revolver and pointed it at Duke. "No fuck you man! You left me for dead. Do you know how many times I have thought of killing you since then? Of paying you back for what you did to me?"

"I made a mistake."

"I nearly died because of your mistake."

"You want revenge, you want payback. You want me dead. Then go ahead," Duke dropped his pack and the hatchets and then stepped forward until the revolver muzzle touched his forehead. "Go on then. Since you can't forgive me, pull that fucking trigger."

Xavier shook his head.

"Kill me you fucking pussy! Get your revenge and live forever with my blood on your hands."

Xavier looked into Duke's eyes and Duke stared back at him defiantly. He then closed his eyes and waited for the gunshot. Time froze for Xavier and the moment stretched into infinity. He took a deep breath and when he exhaled it was as though the anger also left. He lowered the gun.

Duke, feeling that the muzzle was no longer on his forehead, opened his eyes. Xavier had lowered the gun and was holding back tears, liquid snot ran from his nose down his face.

"I know I fucked up back there and I'm sorry. But let me make it up to you," said Duke.

"How? How can you do that?"

"I left you for dead before, so let me get you out of this alive," Duke stepped forward and hugged Xavier, "I've wasted my entire life. I've just cruised through it and haven't done shit, haven't been shit. But if I get you out of this alive, get you home safely, then at least I've achieved that one thing. It might not be much but it's a step up from nothing." Duke let Xavier go and stepped back. "Let me do this one thing."

Xavier nodded, wiping his face.

"Fucking aye Frenchy. You're going to make it."

"Look Duke now that we've had a hug maybe you can drop the Frenchy thing and call me Xavier."

"It's going to take more than a hug for that Frenchy."

Duke grabbed the hatchets and tossed one to Xavier. He moved to the door and stood next to it.

"I'll take them out, you back me up with the revolver."

Xavier wiped his face one more time before nodding in agreement. Duke put his hand on the handle and was about to turn it but stopped and looked back at Xavier.

"So we good?"

"We're getting there," Xavier responded.

"I can live with that," he said as he pulled open the door and daylight poured into the room.

CHAPTER THIRTY FIVE

NO GO NOVY

The camouflage UAZ roared into Novy Sobor at high speed. As it tore down the road the engine sound attracted the nearby infected. Oleg was driving with Timor in the passenger seat. Grigory, The Dunce and Pavel were squeezed into the back. The Dunce was scared and held onto Grigory's knee. Grigory patted his hand but The Dunce's face was ashen white. At this point Grigory was just glad that Rory was still with them, not concerned about the vice like-grip on his knee.

It took all of Grigory's powers of persuasion to stop the others from shooting Rory as soon as they saw him. Grigory asked Rory to repeat his story and Timor was very interested until he heard Rory's ship had sunk. As they were pressed for time and Timor was concerned about ambushing the bus Grigory managed to buy Rory a reprieve from the firing squad for that day at least. *Hopefully I'll find a use for Rory that would keep him alive for longer.*

On the drive over Timor peppered Rory with questions. It was obvious to all that Rory wasn't very bright but he was open and honest with his answers. For this, Timor was grateful as it gave him valuable intelligence on the adversaries he was planning to ambush. It was clear that Rory was kept out of the loop but he was able to give them the names of the Bandits and kept repeating they were bad men. He described how The Butcher had murdered one of his shipmates for a shotgun and Timor was very interested in hearing what weapons they had. As Rory had no real gun knowledge, apart from knowing they were bad, he described the guns as best he could.

Timor was also curious about the other men from the ship. Rory had explained that some were killed by the monsters but there were still many missing. He told of how he had encountered Janik during the night and of how another had shot Kai from very far away. Timor mulled over everything Rory had said while Oleg drove. *This means there are at least three distinct groups that are travelling around. It has been weeks since we've seen another human and now we have three different squads to contend with. First we sort out the bus group, then we'll work out the others.*

As the UAZ swerved past abandoned cars and debris on the road, it approached the crossroads of Novy Sobor. North were the unpaved roads that lead to Gorka, West was Stary Sobor. Timor had rightly guessed that the airport they were interested in was the Chernarus International Airfield in the North West, rather than the domestic airfield in the North East. The most obvious route for the Bandits to take would lead them through Novy Sobor and onto Stary Sobor, the next town across. This route was on sealed roads and the most direct, but it was possible to detour here at Novy. They could decide to go north and get to the airfield the long way around. Timor's plan was to make sure that they didn't take the long way around, and slow them down in Novy.

"Stop here, just past the crossroads," Timor said as he pointed ahead, "everyone get ready. When we stop I want everyone out and dealing with the shamblers first. Rory you stay back as we've done this lots of times but still I want you to watch our backs. Any infected that you see on the ground might look dead, but they could still attack. So unless you see their head chopped off or a hole in their skull, assume they're still dangerous."

The UAZ screeched to a halt and everyone jumped out of the car. Oleg kept the engine running in case they needed to make a fast getaway and pulled his scythe out from its sheath. Timor and Pavel spread out left and right respectively with their guns raised and ready. Grigory stayed back and watched the rear, having swapped out his AS-50 for a more appropriate MP5 sub machine gun. Rory stood near Grigory, his axe raised and ready.

Oleg charged into the fray, swung his scythe and decapitated the first shambler he encountered with a single stroke. There were two more approaching from the right, and with his large leg he kicked the closest one back and swung the scythe in an uppercut, jamming it into the second infected's head from under the chin. Oleg pulled the scythe forward through the face, splitting it into two, and the infected dropped to the ground. The second one that had been kicked down rose up and charged towards Oleg who cut him with the now dripping scythe. The curved blade carved through the top of its skull with a sickening crunch and it fell down dead. Timor observed a crawler move along the road towards Oleg. "Oleg, crawler at 10 o'clock" he called out.

Oleg moved towards the crawler who had both legs attached but for some reason not functioning. He raised his combat boot and crushed the crawler's skull with one gigantic stomp. Oleg wiped his boot on the dead crawler's clothes as he turned to face three more infected that charged towards him. The first dropped before getting close, shot by Pavel and his silenced Bizon PPR. Oleg swung and decapitated the second, spinning around and using his momentum to charge into the third. It flew comically into the air and landed on the hard asphalt with a bone crunching thud. Oleg ran towards it and used his scythe to slice its head off, kicking it away. He looked around for any more infected.

Timor and Pavel also scanned around. There were no more infected charging towards them.

"Clear?"

"Clear!"

"Clear!" Oleg called as he wiped the black bile off his scythe.

Grigory called out, "clear back here!" They all looked around once more before they relaxed and lowered their weapons.

Rory walked towards Oleg, his mouth agape in awe. "Oleg you are a monster slayer, like a knight in the stories."

"Let's not start fucking each other just yet. We need to get this street cleared and sorted," said Timor.

Oleg patted Rory on the shoulder as he passed him and walked back to Timor.

"What's the plan boss?" said Oleg.

"I want to funnel them towards Stary Sobor and make sure they don't take this road north. It needs to be done quick but smart, that old guy is sly and he'll spot anything that's too obvious."

"So what do you want?"

"Oleg, you and Rory start pushing these cars to block both roads. Make it look like lots of cars were abandoned at these crossroads. Just put the larger ones and trucks blocking the northern road and the smaller ones blocking the road to Stary. Grigory, once the cars are in place, go through and check them. I want them in park, fuel caps closed and lock the ones on the northern road but break the glass. Take any keys you find but leave the southern ones in obvious places, under seats, in the glove boxes and so on.

"The northern cars' keys I want hidden away in houses, bins, wherever. Just not all in one spot. If any of these cars are running I want you to disable them, but leave the fuel. I want them to be forced to stay on the bus when they drive into Stary. Pavel, you clean up these infected, just get them out of the way. You have 20 minutes men, before we move on to Stary. I want it done."

The men split off into their assigned tasks. Timor peered down the road with his binoculars, looking for any sign of the bus.

CHAPTER THIRTY SIX

STAROYE

Janik had an uneventful ride to Staroye. There were a few cars along the way that he stopped and checked. They seemed to be in working order so he marked them on his map and kept riding on. The roads were clear of infected and the sun shined. Janik enjoyed the moment while it lasted.

As he approached Staroye, Janik slowed down and examined the town ahead. The town was spread out across multiple streets and along the approach there was a fuel station. There were hand painted signs out the front and hanging off the pumps and although Janik couldn't read Cyrillic he guessed that they indicated there was no fuel.

There was a line of abandoned cars that led up to the fuel station. Their doors were left open and bags or suitcases had been tossed out, their contents now spread across the road. As Janik rode past he looked down but saw there was nothing of value left - well new-world value. There were plenty of iPods, jewelry, mobile phones, but no food, water, ammunition or warm clothing.

Janik stopped at a large Ural and rested his bike next to it. It was a large yellow tuck with a three seat cabin in the front and a large canvas covered tray in the back. He flicked open the canvas cover and noted the two rows of seats on each side. The truck was clearly designed to carry a large number of people. He climbed into the cabin and saw that the keys were in the ignition. He turned the key and the car sputtered and whined, but wouldn't start. The fuel gauge indicated empty but there were no other red lights on the dashboard - a good sign. Janik marked it on his map, climbed out of the seat and onto the roof of the Ural.

The metal roof was hot on his hands as he pulled himself up, but once he was on the roof, he had a great vantage point of the town. Staroye was split into three parts - the middle had a large groups of houses, the left and right were farms and barns. As Janik looked around the town he noted it was quiet and many of the house doors were open.

It took Janik a couple of minutes of scouting around before he put his finger on what troubled him. The town was quiet, eerily so. There were no infected roaming as far as he could see. He looked all around but there wasn't any movement at all. In some places he saw bodies lying on the roads or at house entrances but from this distance it was impossible to make out if they were infected or people.

"HEELLLLOOOO!" he shouted out. The sound echoed from the hills and Janik looked around. Nothing. No movement, no swarm of infected rushed to him, just silence. He climbed down from the Ural and hopped on his bike. Janik rode cautiously along the main road, looking around for any movement.

There were dead infected all around. Many were decapitated, some had bullet holes in their heads, and with some he couldn't tell how they died. Janik observed that all the doors into buildings had an X carved on them. There were also scattered items on the road, and none of the windows had a covering. All blinds were up, all curtains were drawn open. Janik slowed down the bike and stopped in front of a house. He rung the bike bell a couple of times. "Hello. Anyone inside?" he called out. The only response he got was silence.

Janik unslung the crossbow and crept towards the house's entrance. The door, like all the others, had an X carved into it. There was a dead infected that had been pushed aside from the doorway. Janik stepped over its arm and into the house. He gazed around and noticed that all the drawers were open, their contents strewn all over the place. The room to his left was a lounge room and it looked like everything had been rifled through. There was a dead infected on the floor, its head still attached to its neck by only a few sinews of flesh.

Janik turned right into the kitchen. All the cupboard doors were opened but there wasn't any food left. Just cleaning products, plates, cups - nothing useful. *Picked clean,* Janik noted, as he walked out and back onto the street.

It took Janik an hour and three more houses to determine that the entire town has been raided. Whoever did it was methodical and anything useful had been taken, so only junk remained. Janik studied his map, he needed to find another town for the Survivors to obtain supplies now that Staroye was a bust.

He had been to Msta which was about one and half kilometers west. Although not cleaned out like Staroye, it did take Janik a couple of houses to find any food or water. There were infected roaming there so it might still be viable and he was just unlucky, or it could have been raided by people not as methodical. Janik examined the map and noted there was also two towns nearby, one north and one north east. He could ride ahead to those and scope them out, that way at least he'd be able to give Robert a couple of options when they met up again.

Now for which town. The town due north was Shakovka, it was closer and larger. Further away North west on a different road was Guglovo. On the map it looked like a smaller town and it was further away. *So which town Janik? You wanted responsibility, well, now you got it.*

Janik looked around. The men who cleaned this town out were precise and methodical. No house was left. They marked the doors so no one wasted time. The infected were killed with knives or blunt objects, they weren't many bullet holes. Janik could tell they were well trained, well-armed, and well led. With so many people, a small town like

Guglovo wouldn't be any use. *If I were them I'd go to Shakovka next. It's closer and larger.* Janik looked on the map. *Yep, that's where they would have gone next, so I'll go to Guglovo.* Janik packed away the map, hopped onto his bike and started riding out of Staroye.

CHAPTER THIRTY SEVEN

THE RUINED CHURCH

The heat of the day and the lack of water had gotten to Lucas. He walked through the woods, up and down hills, without seeing any sign of life or another town. Lucas had been hiking before so he had an idea of how to survive, but without a weapon, without a container to gather water, without anything at all, he didn't like his odds.

As he trekked up the last hill, he saw the spiral of a church peeking over the horizon. Invigorated by this sight, he pushed himself forward and crossed the crest of the hill. Before him was a valley and off in the distance, a church and other buildings. Lucas smiled, at least now he had a chance.

But as he crossed the valley and got closer to the church, his smile faded. He noticed that there were holes in the walls, that plants were growing along the walls and then he saw that the roof of the church was gone, burnt away with only charred black beams remaining. The other buildings around it hadn't fared much better. They were all damaged or ruined and by the look of it, a long time ago. Lucas cursed. He wanted to scream out loudly but he knew that wasn't a good idea so he held back.

He walked through the ruins of the town and church looking for something, anything that could be of use. But there was nothing. Whatever was here was long gone, but Lucas took consolation in the fact that at least he now had a road to follow. He looked down to the left and saw a small cottage part way down the road.

Excited, he ran towards it. This cottage, unlike the ruined ones, was modern and had a roof. Right now it was his best chance at survival. As Lucas got closer he spotted a Cyrillic sign he couldn't understand a with a picture of the ruined church underneath. The door had frosted glass on it, with more Cyrillic words above a blue **i**.

He tried the door but it was locked. The windows were all closed and curtains covered them so he couldn't see inside. He circled the cottage and although there was another door it was also locked and all the windows were closed and covered. Lucas put his ear to the door and strained to listen. It sounded quiet inside.

He looked around. There wasn't anyone, living or dead, nearby. He rapped his fist against the door, over and over, and then stopped and listened again. No sounds came from inside. Satisfied it was safe, Lucas grabbed a nearby rock and smashed the frosted glass on the door. He reached in and turned the doorknob from the inside, unlocking the door. He removed his arm, pushed the door open and stepped back.

The interior was dark and mercifully quiet. Lucas looked but he couldn't see anything past a few feet where the light entered from the door. He stood back from the door and peered in, pondering his next move. If he had a weapon it would be a no brainer to enter and clear the rooms, search the place and take anything useful. But without a weapon and without being able to see, Lucas was not so sure. The risk was high. There could be an infected or a person inside there just out of sight. Lucas walked to a nearby tree and he kept his eyes on the entrance the entire time. He grabbed a sturdy branch and, using his weight, pulled down on it until it snapped off. The branch broke with a sharpened point and Lucas peeled back the weakened parts until the point was more pronounced.

It's not much but it's better than nothing, he mused as he returned to the entrance and stepped inside. Inside, the darkness now felt more pronounced. Lucas stopped just inside the entryway and waited for his eyes to adjust. As they did, he could make out details, there was a high counter at the far wall, he saw posters on the wall and shelving with assorted souvenirs. With his eyes now fully adjusted, he walked slowly towards the counter, trying to peer over it to the only part of the room he couldn't see. He grabbed a coffee mug off a shelf and threw it over the counter. It hit the floor with a satisfying thunk, indicating to Lucas there was no one behind there. As he circled around he kept his stick out in front ready, until he could see behind the counter. Apart from a chair and some boxes, it was empty. Lucas grabbed the curtain from the window and pulled it open. Light flooded into the room and he turned and opened the door into the second room.

With the light from the window he could see more detail in the second room. It was smaller than the first and there was a round table in the middle with some chairs. Against one wall there was a small kitchenette with cupboards that ended at a sink next to a fridge. Lucas slowly stepped in and looked around. There were no blind corners, and the room looked empty. He walked up to the closest window and ripped its curtain down and once again light poured into the room. He did the same with all the other windows until the room was bathed in light. This backroom looked like a combination change room and kitchen, most likely for the church's tour guides. There were some lockers along one wall that ended near the final door.

Lucas crept slowly to that door which was pulled shut. He listened against the door but couldn't hear anything inside. Cautiously, he pushed the door open and as it slowly widened he looked inside to find a small shower and toilet. Lucas yanked back the shower curtain and there was nothing behind it - it was clear.

He returned to the kitchen and opened the fridge. The odor of rotten food hit him like a freight train and he winced. Using the stick, Lucas pushed aside all the spoiled food looking for something edible. There was nothing that wasn't long spoiled but thankfully he found a half full water bottle with 'Alex' written on it.

"Thank you Alex," said Lucas as he drank the water. He took the now empty bottle into the bathroom and pushed off the toilet cistern lid. Inside, the water was a reddish brown from the rusted flushing mechanism and Lucas cursed. It was not drinkable.

Lucas spent the next twenty minutes turning the building upside down but didn't find anything else useful. Using a hammer, he broke into the lockers where he found plenty of clothes, deodorant cans, shaving gear, but no food and nothing he could use to help him survive. One locker did have a small backpack and Lucas emptied it of its useless contents and put in his empty water bottle. On the wall there was a mounted white box marked with a red cross. Lucas opened it and threw the bandages and pills into the bag. He took his sharpened stick off the kitchen table and left the building, shutting the door behind him.

Lucas stepped back out into the street and scrutinized around him. The sun had passed from overhead and the ruined church was still quiet. In front of him was the valley he just crossed and to his left were the building's power lines. They ran up the hill and Lucas couldn't see where they ended. *May as well follow that, power lines have to lead somewhere*, Lucas thought, and he walked up the hill. The power lines turned to the left and Lucas turned and followed them into the clearing.

CHAPTER THIRTY EIGHT

THE HELI CRASH SITE

Private Barnes had been feeling feverish all day but he had worked hard to keep it to himself. They'd been ordered by the higher-ups to report any signs of fever and any bites but Barnes noted that anyone who reported was never seen again. *Fuck that,* he thought, *I'm not dying out here in this shit hole Russia.* Barnes was on a UH60 Helicopter on his way out. *Just keep it together, no one needs to know one of them bit you.* He looked around at the crew, pilot, co-pilot, two gunners and three soldiers in back. Barnes was in the middle of the three and he looked past Willis and out the open door.

There were smoke stacks all around. Some smaller ones from cars on fire, other larger ones resulted from the use of small ordinances. Chernarus was lost and the brass had finally got their shit together and started evacuating the troops. Barnes looked down to see a ruined church below him.

"Pretty neat huh?" said Willis as he looked at the same church. Barnes tried to answer but started coughing instead. The coughing became more insistent and Willis turned to look at him.

"You alright Barnes?" he asked. Barnes nodded unable to stop coughing. But when he pulled back his hand from his mouth there was blood on it.

"Oh shit he's infected!" Willis cried out. Everyone in the helicopter turned to face Barnes as he coughed up more blood. "Muthafucker's infected and didn't say anything," Willis called out as he grabbed his pistol from the holster and shot Barnes in the head.

Blood sprayed from the wound all over the interior of the chopper. Barnes' hand was resting on his M4A1 assault rifle and contracted when he died. The rifle went into full auto - firing and sprayed bullets across the pilot and co-pilot, wounding both.

The chopper spun out of control and hurtled towards the ground as Willis screamed, "it's in my mouth. The blood's in my mouth."

A month later, Willis was now shambling around the crash site where the helicopter went down. His clothes were covered with blood from Barnes and the door gunner he had feasted on when he first turned. The pilot and co-pilot also roamed with him, their helmets still stuck on their heads. Nearby another infected solider walked through the long grass. Further away was the carcass of a dead cow that had made the unfortunate mistake of getting too close to the crash-site.

Janik watched the infected roaming around the helicopter crash site through his binoculars. The crashed helicopter was in a field south of Guglovo and Janik detected the movement as he rode toward the town. The infected crew continued to roam around and Janik couldn't see anything useful around the helicopter. He was about to lower his binoculars when he noticed movement on the other side of the clearing, well past the crash site. Janik assumed this was another infected walking in the distance until he noticed that it stopped. It was too far to tell for sure but Janik thought he saw him raise his hand to shield the sun from his eyes.

Oh shit that's a man, he realized as he knocked the bike down flat and darted towards the nearest trees. Janik raised the binoculars and watched the man as he turned and walked towards the helicopter crash site. He was still too far away for Janik to identify, so he stayed hidden and watched, using the trees to conceal himself as much as possible.

Lucas stopped and raised his hand to block the sun. He couldn't tell for certain but it looked like there was a helicopter wreck in the distance. There was movement around the helicopter but Lucas was fairly confident it was just infected. He crouched down low and edged closer to it.

Janik watched as the man moved towards the helicopter crash. He was still too far off to identify.

As Lucas got closer to the crash site he saw that there were four infected roaming around, two of them wearing pilot helmets. "Fuck," he cursed, "why can't it ever be easy?" He slowed down and crept towards the helicopter, watching the infected. As he moved closer he circled around, trying to ascertain if he could see anything useful inside.

Janik watched as the man circled around and away from him. The helicopter wreck was now between them and Janik had lost sight of the other man. He contemplated moving to get a better view but decided against it, as he would be exposed in the open field. He instead continued to watch the crash site, waiting for the man to be visible again.

Lucas continued to circle around but with the long grass in the field he was unable to see if there was anything on the ground. On the side of the chopper he saw the United States flag was painted. *Fuck, that's a military helicopter! There's got to be something useful on that.* He got onto his belly and crawled through the long grass towards the chopper wreck.

Janik watched the crash site. He couldn't see the man and couldn't see any movement except for the roaming infected. He looked around but there didn't seem to be anyone nearby. The grass was long so Janik decided to chance it and get closer. Keeping the crash site in front of him, he slowly walked towards it, prepared to drop to the ground and hide in the grass if he saw the mystery man.

Lucas was now close enough to hear the shuffles of the infected as they moved through the grass. He slowly rose to get a better look and came face to face with the infected Willis. Reflexively, he jammed the sharpened stick into Willis' head, providing him with a quick and dirty lobotomy. Willis fell to the ground dead - for a second and final time. Lucas patted down Willis but couldn't find a gun on him, although there were some pistol magazines which he grabbed and put into his pack. Lucas dropped back to the ground and crawled towards the chopper wreck.

Janik scanned for the man but couldn't see him anywhere. He was now 100 meters away from the chopper and peered through the grass. He could see the blades of the helicopter and one of the infected walked past it, but no sign of the man. Janik took the crossbow off his shoulder and looked down the site, scoping out any targets.

As Lucas crawled closer to the chopper he noticed an M4A1 assault rifle in the hands of a dead man seated and still strapped inside. *Jackpot,* Lucas thought and moved towards it. He could see the two infected on the other side of the chopper but he couldn't locate the third one. Slowly he crawled towards the chopper and reached inside. He stretched for the gun and pulled it from the shoulder strap. The dead soldier's hands were still holding onto it so Lucas pulled even harder, trying to pry it loose. One of the dead man's fingers slipped onto the trigger and the gun fired forward.

Janik hit the deck when he heard gunshots coming from the helicopter. He peered through the crossbow sight as the infected rushed towards the shots.

"Oh shit," Lucas exclaimed at the shots. The rifle recoiled back from the shooting and slid away from him. He looked past it to see the infected pilot rush towards him. Lucas grabbed his stick from the ground and thrust it into the pilot's face. The stick snapped off when it hit the back of the helmet and the pilot fell down, dead. Lucas looked down at his stick, he was now left with a truncheon instead of a spike. The also helmeted co-pilot rushed from Lucas' left and he swung at it with his now broken stick. He struck the helmet and the momentum knocked the infected to the ground but the helmet protected it from any damage. "Fuck!" Lucas exclaimed as he climbed into the chopper and reached for the gun.

Janik looked down the crossbow sight and saw Lucas inside the helicopter, trying to get to the rifle. Lucas hadn't seen the last infected come around from the rear and rush towards him from Janik's side. Janik stood up and lined the infected up in his crosshair. When he was certain of the shot, he pulled the trigger.

Lucas heard a thunk and looked up to see another infected stand over him with a crossbow bolt embedded in its head. It collapsed to the ground and he saw Janik standing in the grass behind it. Lucas smiled and grabbed the rifle from the ground as the infected co-pilot climbed into the chopper. He spun, supported the rifle on his shoulder and pulled the trigger, having no idea that the rifle was still set to full auto firing. Bullets riddled the co-pilot as the rifle recoiled up, landing first in the chest, then neck and finally the kill shot in the left side of the face. The co-pilot dropped down dead as Lucas held the trigger, but only a clicking sound was heard as the magazine was now spent. Lucas slumped to the floor of the helicopter and watched upside down as Janik approached.

"Damn are you're a sight for sore eyes," he said to Janik.

"Lucas, glad to see you made it out of Elektro."

"Just barely."

"The others will be pleased to see you too," said Janik.

"Good, so they made it out?"

"I'll take you to them, but first, let's see what we can find in here," Janik held out his hand and helped Lucas up.

CHAPTER THIRTY NINE

GUGLOVO

Janik and Lucas were in the process of searching through Guglovo when they heard the bus approaching. The raid on the helicopter went better than expected, Janik came away with a M4A1 CCO SD which was a silenced version of the assault rifle that caused the initial crash, while Lucas found an M107 50 caliber sniper rifle stored in the chopper. The M107 was designed to take out vehicles and helicopters - one round can pierce an entire engine block and still have enough velocity to kill the driver. The problem was it only had one magazine of 10 12.7x99mm rounds, so Lucas kept it in his pack and carried the regular M4A1 instead.

The town of Guglovo was a small hamlet that had its own access road off the main road. Janik used the crossbow to take out the infected while Lucas covered him with his assault rifle. Although the silenced rifle would have been more effective, they both decided to be prudent and save the ammunition. Fortunately for them, they were inside a house looking for food when they heard the roar of the bus down the main road.

Both immediately stopped scavenging and looked out the windows at the direction the sound came from.

"Did they get a truck running?" asked Lucas.

"There was a Ural I saw back in Staroye but they couldn't have gotten there yet," Janik replied, as he looked out a window that faced the main road. Lucas searched out of a different window that backed onto the field behind Guglovo. All he saw was the helicopter crash far off in the field.

"There," Janik called out, "I see something coming down the road." He pointed off into the distance. Lucas looked out the same window and saw the approaching bus and dust cloud it kicked up. "Shit, it's a bus!"

"I've seen that bus before, it's Shutov and the Bandits, they were almost ambushed by the military guys I was telling you about."

"What should we do?" Janik asked.

"We stay out of sight and wait for it to pass."

"Too late, it's slowing down!" exclaimed Janik.

"Shit, it is too!" exclaimed Lucas, as he dropped the M4A1 and took out the M107 sniper rifle.

Vuk was the one who spotted the helicopter wreck as the bus drove down the road to Guglovo. Still concerned about ambushes, he was on edge and looked through the windows for any potential threat. Shutov was reluctant to stop but did anyway when Vuk convinced him that it was a US military helicopter.

This time when the men unloaded from the bus they were all business, guns up and ready, eyes scouting around for any signs of trouble. Shutov ordered them into position as he stepped off.

"Butcher, Sam, take the front and cover the north and west. Watch for any infected coming from the town. Luther, Harrison, I want you watching the south and east. Vuk, Alejandro, you're with me, checking the crash site. I want everyone focused. Call out any targets. Let's do this quick because we're out in the open here." Shutov checked his CZ550 and moved towards the wreck as the others fanned out.

Janik and Lucas observed them from inside the house. "You think they know we're here?" Janik asked.

Lucas looked down the scope of the M107. "No they're going for the chopper. How far away do you think they are?"

"2, 3 hundred meters why?" answered Janik.

Lucas zeroed the rifle's scope to 300m, "we can end this right now."

"Lucas, don't! You can't just shoot them."

"Why not? They'd do the same to us. That's what they did to Mitch. I sent him out there to talk and they just executed him."

"It's not your fault, you didn't pull the trigger."

"You're right. But this time I will," Lucas watched as Shutov stopped near the wreck. He had Shutov lined up in the sniper scope and his finger tapped the side of the gun, itching to squeeze the trigger.

Shutov watched as Vuk and Alejandro searched through the chopper. "Dead, all of them," Vuk called out.

"How long ago?" Shutov asked.

"With the infected I can't tell. But the guy missing most of his head and the chewed up gunner looks pretty old," Vuk answered as Alejandro climbed out of the wreck.

"Nothing inside Sir," Alejandro said once he'd hopped out. "Let's get back on the bus then," said Shutov.

Lucas was still watching Shutov through the scope as Janik pleaded with him.

"Look, I want them dead as much as you do, but not like this. Not just straight-up murder."

"Fuck that, those rules don't apply out here."

"Fine then, what about common sense? You might get one or two of them but what about the rest. Each shot will paint a big target here for the others and any infected nearby. It's suicide. There are more of them and they have more guns. You want our last stand to be like this, here in this town and just for revenge?"

"Are you afraid to die?" taunted Lucas.

"Yes! Why, aren't you?" sneered Janik.

Shutov and the other men moved back towards the bus.

"See, they're leaving. Let them pass and at least give us a chance to survive."

The Bandits got onto the bus and Sam closed the door. He started the bus and continued down the road past Guglovo. Vuk watched as they passed the town. He saw some infected still shuffling around but there were no abandoned cars on the road.

Janik rushed out of the house once the bus passed and hopped on his bicycle.

"Where are you going?" Lucas asked.

"I'm going to follow them and scout out where they're going. Take this road back the other way, there's a town two kilometers back called Staroye. It's cleared of infected so you should be safe to go through the town. Wait on the other side at the fuel station for Robert and the Survivors. Tell Robert about the yellow Ural in the gas station, he should be able to get that baby running. You can use that to get everyone back here where we'll make camp for tonight. I'll come back here but if you're not here by sundown, I'll ride on to Staroye."

"Got it. Are you going to be okay?" Lucas asked.

"Don't worry about me, I'll be fine." He started to ride off but stopped, "Lucas, thanks for being smart back there."

Lucas nodded and Janik returned the nod before riding off down the road after the bus.

CHAPTER FORTY

GOOD NIGHT NOVY

By the time Janik had caught up with the Bandits they were well entrenched in Novy Sobor. Timor's plan to slow them had worked and they were busy clearing the roads and siphoning petrol out of the abandoned cars. The bus was parked further back in town and Janik watched as the men searched through the cars while Shutov, Alejandro and Vuk looked over a map they had spread out on a car hood. Janik watched them hidden in the trees, wishing he could hear what they were saying.

Shutov had his finger pointed on the map at where they were in Novy Sobor.

"So from here we can go north or west to the airfield."

"With these cars in the way neither option is viable right now," interjected Alejandro.

"I want them moved. What's taking so long?"

"They're going as fast as they can."

"Not good enough. We need to get to the airfield tonight."

"Sir, is that a viable option," Vuk asked.

"If I say it is, then it's viable," answered Shutov curtly.

"Everything is possible, but why should we rush?" asked Vuk, "another day will make no real difference but it may keep us alive. Look around at this town. It's pretty safe, there are buildings, we can see if anyone approaches, and the afternoon is already waning. We won't make it to the airfield by night."

"Are you proposing we should stay here?" Shutov challenged.

"I'm just giving you options. We could move on or we could stay, in the end the decision is yours. I just think there's a lot of unknowns in moving out and far less in staying here."

Alejandro looked around, visually scouting out the area.

"It is a good location. We can sleep in the long barn tonight - the fence surrounding it seems to be in good condition. That fence will hold back any infected that try to wander in," said Alejandro.

"And the wait will give us time to get all the fuel out of cars and into the bus. If we find enough then we should be able to make it straight to the airfield without another fuel stop," Vuk looked down at the map, "taking this route should get us there by late afternoon." He traced a route north from Novy with his finger, "we'd be slower on these dirt roads but it would be safer as we'd only have to pass through one town."

"But why take north when taking west would be quicker?" queried Shutov

"There's less chance of an ambush north."

"I'd say there's more of a chance, not less. Look at how forested it is. The last ambush we saw was in a similar location. I agree we should stay here tonight, but I think we should go west tomorrow, through Stary Sobor, then Kabanino and straight on to the airfield. We'll be having lunch on the runway."

"If you say so, you're the boss after all," Vuk said as he held up his hands.

"I'm glad you remembered. Alejandro, scout out the barn and stables. I want that whole area locked down and cleared straight away so we can set up camp. Vuk, you go with Sam and start clearing out these houses, see if you can find some more food and furniture for firewood."

Janik sat up in the hills and watched the Bandits until the sun started to set. He watched as the cars were drained of fuel and pushed off the side of the road, watched as the bus was moved to beside the barn, watched the men as they unloaded supplies from it into the barn. Once he was certain they were staying in Novy Sobor for the night, he climbed onto his bike and rode back towards Staroye, ready to report all he had seen.

CHAPTER FORTY ONE

LUCAS WAS JUMPED

As Lucas walked through the eerily quiet town of Staroye he found himself becoming more agitated. Although it was still light, the setting sun cast long shadows that kept parts of buildings in the dark. He spun around at the sound of a swinging rusted gate – thankfully only caused by the wind. Lucas tried to calm himself down but this was the first town he had ever seen that was dead. No living. No infected. No sounds. Nothing but wind and corpses all around him. Many corpses were the infected but there were still a few well decomposed ones that weren't.

As Lucas walked down the main street he tried to peer inside the windows of the buildings around him. The interiors were dark and he imagined that inside there were infected watching him, waiting for him. Ahead, just out of town, he could see the fuel station along with the line of abandoned cars continuing down the road. This was the rendezvous point but he couldn't see anyone around.

"Lucas, I'm coming out," a voice called out from in front of him. Yuri stepped out from behind a makeshift barricade that blocked off half the road.

"Yuri!" Lucas called out relieved. Yuri raised his hands to show he was unarmed.

"As you can see, I don't have any weapons. Now Lucas, I want you to take off your pack and put in on the ground. Then I want you to put your gun next to it and step away from both," said Yuri, as he stepped out onto the road, palms still showing.

"Yuri what the fuck? I'm not going to hurt you," said Lucas, confused.

"I know that, but you need to show them that," said Yuri and then he whistled. From around Lucas, once hidden men appeared from behind cover, all were armed, and all had their guns pointed at him. Lucas recognized them from the ship and was relieved to see that some of them were watching him from inside the darkened houses.

"So you think I'm with them now?" asked Lucas.

"You've been gone for a few days, the last anyone saw of you was when Shutov and his Bandits had surrounded you in Elektro. Now you're back and packing some serious firepower. We arrive here to find everything living and dead destroyed. You've got to understand why we're suspicious Lucas. Now I'm sure you have a good story to tell but right now you need to show us some faith."

"Okay. Okay. Everyone chill the fuck out, I'm going to do as you say. I'm dropping the pack first," Lucas called out as he looked around at the men pointing guns at him.

"Slowly," Robert ordered, "leave it on the ground."

Lucas gingerly took off his pack and put it down on the road in front of him.

"Now the sniper rifle," said Yuri.

Lucas unslung it from his shoulder and held it forward.

"I'm going to take the magazine out first. Everyone stay cool," said Lucas. He pointed the rifle to the ground and popped out the magazine. Then he lay it on the ground along with the rifle and stepped back from them.

"Good," said Robert, "Now we can have a civil conversation." Robert put down his own gun and stepped forward. "I want to apologize for the precautions but we're missing a man and we can't be too careful."

"Janik, I know," said Lucas.

"What do you know?" Yuri asked.

"He sent me here to meet you. He's off scouting out the Bandits."

"They were here?"

"No, the next town over, Guglovo. I just came from there. Shutov and the Bandits drove past in a bus. Janik followed them on his bike and told me to come back and fill you guys in."

"So how can we trust you? How do we know this isn't a set up?" asked Robert.

"Like Yuri said you are going to have to have some faith," Lucas smiled, "we're losing the light, so let me fill you in as we get that yellow Ural running. We want to get back to Guglovo before sun down."

Lucas walked back to his pack and gun, "so can I pick this shit up again?"

Robert looked around at the men for acknowledgement and they nodded in agreement, "of course, we're all friends here."

Yuri walked up to Lucas and bear hugged him, kissing him on each cheek.

"I think I liked it better when the guns were pointed at me," joked Lucas.

"Lucas, I want to hear all of your adventures, but first thank you. We all thank you. You saved all of us back in Elektro. How can we ever repay you?"

"Some food would be nice. Got to say I'm pretty hungry over here."

"Then I will give you a feast," Yuri declared.

"Well, a feast of beans and sardines," corrected Alfie.

"At this point that is a feast," Lucas said.

"Hah, the man really is hungry!" Yuri joked and he grabbed Lucas by the shoulder and walked him towards the fuel station and the yellow Ural.

CHAPTER FORTY TWO

BETRAYAL

Doc knew he was in for another sleepless night after finishing his guard duty shift. Pablo had relieved him and he tried to sleep but couldn't. He had just spent his guard shift running over what he'd heard as he watched the road towards Novy Sobor, the road that led to the Bandits. Now that he was off-duty he tried to switch off but couldn't, the sounds of fast asleep men around him didn't help. Instead, he gave up, walked outside to get some fresh air and hopefully clear his head.

Janik had returned to Guglovo at sunset just as the Survivors finished clearing the town. Doc wanted them to keep one infected alive so he could study it, but he was vetoed by the others, "All we need to know is how to kill them," was Yuri's answer.

When everyone had settled down for the night, Doc changed the dressing on Robert's arm. The wound was clean and there was no sign of infection, to Doc it seemed that Robert was going to be in the clear. Robert didn't even thank Doc, he just went back to studying his maps and listened to Janik's report.

Doc had taken his time so that he too could hear what Janik had to say. Janik told them how the Bandits were faring, and to Doc it seemed much better. He told them of the weapons, of how they cleared out and took control of Novy Sobor, and of their other provisions such as tents and sleeping bags. Doc's bed consisted of squeezing between two men on the floor of a house with an old blanket to keep him warm. Robert had insisted that they don't start any fires as the smoke or light might attract attention.

Doc looked down the road to Novy Sobor as he recalled the conversation between Robert and Janik. Robert's plan was to avoid the Bandits, they would travel north and let the Bandits go west. No one knew what was in the airfield but Robert had decided to let the Bandits have it for themselves. Talk among the other men was that the airfield was where the last people were hiding out, where planes were landing to fly people home. Doc wasn't sure if this was true or just rumor, but it seemed that the Bandits were in a big hurry to get there, so it was something they considered worth rushing for.

Once he'd reported everything he'd seen to Robert Janik volunteered to go back and watch the Bandits throughout the night. Robert was impressed, but insisted that Janik take someone else with him. Janik retorted they had only one bicycle and it made movement much easier. He assured Robert he'd be safe, all he would do was observe from high up in the hills. Sure he wouldn't get any rest, but at least they'd know what the Bandits were up to. Robert reluctantly agreed, so Janik took some food and rode off into the night.

Doc just didn't trust Janik. It seemed to him that he was too eager to go off and 'watch' the Bandits. What was Janik planning? Was he playing both sides against the middle? Did he plan to join up with the Bandits and hitch a ride to the airfield? What did he know that he wasn't telling anyone else? Doc didn't voice these questions to anyone else but they gnawed at him. The Survivors had guards posted at both town entrances, so any attempt to attack them at night would be difficult. And what would the Bandits gain from such an attack? *We have barely any food, a mishmash of guns, and a beat-up old Ural. Even if the Bandits knew where we were they'd most likely just ignore us and continue on to a more valuable prize - whatever was at the airfield.*

Doc thought Janik's plan would most likely be meeting with the Bandits during the night to leave with them in the morning. It wasn't a bad plan. It would take hours after sunrise before questions would be asked. Then they would slowly make their way to Novy to find the Bandits were gone, and no sign of Janik. And since Robert was insisting on avoiding the Bandits, Janik's betrayal would never be discovered, some other reason would be given. He was taken by an infected, fell while riding and knocked his head, any reason but the one that was obvious to Doc.

He looked around as it had suddenly become very quiet. It was dark and he realized he had been walked along the road to Novy Sobor while lost in his thoughts. He turned and looked back to Guglovo, but he could see no sign of the town - like it had evaporated into mist, such was the darkness that surrounded him. All Doc could see was the road ahead. The road was salvation, the road was a way out.

He may have started the walk to Novy unconsciously but he would finish it in the full knowledge of what he was doing. *Fuck the Survivors and their plans to run and hide.* He would live. He would join the strongest team and make it out of there. Doc continued down the dark road - nothing with him but the clothes on his back and hate in his heart.

All night as he watched the Bandits, Janik was surprised at how brazen they were. Once again they used fires to light up a perimeter, this time around the long barn. Two men patrolled the perimeter all night, relieved every two hours by the next shift. Janik fought hard to stay awake and when the night lightened to signal the coming of dawn, he slapped his face a couple of times to stay awake.

Janik scoped out the road where he saw an unarmed figuring walking towards town. The figure was too far away for the Bandits to see but from Janik's vantage point he could just make him out. He raised the binoculars to get a good look and was stunned to see it was Doc. No pack, no gun, just walking along the road as if in shock. *Shit something bad has happened,* Janik pondered as he gathered up his things and rode down the hill to Doc.

Doc heard the wheels of the bicycle and turned to watch Janik ride towards him. He stopped and waved, a meek little 'hiya' wave.

"What happened?" Janik asked, leaping off the bike.

"Take me to the Bandits, where are they?"

"I've been watching them all night. They haven't moved. Did someone attack the others?"

"Not that I know of."

"Then why are you here?" Janik asked, confused.

"Why are you here?" Doc asked back.

"Observation. Did Robert send you to check up on me?" asked Janik.

"Come on Janik, don't bullshit a bullshitter."

"Now you've completely lost me. We need to move into cover."

"Oh yes, we wouldn't want your friends to see us."

"Have you completely lost your mind?"

"I know you're working with them. I know you're planning to go to the airfield today. Look Janik, I'm not judging you, it's a smart play. I just want in."

"Doc, I have no idea what you think you know, but I'm not working with the Bandits. I'm here observing them to see if we can learn anything new."

"A job you conveniently volunteered yourself for."

"Yes, I chose to sacrifice sleep just in case they did anything overnight. What about you? What have you sacrificed lately?"

"Look at you Mister high and mighty. You've always been a little worm, so don't try to make out you're some kind of hero to me. I know you're a pussy and you wouldn't do anything that didn't benefit you first."

Janik got angry, "what did you say?"

"You'd sell us all out if it would save your own ass. You've only hung around because it keeps you alive and now that there's a better offer, you are going to run and take that."

In a rage Janik grabbed his crossbow and pointed it at Doc. "Just give me a reason muthafucker," Janik growled through gritted teeth.

"You haven't got the balls. Lucas told us how you wouldn't let him shoot Shutov yesterday. Pretty convenient, wouldn't want to lose your ticket out of here. You've always been a coward and you always will be."

They eyeballed each other – neither man backed down. Doc saw the hesitation in Janik's eyes and played off it. "Just as I thought. I guess I was wrong about you Janik. You don't even have the balls to go over to the winning side when you have the chance," Doc turned and walked down the road towards Novy.

"Fuck you. I don't need to pull the trigger, those assholes over there will do it for me," said Janik as he lowered the crossbow.

"I'm a Doctor, I have a special set of skills that I can offer. What the fuck can you offer anyone besides a bit of target practice?"

Janik raised the crossbow and pointed it back at Doc. Doc kept walking, unconcerned by Janik. He didn't even bother to turn back. Janik watched him for a moment before he decided against killing him and got back on his bicycle. He rode back towards Guglovo as fast as he could.

It took a moment for Alejandro to register that there was a man walking down the road. He whistled loudly and called out, "I have a contact 200 meters down the road and it's not infected." Everyone came rushing out of the barn, in various stages of wakefulness. Shutov pushed through to the front and peered down the sight of his CZ550.

"Well looky here, it's Doc!" said Shutov.

"Is he alone?" Vuk asked.

"Appears so. He doesn't have a rifle or a pack and he's walking with his hands raised," answered Shutov.

Vuk looked around for other Survivors, "I don't like it. An unarmed single man with no gear just happens to be walking into the town we are in. It has to be a trap."

"Agreed," Shutov lowered the rifle, "everyone spread out I want eyes in every direction. Watch for anyone coming, especially from behind. Vuk, Butcher, you stay close to me, and keep your guns on him at all times. If he so much as sneezes I want him killed."

"Let's just take him out now. What happened to protecting each other at all costs?" The Butcher demanded.

"Relax Butcher, your beans are safe and sound. His presence intrigues me right now, and that buys him another 10 minutes. He's still on a ticking clock, so feel free to shoot him if he so much as looks the wrong way."

Vuk anxiously looked at Doc, "How could he have gotten so far inland without a gun? He's got to be working with someone else."

Shutov called out, "Alejandro, did you see him with the Survivors at Elektro?"

"No he wasn't among them."

"Mmmmm," Shutov mused, "Doc, Doc, Doc. Where have you been hiding all this time and why have you suddenly appeared in my backyard?"

Doc walked apprehensively towards Shutov, Vuk and The Butcher. He wanted to wipe off the long bead of perspiration that ran along his cheek but didn't dare move his hands. Both Vuk and The Butcher kept their guns trained on him while Shutov stood between them, just watching him.

"I'm not armed. I'm not dangerous," Doc called out.

"It's not you I'm worried about. It's your friends who are hiding that have us concerned."

Doc kept walking towards them, "I'm alone," he yelled back.

"So you say," the Butcher shouted.

Doc continued to walk with his hands raised. When he was eighty meters away they called out to him again.

"That's far enough," said Vuk, "Stop there, and very slowly raise your shirt."

"What?"

"Do as he says," Shutov called out.

Doc lifted his shirt, exposing his white podgy belly. "Now turn around," Vuk called out and Doc complied.

"No hidden weapons, no explosives," Vuk said quietly to Shutov.

"Okay. You can keep coming, keep your hands behind your head, fingers interlocked. Don't move them or we will shoot," Shutov commanded.

Doc nodded and followed the order as he walked towards them. Vuk grabbed a wooden crate and turned it over to form a makeshift seat.

"Sit there and keep your hands on your head," Vuk commanded.

Doc sat on the crate and The Butcher circled around to stand behind him.

"So Doc, you and I are now going to have a little chat." Said Shutov menacingly, "and if I think you're lying to me or I just don't like your answers, then you'll be the one who needs medical attention."

Janik rode into Guglovo to find the town quiet. There were no guards stationed at the entrance and all the house doors were closed. He stepped off his bike and searched around for the others. Suddenly, they all appeared around him as they came out from cover, weapons raised and pointed at him.

"Guys, friendly remember?" said Janik.

"Doc's missing," Yuri explained.

"I know. I saw him walk over to the Bandits this morning."

"What? Why?" asked Lucas.

"He told me he's joining them."

"Son of a bitch!" exclaimed Robert, "that bastard sold us out."

"This means we're compromised," said Yuri, "they could be on their way here right now."

"Pack everything up into the Ural. We leave in 5 minutes. Lucas get behind some cover that overlooks the main road.

If you see their bus coming towards us, you disable it. Try to avoid casualties. Slow them down, don't kill them." Lucas nodded and ran off as Robert took out a map.

"Janik, show me where you watched them from." Janik pointed out a tree line west of Novy Sobor. "I want you to ride back there, but travel off the road, go through these fields. Once you're back there, watch the Bandits until we arrive."

"You're going to them?" Janik asked perplexed.

"It's the only play they won't expect. We can't stay here and fight, they're better armed and there are more of them. If we run and they chase, we'll have to stop eventually. Since they have more fuel, they will catch up to us and we'll still be out gunned. But if we go along the main road, travelling slow with Lucas providing cover, they won't expect that. Shutov's not stupid, he won't drive down the main road with everyone in the bus. But if for some reason he does, and Lucas sees him first, then his 50 cal will disable them and then we'll be able to escape. They'll be more likely to go a different way around or even decide to keep going to the airfield. The one place I know they won't be very soon is Novy, so that's where I want to be. If they happen to still be in Novy when we get close then we'll know because you're watching. Now get to it - we don't have much time."

Janik was about to argue some more but saw the futility of it and once again hopped on his bike and rode off. Yuri shook his head.

"Look Yuri, I know it's not much of a plan, so please, if you have something better, then tell me. But we're short on time and even shorter on options," pleaded Robert.

"You're right. It's not much of a plan, but we'll make it work," said Yuri.

"Good man, now get that Ural started."

Yuri walked over to the Ural and climbed into the driver's seat. Robert looked off down the road to Novy Sobor.

"Fuck you, Doc! Fuck you for doing this," he muttered

under his breath.

By the time Janik had returned to his vantage point in the hills, the town of Novy Sobor was silent. He looked back across at the barn where the Bandits were the night before - but it seemed deserted. There was no one moving around and the bus was also gone. Using his binoculars he scouted around the town, deserted, as was the surrounding fields.

He watched for a while and still saw no movement. The temptation to sleep began to overpower Janik. He had spent the whole night watching them and now in the day there was nothing to see and he was bored. He wanted to sleep, snatch a few hours. Then Janik remembered that others were relying on him, that if he slept it could mean their death. He poured some water over his face in an attempt to wake up and returned to scouting around for any signs of the Bandits.

Mercifully, Janik didn't need to wait for long until he heard the sound of the Ural approaching. He was about to gather his things when he heard the click of a pistol cocked behind his head.

"Bang - you're dead," said Lucas.

"Oh fuck Lucas! You scared the crap out of me," panted Janik.

Lucas holstered the pistol and scanned the town through his M107 scope. "You really oughta watch your six," he said, "how's Novy looking?"

"Empty. Their camp was at that barn on the other end of town but it's gone, and so is their bus."

"How long have you been here?" asked Lucas.

"About 40 minutes, took me longer to get here travelling overland."

"That gives them enough time to break camp and move on. It's a good spot up here. Tell Robert I'll stay here and provide overwatch while they go in. Signal me when it's all clear."

"Sure thing," said Janik and he climbed on the bike and

rode down the hill to meet the Ural.

The Ural had stopped on the road 300 meters out of town. The Survivors were all out and watched the surrounding area while Janik relayed the information to Robert.

"It could be a trap Robert," offered Yuri, "they may be hiding in the buildings, waiting for us."

"No, it's empty as I predicted. They're either looking for us in Guglovo or they've moved on towards the airfield."

"I don't like it. We have nothing to gain and everything to lose going in," said Yuri.

"There's nothing to worry about, there's no ambush in town."

"How can you be so sure?"

"Because they won't expect us to come straight to them, so they won't have set up an ambush. It's the roads out of Novy that are the issue. If they were going to ambush us that's where they'd do it," explained Robert.

"So we go back then?" offered Alfie.

"We can't go back, they could be in Guglovo by now," replied Yuri.

"That's right, we have to go forward. We'll be fine, Lucas is covering us. Janik hasn't seen any movement since he's been here. If they were planning on ambushing us he would have seen it."

"There are parts of the town I can't see from up there and without x-ray vision I have no idea what's happening inside the buildings."

"You're all going to have to trust me. We'll be okay," said Robert.

"You're taking a big risk with all our lives," said Yuri.

"I know you think that, but there is no risk. The Bandits aren't there. Everyone back in the Ural - we're going in."

The men climbed into the back of the truck and Janik handed them his bicycle. They loaded it in and pulled Janik up. Robert and Yuri climbed into the cabin and Yuri started the engine.

"I hope you're right Robert," said Yuri.

"I'm right - you'll see."

Robert was right. The Bandits were no longer in Novy Sobor. Alejandro was just out of town in a tree line looking back in, and technically, outside of Novy. Hidden in the bushes next to him was a dirt bike and he watched Doc through his binoculars. Doc was bound and gagged and still sat on the wooden crate.

Yuri and Robert turned a corner driving through Novy when they both saw Doc tied to the crate.

"It's Doc!" exclaimed Yuri.

"Cut the engine, we'll go in on foot," said Robert as he climbed out of the cab. He banged on the Ural's side and the men climbed out from the back. Robert pointed to Doc and indicated they should spread out.

The Survivors fanned out - guns up, looking for any threats behind cover. They slowly made their way towards Doc, with Robert and Yuri leading. Yuri had the M4A1 rifle from the chopper while Robert carried the silenced version.

Up in the hill, Lucas watched through his M107 scope as the Survivors spread out. *Oh shit, something's wrong,* thought Lucas as he scanned around the hills for any threats.

Doc saw them and wriggled around, trying to free himself. Robert waved his hand to indicate he should calm down as he slowly made his way towards Doc.

Alejandro watched them through the binoculars as they approached Doc. He had an AK-74 on the ground beside him, but left it there as he watched the men. Satisfied the area was clear and there were enough guns pointed at Doc, Robert removed his gag.

"You son of a bitch," said Robert.

"You have every right to be mad," replied Doc.

"Mad? I'm not mad, I'm fucking furious! You do this to me after I save you countless times. You would have been long dead if it wasn't for me."

"I just wanted to talk to them, find out what they know," pleaded Doc.

"Bullshit," interjected Janik, "You told me you were joining them."

"I tried, but they wouldn't have me. They said they didn't want the extra mouth to feed."

"What about your special skills?" mocked Janik.

"Shutov said that unless I had a cure for the infection, he didn't need someone to fix his 'boo boos'. The guy's always been a cock," answered Doc.

"So why didn't they shoot you there and then?" Yuri asked.

"He said I wasn't worth the bullet. Said he'll leave me for the infected to eat."

"Sounds like a trap to me," Robert said.

"I don't believe him either," said Janik.

"So don't believe me - I'm past caring. If you want to kill me then do it now with a bullet - I don't want to be eaten alive."

"It's what you deserve," said Robert, venom dripping from each word.

"I know I fucked up. I don't expect you to forgive me but you can't do this. You can't just leave me here to die like this," pleaded Doc.

"I'll shoot him," said Yuri raising his rifle.

"No," called out Robert, "we're better than this. Better than him."

"So what then?" asked Yuri.

"We untie him. Give him some food and water and let him go," said Robert.

"Straight back to the Bandits?"

"They left him to die. He's on his own now," Robert turned to Doc, "we'll see how long you last out there by yourself."

"What about a gun? I'll need a gun," pleaded Doc.

"You've got to be shitting me, the balls on this guy!" exclaimed Janik.

"No gun. You lost that privilege the second you betrayed us," answered Robert.

"Then you may as well shoot me now."

"Don't tempt me," said Yuri.

"What about an axe?" asked Doc.

"I don't think you're in any position to negotiate," answered Robert.

"I think I am. How about we trade, an axe for information on the route the Bandits took."

"You saw which way they went?"

"They gagged me, but they didn't blindfold me, so yes, I saw which way the bus went," Doc answered.

Robert looked down the roads, there was no way to tell which of the three roads the bus took.

"How can we trust you?"

"You can't. What did you say before in the warehouse... someone has to be the bigger man. I'll trust you and tell you anyway. They went north," Doc said, indicating the dirt road with his head, "they took that road north to the airfield. Now, before you leave at least give me a chance to live - just one axe, that's all I ask. I know there's a bunch in the Ural. You don't trust me and I accept that. So just leave one on the road next to a pack and I'll collect it when you leave."

Robert stepped away from Doc with Yuri and Janik. He pulled out the map and examined it.

"He could be telling the truth. North's the longer way around but it's safer, less towns to go through," said Robert.

"I don't buy it. He's covering up something, I feel it."

Alejandro watched them as they conferenced over the map - his AK-74 was in his hands, ready to fire.

"But if he's telling the truth, which way do we go then?" asked Janik.

"I say west to Stary Sobor," said Robert, "Yuri?"

"It looks like a big town and we do need fuel and supplies. If they have gone north then they'll bypass it completely which makes it safer for us," Yuri studied the map, "there really isn't another viable option nearby."

"We could be driving into an ambush," said Janik.

"Yes, it's a risk, but everything's a risk nowadays. Besides, what choice do we have? We'll run out of fuel before we get to another town south. If we drive north we could be driving straight to them. We know they've cleaned this town out so there's nothing left here for us," Robert said.

"I don't like it."

"Neither do I, but we don't really have a choice. We'll try to be careful," said Robert as he folded up the map. "Untie him," Yuri untied Doc while Janik covered him with the crossbow. "We're going west Doc. We're going to leave you a pack with food and an axe on the road out of town. I say you collect that and go a different way to us, because if I see you again I'm going to shoot you myself. Is that clear?"

"Crystal," answered Doc, begrudgingly.

"Janik, signal to Lucas to come down and then get this shitbag's pack and axe ready," ordered Robert, "everyone else back in the Ural, we're going to Stary Sobor."

Doc watched them from his seat, rubbing his wrists, as they drove away. He supposed he should have felt some sort of guilt or remorse but he felt nothing – just emptiness. Was this what the new world would be like? At least now he was on the stronger side. At least now he'd have a chance to live.

He watched as the Ural stopped further down the road. A pack and axe were tossed out the back and Janik gave him the double finger as the Ural continued on down the road. *Charming*, Doc thought, as he got up and walked down the road.

Alejandro stepped out from his cover behind the bushes and onto the road. He had his AK-74 up and pointed at Doc.

"How was that?" Doc asked him.

"They're going the wrong way? You were supposed to get them to go north."

"I did what Shutov asked, I told them you went north."

"Then why did they go west?" asked Alejandro.

"Because they're not interested in you, they're trying to avoid you by going a different way."

"And now they're going the wrong way, Shutov will be pissed."

"What will happen to them if he finds them?"

"Come on Doc, you're a big boy, what do you think?"

"All of them?" queried Doc.

"It's a tough world nowadays. Can't have too many mouths to feed," answered Alejandro.

Alejandro followed Doc down the road but slowed down so that he was eventually behind him. "What's in the bag?" he asked.

"Some food and drink. Enough to last me a couple of days I suppose," answered Doc.

"So you go and betray them and they still help you out. Geez Doc, you really fucked this one up."

Doc stopped and turns around, "what do you mean?"

"I mean we'd never do that. We'd kill a betrayer as soon as we found out." Alejandro raised the AK-74 and looked down the iron sight.

"What are you doing? Shutov and I had a deal."

"Did you really think he'd trust you after what you did to your friends?" Alejandro asked, as he shook his head. "Doc you know this is the only way this could end."

"But I did as he ordered. I told them you went north," begged Doc.

"This is not about which way they went, it's about you. Sure, sticking with them may have got you killed in the long run, but you would have lasted longer than you did by betraying them. Sorry Doc," said Alejandro as he pulled the trigger. The AK-74 fired and the sounds burst through the stillness of the day. Doc's chest was pocked with bullets and he was flung back, hitting the road hard.

Alejandro walked past him, looking down at the bullet riddled body. Doc's eyes stared up into the sky, vacant but still accusatory.

"Sorry Doc, just following orders," he said picking up the pack and emptying the contents into his larger pack. He tossed the empty bag onto Doc's corpse and rode off into the valley north.

CHAPTER FORTY THREE

STARY SOBOR

Rory looked up at the clear blue sky, it was a nice day, 'a good day for gardening' his mother would have said. He was perched on the end of a rubble pile, lying down watching the shapes of the clouds. The Russians had been good to him, they gave him food and water, and Oleg showed him how to use a scythe. Together Rory and Oleg were pretty formidable at clearing out the infected from Stary Sobor, which was surprisingly not that many.

It had been a busy night for all of them. Once the infected were cleared out, Timor had them moving cars and carrying heavy items out of houses and onto the road. The plan was to use these items to create an artificial cul-de-sac in the middle of the main road into Stary Sobor. The barricade could not be seen by anyone until they turned the corner but by then it would be too late as there was no way to go around.

Rory sat on the end of the cul-de-sac eating his apple as Grigory had told him to. The Russians had left him there and went away, they said they would be back soon. They told him that his friends from the ship would be by soon and they would all have a little chat - Rory remembered there was some smirking at that. He wasn't concerned though as he was high up on the barricade and out of the reach of any infected. He still had his axe, he had food and water and it was a nice day. Life was good.

His serenity was broken by the sound of a distant rumbling along the road. Rory looked down the road but he couldn't see anything. The Russians told him that when the others came they would be in a big car or a bus. They told him he should sit perfectly still and not touch the axe. Rory was worried, but Grigory reassured him he'd be okay, that he'd be watching him from far away to make sure. Rory liked Grigory, he was nice. He hadn't called Rory stupid once, and the only other person he could say that about was his mother.

Grigory also heard the sound as he watched Rory from up high on the hills. He was west of Rory up in the hills that overlooked Stary Sobor, hidden between trees and brush. He had spent the morning subtly moving braches and pulling off leaves so as to have the right balance of vision and concealment. Grigory viewed Rory through the AS-50 scope. Rory looked calm, sitting there eating his apple. To Grigory, Rory could be in any number of situations and in many ways he wished he was, any situation other than the one that was about to unfold.

Grigory took out his rangefinder and scoped out around him again. He checked ranges off against landmarks and double checked them against the notes he had written. They were all correct but he triple checked the most important one, the one from him to Rory - it was two hundred and forty meters. Between him and Rory was an empty road with the US Military Forward Operating Base set up beside it.

Grigory recalled that at the height of the crisis there were rumors of US military being within the area, a roving death squad that attempted to control the infection with extreme prejudice. Whether they were invited or volunteered to help was information well above Grigory's rank but it seemed they had been using Stary Sobor as their operating base.

A tract of land had been cleared and various military tents were set up. Behind the tents were the neat rows of dead US soldiers in body bags. They had been abandoned at some point and were now left rotting in the sun. The stench was initially overpowering but Grigory was used to it now and it no longer bothered him. The tents had also been abandoned but what had been left behind was much more useful. There was a treasure trove of guns, left in foot lockers, lying on racks or still clutched in the hands of dead soldiers. It appeared that at some point the base had been overrun and the men had either retreated hastily or were left to die.

The Russians had all traded up except for Grigory who was still happy with his AS-50. Oleg left behind his military issued assault rifle and took up a US SAW 249. SAW stood for Squad Automatic Weapon and the gun was massive - a large machine gun with a belt feeder that Oleg carried around as though it were a pistol. Pavel traded his AK-107 for an M16A2 with under-barrel M203 single-shot 40mm grenade launcher. Timor left his AKM and took a silenced M9, a strange choice but for what he had planned he needed stealth over stopping power. Having seen the worst of him, Grigory knew there was a special place reserved in hell for Timor but he still had to respect him. Unlike many other leaders, Timor always took the hard jobs on first, he was always in the firing line and he didn't ask his men to do anything that he wouldn't do himself.

Other guns and explosives, including another SAW 249, were loaded into their camouflage UAZ that was now parked far back in the trees behind Grigory. Yesterday they were on the verge of starvation, risking their lives to raid a small town, but today, after raiding Stary Sobor, they were kings again. The problem was - for how long does this last, how long until it was famine time again? This time they were not short on guns and ammunition but they were short on other people to use them against. Initially it was very easy to survive, so long as you didn't mind killing others. Over time the number of people to kill had decreased and the provisions they had on them also became scarce. So these new survivors, the ones off the boat, they meant food and more importantly, information. It was for this reason Timor had gone to all the trouble of setting up this ambush, with poor Rory as the bait.

"I hear a vehicle," crackled Timor's voice on Grigory's radio. He dropped the rangefinder and spoke into it.

"I don't see them yet but they're coming from the main road east as expected."

"Do you have good a line of sight?" asked Timor.

"I can see the entire ambush zone except for where the green house blocks part of it. Oleg are you still inside it?"

"Yes," Oleg answered.

"Remember, nobody shoots unless I give the order," said Timor. "I'll keep my radio on so you can hear me speak - Pavel you're covering the east side. Grigory - if we need to prove dominance then I want you taking the kill shot. Everyone else - stay hidden."

Grigory spoke into the radio, "I remind you that this gun is designed to take out cars, it will absolutely decimate a person."

"Good," Timor responded, "hopefully that death will be enough to placate them."

Grigory dropped the radio and picked up his rangefinder, watching for the vehicle to reach the crest of the hill.

Inside the bus, Sam was driving down the road towards Stary Sobor. The men in the bus were relaxed, smoking, making jokes - which even Shutov joined in. Vuk was the only one on edge; he stood up and looked back and forth, watched the scenery through the windows. He scanned in front of them and behind them for any movement, any sign of people.

"Vuk, sit down - you're making me dizzy," said Shutov.

"I'll sit when we're safely at the airfield," answered Vuk.

"What are you looking for? This land is dead, the people who set up that ambush are long gone."

"What about the other Survivors from the ship, the ones Doc told us about?" asked Vuk, looking out a window.

"I've taken care of it," answered Shutov, "Doc will tell them we've gone north and they'll chase after us that way. If they even make it to the airfield we'll be long gone by the time they get there."

"Why? What's at the airfield?"

"Hope, Vuk," Shutov said cryptically, "hope is at the airfield."

"Town up ahead," called out Sam, looking down at his map, "must be Stary Sobor."

"Drive straight through Sam, and onto the airfield."

"Can't," answered Sam, as the bus turned the corner, "look ahead - the road is blocked."

"There's a man up there," yelled out Vuk as he pointed out Rory seated on the barricade.

"Infected?" asked Shutov, standing up and looking ahead.

"Can't tell," answered Vuk.

"Oh fuck, he's waving," called out Sam, as the bus slowed down to avoiding hitting the barricade.

That comment put everyone else on edge and they dropped what they were doing. Guns were pulled out and everyone was at the windows looking for movement.

"Turn us around Sam," called out Shutov.

"I'm trying to, but this is a freeking bus and there's shit all around us," he said, as he put the bus in reverse, "everyone move back from the mirrors, I need to see."

"Is that The Dunce?" asked Alejandro, "It is him, isn't it?"

"Wasn't he killed in Elektro?" asked Luther.

"What the fuck is going on?" yelled out Harrison panicked, "how the fuck did that simpleton get here ahead of us?"

Shutov stood up and yelled out, "everyone calm down. Sam, stop the bus and open the doors - everyone get out and establish a perimeter, but stay close to the bus."

The doors opened and the men peeled out. The Butcher and Alejandro covered the rear, Luther took the right, Vuk covered the left while Harrison moved forward and trained a gun on Rory who just sat there on the barrier, still chomping his apple and waving.

Once they had the perimeter set, Shutov stepped off the bus and walked towards Rory, his CZ-550 lowered to Rory's chest.

"Hi boss," said Rory casually to Shutov.

"Dun... Rory what are you doing out here?" asked Shutov.

"Eating," answered Rory holding up the apple to emphasize his point.

"I can see that, but I meant – here - in the town. How did you get so far inland?"

"Ride, I got a ride," Rory's answer set off the Bandits and they all scanned around for any threats.

"Rory, who gave you the ride?" asked Shutov slowly.

"The Russians did."

"Russians, like me?"

"No, not like you - they're soldiers," answered Rory.

Vuk stepped forward, "Sir, we need to get out of here, this is not safe."

"Rory, now this is very important, where are the soldiers right now?"

"Gone," said Rory, as he tossed the apple core away.

"Where did they go?" asked Vuk.

"Maybe I should answer that," replied Timor's voice from inside a nearby house. All the Bandit's guns swung towards the house but it was too dark inside for anyone to make out any details.

"Ohhhh, so many guns. I suppose I should be scared," mocked Timor.

"Who are you?" asked Shutov.

"Call me the Toll Collector. If you want to pass you're going to have to pay," said Timor, as he walked out, hands up to show he had no weapon.

"And what is this toll?" asked Shutov, amused.

"All your food and water... oh and information on what is at the Northwest Airfield," Timor replied calmly.

"Fuck him," said The Butcher, holding up his AKM, "I've got payment right here."

Timor turned and looked at The Butcher, his face was serene while The Butcher's was filled with rage.

"I think you'd better call back your dog," said Timor, turning back to Shutov, "you are in charge of this motley crew are you not?"

The Butcher firmed his grip on the AKM and prepared to fire. Shutov sensed his volatility and turned to him.

"Stand down, Butcher," he ordered.

The Butcher hesitated and turned to Shutov. Shutov nodded, indicating with his hand to lower the rifle. The Butcher did so, but still kept it trained on Timor.

"That's an interesting name, Butcher – you remind me to find you if I ever need a cow gutted," mocked Timor.

In the back of the yellow Ural the Survivors were arguing as it continued to drive towards Stary Sobor.

"We should have just killed him," said Janik to the group.

"Weren't you the one who stopped me from shooting Shutov before?" asked Lucas.

"Yes, but that was different - it was riskier and he hadn't done anything to us. Doc betrayed us, he tried to go over to the Bandits."

"And they kicked him out," responded Lucas.

"How do we know? Maybe they wanted us to think that. Maybe this is all part of their plan."

"What plan?" asked Alfie.

"I don't know, I just have a feeling that some bad shit is about to go down," replied Janik.

"You're either suicidal or delusional my friend, I just can't tell which." said Shutov to Timor.

"I assure you I'm both, but in this world, even getting a tin of food is a suicide mission, that's why we have the toll."

"And if we don't pay the toll, what then?" mocked The Butcher.

"Then you all die and I take what I need. Either way I get your food."

"How are you going to kill us? With harsh words?" asked Shutov.

"In a way, yes," replied Timor, "Grigory, do you hear me?"

"Yes," crackled Grigory's voice through the radio in Timor's pocket.

"So there's another voice, why should we be afraid of him?" asked The Butcher.

"You all mocked poor Rory here," said Timor, "but to me it seems like you are the stupid ones. He told you there were Russians, as in, plural. I'm standing here empty handed and telling you to give me everything you have. Let's see if someone can put the pieces together."

"There are other guns trained on us right now," replied Shutov wearily.

"I guess that's why they made you the leader," mocked Timor as he slow clapped.

"Bullshit!" exclaimed The Butcher, "He has a radio and a voice on the other end, he's bluffing."

"I don't bluff - about that you'll have to believe me."

"What if we don't?" asked Shutov.

"I can make true believers out of you, but it's going to be... messy," replied Timor coldly.

Shutov looked around at his men - they were alternating between looking at him and Timor. Some shook their heads, others just itched to pull their triggers. Shutov was torn, he couldn't show weakness in front of his men, but he also believed Timor. The man was too calm to not be in charge of the situation.

"I'm sorry but it looks like we'll have to call your bluff," said Shutov.

"Are you sure?" asked Timor.

"What would you do in my position?" replied Shutov, shrugging his shoulders and holding his hands out.

Timor exhaled loudly, "I guess I'd do the same. It's a shame, but that's how it is." Timor looked the Bandits over, "so tell me, who's your most expendable man?" "What?"

asked Shutov.

"Your most expendable man. I told you it would be messy and now you must lose a man," Timor turned to The Butcher, "please tell me it's him."

"Why?"

"Because I'd love to see him die at my feet."

"Just you try it," growled The Butcher.

"So who will it be, which of your men will die so I can prove my point?"

Grigory listened to the exchange via his radio while he looked down the scope of the AS-50. He moved from man to man, lining up the shots but lingering a little too long on The Butcher, he also hoped it would be him.

"The Dunce?" replied Shutov's voice through the radio.

"Who?" asked Timor.

"The Dunce, Rory. That fool sitting up there. He's my most expendable man."

Grigory moved the scope to Rory who was seated up on the rubble, oblivious to the enormity of the exchange occurring below him. Grigory's hands were shaking, he moved his eye away from the scope and rubbed the sweat off his face.

"You can't do that, he's not your man," Timor replied.

"Oh yes he is," answered Shutov, "Rory who do you work for?"

"You Mr. Shutov, you and the Captain are the boss," replied Rory automatically.

"I'd say that makes him my man. You wanted a body, I just gave you one."

Timor rubbed his bearded chin, thinking it over.

"Just remember you're the one who's killing him, not me. Are you sure you want it this way? It doesn't have to be like this?" asked Timor.

"If you want to be the boss then I'm afraid you've got to prove it," replied Shutov.

Timor turned to Rory, "I'm sorry Rory," he said, "Grigory take the shot."

"But sir..." crackled the radio as Grigory trailed off.

"Ahh hesitation, perhaps you're not as strong as you thought," offered Shutov.

"Grigory take the shot, that is an order!" commanded Timor.

Grigory looked down the sight of the AS-50. Rory just sat there, placid, not a care in the world. *I can't do it, not to him. He's an innocent.*

"Grigory God dammit, you-take-that-shot!" yelled Timor through the radio.

Grigory's face was ashen as he looked down the scope. His closed eye leaked out a single tear as he said softly, "sorry Rory," and squeezed the trigger.

At the ambush point everyone watched Rory, waiting to see what would happen. He noticed all the attention and looked around confused, wondering why everyone was watching him.

The bullet impact hit him before anyone heard the noise. Rory's upper torso burst open into a cloud of pink mist that splattered out along the houses behind him. He was flung back from the barricade and hit the ground hard behind him, his upper body almost completely obliterated.

Then the sound of the bullet rushed across them from the hills to their east. It was almost a sonic boom and some of the men put their fingers in their ears to make them pop. They stood staring at the spot where Rory was, now replaced by the pink spray on the walls. Everyone was stunned and they just stared, trying to comprehend what had just happened.

"Well you promised messy and in that you definitely delivered," joked The Butcher.

In the Ural they also heard the shot over the roar of the engine. Yuri immediately slammed the breaks and cut off the engine. The area was suddenly quiet and they saw birds flying off from the trees in the distance, scattering in every direction. Robert banged the rear of the cabin and called out, "everyone out."

They all climbed out of the Ural and congregated at the back. Janik and Lucas were scouting around with binoculars while Robert consulted his map.

"What was that?"

"Fifty caliber shot," said Lucas, "can't be sure where but it sounds like it came from that way," he pointed to the hills near Stary Sobor.

"The Bandits?" Janik asked.

"They could have circled around," Yuri said, pointing to the map.

"Or Doc could have lied to us and they went this way," said Janik.

"That shot wasn't at us though, its direction was away," Lucas offered while looking around.

"So where did it land then?" asked Yuri.

"No idea, I was in the back of a truck remember?" replied Lucas.

"We have too many questions and no answers. Yuri, stash the Ural in the trees here. Lucas, circle around and see if you can find the shooter. Janik, are you up for another scouting mission?"

"Just tell me where boss," said Janik, as he unloaded his bicycle from the Ural.

"Go into town and get me some intel. I want to know who is shooting at who. But be safe and meet us here," he pointed to the top of a hill overlooking Stary Sobor, "Lucas this is the rendezvous point. We'll go straight there and watch the town. Everyone, be careful with your fire. We don't know who's shooting at who or why they are, for all we know there might be other survivors in Stary Sobor. Janik it's all on you, we need you to find out what's happening. Lucas, you keep him safe and spot that shooter."

"Will do. Come on little man, I want you so stealthy in Stary I don't even see you crawling round down there," said Lucas.

"You won't. See you at the rendezvous point," replied Janik, and he rode off into the trees.

Alejandro had also heard the shot as he rode through the valley behind Stary Sobor. His map had marked the area as *Old Fields* and around him were rolled up bales of hay. Feed for farms that would never use them.

Alejandro stopped the motorbike and looked down across the field back towards Stary Sobor. In the distance all he could see was the large white water tower that stood high above the town. He looked down at his map, around at the field and then listened. There were no other shots. *I should check it out, Shutov will want to know if there were others around.* Decision made, he turned the bike away from the direction of the Northwest Airfield and south towards Stary Sobor.

"Just leave the guns in a pile right here for now. We're not interested in your puny weapons but I'm getting sick of you pointing them at me," Timor called out as the Bandits unloaded their guns at a pile near his feet. Rory's death had quickly dispelled any qualms they had about obeying Timor.

Shutov was the last to disarm himself and he returned to the head of the line of men standing next to the bus. The men were all leaning against the bus facing the hill where Grigory fired. They looked up into the hills, nervous, trying to spot where he was.

"Ohh it's like a firing line, which you should remember is exactly what you are," said Timor, "Oleg come out and say hello to our new friends."

Oleg stepped out of the green house carrying his M249 SAW. Some of the Bandits gulped when they saw his formidable size and the large weapon he carried.

"Oleg, these are the ducks. Ducks, this is Oleg," said Timor.

Oleg smiled at them as he rested his M249 on the edge of the side barricade. He pulled back on the loading mechanism and the sound caused some of the men to flinch.

"Oleg is going to watch you for a moment while I have a chat with your boss. You two on the end - I want you to get on the bus and take off all the food and water you have. Put it all in a pile in front of this house. If there are any guns on there don't even think of touching them. If Grigory sees one in your hand he will not hesitate to shoot. I'm going to check the bus myself when you're done and if I find any hidden food or water I will shoot you both in the legs and leave you here to feed the infected. Is that understood?"

Luther and Sam nodded in assent.

"Grigory?" Timor said louder.

From the radio came Grigory's response, "yes sir I have eyes on the two of them."

Grigory dropped the radio and wiped tears from his eyes. *Pull yourself together man, you've done worse shit than this.* Grigory sobbed, choking back more tears. *You should be looking down the scope, watching them, not crying like a little girl. Sure you killed him but it's done now, you can't change that. He would have most likely died anyway, how long could someone like that last out here?*

But it wasn't working, Grigory couldn't justify it to himself. The guilt, the pain, it was too much for him to handle. It stemmed from more than just Rory's death. It derived from all the people he killed, the women he raped, the things he had done. *Hell - that's where you're going now. Killing Rory just made sure your ticket was one way.* He couldn't stop the thoughts from running around in his head.

Nobody deserves to die, not like that. Well that's not true, I do. I deserve to die like that and so do the others. He made a fist and pounded his head hard, trying to drive the thoughts out. The pain worked momentarily, distracting him enough to focus. And that's when he heard it - the snapping of branches.

He turned to see a group of men crouched along the ridge line behind him. They were barely one hundred meters away but so far they hadn't spotted Grigory. He ducked down and crawled behind some brush, pushing the leaves aside so he could see.

Robert, Alfie, Yuri and Joseph all walked along the ridgeline, trying to stay low. They were on the edge of a valley and desperate to get to the next tree line. It was because of this desperation that they hadn't noticed Grigory as they went past him, instead they focused ahead as though by sheer force of will they could make the next tree line come closer.

Robert hated being out in the open like this but they had no choice. The shooting had stopped and this was the quickest way to get to the hill that overlooked Stary Sobor. Unfortunately, it was also the riskiest.

Lucas watched the Survivors through his binoculars as they walked along the ridgeline. He had given up on scouting around for the 50 Caliber sniper as there were too many trees and he didn't have any real sense of which direction the shot came from. Lucas used all of his hunting skills- knowledge taught and retaught from such a young age that it was now innate. He lay perfectly still on the dewy grass, the only movement was the slight adjustments his hands made as he scoured the trees, hunting for that sniper.

Grigory watched the men as they brazenly walked across the field. He had the drop on them, he could take them all out.

"So boss man what's your-" Timor's voice over the radio was silenced as Grigory hastily turned it off. He turned back to watch the group of Survivors. They continued to walk, oblivious to the sound.

Grigory took out his rangefinders and obtained the distance to the men. Two hundred meters and moving further away. He grabbed the AS-50 and adjusted the scope before he stopped himself. *No more,* the thought burst into his head with such clarity that it startled even Grigory. *No more killing. Rory was the last - that will at least make his death special, make it mean something.* Grigory watched the men. They were walking away from him, they were not a threat, there was no need to kill them. But there was also no need to kill the others and yet he did. He raised the sniper rifle and looked down the scope at the lead man, Robert.

Robert was walking along, oblivious to the present danger he was in. And then Grigory flashed back to Rory. Kind, gentle Rory. Trusting, stupid Rory. Rory who disappeared and left a cloud of pink mist behind. Grigory hit his head harder, trying to knock the memory out of his mind. It wasn't working.

"Fuck," he whispered as he lowered the rifle. He couldn't do it. Not now, not ever again. Grigory grabbed the radio and was about to turn it on and report back to Timor. *That's like pulling the trigger yourself,* his mind berated him. *Don't go back, go forward,* and suddenly it was clear to Grigory what he must do.

These men would be his salvation. He would go to them, offer himself up to them as no threat. If they kill him, then he got what he deserves. If they let him live then he knew they were good men and maybe he could be redeemed. Grigory stood, almost as if in a trance. For the first time in a very long time he was at peace. In the next moment he would either die or be reborn again. He shouldered the AS-50 and walked towards the Survivors.

Although the walking Survivors didn't hear the radio chatter, Lucas did. Perhaps it was because he was still and silent, or perhaps because his ears were more able to tune out the noises of the forest. Regardless he now had a possible direction that the sniper could be in.

As he searched out the area he believed the radio sound came from, he was surprised to see the sniper had just stood up. On his back was a large AS-50 sniper rifle, which Lucas assumed was the one he heard before. Lucas watched as the man walked, astounded that he has just exposed himself like that.

And then he remembered the others and realized the man was walking towards them. Automatically, Lucas dropped his binoculars and picked up his M107 rifle. He looked down the scope and used the mildots to estimate that the sniper's range was about 300 meters. He turned the dial on the scope to 300 meters and looked back down, lining up Grigory for the kill-shot.

It was the groans that got Janik's attention. A continuous cluster of moaning and the occasional thumping that came from the large red shed. Like the white ball-shaped water tower, the red shed was large enough that it could be seen from a great distance. It was located on the eastern edge of Stary Sobor. Janik planned to leave his bicycle there while he searched the town on foot.

As he got closer the groans and sounds coming from inside turned his stomach to ice. There were infected inside, lots of infected. Janik peered through a gap in the corrugated iron and looked inside. It took his eyes a moment to adjust before he was faced with a gruesome sight. There were at least fifty infected in there, many weak and emancipated. There were body bags on the floor, most were open, and the doors were chained shut. To Janik it appeared they were just locked in there and forgotten. He crept away cautiously, glad for the chains that kept them locked inside.

Lucas watched the sniper through the scope. The man had some sort of military uniform on, although torn, Lucas could make out the patches on his arm. *Maybe he is one of the other survivors Robert spoke of, the last shred of Government in this land.* He recalled Robert's specific orders - don't shoot unless necessary. The sniper at this point appeared to be no threat, the rifle was holstered and he was walking quickly towards the others. Lucas decided to hold off and watch, adjusting the scope range again as the man moved further away. If the sniper reached for any weapon he would be dead before his fingers could touch the steel.

Timor put his arm around Shutov as he led him away from the others. Shutov breathed in the odor that came off Timor and visibly winced.

"Bit ripe am I? No time for showers and soap in this chaos," Timor said as he pulled Shutov closer.

"How long have you been out here?" Shutov asked.

"I'll be the one asking the questions. Let's start with how you got here. Rory tells me, whoops I mean told me, you all came from a ship that sank off the shore."

"That's correct," answered Shutov.

"Why the fuck would you have come here? Did you know about the infection?"

"We'd heard rumors, there were transmissions we picked up on the civilian channels. But they were crazed, we didn't believe them. There was mention of a place called Green Mountain."

"And what about the military frequencies, news broadcasts?"

Shutov shook his head, "Nothing. No mention of an infection."

"You've got to love the Russian Military, the only thing they're effective at is a cover up," said Timor, "so why did you come?"

"Our Captain. This was his homeland, I think he wanted to be certain. So we came."

"And where is your Captain now."

"Dead."

"Infected?"

"No, he was shot."

"By you?"

Shutov shook his head, "Suicide."

"He might have been the smartest one of you all," said Timor as they continued to walk down the road.

Robert was so focused on getting up the hill quickly he didn't initially notice the tapping on his shoulder. When it became more insistent he turned around and was stunned to see everyone else had stopped. About 50 meters behind them, Grigory was walking towards them, his arms up but carrying an ominous looking rifle on his back. Robert then noticed that Alfie and Yuri had their guns trained on him.

"Lower your damn guns. If he wanted to hurt us he would have already," snarled Robert.

Yuri and Alfie complied and lowered their guns. Robert waved Grigory over, who nodded in acknowledgement. Robert signaled to the others to stand down and make a path as Grigory ran towards them.

Lucas watched the exchange through his binoculars. Grigory came close to Robert who held out his hand and Grigory tentatively shook it. Satisfied that the Survivors were safe, Lucas turned his attention back to the town and looked for Janik.

"Wow are we glad to see you," said Robert noticing the uniform, "are you military?"

"Was - Private Grigory Roudenko – formerly of the Russian Federation. That was then, before it all went to shit, now we're just trying to live. You're from the ship that wrecked earlier?"

"We are. You said 'we' before, are there others with you?"

"The remainder of my squad, they're in the town."

"Great, let's go down and speak with them."

Grigory shook his head, "bad idea, they're not exactly... good, people."

"Was that you we heard shooting before?" asked Alfie looking over the AS-50.

"Yes," Grigory hesitates, " I was following orders."

Alfie was about to ask another question but Robert shook his head to stop him.

"So Grigory why did you come to us?" asked Robert.

"I don't know," replied Grigory, "I saw you walking and I

thought maybe... we could help each other."

"Do you need food, water? We're happy to share."

"No nothing like that. It's just... I did a bad thing and now I'm... hoping to do a good thing. Come, let me show you."

Grigory led them to the crest of the hill. From up here they could see most of Stary Sobor including the ambush site. Grigory took out his rangefinder and looked back into town. Robert, Yuri and Alfie, who all had binoculars, followed suit.

"Do you see the group unloading the bus?" asked Grigory.

"Yes, I recognize them from the ship. They are the Bandits. We've, shall we say, had our differences."

"My squad are robbing them right now. See down there? Oleg's watching over them with the M249. And look further up the main road, that's our leader Timor-"

"Talking with Shutov," interrupted Alfie.

"I wish we could hear what they're saying," said Robert.

"You fool, of course we can," chastised Grigory as he took out his radio and turned it back on. Timor and Shutov's voices came through the radio as the four men listened while watching them through the binoculars.

"You've done well Shutov, I wish we had more men like you in the army. Maybe then this place wouldn't have gone to hell."

"So then it's agreed - you'll take three of us to the Northwest Airfield and we'll cooperate with you."

"Ah yes - but which three?"

"There's myself and we definitely need Sam, so that's two," Shutov looked over at his men lined up at the bus.

"Oh shit, we don't have much time," exclaimed Grigory.

"Why, what is it?" asked Robert.

"Timor's plan was to rob them of food and water, find out what they know and then execute the entire group. It seems their boss has struck a deal that saves some of them but the rest won't be so lucky."

"You have a sniper rifle, just take them all out."

"No, I will not kill another man. I'm done with that," said Grigory sternly.

"You said yourself these are bad men so what's the problem?" asked Alfie.

Grigory looked over the houses stained with Rory's blood. "I can't make exceptions - that's how this all started. First it was "they have food and we're hungry" - so we kill them.. Then it was "they fired at us first" - so we kill them. Finally it was "they may kill us" - so we kill them. But it was all just excuses for doing the inexcusable. I will never kill another person again."

"What then?" asked Robert.

"Distraction. I'll buy you some time, enough to get out of here. This rifle will disable the bus - probably permanently - so they won't be able to follow you," Grigory took out his map and handed it to Robert, "across this field behind us is another hill, on the other side of that hill is a camouflaged UAZ, it's marked on the map. Take the car," he handed Robert the keys, "there are more guns inside, along with some food and water. Use the car to escape."

"What about you?" asked Robert.

"I've been out here long enough, I'll be fine."

"Do you want one of us to stay back and help?" said Yuri.

"Unless you're a priest, there is no help for me. Now go, I don't know how much time I can buy you and you'll be wide open crossing that field," said Grigory looking down the scope at the bus.

Janik was hidden inside a house, watching through a window as the Bandits unloaded their food from the bus. He could see Shutov and Timor talking further down the road, but since there was no safe path to reach them he decided to stay hidden. At least here he was in earshot of the Bandits and Oleg.

The wind cracked as the front right tire of the bus burst apart, rubber and shrapnel hitting some of the men. One piece of shrapnel embedded itself in Luther's neck and he crumpled down, bleeding. The other Bandits all ducked down, no longer concerned about Oleg and his M249, instead they tried to find cover. Another round hit the bus' engine.

"What the fuck man, you said we'd be safe?" Sam screamed to Oleg.

"I don't know why he's shooting," bellowed Oleg as he took out his radio and yelled into it, "Grigory hold your fire, what do you see?"

Janik watched Shutov and Timor also get behind cover from the firing and move back towards the Bandits. He could hear Timor's voice through Oleg's radio.

"Grigory, stop the shooting - that is an order!"

Oleg gazed over at Timor and shook his head. Timor moved closer as another round hit the bus, taking out a rear tire.

"Oleg, what did they do?" yelled Timor.

"Nothing, they were complying when he just started shooting."

Timor scrutinized the bleeding body of Luther, "What about him?"

"Just unlucky, he just got hit by shrapnel."

Timor turned to Shutov, "do you have any more men around here?"

"Only one, but he's going straight to the airfield so it wouldn't be him."

"Well it's not my man up there. Grigory doesn't miss, so if he *was* shooting, there'd be more dead people around here."

"The Survivors. It must be one of them."

"Who?" demanded Timor.

"Others from the ship, they've been stalking us for days. One of them must have taken your man out and is using his rifle to shoot at us."

"Shit," Janik whispered to himself listening to their conversation.

"Oleg, Pavel, circle around to the left past the red shed, try to get him from behind," Timor yelled across the road.

Pavel stepped out from a nearby house and ducked behind the bus.

"Can you control your dogs if I take them off the leash?" Timor asked Shutov.

"They'll do as ordered."

"Good, tell them to pick up their weapons and move across the town to the west, see if they can cut him off from the other side."

Janik watched this exchange. He was safe in the house as Oleg and Pavel walked towards him. *Fuck I need to do something or they'll decimate the others.* He raised the crossbow and aimed it at Oleg's leg. Janik pulled the trigger and the bolt tore out and embedded itself into the flesh and muscle of Oleg's upper quad.

"Yurrgh!" bellowed out Oleg, dropping the M249 and clutching his leg.

The idea worked to slow down Pavel and Oleg, who were now looking for where the bolt had come from. The distraction gave Janik enough time to slip out the back door. He ran towards the red shed.

The movement caught Shutov's eye and he turned to see Janik running across the open ground.

"There!" hollered Shutov and he reached around for his rifle before realizing it was no longer on him.

Timor also spotted Janik and pulled out his concealed M9 SD. He shot at Janik but he was too far away and ran too fast for Timor to hit him. The bullets kicked up dirt on the ground around him. Frustrated, Timor whistled to Oleg and Pavel.

"There – southwest, heading towards the big red shed!"

Oleg and Pavel looked but they couldn't see him as the house Janik had previously been hidden inside of now obscured him from them.

Oleg seized the protruding part of the bolt and snapped it off, leaving only a small amount exposed.

"It's that little prick Janik from the ship, I told you the Survivors were here. They're the ones who took down your man," yelled Shutov.

Shutov watched helplessly as Janik made it to the red shed and stopped at the large chained-up double doors.

Janik shouldered the crossbow and took out a small hatchet that he kept in his pack. He pounded at the chain - the sound of each blow attracting more infected towards the door. With each hit the chain became a bit weaker and the door strained as more and more infected pushed against it.

Lucas also watched Janik from the hill, waiting for him to come around so they could leave. *What are you doing Janik?* he wondered as Janik continued to hit the door. Lucas spun his binoculars around and surveyed the Survivors as they ran across the field - they were a quarter of the way across and running full pelt.

Lucas turned the binoculars back around at Janik and saw bullet-sized holes suddenly start appearing in the steel door. Janik dropped instinctively and turned to see more bullets coming at him fired from Oleg using the M249. Lucas dropped the binoculars and picked up his M107.

He looked down the scope at Oleg as bullets continued to fly out of the M249, fortunately for Janik they were going wide as Oleg was not used to the recoil on the gun. Lucas lined up Oleg in his sight, sucked in a deep breath of air to sturdy himself and pulled the trigger.

The bullet missed Oleg and hit the dirt behind him. Oleg dropped, panicked, and the reprieve gave Janik enough time to escape. Lucas squeezed the trigger a few more times, purposely shooting wide in order to force Oleg to scramble back behind cover without hurting him.

Lucas shifted the rifle around to Janik and saw him pointing at the shed. Lucas lowered the scope, waved Janik towards him and then raised the M107. He made some adjustments on the scope and lined up the lock on the shed. Once Janik was clear and around the far end of the shed, Lucas squeezed the trigger.

The chain and a lock disintegrated and left behind a hole from which a black cloud of gore burst out from. The shed doors flung open and a horde of infected charged out, looking for any living being to devour.

From behind the shed, Janik lobbed a smoke grenade past the infected and towards the Bandits. It landed near the damaged rear of the bus and the effect was immediate, all the infected turned focus towards the smoke and ran at it, roaring.

Grigory also watched the shed as the horde rushed towards the smoke. He was so focused on the events down below he didn't notice Alejandro creeping behind him with an AK-74 aimed at his head.

"Drop the rifle," Alejandro hissed.

Grigory did and put his hand behind his head.

"You must be Lucas. Look, I'm helping you, trying to keep them pinned down while Robert and the others get to our UAZ. If you have a map I'll show you where."

"Lucas from the ship, he's here?"

"Wait who are you?" Grigory asked as he turned around.

"The man with the gun," answered Alejandro.

Shutov's voice emitted from the radio on the ground, "Forget the Survivors men, focus on the horde of infected."

Alejandro turned to the radio.

"That's Shutov. Where are they?"

"In town being overrun by infected," said Grigory as he pointed to the chaos behind him.

Alejandro watched the Bandits as they blindly fired on the charging infected. They had set up positions behind cover and Oleg's M249 was making mincemeat of many of them. The number of infected was still too great and it was hard for them to see through all the smoke.

"Tell me where the Survivors are and you might just live."

"Fuck you."

"Fuck me?"

"Yeah, fuck you! They're good people so if my death helps them escape then at least I can manage one good thing in my miserable life. You want to kill me, then do it, I'm less afraid of dying than I am of spending another day like this."

"If you insist," said Alejandro and he shot Grigory in the head. Grigory slumped down dead, part of his face turned to mush where the bullet exited. Alejandro snatched up the AS-50 and the radio from Grigory's body and moved towards the town.

Oleg continued to spray bullets into the smoke as infected poured out of it like some twisted nightmare.

"They just won't stop," shouted Oleg.

"Keep shooting," instructed Timor.

"I'm nearly out of rounds. I'll need covering fire while I reload."

The Bandits were also lined up behind cover with their weapons drawn and ready. Any previous animosity was gone, they were now all focused on surviving the infected horde.

"Shutov! Shutov can you hear me?" came Alejandro's voice through the radio, "the Survivors, they're leaving in a car."

"That's my man Alejandro, the one that was going to the airfield," Shutov told Timor.

"Looks like he got waylaid then," said Timor.

"Can I have the radio? I'll find out what's happened." Timor considered it briefly, and seeing no threat, decided to toss Shutov the radio.

"Reloading!" shouted out Oleg as he opened the M249 and popped out the magazine belt.

The Bandits fired into the smoke and infected, forcing Shutov to move back from them so he could hear the radio over the racket from their guns.

Lucas watched the horde through his binoculars as Janik advanced up on him

"Did it work?" asked Janik.

"Oh yeah, they're knee deep in infected down there."

"Great, let's get to the rendezvous point."

"The others aren't there anymore. They've moved across the field, but they left a Guardian Angel over there. Take a look."

Lucas watched the Survivors crossing the field while Janik surveyed the hill.

"You mean Alejandro is with us now?" Janik asked, perturbed.

"What? No, some Russian military guy."

Lucas focused his binoculars to the hill to see Alejandro talking on the radio. Janik watched back in town and saw Shutov was also talking on a radio as the M249 fire started up again.

"Looks like he's talking to Shutov," said Janik.

"Yeah and our guy's dead, see the corpse on the ground near Alejandro. I'm guessing Al took him out."

"Forget them, they can have the town, let's bug out."

"We can try but we won't get all the way across. We'll be able to crawl and use this tree line as cover part way there, but if we run across that open field he'll see us moving and we'll be done for."

"So, shoot him! He's a confirmed killer."

"I would like nothing better but didn't you tell me to be judicious with the shooting? This thing is loud, if I fire it now it will bring all the infected and the Bandits upon us. For now we're stuck here until Alejandro moves on."

Everyone was out of breath and gasping as they arrived at the woods on the other side of the field. Robert turned and looked back across the field they had just traversed. There was no movement, no one chased after them. He couldn't hear any gun shots. "Looks like we're in the clear," he said.

"What about Janik and Lucas?" asked Yuri.

"Grigory will tell them where we've gone," said Robert consulting his map, "the UAZ should be on the other side of this hill. Alfie stay here and watch the field for Lucas and Janik, everyone else to the car."

"I want to stay too," Yuri said.

"You have a shotgun Yuri, it doesn't have the range of a Lee Enfield," said Alfie.

"Get a better gun from the car and then come back and help Alfie," Robert offered.

Placated, Yuri followed the others as they labored up the hill. Once at the top they looked around for the car and Yuri spotted it on the other side, just off the dirt road.

"There," he said as he rushed down towards it. Robert and the other Survivors followed him to the parked car.

The rate of infected that came through the smoke slowed as the smoke also dissipated. The fastest sprinters had been killed and only the crawling and injured ones remained. Oleg stopped firing as he could now see to the red shed. Heat waves shimmered off the gun through his vision and he wiped the sweat from his face.

"Save the ammunition," said Timor, "you three take your shotguns and pistols and clear out the remaining crawlers."

Shutov returned to Timor, "Do you have a car nearby?"

"That's none of your concern," replied Timor.

"Well it is now, my man just said that your sniper sold you out. He told the Survivors where your UAZ was hidden and now they're on the way to it."

"What?" exclaimed Timor as he snatched the radio out of Shutov's hand, "Who is this?"

"Alejandro of the MV Rocket. Who are you?"

"I'm the man who's about to kill all of your friends if you don't stop fucking with me. Where is Grigory?"

"If you're talking about the brown haired guy with a beard and Russian uniform, he's lying dead in front of me."

"Who killed him?" demanded Timor as he turned his back to Shutov.

"I did, after he tried to attack me. He thought I was one of the Survivors and when he discovered I wasn't, he attacked me. I did what I had to."

"Then you're a dead man," growled Timor.

Shutov called out, "I don't think you're in any position to make threats."

Timor turned around to see that the Bandits had surrounded Oleg and Pavel, their guns pointed at them. Oleg and Pavel had dropped their weapons and held their hands up.

Timor absorbed the turn of events. "Do you want to start a pissing contest Shutov or do you want to get me back my car? Your bus is destroyed and that car has food, water and a large collection of guns. If these Survivors are as dangerous as you say, I doubt you'd want all that getting into their hands."

Shutov thought it over, "okay, but we need to be quick, Alejandro saw them already cross the field."

"Dammit that means they're getting close," cursed Timor as he studied the group, "Oleg you're in no condition to run, so you stay here."

"Butcher, you watch him. The rest up the hill to Alejandro," Shutov pointed to Timor and Pavel, "pick up your guns but stay in the front, if you turn around once we will shoot you."

The two prisoners grabbed their guns and were marched up the hill as Oleg sat on a low wall and raised his injured leg.

Robert couldn't help but laugh, "that gun suits you Yuri."

"It's bloody heavy but it'll do the trick," said Yuri as he heaved the second M249 SAW onto his back, "I'll get back to Alfie." Robert nodded and Yuri took off, charging up the hill as fast as he could with the extra weight on his back.

"Right, everyone else spread out, watch for anyone coming down the road or over the hill. If we don't know them then get them disarmed, warning shots over the head first. If they don't disarm at that point, you decide, but remember it's probably going to be you or them, so play it safe."

The men dispersed around the UAZ as Robert watched Yuri run over the top of the hill.

Lucas and Janik were covered in dirt and grass, they had tree branches sticking out of their belts as they crawled along the ground. They had made it partly across the field by crawling underneath trees and shrubs but now they were stuck as there was no further cover. They used their binoculars to watch Alejandro as he stood at the top of the hill, scouting around with his own binoculars.

"Why doesn't he move?" asked Janik.

"I don't know, but he's definitely looking for someone."

"Us?"

"Could be, could be the others - oh shit, look further down that hill."

Janik adjusted his binoculars and saw Timor and Pavel being marched up the hill by the Shutov and the Bandits.

"That's not good."

"Not at all," said Lucas as he looked towards the next line of trees around one hundred and thirty meters away from them, "we could make it there in 20 to 30 secs tops, but they'd see the movement."

"Then let's get prepared to sprint while we keep an eye on them, if they get distracted we'll be ready to run," replied Janik.

Janik zipped his pack closed and checked everything was stowed away before he raised his binoculars and continued to watch the Bandits.

"So this is the dead man?" said Timor as he looked over Alejandro.

"Funny, I could say the same thing about you," replied Alejandro.

"I've been dead for a long time my friend."

"Quit it, both of you," said Shutov. "Have you spotted the car or the Survivors?" he asked Alejandro.

"Negative, there's been no movement at all out there."

"So where's my car?" Shutov asked Timor.

"Oh I think you're mistaken, it's my UAZ or it's the Survivor's UAZ, but it will never be *your* UAZ. Now I gave you a chance to negotiate so if you afford me the same you just might get a ride in my car."

Shutov grabbed the pistol out of Sam's hand and held it to Timor's forehead. Timor didn't flinch.

"I hate to break it to you Shutov but this isn't the first time I've had a gun held to my head. Death holds no fear for me my friend, I've been looking into that bitch's eyes for a while now."

Shutov looked him over and recognized the steely determination in Timor's face.

"I believe you," said Shutov while he turned the pistol to Pavel, "but your friend here."

"If I care so little for myself why would I care for him?" asked Timor.

"I'm more concerned with how he would feel about his own life," Shutov said as he returned the muzzle to Timor's head and pulled the trigger. From such a close range the bullet went clean through his skull, spraying blood, bone and brain matter onto the tree behind him. Timor instantly dropped dead.

Alfie, Lucas and Janik were all watching the moment through binoculars. They flinched and called out in shock as Shutov executed Timor.

"So Pavel, now will you tell me where this car is?" asked Shutov, turning the gun to him.

"No," answered Pavel, "but I'll take you to it if that keeps me alive."

"Good man, first smart thing one of you soldiers has done all day. Now, which way?

"Across this field, but we'd better hurry," said Pavel.

"It's too wide open out there Shutov, we should circle around instead," Vuk implored.

"It will take too long," insisted Pavel, "the UAZ is not too far but we need to move."

"You're right Vuk but so is our friend, you circle around the left, Sam you circle to the right. Both of you cover us as we go through the middle."

Vuk and Sam nodded as they peeled off left and right respectively.

Yuri was at the edge of the tree line on the other side of the hill, searching around for Alfie, "Pssst Alfie where are you?"

"Up here in the deer stand," said Alfie turning around and looking down at Yuri. "Damn that's a big gun."

"What's happening?"

"Shutov just killed someone, I didn't recognize who. Lucas and Janik are stuck in the brush on the edge of the field due south of us. They can't get across because Shutov and the Bandits are watching from the other side."

"Oh, I see them," said Yuri spying the Bandits, "they're moving out from the hill."

"Shit, they're spreading out and coming this way!" exclaimed Alfie.

"I'll slow them down. You get back to Robert and tell him to drive down the road and scoop up Lucas and Janik."

"Won't they hear the car?" asked Alfie.

"Not over the sound of this baby, they won't," said Yuri as he set up the machine gun under the cover of a thick pine tree.

"We're fucked, that's what we are," said Janik as he watched the Bandits cross the field.

"No, they don't know we're here, and if they get too close I still have the M107."

"Sure, but how are we going to get across the field?"

"Same plan as before - the second they're distracted long enough for us to cross - we run."

"So I guess you're going to kill me anyway?" said Pavel as they ran across the field.

"Shut up and get me to the car," rebuked Shutov.

"This is stupid, they'll see us coming from far away," complained Pavel.

"That's why you're in front," answered Shutov.

"Shhhh. I hear a car," said Harrison.

"Where? Which direction?"

"That way," Harrison said as he pointed north east.

They all strained to listen but the silence was broken by the sound of machine gun fire landing near them.

"Jesus," Harrison exclaimed as he hit the ground. Shutov and Pavel were also lying flat on the long grass as bullets whooshed over their heads.

"What is that?" Shutov asked.

"That's the other M249 we found last night. That means they've got to the UAZ," replied Pavel.

"Fuck! We need to get to cover," called out Harrison as he spun around. Fortunately, the grass was high enough to conceal them from the shooter.

"Those trees to the left, stay low and crawl over there," said Shutov as crawled through the grass. The bullets continued to whiz over their heads as the others followed him.

"Now's our chance," said Janik as he watched the Bandits crawl away.

"Can you see who's shooting?" asked Lucas, scanning the far tree line with his binoculars.

"No and I don't care, so long as they keep shooting at them and not us, we're good. Let's go."

"Alright then, on three," said Lucas looking around, "one...two...three."

Both men lept up from the ground and rushed across the open field towards the next tree line.

From across the other side of the field concealed in a brush Vuk noticed Lucas and Janik running. From this distance they were too small for him to recognize and too far away to do anything about. He turned back to where the firing emanated from - which was much closer - around fifty meters from where he was.

Vuk saw where the bullets originated from but was unable to see the shooter, who was concealed underneath a pine tree. Vuk searched across the field where Shutov, Harrison and Pavel were, but they couldn't be seen. The bullets were flying over their last known location, where they were most likely now dead in the tall grass.

Vuk peered down the sight of his AKS-74 Kobra. The bullets kept coming from beneath the pine tree but the shooter was hidden, all he could see was the muzzle flash and puffs of smoke. Vuk lined up where he thought the shooter might be, and steadied his aim. He braced for the recoil as he squeezed the trigger.

AK rounds streamed out of the rifle and into the pine tree, instantly stopping the barrage of M249 fire. Vuk stopped shooting and listened, watching the pine tree for movement. There was none. The field was silent once again. He kept his gun trained on the pine tree as he walked slowly towards it, ready to shoot at any sign of movement.

As he got closer he heard the groan of a man in pain and the wet coughing of blood. Vuk recognized the voice and slung the rifle over his shoulder as he ran towards the coughing.

"Yuri!" he called out.

"Vuk! Over here."

Vuk ran around the pine tree to find Yuri lying on the ground, the clothes on his right side had turned a dark shade of maroon as more blood seeped from the wounds. Yuri was on his back looking up at the sky.

"Was it you?" Yuri asked.

Vuk nodded, trying to hold back the tears.

"If it was going to be anyone then I'd want it to be you," said Yuri.

"I'm sorry I didn't know it was you. I wouldn't have-"

"Save it. Excuses are for the young and stupid and you, my old friend, are neither," the words took an effort for Yuri to splutter out and he coughed up more blood as he finished the sentence.

"What can I do?"

"Nothing, it's too late for me," said Yuri holding up a bloody hand, "did the others make it away?"

"I think so," replied Vuk, searching the field for them.

"Then I die for a reason, and it is a good day to die, what more could an old man ask for?"

Vuk grabbed Yuri's hand and tenderly held it in his, as he looked into his friend's eyes.

"It's not too late for you Vuk," said Yuri, staring back at Vuk.

"I'm an old dog, I don't have any new tricks."

"You're still a good man and that's no trick," chastised Yuri.

"What would you have me do?" pleaded Vuk.

"Whatever is in your heart," and with those words Yuri's eyes went vacant and his labored breathing stopped.

Vuk stared down at him, still holding his bloody hand. He bent down and kissed Yuri on the forehead.

"Goodbye old friend. I'm sure I'll see you again soon," said Vuk as he closed Yuri's eyes. He sat there motionless, watching an ant crawl across Yuri's arm.

Vuk rose, his clothes now stained with Yuri's blood. He picked up the M249 SAW and carried it as he walked out of the tree line and into the field.

Shutov, Pavel and Harrison watched as the bloody visage of Vuk walked towards them.

"Is he down?" called out Harrison.

Vuk nodded and continued walking, almost in a daze.

"Vuk the killer," yelled out Shutov proudly, "and look, he carries the spoils of war."

Lucas and Janik also watched Vuk from the other side of the field, although he was too far away for them to recognize even with binoculars. From behind them, they heard the sound of a car rolling to a stop. Alfie climbed out and walked towards them.

"Can you see Yuri?" asked Alfie.

"No. Where is he?"

"He was covering our escape with the machine gun fire. Over near that deer stand."

"Then he's dead," said Janik handing Alfie his binoculars, "whoever that is, killed him and took his gun."

"Fuck!" cried Alfie, "is this what it's going to be like from now on? Is this the only life we have left to look forward to? What about Grigory, did he make it?"

"Who?" asked Lucas.

"The Russian who told us about the car, he was on the hill giving us cover."

"No," Lucas said shaking his head, "Alejandro took him out."

"Motherfucker!" exclaimed Alfie.

Lucas lifted up his M107 and pointed it towards the figure walking across the field.

"No, not now, not like this," said Janik.

"Why not? He murdered Yuri."

"It is an unnecessary risk. Will killing him bring Yuri back?"

"It would make me feel better."

"Like killing Kai did?" chastised Janik, "look it's still a man's life you're taking, however you try to justify it. What it comes down to is that either we can be like them, or we can be better than them. He doesn't know we're here, he's no threat to us - killing him would be murder. If we let him go we can make a clean getaway."

Lucas mulled this over before nodding and lowering the rifle.

"Not quite a clean getaway," joked Alfie.

"What do you mean?" asked Janik.

"The UAZ holds 5 but you two make six, so - shorty - looks like you're lying across three men's laps in the back and none of them have bathed in days."

"Oh shit. First I lose my bike and now this," said Janik as he skulked off to the UAZ.

Pavel was marched back to the bus ambush site where The Butcher was waiting. Oleg lied on the ground dead, bullet holes punctuating his chest.

"I take it we didn't get the car then?" asked The Butcher.

"What happened to him?" demanded Shutov.

"He tried to run away so I shot him," said The Butcher calmly.

"He tried to run with a broken leg?" accused Vuk.

"I said he tried to run away, I didn't say he was smart about it," The Butcher coolly replied.

"Enough! It matters not anyway," said Shutov, "without medical attention the wound would have killed him anyway. And since we're... short on doctors, he would have just slowed us down," Shutov turned to Pavel, "as for you. Convince me to keep you alive and I will."

Pavel eyeballed the Bandits pointing guns at him, his mind racing to come up with the right answer.

"Knowledge," said Pavel, "I can give you knowledge. You've been here for just a couple of days, I've been living in this shit for weeks. I know about the infected, about raiding towns, where the uncontaminated water is, the best places to get fuel and vehicles. You want to survive and I have the knowledge to help you do it."

"I'm not entirely convinced but you have tonight to sell it to me," said Shutov, "now, show me where you slept last night."

Pavel nodded and walked down the main road towards the church and general store.

"The rest of you gather our things off the bus and take them into shelter. Sam, check over the bus, I'm sure it's a write off but make sure."

As the men dispersed, Vuk walked up to The Butcher and held his hand out to stop him. He leaned in close and said quietly, "If he tried to run away then why are the bullet holes in his chest and not his back?"

The Butcher looked down at Oleg's corpse - it was clear he was facing his killer at the time he was shot.

"So you're not the only one with blood on their hands," challenged The Butcher as he walked away. Vuk stared down at his hands, his bloody clothes and then back to Oleg's corpse.

It was almost getting dark when the Bandits had finished unloading their provisions into the large two story red house that Pavel led them to. Vuk sat out the front watching the sun set. His hands were now clean, although he picked at the blood under his fingernails. He had changed out of his old shirt into a new shirt that was two sizes too big for him, but was at least free from Yuri's blood.

Shutov sat down next to him, "what is it Vuk? You've been quiet all afternoon. Is it Yuri? Is that what troubles you?"

Vuk nodded, "It's been a long time since I've had to kill a man."

"Yuri was not just a man though was he? He was also your friend."

"Yes, I suppose he was," contemplated Vuk.

"Although it is an unfortunate event Vuk, it pleases me to know that you would kill a friend to save your brothers."

"I did what I had to do, but I can't leave him like that."

"Like what?"

"Out there, food for the infected. It's not right. He deserves better. I want to bury him."

"It's folly to go back," said Shutov, "you'd be risking all our lives."

"I'll go alone, in fact, I need to go alone."

Shutov was about to argue some more but was stopped by the steely determination he witnessed in Vuk's eyes.

"Do what you must to be at peace with it," said Shutov.

"I wasn't asking you for permission."

"And I wasn't offering it, just my advice. The dead don't care what happens to them, only the living. So you do what you need to do to get this squared away because I, no *we*, need you back to one hundred percent."

"I'd say you have other people to worry about than me Shutov," said Vuk.

"You speak of The Butcher."

Vuk nodded, "Killing Oleg was a stupid move, and not his first."

"We'll never know what really happened between him and Oleg, so we have to let it go," replied Shutov.

"But you don't believe his story?"

Shutov stood up, "I know most men don't run away backwards," he said before turning and walking away.

Janik bounced up and down on the legs of Lucas, Pablo and Joseph as the UAZ travelled along the dirt road.

"Will this road never end?" Janik complained.

"We're nearly there," said Alfie, seated in the passenger seat holding a map, "just past the gate and keep following this road."

The UAZ continued along the road and turned into a clearing. It was at the southern end of two long runways.

"Holy shit," said Robert

"Is that what I think it is?" asked Alfie.

"I'm guessing that's what got Shutov so excited," replied Robert.

He stopped the car, the men in the back all used the opportunity to leap out - Janik was the first. They all stared down the runway at what had Robert and Alfie lost for words.

"Let's go to it now," said Pablo, excitedly.

"Too risky, look at all the infected down there," replied Janik.

"Besides, the light is almost gone," added Lucas.

"They're right, we'll take one of the hangars and bunker down in there tonight. That will give us time to think and work out a strategy."

"Just look at them all out there, there must be over a hundred," ruminated Janik.

"I'd say more, these are just the ones we can see," interjected Lucas.

"Forget it for now, let's take the hangar on the far left. Janik, Lucas, you go first and clear it out. And be quiet we don't want to stir up the hornet's nest."

Janik took off his crossbow and Lucas grabbed an axe out from the car. They began to creep towards the closest hangar.

Robert removed his binoculars and stared back down the runway.

"What are you thinking boss?" asked Alfie, lighting up a cigarette.

"I'm thinking that we just might have a chance Alfie, we just might have a chance."

CHAPTER FORTY FOUR

GREEN MOUNTAIN

Far from all the death and mayhem at Stary Sobor, Duke and Xavier were busy scaling Green Mountain. The mountain was essentially a large hillside with its only feature being the large radio tower at the peak that could be seen for miles in any direction. Duke felt the tower would be a great place to plan their next move and work out which direction they should travel.

As they got closer to the tower, they reached a dirt road that led up and down the hill. Duke and Xavier stopped at the road and assessed the situation. Xavier took out his binoculars and scanned up the road towards the tower. The dirt road that they were on led to the facility entrance which had debris and abandoned cars piled at the front. There were dead bodies lying on the road, many in military uniform, while the infected roamed around the cars. The main gate was closed shut, no way in through there.

The Green Mountain facility consisted of a couple of buildings surrounding the massive radio tower that extended high into the sky. The entire facility was surrounded by an eight foot concrete wall and then a chain link fence, with the only visible opening being the gate and guard station at the front.

"That entrance is locked and there are infected swarming all around out there," said Xavier handing Duke the binoculars, "perhaps we should give it a miss?"

"No, it's too good an opportunity to waste, that tower is the tallest building around, if we can get up there we'll be able to see for miles."

"I understand that, and it did seem like a good idea back at the house, but here and now, I'm suddenly cold on it. This place gives me the creeps."

"Well suck it up Frenchy cause we're going in. Let's see if we can sneak in from the back."

Xavier packed away the binoculars and followed Duke back into the forest to circle around the facility. They found a small gap within the chain link fence and Duke kicked it wider to make space for them to squeeze through.

Once they had arrived at the concrete wall, Duke held up his hand to signal Xavier to stop. They both listened. There were sounds of shuffling on the ground - crawling and shambling infected could be heard from over the wall. Duke signaled to keep moving and Xavier followed him as they travelled along the wall.

They turned the corner and found there was a gap in the fence. It was a small opening at the bottom of the wall where the concrete had given way. Duke got on his belly and peered through the gap - it was tight but he could squeeze through.

"We'll get in through here, but let's go in light. Just take in weapons and the map, we can leave our packs out here." Xavier unloaded his own pack and pulled out the small hatchet and revolver. Duke did the same and they both stashed their packs in a nearby shrub, covering them with branches.

"I'll go in first," said Duke, holding out his hatchet, "we keep it low and quiet. We get to the tower and climb up there, only engage if we have to and with hatchets only."

"You sure about this?" asked Xavier.

"You'll be fine. I said I'd keep you alive and I will. Just stay close to me and follow my lead," Duke replied. He dropped to the ground and crawled through the small gap.

Duke came out the other side behind the main building of the Green Mountain facility. There were infected in the distance but none had noticed his intrusion and continued to roam the facility.

"Alright Frenchy, it's clear, come on through," Duke whispered back through the gap. Xavier squeezed through and pulled himself across to the other side. He stood up and crept over to Duke who continually watched the infected.

"We got a couple around here but seems pretty clear inside. Looks like most of them were locked out. I say we go around the back of this building and across to the tower."

Xavier nodded, agreeing, and followed Duke. They slowly stalked along the wall, constantly checking behind them for any surprises. As they neared the edge of the building Duke peeked out around the corner.

"Sweet mother of mercy," exclaimed Duke as he discovered an ATV parked at the building near him.

"What is it?" Xavier asked.

"It's the end of hiking Frenchy, that's what it is," answered Duke as he slowly crawled towards the ATV. Xavier turned the corner and saw what Duke was so excited about. The ATV, an acronym for All-Terrain Vehicle, was a four wheeled outdoor quad bike designed to travel along most surfaces. It had two seats and a gear sack for any equipment.

Duke examined the ATV as Xavier crawled towards it.

"How is it?"

"No keys, so I can't tell, but she looks in good condition and I could probably hotwire it," Duke looked at the instrument panel, "she has a quarter tank of fuel."

"Great."

"Well, not for you - you're going to have to ride bitch."

"Hey if it cuts back on the walking, I don't care."

"We'll come back to it. For now, let's get up the radio tower," said Duke, patting the ATV affectionately. They both got on their bellies and crawled past two damaged Urals on their way toward the radio tower base. The circular base of the tower had a large steel door at the entrance that was thankfully open.

Xavier and Duke rose up at the entrance and crept towards the door. Duke looked around and down the corridor, which extended for about 5 meters before making a 90 degree turn. The corridor looked clear and they stepped inside. Once they were both inside Duke reached past Xavier and slowly closed the door, blocking out most of the light.

"We can't see a thing now," whispered Xavier.

"They see worse than us. Give it a minute," replied Duke.

They both stood and waited as their eyes slowly adjusted to the darkness. From around the corner a small pool of light was visible.

"I'll take the front," said Duke. He had his hatchet out and ready as he walked down the corridor. He prowled slowly to the corner where he stopped and listened for any sounds. There was nothing except for the sounds of their own breathing. Duke slowly peeked around the corner, the rest of the corridor was dark but he could just make out a ladder at the end. The light spilled in from the top of the ladder and showed the corridor was clear. Duke walked to the ladder and looked up it. It extended for 20 meters onto the next level.

"We should be safe up there, we know they can't climb ladders," said Duke as he started to climb.

"Assuming there are none already up there," replied Xavier, climbing behind Duke.

As he neared the top Duke slowed his rate of climbing and peered over the edge. He looked into a small room, some safety equipment ran along the wall which included abseiling ropes and harnesses, but there were no infected. The door to the outside balcony was open and Duke could see far off into the distance through it.

He climbed up onto the floor and called back down, "it's clear Frenchy, come on up." As Xavier climbed up, Duke walked outside, hatchet ready. The balcony circled the radio tower and Duke discovered a dead body on the floor near the doorway. The body was wearing a lab coat and a Makarov PM pistol rested in one hand. He appeared to have committed suicide a long time ago as the body was quite decomposed.

"Oh fuck," said Xavier at seeing the body.

"Poor bastard," said Duke looking around, "looks like he wanted to see the view one last time. Leave him for now, we need to clear this floor out, I'll go left, you go right."

They split off and circled around the circumference of the balcony. Apart from the communications dishes hanging from rails, there was nothing else of interest and they arrived back at the decomposing body.

"Nothing?"

"Nope, just this poor bastard," replied Duke. He reached down and took the pistol from his hand and looked it over, popping out the magazine.

"Pistol's rusted to shit but the ammo's good," he said, pocketing the magazine and tossing the pistol over the rail.

"Jesus Duke, how about a bit of respect for the dead?" implored Xavier.

"Why? He doesn't need this shit and we do," replied Duke, patting down the body. He found a wallet which he tossed, electronic swipe card which he pocketed and a can of Mountain Dew.

"You want this," said Duke, showing Xavier the soda. Xavier waved it away and Duke shrugged before pocketing it. "Let's see what's on the next level," Duke said as he walked back inside.

Inside halfway along the wall there was a small wall mounted ladder that led to a red hatch on the roof. Duke climbed up the ladder and pushed against the hatch, it was locked shut. Beside it there was a black swipe card contact panel. Duke took out the dead man's swipe card and tapped it against the contact strip - nothing. He pulled it back and swiped it again. Still, nothing happened.

"Didn't really think that would work, but worth a shot," confessed Duke, looking closer at the contact panel. There was a small led light that was not illuminated. Duke looked at the hatch and noticed it had a key hole.

"Power is out and it looks like the backup battery's gone too. But this thing has a key hole so we might just be able to get in."

"Let's just go, I don't like this place," pleaded Xavier.

"Why?"

"Just a feeling."

"That's just stupid, sorry to say. Look here on the map - there's nothing nearby, we could bunker down here for a couple of days. We could easily clear out the few infected, check all these building and cars for weapons or supplies. If we get that ATV up and running we'll be much faster and if we can get higher up the tower we'll be able to see for miles around. This may be our new home."

"You're thinking of staying here?"

"At least for a while. Look, even if we don't find anything here there are still lots of towns nearby we can raid, using this as a base for operations. Once we clear out the infected inside, we would be pretty safe from any attacks. I don't see any reason not to stay."

Xavier ruminated on Duke's point but was still uncomfortable with the idea of staying.

"Apart from your 'feelings' can you think of one rational reason not to stay?" asked Duke.

"No," replied Xavier reluctantly.

"Okay then, let's get this area cleared and start searching those buildings."

Duke climbed down the ladder and Xavier halfheartedly followed him.

CHAPTER FORTY FIVE

THE U1H1

Sure it was painted in a drab olive green and was just a collection of steel and electronics, but to the Survivors, it was a thing of beauty. Sitting there in the middle of the runway, the U1H1 helicopter represented hope, a way out of this hell hole. While Lucas and Janik cleared the hangar, Robert just stared at it - he'd always loved machines and how they worked, but this helicopter, this beautiful machine - he'd marry her and treat her right forever if he could.

During the night they planned how to clear out the infected from around the helicopter so that Robert could get close enough to examine it. *The plan wasn't that complicated and it looked like it would work,* thought Robert as he watched the UAZ roar towards the helicopter.

During the dawn light the Survivors were able to truly assess the situation at the Northwest Airfield and it wasn't good. The airfield appeared to be humanity's last stand against the infected and they'd failed miserably at it. There were many dead bodies and it was more densely populated with infected than they'd encountered in any other location. It seemed that many of Chernarus' population came here to escape but found only death instead.

Robert decided that it would be foolish to try and clear the place out; a task of herculean proportions that would take days. Instead, he decided to draw the infected away from the helicopter and buy them some time to examine it and move it to a safe location. Last night the excitement at the prospect of flying out of here was infectious and it fell on Robert to give them a reality check. They didn't know if the helicopter was working, if it had fuel and who could fly it. At least today they'd answer two of those questions, but who could fly it was still going to be a problem.

Alfie drove down the runway in the UAZ using the car horn to draw infected towards him and away from the helicopter. Every time they got close, Alfie sped away and then waited, blasting the horn so that they all swarmed at him again. Robert watched through the binoculars as the infected near the helicopter chased after the car. Some remained near the helicopter but their number was manageable, so the Survivors moved in.

Janik and Robert took point, Janik with the crossbow and Robert with the M4A1 CCO SD. At the hangar, Lucas provided overwatch with a camouflage SVD he found in the UAZ, while Pablo and Joseph circled around left and right to stop any of the infected on the edges of the runway getting too close.

Inside the UAZ they had found a large collection of guns and provisions, and for once, the Survivors felt like they had a fighting chance. They now had plenty of food, water and ammunition and, if they could get the helicopter working, a way out.

A crawler shuffled through the long grass near them and Janik shot it in the head with his crossbow. Robert covered him as he retrieved the bolt and reloaded the crossbow.

"Thanks," Janik said, and Robert nodded, continuing to the chopper. There were two infected in front of them - Robert pointed out the one to the left and Janik nodded. He shot the left one with a double tap to the chest, knocking it down. Janik took out the right one with a single kill shot to the head. Robert moved in to the knocked-out infected and shot it once in the head from close range, its face caved in like a squashed melon.

"Still can't get used to that," he said to Janik.

"Won't need to. Once we get the chopper up we'll be home free."

"You know Janik, you're a smart guy, a reasonable guy."

"Yeah, so?" said Janik loading up the crossbow again.

"So, even if we manage to get the chopper up, and that in itself is a big 'if'. Then what? Where do we fly to?"

Janik considered this prospect, "I don't know but I'd prefer to have that problem than the ones we've had previously."

"Fair 'nuf. Then let's see if we can get this baby up," said Robert, as he slung the rifle over his shoulder. He climbed into the chopper as Janik stood guard outside, watching for any approaching infected.

CHAPTER FORTY SIX

THE DAY AFTER

Shutov woke up with a start, hitting his hand against the wall as he fended off the infected from his dreams. He nursed his hand and was glad that he had a room to himself. One of the perks of being the boss, he thought, before memories of the previous day flooded back.

His heart was immediately consumed with hate, hate for the men that got the better of him. Hate for the fact that he was losing control. Hate that he was now stuck in this God forsaken town without any transportation to get to his airfield. It was his airfield and he would be damned if he'd let the Survivors take it.

They had spent the night hunting through the abandoned cars for one that was working. Plenty were operational but they were now all part of the barricade that started this mess off. There wasn't a drop of fuel left in any car. Pavel informed him that they had emptied them all out and loaded up jerry cans into the UAZ the night prior.

Pavel had bought himself another day with the living by sharing all he knew with Shutov. He provided a map to the Russian's camps, the locations of other working vehicles, and intelligence on how to fight the infected. Shutov cared for none of it, he wanted the airfield - his precious airfield and the helicopter that would take him home. And if he was honest with himself he wanted revenge, a way to save face in front of his men.

His grasp on them was waning, already that fool Vuk had spent the night burying one of the Survivors. Once word got around about that he felt the tension between the men. When Vuk returned they grilled him about it but Vuk stonewalled them, refused to answer any questions and charged off into another room to sleep. It fell on Shutov to convince them that Vuk was still with them, that he had just killed his friend to save all of their lives. He told them that Vuk's loyalty was not to be called into question. It was a tiring night and he was sure Vuk heard most of the arguments, but in the end, logic prevailed. Vuk had proven himself and if he wanted to bury his friend then who could reasonably argue against that.

Outside the window, the sounds of the men talking was broken up by the honking of a loud horn. Immediately the men went quiet and moved into position, looking down the road at the sound, guns ready. Shutov grabbed his CZ550 and went to the window, he was one story up and could see the road from his window.

Up ahead he saw a yellow Ural drive towards them, the horn honking with glee. Shutov peered down the scope and saw that Alejandro was in the driver's seat. *The man works fast, I only sent him out a few hours ago to look for a car in the nearby towns.* He lowered his rifle and leaned out the window to yell down to the men below.

"Stand down men, it's Alejandro, with our new transportation." The men visibly relaxed and lowered their guns as Alejandro turned off the main road and through a front garden, knocking down the low fence. He drove overland around the barricade and came back up on a small dirt road beside the church. Having passed the barricade he returned to the main road and drove up to the red house they were staying in.

Shutov stood at the entrance and when the engine shut down he gave Alejandro a clap.

"You work fast I see."

"I got lucky sir, that's all. This was parked in the trees just out of town, keys still in the ignition."

"You think it could be the Survivors' truck?"

"I think so," Alejandro replied.

"Well good, they owe us something after yesterday's troubles."

"How does it run?" Sam asked Alejandro.

"Seems good, fuel's a bit low."

"Sam, you check the truck over. If it's good then we'll load up and drive to Lopatino, we should find fuel there. Men it's been a minor setback but we're still going to get to the airfield today."

The men cheered and some patted Alejandro on the back as they loaded up the truck.

CHAPTER FORTY SEVEN

THE HORDE

Duke and Xavier found the outside area of the Green Mountain facility relatively easy to clear of the infected. The few that were there were easily dispatched with their hatchets, which allowed them to conserve ammo. They searched the dead soldiers outside for more weapons or ammunition but there was nothing of use. The Urals and the burnt out Humvee likewise had nothing to offer.

The buildings on the other hand proved harder to breach. Unlike in the movies, Duke found it impossible to kick down the doors and get inside. They'd decided to start with the smallest building, figuring it would be the easiest to loot. Unfortunately the door was reinforced and the windows were barred which meant they couldn't break them to climb inside.

Duke kicked at the door again, more out of rage than from any hope of getting inside.

"Fuck it! We'll come back to this one, we'll need a crowbar or something to get the door open," he said, pulling his shirt up to wipe his face.

"Fine, then which one next - the big one or the storage shed?"

Duke scrutinized both buildings. The storage shed appeared to be a maintenance building, there might be another ATV in there or even the keys to the one outside. The larger building seemed to be the main focus of the facility. It was two stories with two entrances but the windows had a reflective tint on them so they couldn't see inside.

Xavier took his water canteen and had a drink while Duke deliberated. Watching Xavier made Duke thirsty. He hunted around for his canteen.

"Where'd you put the packs?" he asked.

Xavier didn't stop drinking to answer but pointed up to the radio tower.

"Fuck that, can I have some of yours?" asked Duke.

"Sorry," said Xavier tipping the canteen over to show it was empty.

"Dammit! Won't something go right today?" Then he remembered he still had the can of Mountain Dew in his pocket. He pulled it out and made a big show of it before he pulled the tab. The can made a hissing sound as yellow soda bubbled out from the opening. Duke put his lips to the can's edge and sucked up the soda before it all ran out.

"Ewww hot soda, what does that taste like?" asked Xavier, as he watched Duke greedily gulp down the Mountain Dew.

"Success Frenchy, it tastes like success," replied Duke, having finished off the can in one large pull. He belched loudly and pointed to the largest building.

"That one, that's the one we open next. I have a good feeling about it."

Xavier walked to the doors and tried them, both were locked. He turned to Duke who had grabbed a large rock from the ground and rushed up to the closest tinted window.

"I'm done trying to kick doors down," he said throwing the rock at the window. The rock hit the tempered glass and bounced off it, creating a spider's web effect at the impact point, but didn't break it.

"You've got to be shitting me," said Duke, as he took a larger rock and threw it with much harder force at the cracked glass. The rock smashed through the tempered window, which broke into hundreds of small granular chunks that fell to the ground. The broken window revealed a horde of waiting infected inside who all groaned in unison and started to pour out of the now open window.

The horde climbed all over each other to get out, quickly damming up the windows and stopping any of them from getting through. They groaned and reached out at Duke, trying to get at him.

"Fuck me!" exclaimed Duke, stunned.

Xavier searched around for somewhere to run as the infected pushed against the other windows, causing them to shake. The groans of the infected inside the building had attracted the ones outside the facility who were now all congregating at the gate, pushing hard against it.

"That gate's not going to hold much longer," yelled Xavier.

"Neither are those windows," cried back Duke, as more windows begin to crack from the force that pushed against them.

"Quick, up the tower!" Xavier called out, running towards the radio tower entrance. Duke ran after him and once through the door, looked back and witnessed the front gate collapsing and the windows breaking open. The infected charged in from both sides towards Duke who slammed the door shut and locked it.

"Oh God, what have I done?" murmured Duke.

CHAPTER FORTY EIGHT

NEGOTIATION

Robert looked over the cockpit of the UH-1H helicopter and groaned. The cockpit was a dazzling array of gauges, dials and switches along with two pilot seats - both with flight sticks in the middle. He had no idea what most of the gauges meant, but fortunately, it was an American helicopter and therefore English was written on the dials. He climbed into one of the seats and examined the gauges.

Amongst the gauges he saw the one that read 'Fuel', with the needle pointed at 3000lbs. Robert tapped it a couple of times but the needle stayed in the same position.

"Good, good," he muttered to himself as he looked over the other gauges. Some were inactive - some indicated levels he didn't understand and most of it was just Greek to him. Robert flicked a few of the switches at the head of the console but nothing happened so he flicked them back.

He climbed out of the pilot's seat into the cabin and counted the seats. The helicopter had seating for eight, including the two pilots and two men on the gunners seats. He jumped out of the cabin muttering to himself.

"We're six Survivors but there are eight seats, that will help."

"Help what?" asked Janik.

"I'll explain later. Let's get this into the hangar. I'll stay here and guard for infected. You take Pablo and Joseph and bring back that Heli dolly so we can wheel it out of here."

"So it's working?"

"Tail rotor is out, but it has fuel, so that's a good sign. I want to get it safe and sound inside before I really turn it over, but the rotor is a problem."

"Can you fix it?"

"With help I can, but not out here."

Janik nodded and moved off back towards the hangar.

"God dammit, why isn't anything easy?" Robert muttered to himself. He watched as Janik walked away and met up with Pablo. *I'm now responsible for their lives - all of them, when did that happen?* he asked himself.

Robert took out a spare radio that was in the back of the UAZ and turned it on. He left it on the frequency it was set at and stared at it, gathering up the courage to transmit. He brought it up to the side of his head and spoke into the microphone.

"Shutov! Shutov, do you hear me?" Robert waited for a response, "Shutov! Shutov! Can you hear me?"

The sound of Robert's voice echoed across Stary Sobor from both the radio on Oleg's corpse and the radio Alejandro took from Grigory. Shutov stopped studying the map and he heard his name called out again.

"Shutov! Shutov, this is Robert, can you hear me?"

Shutov turned to Alejandro who was near him with the radio in his pack.

"Your radio - give it to me right now!" Shutov ordered. Alejandro fished through his pack and handed Shutov the radio. "Find the other two dead bodies and take the radios from them too."

Alejandro nodded and rushed over to Oleg's corpse. Shutov signaled to Pavel to come over to him.

"What's the range of these radios?"

"They get around four kilometers, maybe less with the hills around us."

"Do you have any other men around?"

"No, I told you I'm the last of my squad, all the other men are dead. But their radios were in the car."

"Shutov I want to talk with you," the radio broadcast.

Shutov picked up the radio and spoke into it.

"You know Robert, proper radio etiquette is to say 'over' at the end of a transmission. Over," mocked Shutov.

"Take a guess what I'm looking at Shutov?"

"Ah, ah, ah, you didn't say over. Regardless, I'll hazard a guess you're looking at your group of soon to be dead men. Over."

"That's where you are wrong. I'm at the North West Airfield Shutov. I know all about this helicopter here. I'm about to punch my ticket out of here, I just need your help."

The men who were listening in went wild and started talking over each other. Shutov snapped his fingers to silence them. Robert continued through the radio.

"...that's why we're talking. You and I both know what I need. Send Sam to me to get the helicopter operational and we'll negotiate about who goes out first."

Shutov contemplated Robert's offer as everyone looked to Sam. Vuk, who was standing next to him, leaned over to him.

"What makes you so special?"

"Before I worked on the ship I was discharged from the Air force with a specific MOS."

"MOS?"

"Military Occupational Specialty, in my case, helicopters. I guess they think I'm the only one who can fix it."

Shutov studied Sam and Vuk as they spoke.

"And why would I give you my only bargaining chip?"

"Look, the helicopter holds eight but there's only six of us here. If you send Sam and we get it repaired then I'll give up two places so you can have four of your own men fly out."

The ruckus amongst the men commenced as they yelled and screamed to be heard, some at each other, some at Shutov. This time Shutov couldn't quell them for all the finger snapping in the world. He held the radio out to transmit the yelling. "Do you hear that? How can you expect us to choose four men to live while the rest die?"

"It won't be like that. The ones who leave will get help, they'll get someone to come back for the rest."

"Why would we believe that?" asked Shutov.

"Because I'll be one of the two that stays behind. If we work together instead of fighting each other we can survive out here."

Shutov regarded his men. They all pleaded to be one of the ones that went on the helicopter.

"The catch is, you have to stay too. From what I understand, you're Captain of the ship now, therefore you're the last to leave."

Well played, Shutov ruminated, *I can't exactly say now I want to be one of the first group out.*

"I'll need to talk about it with my men before I give you my response."

"Fine, but while you're deliberating we should at least have Sam start repairing the chopper so as to not waste any more time. Tell him to be at the Southern runway at 4pm with a radio in hand. He is to come unarmed and alone. No harm will come to him, you have my word."

"How will he get there by that time? We don't have any transportation now that you shot up our bus."

"He can use Alejandro's motorbike," Robert paused, "didn't think we knew about that, did you? As for the rest of you, we have a Yellow Ural stashed nearby that you can use to get here."

"Do you now?" said Shutov, looking over the Ural in front of him.

"Yes, but I won't give you the location until the helicopter is repaired. We'll speak again at 4pm today. And no tricks, I have the airport locked down and Lucas will be watching with the 50 cal. Sam, alone, unarmed, 4pm."

"Looks like you're holding all the cards."

"No Shutov, you do. You hold all our lives in your hands. I gave you my word, now you give me yours."

"Like I said, I'll talk to my men and get back to you, over and out," and with that Shutov turned off the radio before Robert could reply.

Robert yelled into the radio. "Shutov, Shutov, you son of a bitch." He switched the radio off and returned it to his pack. Janik, Pablo and Joseph had returned with a large helicopter transport dolly that fitted under the skids to move it around whilst on the ground. They had caught most of the conversation.

"You're not really going to go through with it are you?" Janik asked.

"What choice do we have? Without Sam, the helicopter won't be usable for anyone."

"Yes but this is Shutov, we can't trust him."

"Janik, have faith - people are innately decent and good, even Shutov."

"I hope you're right because you're taking a big gamble with our lives telling him where we are."

"I know that Janik, but we're going to minimize that risk as much as we can. First we get this helicopter out of sight, then we'll go through the plan for this afternoon."

CHAPTER FORTY NINE

SACRIFICE

Duke and Xavier were on the first floor balcony of the radio tower looking down at the infected horde below. There were over fifty infected, crawling and banging against the door in an attempt to get at them. The cacophony of groans that rose up from the infected, coupled with the sounds of them pounding on the steel door, created an awful din. Both Duke and Xavier stared back down, numb.

"Maybe when they get inside and can't find us they'll give up," Xavier offered.

"I doubt they'll even get through that door - it's pretty strong. But if they don't, they're not exactly just going to walk away – they will still hang around here."

"What is our food and water situation like?" asked Xavier, walking back inside. Xavier tipped his pack up and Duke copied. They looked over the tins of food, cans of soda and water, along with the few random magazines of ammunition they had found along the way.

"Looks like we have five days' worth - maybe eight if we really stretch it out," said Duke, sorting through the supplies.

"So that's good, in five days a lot of them might have moved on."

"Do you hear that racket out there? We have to do something and we have to do it fast, because that noise will attract every infected for miles around here. In five days' time there might be hundreds down there."

Xavier sorted through the ammunition while Duke searched around for something, anything that might help. He noticed the abseiling gear mounted on the walls and grabbed it, walking outside. Curious, Xavier followed him back out.

Duke walked around to the opposite side from the door and looked down to the ground. There were no infected roaming around there. He tied the rope with its harnesses on to the balcony.

"Good idea, we'll rope down here and bug out while they're all at the front."

"No, it's half a good idea. We can get down fine, but the only way out is through the front gate or the back hole in the wall. Either way, we run the risk of one of them seeing us and bringing down the whole horde on us."

"So what do we do then?"

"Not we, I. You gather up all the food and water into your pack and rope down the back. I'll go down and open the door and make a last stand down there. I could probably take a couple out and still make it back up the ladder."

"That's suicide!" exclaimed Xavier.

"No it's not. That corridor is pretty narrow, so they'll have to come at me one at a time. I'm getting good with the hatchet, I'll make it back to the ladder."

"You're going down with just a hatchet, this is crazy."

"You take the guns and ammo, you take the food and water, and you stay alive. I told you before that I'd keep you alive and that's exactly what I intend to do."

"I won't do it."

"Yes you fucking will, Frenchy!"

"No I fucking won't," said Xavier, grabbing Duke's head with both hands and pulling his face towards his own, "look Duke, you don't need to do this. I forgive you-"

"It's not about that."

"Yes it is. I don't need you to make this sacrifice, you have nothing left to atone for."

"It's not about atonement."

"It better fucking be, because I don't want you suicidal."

Duke and Xavier eyeballed each other. Duke put his own hands behind Xavier's head, both hands were shaking with rage.

"Fuck you, Xavier. You forget about me and you stay alive."

"Not at your expense. You're a good man Duke, you don't have anything to prove."

Duke's eyes welled with held back tears and he sniffed to stop from crying. Xavier just looked into his eyes and nodded.

"We're in this together Duke. We make it out together or we go down together."

Duke glowered back at Xavier and then his face softened, a smile almost forming. He nodded. Satisfied, Xavier let him go and the two men sprang apart.

"So what now then? We both climb down the back?" asked Duke.

"No you were right the first time, it would be suicide. We'll follow your plan. We open the door and we fight them together. If we're smart and a bit lucky we'll take a fair whack of them out before we have to climb up the ladder."

"And while they're inside banging at the ladder we sneak out the back."

"Exactly! The corridor's pretty long, so most of them should be inside. That means we should be able to sneak out without any one of them seeing us."

"Oh we aint sneaking out," said Duke looking over at the ATV, "we're riding out in style."

Duke slowly lowered the second pack down the rope and onto the ground, right next to the first pack. He looked down at them, all that remained of his worldly possessions squeezed into two bags. With both packs safety on the ground, Duke threw the rope over the side where it hit the ground. A nearby infected turned towards the sound, but once he saw there was no movement he returned to roaming the grounds of Green Mountain.

Duke went back inside and climbed down the ladder to find Xavier seated on the floor of the corridor. Xavier examined his revolver, turning it in his hands. He handed it to Duke.

"Here, you take it," he said.

"No, you need a gun."

"We both know you're the better shot. You work both pistols, I'll use the hatchets."

Duke thought it over and nodded, there was no time to argue and it was a solid plan. He handed Xavier his hatchet and double-checked both pistols. Once he was sure they were both locked and loaded, he nodded to Xavier.

Xavier walked down the corridor with Duke behind him.

"So this is it?" Xavier said

"Not bad for a last stand."

"Last stand my ass, you promised you'd get me out of this alive and I'll be fucking holding you to it."

They arrived at the door which had a hoard of infected waiting on the other side. The door shook as they pounded against it. Xavier held on to the handle and Duke stepped back, both guns in his hands and pointed at the door.

"You ready?" he asked Xavier.

"No, but fuck it!" exclaimed Xavier as he opened the door and the infected horde charged in.

CHAPTER FIFTY

NWAF

The roar of the approaching motorbike put everyone on edge, even though they had been expecting it. Lucas had set himself up at the top story of the ATC tower of the airfield, which gave him a 360 degree view of most of the airfield. He had his trusty M107 sniper rifle set up on some boxes he found inside the tower. A radio rested on a box next to the rifle. He watched the hill - from where the sound of the motorbike could be heard - through the sniper rifle scope.

To the right of Lucas there was a firehouse similar to the one he was up on back in Elektro, in what felt like a lifetime ago. This time Alfie took up position inside the tower looking for any sneak attacks from behind. Although he should have been watching to the north, he couldn't help but continue turning back towards the sound of the motorbike, eager to see it clear the hill.

Across the runway at the other side of the airfield Janik was well hidden in the cooling shade of a tree. Behind him there was a southern cluster of buildings that Janik had been watching for any activity. The buildings only had infected roaming around and their movement kept distracting Janik. He also had a radio next to him but, because of the proximity of the infected, its volume was kept very low.

In the hangar Robert, Joseph and Pablo watched the motorbike through a small gap in the hangar doors. Behind them was the helicopter, still on the transport dolly. Along with their spare provisions: food; water; guns; and ammunition, taken from the Russian's UAZ.

The UAZ itself had been abandoned by Alfie in the northern part of the airfield. This ensured that most of the infected were there, still drawn to the sound of the running engine, and therefore away from the Survivors who stayed in the southern part.

The three men all looked through binoculars at the hill on the southern end of the airfield, waiting for the motorcycle to clear it. Being the highest up in the ATC tower, Lucas was the first to see the motorcycle and rider clear the hill. The rider was alone and rode down the hill to the runway.

"I've got eyes on," said Lucas into the radio.

Robert saw the rider come down the other side of the hill. He rode straight towards the runway.

"I see him," Robert replied into his radio.

Janik saw him too and just nodded rather than saying anything across the radio.

The rider slowed down and stopped the motorbike at the runway's edge. He climbed off and removed an axe strapped to his shoulder. Lucas caught the movement.

"Weapon," he called into the radio.

"It's an axe and that's not Sam," said Robert as he looked at Vuk through his binoculars. "Sam you seem to have aged," he said into the radio.

Vuk took the radio off his belt and spoke into it, "And got a lot more handsome too, I hope. Robert, how are you this fine evening?"

"Pissed. You don't seem to be Sam but you do seem to be armed, so Shutov disobeyed me twice."

"Yes, I felt I would be the best one to deliver the bad news. Shutov won't acquiesce to your demands, he won't give up Sam so easily."

In the back of the yellow Ural Shutov and the other men listened to the radio conversation. He smiled at Vuk's response.

"So they sent you?"

"Well, actually, I volunteered. We weren't sure how you'd take the news and the loss of an old man is no real loss at all. I assure you the axe is only for the infected - I mean you no harm."

Robert looked back at the helicopter before turning back to Vuk. "So what is Shutov proposing?" asked Robert into the radio.

Vuk looked around but couldn't see anyone else on the airfield. He felt very exposed out here and knew there was a sniper crosshair on him.

"He still agrees to the terms of your deal - there's just a slight adjustment."

"And that is?"

"He wants a hostage. One of your men is to take my motorbike and return to Stary Sobor. I will take his place and be your hostage. The two hostages will be there to ensure compliance - if his four men make it safely on board the helicopter, then the hostage lives. If you betray him, the hostage dies. The same applies for me."

"Why do I get the feeling he doesn't really care if you live or die?"

"It's in all of our best interests to work together, the hostages just ensure there's no betrayal once the job is done."

"I don't like it," said Robert.

"I agree boss," said Lucas into his radio, "Shutov's up to something."

"If the terms are not amenable then I can leave, but I'd rather we speak face to face." Vuk held the radio up high and shook his head, pointing at it.

"What's he doing?"

"The radio, he doesn't want to talk on the radio."

"Why?" asked Pablo.

"Of course," said Robert to himself, "there's more than one." He turned to Pablo, "Shutov's listening in, that's why."

"It could be a trap," offered Pablo.

"It's possible," he said to Pablo before speaking into the radio, "Vuk raise your shirt and turn around." Vuk complied and Robert watched him through the binoculars.

"Fine, now drop the axe and take off your pack. Leave both on top of the bike," ordered Robert through the radio.

Vuk did so and left the axe and his pack on the ground.

"Lucas, what's the perimeter like?" asked Robert.

Lucas scanned the airfield slowly with his binoculars. Apart from the infected at the northern end crowding the abandoned UAZ, it appeared clear. He picked up the radio and spoke into it.

"Looks clear boss," answered Lucas.

"I said I was alone," said Vuk.

"I'm sorry if your word doesn't carry any weight Vuk," replied Robert, as he stepped out of the hangar. "Can you see me? Look around but only say yes or no, don't give any position information away or Lucas will kill you."

Vuk scanned the airfield slowly and saw Robert standing in front of the hangar, "Yes."

"Good. Turn off the radio and leave it on your pack. Walk straight towards me, slowly with your hands up. Remember, Lucas has you in his sights."

"Understood," said Vuk, and he turned off the radio. He left it on the pack and walked towards Robert with his hands raised high up in the air.

The yellow Ural stopped and Alejandro banged hard on the back of the cab.

"We're here," he called out. The men all jumped out of the Ural and checked their weapons. They were on an indiscriminate dirt road near a forest.

"Does everyone know what to do?" asked Shutov.

The men all nodded.

Alejandro handed the Ural keys to The Butcher and looked around for a rock.

"Everyone check your watches – Butcher, Alejandro, it's all on you. We need 15 minutes to get into position then you know what to do."

The Butcher nodded. He jumped into the driver's seat and Alejandro climbed into the back of the Ural. He smacked the back of the cabin to indicate he was in, and The Butcher drove off down the road.

Harrison checked his watch before he peeled off to the right and into the forest. Sam handed Shutov a roll of duct tape and an AK-74. Shutov took both and walked to Pavel, handing him the AK-74.

"Hold that and don't try anything funny, it's not loaded."

Pavel held on to the gun and Shutov used the duct tape to stick it to his hands. The tape ensured that Pavel couldn't drop the rifle.

"What are you planning?"

"All in good time," Shutov said, as he pushed him forward, "now, into the forest."

"That's far enough," yelled Robert, and Vuk stopped ten feet away from him. "You see the three of us, yes? You see the guns pointed at you?" Vuk nodded. "Good. We don't want to kill you so don't give us a reason to, fair nuf?"

"That's fair," Vuk replied.

"Now what was so important that you couldn't say over the radio?"

"Shutov is listening. He plans to attack you tonight."

"What!" Pablo said.

"He's coming to the airport, they already have the yellow Ural and they're on their way here.

"Why are you telling us this?" probed Robert.

"Like you, I'm sick of the fighting. When I heard Shutov planned to betray you, I volunteered to be the one that would deliver the message, to at least to give you some warning."

"Why should we believe you?" said Joseph.

Vuk sighed, "I'm an old man who buried an old friend last night. I have no time left for lies and schemes."

"Yuri?" Robert asked.

"Yes, Yuri. I don't want to lose any more friends, and we were all friends once. There's no reason for us to be fighting each other."

"I agree."

"But Shutov doesn't, he sees the world as polar. Us and them. He wants the helicopter and he'll kill you all to have it."

"But I offered him four places."

"You slapped him in the face when you said he couldn't be part of the first group. Shutov would never stay behind, so now, in his mind, he has to take the chopper. You showed weakness Robert. You gave him too much information. He knows you're only six, he knows where you are, and he's on his way here to kill you all and claim the helicopter. End the violence, leave the helicopter for him and just go."

Robert looked around the warehouse and back at Vuk, mulling it over.

"They're taking the long way around to sneak in from the north under cover of darkness. You have time to get out with your men unscathed. Don't fight him, it will only lead to more death."

"I can't just let him win."

"It's not a game, these are people's lives you are toying with."

"So is Shutov," accused Robert.

"Yes, but he doesn't care. I'm hoping you do."

Robert let Vuk's words sink in.

"He's coming from the north you say?"

"Yes, under the cover of darkness. You still have time."

"Good," he turned to Joseph, "go and tell Lucas to watch the north for the Bandits. Tell him to stay off the radio unless it's an emergency. Same for Alfie in the fire station. Then run across to Janik and let him know."

Joseph ran out and across the runway towards the ATC tower.

"So you're not leaving?"

"I can't. I won't let him prevail through inaction."

298

"Then you've doomed us all."

"No, Shutov did, when he wouldn't cooperate."

"And it won't be over until one of you is dead," muttered Vuk.

"Then I hope for all our sakes it's Shutov."

Janik was watching the runway when he heard the branch snap behind him, immediately putting him on edge. Knowing that the infected were nearby, he slowly turned to see what was moving and was surprised to find Harrison creeping behind him. Harrison was so focused on the infected in the buildings he hadn't spotted Janik who silently pulled himself into the cover of the tree.

Janik scrutinized Harrison as he sneaked along the tree line that ran parallel to the dirt road. Janik watched him and had to make a choice - should he follow Harrison or stay where he was?

Harrison crossed the dirt road and headed towards the hill, circling around to the hangars. Janik looked around and listened, there was no one else nearby. He contemplated speaking on the radio but guessed it was not safe. *What's he up to?* Janik deliberated as Harrison continued over the hill and almost out of Janik's sight. Janik decided it was prudent not to lose sight of him and began to stealthily chase after him, sticking to the same tree line.

Lucas watched as Joseph ran across from the hangar towards him. He looked down the scope but Joseph wasn't being chased by anyone and no one else has come out of the hangar. Satisfied that nothing was amiss, he continued to scan the surrounds looking for any signs of the Bandits.

As he looked towards the south-west, at first he couldn't believe his eyes. Coming at him from the tree line was the yellow Ural, driving straight towards him. He grabbed the radio and shouted into it, "I have a contact southwest, it's our Ural."

"Who's driving it?" asked Robert across the radio.

Lucas looked down the sniper scope to the truck but didn't see anyone inside the cabin, "I can't see anyone in the front."

"Say again," Robert demanded.

"There's no one driving it but it's coming straight towards me.

"Disable it."

"Will do," Lucas said, and he dropped the radio.

Inside the cabin of the Ural, a large rock held down the accelerator while a rope was tied to the steering wheel to keep it on course. In the back, hidden by the canvas, The Butcher and Alejandro held on tight, bracing for the impact.

Lucas lined up the engine compartment at the base of the cabin through the M107 scope. Once he was certain of the shot, he held his breath and fired. The bullet split open a large hole at the front of the Ural, the metal having torn away like shredded paper. Smoke poured out from the engine and it was suddenly silent. Unfortunately for Lucas the Ural had built up too much momentum and was still charging towards him.

Lucas realized it was about to hit the ATC tower and braced for the impact. The runaway truck rammed in to the bricks on the side of the ATC tower, the thunderous crash reverberated around the airfield. Although prepared for the impact, Lucas was still jolted off his feet.

As soon as the Ural hit the wall, The Butcher and Alejandro climbed out of the back of the truck. They shook off the dizziness and squeezed in close to the ATC tower wall so as to not be spotted by Lucas. The Butcher still carried Grace, his beloved AKM, while Alejandro had traded up to Yuri's M249 SAW.

Lucas looked over the side but most of his vision of the Ural was obscured by the steam from the busted radiator and kicked-up dust and debris from the impact.

The Butcher indicated that he would climb up and motioned for Alejandro to go right. Alejandro nodded and circled around the building as The Butcher climbed up the ladder.

Alfie watched the ATC tower from the fire station but the Ural had hit the far side so he hadn't seen either man climb out. He scanned around the airfield but all he could see was Joseph, stopped at the runway, also entranced by the Ural crash.

Alfie turned back to Lucas, who was looking over the side of the building, and watching him yell into the radio. Without a radio of his own, Alfie couldn't hear what was being said. He was about to return to watching the north when he saw Alejandro sneaking around the side of the building.

Alejandro crept towards the ATC tower's main entrance at the front, holding out the M249 SAW in front of him. *That's Yuri's SAW,* Alfie thought, looking the gun over, *Alejandro was the one who killed Yuri.* Alfie looked around for help but Lucas was too focused on the Ural while Joseph was on the opposite side and couldn't see Alejandro. Alfie was stuck, he couldn't yell out without giving away his position but he couldn't let Alejandro get inside the ATC tower.

He lined up Alejandro in the iron sight of the Lee Enfield. Alejandro was so focused on the entrance he hadn't seen Alfie. This was his chance - he could do it - kill the man who murder Yuri. Alfie shook his head, he couldn't just kill him, it wasn't right. He lined the rifle up further away and fired. The bricks near Alejandro chipped and cracked where the bullet impacted, not far from his head.

The shot drew everyone's attention. Joseph circled around from the runway towards the firehouse, his Winchester 1866 shotgun raised and pointed where Alfie had fired. Lucas left the sniper rifle on the roof and took out an M1911. He crept over to the other side where he could see Alejandro.

Alfie called out from the roof of the fire station.

"Drop the gun. I won't give you another chance."

Alejandro looked up and studied Alfie. He was high up with a rifle pointed straight at him. Alejandro realized he was trapped and tried to talk his way out of it.

"Alfie it's me. Al, come on, you're a good guy, you showed that by not killing me. That will count for something with Shutov."

"Look, I don't want to do it but I will - now lower the gun."

"I'll lower it but you got to promise me I'll be okay," implored Alejandro.

"Look, stop fucking around and just drop the gun," yelled back Alfie.

"You wouldn't kill an unarmed man."

Lucas was so focused on the conversation occurring below he didn't notice The Butcher climbing up the ladder behind him. The Butcher slowly climbed and looked up, seeing Lucas with his back facing him. The Butcher smiled as he continued up, withdrew his pistol from a holster and pointed it at Lucas. He walked slowly towards him, the pistol pointed straight at Lucas' head.

Lucas sensed the presence behind him and began to turn his head. "Drop the gun," a voice very close behind him whispered. Lucas' stomach turned to stone as he lowered the gun.

"I'm lowering it, see," Alejandro's voice came from below the ATC tower.

"Good, now turn around slowly," The Butcher ordered Lucas.

Lucas turned to see The Butcher's face smiling at him, the pistol pointed at his head filling his vision.

"Look into my eyes Lucas," The Butcher commanded.

Lucas looked away from the gun to The Butcher. His eyes were bloodshot but cold and black, with no life behind them. The Butcher licked his lips and smiled, his eyes suddenly came to life, before he pulled the trigger and shot Lucas - dead.

Alfie turned immediately to the roof at the sound of shooting, momentarily forgetting about Alejandro. Alejandro, who was waiting for the distraction, seized the opportunity. He raised his M249 SAW at Alfie and pulled the trigger - a torrent of bullets flew at Alfie. Realizing his mistake Alfie returned focus to the ground in time to see the bullets rip through his body. The multiple impacts pushed him back and he fell off the other side of the small roof and hit the ground hard.

Alejandro was so fixated on Alfie, he hadn't noticed that Joseph had circled around until after he had shot at Alfie. Joseph had the shotgun pointed right at him. Realizing the same trick wouldn't work twice, Alejandro showed no hesitation in dropping the M249 SAW, and stepped back from it. He raised his hands and held them up in the air.

Joseph kept the shotgun trained on him as he approached, "Why? Why would you do it?" Alejandro just stared back, not knowing what he could say that would keep him alive.

On the rooftop The Butcher couldn't see Alejandro but he could see Joseph - he had his pistol trained right on him. He had Joseph lined up for a kill shot, but his morbid curiosity kept him from pulling the trigger. *Will he do it?* The Butcher wondered.

"Is it in your nature to destroy?" Joseph asked, but Alejandro remained silent. "You know, Alfie was a good guy, he wouldn't have shot you if you were unarmed." Alejandro nodded at that statement, acknowledging it. "Unfortunately for you, I'm not Alfie."

"Nooo!" Alejandro called out as Joseph squeezed the trigger. Alejandro's chest popped with what felt like a thousand burning pock marks as the shotgun pellets hit him. Each hole felt like it had Tabasco poured through it and he cried out in pain before falling back, dead.

"Feels good, doesn't it?" The Butcher called out from the roof. Joseph gazed up and The Butcher fired, hitting him in the head. Blood poured out from the bullet hole. Joseph coughed before dying, falling forward onto concrete. The back of his head was unscathed as there was no exit wound, but the concrete around the front reddened as blood seeped out.

The Butcher turned back to the roof and picked up Lucas's radio. "Butcher here. Lucas, Alfie and Joseph are all neutralized. I have the sniper rifle so you're safe to come out," he said into the radio.

"Good work Butcher," Shutov replied, "You hear that Robert? You've lost three men already and your overwatch is gone. It's only a matter of time."

"Fuck you Shutov," Robert's voice raged over the radio.

"Very eloquent," mocked Shutov.

Robert put the radio down and returned to pointing his gun at Vuk. Pablo had his MP5 pointed at Vuk as well.

"You lied to me Vuk, you said we had time."

"That's what they told me."

"Three of my men are dead because of your lies," growled Robert.

"It wasn't a lie. I told you what I knew."

"Then why are they here now?"

"I don't know. Shutov told me what the plan was before I rode off. If he changed it afterwards I wasn't made aware of that."

"That's very convenient."

"No it's not. It would have been more convenient if he had followed the plan, then they might have still been alive."

"What do we do now?" Pablo asked.

"Keep an eye outside, especially at the ATC tower. We know that at least The Butcher is there."

Shutov, Sam and Pavel were at the other end of the runway hidden in the trees. Shutov and Sam were both scanning the airfield with binoculars while Pavel stayed low, the AK-74 still taped to his hands.

"Can you see anything?" asked Shutov.

"Just the Butcher at the tower. There are so many buildings they could be hiding in, it will take ages to clear them out."

"Do you see the helicopter?"

Sam searched the airfield, "No."

"Exactly, which means it's in one of the hangars. That's where the three of them will also be."

"But which one, there are still so many."

Shutov slapped Pavel on the back, "that's where you come in Pavel. You're going to run out there and find them for us."

Pavel was shocked, "Just run around the airfield with a gun in my hands. That's suicide."

Shutov held the CZ550 to Pavel's head, "No, that's a chance to live. If you don't run, you'll definitely be dead."

Pavel nodded. "Good boy, one more thing though," said Shutov as he pulled off some tape and put it over Pavel's mouth. "We wouldn't want you to call out our location now would we."

Sam laughed as he put a black balaclava over Pavel's head. From underneath the balaclava Pavel groaned and shouted but the tape muffled the sounds.

"Now, go find us some Survivors," said Shutov, pushing him towards the hangars. At first Pavel stood there looking around, completely exposed. Sam fired a couple of rounds from his PDW at Pavel's feet - that got Pavel moving and he ran across the runway towards the hangars.

Shutov picked up the radio and transmitted, "Men we are coming across the runway, we'll flush out these rats."

Harrison watched from his vantage point up on the hill. He was the closest to Pavel and the hangars, and laughed as Pavel zigzagged across the runway. *Oh that's funny shit,*

Harrison thought as he watched Pavel.

Further back behind him Janik was not amused but confused about the move. *Why would Shutov dodge sniper fire when he knows Lucas is down? And why would he run out in the open like that?* He alternated between watching Pavel and Harrison trying to figure out what the plan was.

Pablo looked out the gap between the hangar's doors to find Pavel running towards them. "I see him," he told Robert. Robert moved over to the door, ensuring his gun was still trained on Vuk, and looked out. "That doesn't look like Shutov," he replied.

"Who then?"

"I don't recognize him," he called Vuk over, "Vuk come here. Tell me who that is."

Vuk walked tentatively to the door and looked out. He recognized Pavel's uniform, even with the balaclava covering his face.

"I think that's Pavel." Vuk answered.

"Who?" asked Robert.

"One of the Russian military guys."

Pablo was wary and trained his gun on Pavel, who ran erratically. "I don't like this Robert," Pablo yelped.

"Is he a threat?" Robert asked Vuk.

"He was their prisoner last night, maybe he escaped."

"It's pretty crazy just running across the runway like that," Pablo offered.

"I agree, it doesn't feel right."

They watched as Pavel got closer to them. "What should we do?"

"Let's hold our fire, get him to disarm. Then find out what's going on"

Pablo called out from the hangar doors, "You, in the ski mask, drop the weapon."

Pavel turned towards the voice and shook his head. He changed direction and started running towards the hangar.

"I said drop the weapon!" Pablo shouted even louder.

Pavel held his hands up to try and show that they were taped. To Pablo and Robert it looked like an aggressive gesture.

"Why won't he drop the gun?" asked Robert pointing his own M4A1 at Pavel. Pablo stepped out of the doors and held the MP5, pointed straight at Pavel.

"This is your last chance - drop the fucking gun!"

From his vantage point up on the hill Harrison saw Pablo step out of the hangar. "Got you, sucker," he mocked, as he looked down the sight of his AKS Kobra. He started firing at Pablo, the shots landing close but missing him.

"Fucker's shooting at me," Pablo called out, having assumed the bullets were coming from Pavel. He sturdied the MP5 and started shooting, the submachine gun bullets hit Pavel in a diagonal line from the left hip to the right shoulder.

"He's down," Robert called out, and Pavel tumbled to the ground.

"Why didn't he just drop the gun?" Pablo asked watching the body to make sure it didn't move. More bullets struck at the doorway near Pablo and he pulled back confused.

"What the fuck? Where are those coming from?"

"Close the damn door," Robert called out.

Sam and Shutov watched from across the runway as Harrison shot at the hangar. "Plan worked beautifully sir, they're in the last hangar."

"I love it when I'm right," replied Shutov, as they both began to walk towards the hangar that the remaining Survivors were holed up in.

Janik watched as Harrison fired at the closing hangar door. The noise from the gun masked the sounds of Janik creeping up to him, crossbow out, pointed directly at Harrison's head.

"Stop shooting," Janik commanded, standing directly behind Harrison.

Harrison stopped shooting and slowly turned around.

"Shorty, we didn't finish our conversation last time."

"Put the AK down and step back from it."

"You won't shoot me," taunted Harrison, "you don't have the stomach for it."

Harrison and Janik eyeballed each other. Janik stared him down, refusing to look away. Harrison decided to try his luck and raised the AKS. Janik caught the slight movement and instinctively pulled the trigger on the crossbow, sending a bolt directly through the bridge of Harrison's nose and into his skull. Harrison collapsed, instantly dying.

"I didn't used to," Janik replied to the taunt, as he watched the hangar doors close. He looked around and dropped down. On the runway one hundred meters in front of him were Shutov and Sam, walking towards the hangar. Fortunately they paid him no mind, instead they were focused on the hangar door as they approached, Shutov talking into the radio.

Inside the hangar the three men listened to Shutov's taunts come across the radio. "Robert, Robert, you may have got one of mine but there's still many more of us left and we know where you are now."

Pablo turned to Robert, frightened. Robert looked back at him, his eyes raging like that of a caged animal.

"If you give yourself up now I'll guarantee you a quick and painless death," Robert shook his head, "but if you make me come in there after you then I'll feed you to the infected myself. Doc told me you'd already been bit."

Vuk and Pablo turned and looked at Robert's arm. Pablo's eyes shot daggers of accusations at him. "It's bullshit, I got scratched by an infected but I'm past the incubation period, there's nothing to worry about."

"You mean you're one of them?" shouted Pablo, as he pointed his MP5 at Robert.

"No Pablo. Look at me, do I look like one of them?" Pablo shook his head. "Be rational, he's just trying to turn us against each other."

Pablo considered this. As he thought it over Robert snatched the radio up, "Don't forget I have your man Vuk, if you try to come in he'll be the first one I shoot."

"Go ahead," scoffed Shutov, "he served his purpose."

"Son of a bitch!" uttered Vuk.

Robert looked around for something else. Then he remembered the weapons cache from the UAZ.

"You might not care about Vuk but I also have your precious helicopter in here too."

Dammit he's right, Shutov thought as he spoke into the radio, "destroy that and you destroy your only way out of here."

"According to you, I'm already a dead man. Why should I care about the chopper?" replied Robert.

Shutov admonished himself for being too quick to speak. "Perhaps we can negotiate." Shutov said into the radio as The Butcher stepped in beside him. The Butcher had the M107 on his shoulder but still wielded the AKM.

"I'm through negotiating with you Shutov. You don't play by the rules so neither will I. If you come in here I'll destroy the helicopter and all your dreams of escape."

Robert put down the radio but Shutov's voice could still be heard insistently calling out his name. "What are you thinking?" asked Pablo.

"Get me that satchel charge the Russians had. I'm going to buy us some time."

Robert kept his gun trained on Vuk as Pablo went towards the pile of weapons at the rear of the hangar.

"I'd like a gun," Vuk said calmly.

"You've got to be kidding me," replied Robert.

"You heard him, I'm nothing to him. But with a gun I can be something to you."

"Not my problem."

"You need to trust me. I don't know why they changed the plan, I didn't betray you and I want to live. If you want the same then give me a gun so you can stop pointing yours at me and start pointing it at the real bad guys."

Robert looked over to Pablo who shrugged, "You're the boss, that means you make the hard decisions," Pablo decreed.

"You'll have to take my word Robert, as a man of honor. If you give me a gun I will help you, I will not betray you."

Robert looked Vuk over, who stood proud looking into Robert's eyes.

"I believe you," he turned to yell to Pablo. "Get him a gun. An assault rifle would be good."

"You sure boss?" asked Pablo.

Robert gazed over at Vuk who held his fist across his heart. "Yes," he replied.

Janik watched as Shutov, Sam and The Butcher conferenced fifty meters from the hangar entrance. They used the shell of a burnt-out tank as cover from the hangar doors. Janik kept low, hoping that the trees and the grass kept him obscured from the three remaining Bandits. Between him and the Bandits was Vuk's motorcycle, still lying on its side with the pack and axe on top of it. *If things go bad at least I'll have a fast way out of here,* Janik couldn't stop the thought as it popped into his brain.

"Where's Alejandro?" asked Shutov.

"They took him out," replied The Butcher.

"Why didn't you say anything on the radio?"

"I didn't think you'd want them to know our numbers. What about Harrison?"

"He was up on the hill shooting into the hangar," replied Sam. They all looked up the hill towards Janik, who was lying low. None of the three men spotted him.

"Is he gone?" demanded Shutov.

"Either they got him or he ran away," answered Sam.

"So we're three now?"

"And they're four inside there?" tendered The Butcher.

"Look that's seven, we can all fit in the helicopter now, there's no need for this," pleaded Sam.

"We have to kill them all," snarled The Butcher.

"That's madness-"

"No he's right," interrupted Shutov, "it's too late for them now. But how do we get inside?"

The Butcher took off the M107 and pointed it at the door.

"I've seen this shoot through brick walls. It will tear through that steel like it was tissue paper."

"And possibly hit my helicopter you stupid fool," said Shutov, pushing the gun down to stop it being pointed at the hangar.

"Don't call me a fool. I've killed two men today, how many have you killed?"

"The day is still young Butcher," replied Shutov, "and you migh-" Shutov was cut off by the sounds of shooting from inside the hangar. The three men instinctively ducked down but the bullets weren't aimed at them.

They all peered over the tank hulk towards the hangar door as the shooting stopped. Suddenly Vuk's voice came over the radio, "Shutov it's Vuk. I've taken them down."

Janik listened in on his own radio. *Bastard,* he thought.

"Who?" asked Shutov.

"Robert and Pablo, they're both dead."

"And Janik, the little one?"

"Unaccounted for, but he wasn't in here. I'm opening the door, hold your fire."

"Understood."

The hangar doors opened slightly, enough for a man to walk through. Vuk stepped out and signaled for them to come over. Sam and Shutov rose but as The Butcher tried to get up Shutov placed a hand sternly on his shoulder, holding him back.

"You stay here, keep an eye out for the pipsqueak."

The Butcher didn't say anything but eyeballed them as

Shutov and Sam walked towards the hangar. They kept their guns up, trained on the entrance.

Vuk watched them approaching and didn't see The Butcher still crouched behind the tank. When Shutov and Sam were within speaking distance, Vuk called out as he looked around the airfield for the other Bandits.

"Where are the others?" he asked Shutov.

"They're all dead. It hasn't been a good day. Except for you of course – looks like you had a very good day. No hard feelings about what was said before."

"You said what was necessary to remove the leverage," replied Vuk.

"It's good that you're a smart man Vuk, now show me the corpse of Robert. I feel an overriding urge to piss on it."

Vuk pointed to the end of the helicopter where two bodies lay face down. Their guns were pushed away from their hands and there was blood on the smooth concrete of the hangar.

"Watch your fire," said Vuk, "They were planting explosives on the helicopter. Robert was going to blow it up rather than let you have it." Vuk pointed to a trigger device in Robert's dead hand. "See that switch in his hand, that sets it off. I don't know if he got the charge primed before I killed him."

"Ballsy move," said Shutov as he approached the bodies, his gun down by his side. Sam was beside him, having holstered his own PDW.

"Thanks," said Robert as he and Pablo sprung up pointing their hidden pistols at Shutov and Sam.

Shutov turned and saw that Vuk had also pointed his rifle at them. Realizing he was outnumbered he put his gun down and Sam followed suit.

"Good, now maybe now we can have a civil conversation," said Robert.

"There never was a bomb was there?" asked Shutov.

"That's where you're wrong, the helicopter is rigged to

blow. If you try anything funny, we all die," answered Vuk.

"You bastard Vuk!" yelled Shutov in a rage. "You fucking bastard. You betrayed your own brothers. I was right not to trust you," he screamed, his face red, spit flying from his mouth as he yelled the words.

Outside the Butcher heard the shouting and examined Vuk through the doorway. Vuk had his gun up and pointed at an unseen assailant. "After all we've been through Vuk," Shutov's voice yelled from inside the hangar.

"You were the one who betrayed me, you betrayed all of us. You've only ever thought of yourself and look where it's gotten you. We could have worked together but no, you had to be the boss. All of this is on you," Vuk yelled back, so worked up in his tirade he didn't notice The Butcher creep up on him.

Janik observed the Butcher as he crept closer to the hangar but he was too far to hear the conversation. Unaware of the betrayal, he stayed hidden and watched.

All too late Vuk sensed the movement on the runway and turned his head slightly to see The Butcher pointing the AKM at him.

"You remember Grace don't you Vuk?" The Butcher asked.

Vuk nodded, "Never did like that bitch."

"Look at me Vuk," The Butcher ordered.

"Fuck you, you psycho," said Vuk closing his eyes.

Robert and Pablo couldn't see outside the door to whomever Vuk was talking.

"Vuk, what's happening?" Robert asked.

The sound of the AKM firing echoed around the large hangar as the bullets hit Vuk and he collapsed down, dead. Robert and Pablo ducked behind the helicopter and Shutov used the moment to snatch up the PDW and hold it to Sam's head, using him as a human shield.

"What the hell?" asked Sam.

"Shut up," yelled back Shutov, "Butcher is that you?"

"Yeah!" said The Butcher, victorious.

"Robert, your kindness will be your undoing. Now drop your guns and the trigger device or I'll kill Sam and no one flies out of here."

"You wouldn't dare."

"No, unlike you Robert, I would."

Robert looked through the glass screen of the UH-1H chopper at Shutov. He held onto Sam tightly, keeping most of his body behind Sam's. It was impossible to get a shot without hitting Sam.

From behind Shutov The Butcher stepped into the doorway, surveying the scene. He gazed at Shutov as he held the gun to Sam's head.

"You know as well as I do Robert you won't kill yourself, not while there's a chance. Now if you drop your guns and the trigger device, I'll give you that chance."

Robert turned to Pablo looking for help.

"You do it and we're both dead," Pablo whispered.

"I know," Robert whispered back.

He peeked through the glass at Shutov and The Butcher, looking for a way out. The Butcher turned his gun from pointing to Robert to pointing it at Shutov and licked his lips, a wet smile followed his tongue.

"Nooooo!" Robert yelled, and Shutov turned to face The Butcher as he fired on him.

The bullets went through Shutov's side, puncturing his kidneys and severing his spine. As he continued to turn, the bullets perforated Sam's chest, one of them pierced Sam and drove deep into Shutov's stomach.

"Who's the fool now?" The Butcher called out, "I just got me a score of four."

From the hilltop Janik heard Robert's voice yell out. *They're alive,* his mind rejoiced. Janik looked at The Butcher standing at the entranceway of the hangar, firing in. Without any thought for his own safety Janik ran towards The Butcher, Harrison's AKS Kobra in his hand. He was about to run past the motorbike when he got a better idea and lifted it up.

"What the hell Butcher! He was our only ticket out of here," screamed Robert, confounded.

"Who says I want to leave?" hollered The Butcher as he fired at them, "I'm having too much fun to leave all this behind."

Robert dropped the trigger device and used both hands to blind fire his M4A1 over the helicopter and at The Butcher. Pablo joined in and they both shot at him, forcing him to take cover behind the hangar doors.

Janik saw The Butcher step back outside and fire into the hangar as he rode the motorbike towards him. One hand was on the bike trying to keep it straight, the other was holding the AKS, which he started firing. The bullets went wild and Janik roared as he rode straight towards the Butcher.

At the sound of the motorcycle and shooting The Butcher turned to see a demon on a motorbike riding towards him. For the first time, he was afraid. He fired towards the bike but the combination of his fear and Janik's erratic riding prevented any bullets from hitting him.

Janik lept off the bike, shooting and presenting an easy target for The Butcher to hit. He unloaded into Janik but the magazine was nearly empty so only the final two bullets hit him before it fired dry.

Janik landed on top the Butcher and with his last ounce of strength, took a crossbow bolt from his quiver and jammed it into his eye socket. The Butcher pushed Janik off him and spun uncontrollably with both hands trying to remove the crossbow bolt.

He staggered inside the hangar and straight towards Robert who had a bead on him. Robert didn't hesitate and shot The Butcher, putting him out of his misery.

The sound of the motorcycle still whined as Pablo and

Robert kept their guns trained on the door. They saw Janik crawling in and rushed over to him.

Shutov opened his eyes and saw Robert and Pablo rush past him. He scanned the room and discovered that the trigger device was close. Painfully, he turned over onto his stomach and crawled towards it.

"Janik! Janik! Are you okay?"
Robert gently turned him over and surveyed the damage - it was clear Janik was a goner.
"Did I get him?" Janik asked.
"Yeah man you saved us both." Pablo responded.
"You're a hero Janik," said Robert.
Janik smiled. "Hero, who would have thought?" he whispered and with the smile still on his face, he died.

Shutov continued to crawl towards the trigger on the ground. His legs were numb but he pulled himself forward out of blind hatred - closer and closer to the trigger.

Robert reached out and closed Janik's eyes.
"Thank you," he said before turning to Pablo. "Check The Butcher, make sure he's dead."
Pablo moved over to the Butcher, his MP5 still pointed straight at him.

Almost, almost, Shutov drove himself forward, blocking out the pain.

Pablo poked The Butcher's side with his shoe, there was no response. "He's dead," Pablo called out to Robert.

Shutov's hand reached out and grabbed the trigger device. Robert rose up from Janik's body and turned to see Shutov facing him, the trigger device clutched between both bloody hands.
"Shutov, don't do it."

"Death is the greatest of all human blessings," said Shutov, as he pressed down on the trigger.

The fireball that erupted from the satchel charge under the helicopter consumed everything within the hangar in microseconds. The hangar walls imploded and the roof collapsed on top of them. The blood and matter of all the dead men ran together, forming a macabre river that poured out from under the rubble.

EPILOGUE

WEEKS LATER

The ATV rode through the silence of the airfield that had now been given back to the infected. The occupants took note of the dead body on the runway and the collapsed hangar as they rode on.

The infected charged towards this new and very noisy distraction as the ATV zoomed across the runway. The second occupant tapped the Driver's shoulder and pointed to the ATC tower. The Driver nodded and changed direction towards it.

As the ATV got closer it slowed down and the rear passenger lept off. It was Xavier, with a much more pronounced beard and confidence in his step. He raised his M4A1 CCO and started taking down the infected.

Duke turned off the ATV and hopped off, assisting Xavier with infected management. They worked in a well-coordinated fashion, as they moved back into the ATC tower. With the nearby infected taken care of, Xavier rushed in and Duke followed him, shutting the door behind them.

Xavier took out a crowbar from his pack and jammed it between the double doors, holding them shut. From the other side of the doors, the infected pounded and groaned.

"Five minutes tops," Duke said as they pointed the weapons ahead of them and climbed the stairs.

They checked the corners of the second story of the ATC tower. It was clear.

"Clear," Xavier called.

"Clear," Duke echoed, and pointed to the roof.

They both stepped outside and Duke climbed up the ladder to the roof of the ATC tower. Xavier covered him with his gun as Duke peered over the edge to the roof.

"Oh fuck!" Duke said looking over the roof.

"What is it?"

"Dead guy, been here a while. Come up, he has some good shit."

Xavier climbed up the ladder and looked down at the dead body of Lucas. The body had been exposed to the elements and animals and was in bad shape.

"Fuck me that's Lucas!" Xavier exclaimed.

Duke looked closer at the body and recognized Lucas. He noticed the gunshot wound to the head and pointed it out to Xavier, "Shot in the back of the head."

Xavier nodded and looked around. He pointed over to the collapsed hangar.

"Think that's got something to do with this?" he asked Duke.

"Dunno, but there's another two bodies," he pointed down to Alejandro and Joseph's bodies. Like Lucas' body, they had been attacked by the ravages of time and animals, and were in even worse shape.

"One of them could be Alejandro, can't tell the other one."

"Jesus what happened over here?" asked Xavier.

"Greed Xavier, the earth provides enough to satisfy every man's needs, but not every man's greed."

"Amen, brother" said Xavier.

The End.

319

SPECIAL EDITION CONTENT

THE YOUTUBE INTERVIEWS TRANSCRIPTS

INTRODUCTION

These interviews are some of the many that are on my YouTube Channel http://www.youtube.com/ChernoJourno. I chose these particular interviews because of the way they spoke to me - which doesn't mean that the others weren't interesting or worthy. The usual limitations of both time and space meant that I couldn't put every interview into the book.

At the end of each interview I have incorporated **Cherno's Final Thoughts.** Where - just like Jerry Springer - I wax lyrical about the interview and what it meant to me. Fortunately, unlike Jerry, I haven't had to contend with violence during my interviews – except for that one time that Mandalore saved my life.

INTERVIEW WITH NFK
ABOUT HIS FIRST MURDER

This was my first interview with a player as the Cherno
Journo. I had previously travelled the coast chatting, playing
with friends/randoms and gathering stories. NFK was my
first formal interview with a player I hadn't met previously.
NFK chose the top of Zub Castle to meet and was very wary
that he could be walking into a trap.

Cherno Journo
(Lowering his the gun)
It is the free press, I am the Cherno Journo.
(enters Zub Castle tower)

NFK
I hear you, come on up.

Cherno Journo
Okay. Do not shoot. I am the press.

NFK
Can you hear me?

Cherno Journo
Yeah I hear you fine mate, coming up.

Cherno Journo arrived at the top of the tower to find NFK
there with an AKM pointed at him.

322

Cherno Journo

What do you want me to do with this gun? I can drop it in this loot pile there if it makes you feel better.

NFK

Just take the other corner that I'm pointing at and keep your gun trained at the stairs in case somebody else shows up.

Cherno Journo

You want me to raise it then? *(pause)* It's lowered.

NFK

At the stairs in case somebody else pops up.

Cherno Journo

Yep but do you want me to raise my gun? I'd need to raise it for that.

NFK

Yep that's fine so long as it's at the stairs.

Cherno Journo

Yeah, yeah, no probs.

Cherno Journo raises his gun and points it at the stairs. There's a pause as they both watch the stairs.

Cherno Journo

Okay, well you tell me when you feel safe and I'll start the interview. *(looks around)* I can sweep the hills for heat signatures.

NFK

Oh that's right you got the L85. That's space age stuff.
(Cherno Journo sweeps the hills)
Yeah I did a little patrol before you got here and I didn't see much of anything.

Cherno Journo
Well it's a nice location but I don't really want to do the interview so far away because I'd like to do a two shot as I record it. But again this is... to make you feel safe I can do it from here.

NFK
What, do you have an alternate location or something?

Cherno Journo
No I just mean I wouldn't mind getting a little closer so we're not so wide apart for the actual interview stage.
(no response from NFK)
I understand the paranoia so...

NFK
Yeah you can come closer that's fine just don't point the gun directly at me.

Cherno Journo
I might lower it then
(Cherno Journo lowers the gun and walks towards NFK)
This is good, this will work.
(it starts to rain)
Oh rain, it's atmospheric.

NFK
(laughs)
Yeah it's very moody.

Cherno Journo
Not bad, okay well, I'm FRAPSing this, I assume you don't have an issue with that.

NFK
Nope no problems.

Cherno Journo
Okay well NFK we are here at Zub Castle and you've agreed to an interview. We've met up, we're feeling safe. Well you're feeling safe, I don't mind if you kill me because I'll just respawn. Ummm, this rain is very loud but let's see if we can do it anyway. Tell me about your first murder.

NFK
Right well it was at Pustoskha and just to give you a context for what happened the previous two lives I had been killed by players. Both times I had been ambushed in barns. So I had issues with paranoia that time around and I'd had a couple of run in with zombies.

The sequences of events is a little weird because what happened was I was going to Pustoskha, I had a crossbow with me and a hatchet. I had just switched to the hatchet because I'd lost my last crossbow bolt. I saw movement in the supermarket and so I went to investigate, then I heard the shooting, at which point I sort of flattened up on the wall of the building next door to the supermarket and I saw these zombies just running down the street and I heard more shooting. At which point I decided to stay hidden for a while and then I risked it and ran into the supermarket for more cover.

And there was nobody there, whoever was in there had left. So I was thinking if they've left they're not coming back in here so I'm just going to wait out all this crazy shooting.

Cherno Journo
So you didn't plan on killing anyone while you were in there?

NFK
Not really no. My logic was they've already been here so there not coming back and they were just shooting zombies and would run out of ammunition eventually. But it went on

for minutes, the guy had a shit ton of ammunition.

(Cherno Journo laughs)

So the more this goes on the more I'm thinking shit what am I going to do if he runs back here, you know, for shelter or something? Am I just going to sit there and let him come at me holding the axe?

I had found a revolver as well so that's when I decided to switch to the revolver. I knew I could hold off the zombies with the axe if they showed up but the revolver, the revolver was for other players. And that's why I decided to switch to the revolver. I just made a decision - okay I'm not taking a risk. If this guy shows up, through those doors, because I was behind the counter in the corner.

So on this particular go around I'd had a hard time finding gear so I was just playing avoidance. I was just avoiding other players a lot. So when this maniac was shooting up the town I was like I can't just sit here and let him shoot me too. That's when I decided to pull out the revolver and wait.

So within minutes of me thinking if he comes through that door I'm going to shoot him, that's exactly what happens. He rounds the corner and he comes bursting through the door zombies on his tail. He had a revolver in his hand though. And the funny thing was though I feel like there was a pause, we sort of just looked at each other for a second.

And then I opened fire. I don't know if I hit him, I think I hit him. Then he fired back and the rest of it was kind of a blur. We just traded fire back and forth. I reloaded the revolver like three times. He dodged behind shelves and I was behind the counter. Then finally the shooting stopped. I had the revolver trained around a corner which I couldn't see.

So I was waiting and waiting. Then I realized I was bleeding so I had to bandage myself, hoping he wouldn't pop up and shoot me while I was bandaging. And after I'd bandaged myself I though fuck it, I'll check it out. I checked around the corner, and around then he must have died because flies started buzzing. Until then he must have been unconscious or something and I must have clipped him just as he reached that corner.

Cherno Journo
And what did you feel after? Obviously once the heart rate slowed down, breathing came back to normal, what did you feel?

NFK
Well the funny thing was that afterwards I felt pretty shitty about it because, a few hours previous, on this very spot on here at the top of Zub, I logged in. And right after I logged in somebody else was already here. And they didn't shoot me, they actually engaged me in conversation.

All that was on me was a crossbow anyway so I probably wouldn't have been able to get the drop on him even if I tried. But the point was they could have shot me and didn't. I'd made like a pathetic offer to try and trade with them. I was like I've got some flares and bandages what do you want to do? I guess they just figured I was a waste of time and just said nothing as they ran down the stairs.

So somebody else facing in the exact same situation I faced later on in the day, decided not to shoot me. But when it came to me having the exact same situation I did shoot, so I felt kinda shitty about it afterwards.

Cherno Journo
What about vehicles? Have you had vehicles on a map?

NFK
As far as vehicles go I have found an ATV, motorcycles. I

found a Ural once but I didn't keep it because it's so big and noisy. Mostly ATVs and motorcycles. Motorcycles are my favorite, it's like the most awesome vehicle in the game as far as I'm concerned. I've done so much cross country travelling across the northern and western edges of the map, and in the countryside where I've never been ambushed. And that's because I think I take routes that don't go to anywhere, not travelling on the way to Stary Sobor. Or going in between two cities or something like that. I'm always in the middle of nowhere, going to nowhere.

The places I'm most cautious are if I'm approaching Berezino for a medical run or something like that. All the times that I have been ambushed have been places where there is loot, like inside a barn. I went to the Northwest Airfield once and of course I go to the firehouse and I get ambushed there. So generally speaking if I'm in the wilderness I feel much safer than anywhere habited.

Cherno Journo
And so the plan is now to keep travelling north and surviving the apocalypse?

NFK
Yeah I'm going to go back to what I do best which is looking for tents. I'm curious to see if I can still find them because I know that this particular update had a lot of issues with tents so we'll see if people stop using them or something I don't know. But I'm going to look for tents and vehicles.

Cherno Journo
Alrighty well NFK thank you very much for interviewing with the Cherno Journo. This is the Cherno Journo, out.

Cherno's Final Thought

I love the tension at the start of the interview, the transcript unfortunately can't show it. You need to watch it on YouTube to understand, as NFK was my first interview with a player I'd never met before.

Whilst this was my first interview, I didn't put it up because of that - if it was crap I would have let it go. What I liked about NFK's story was the ease in which things can go wrong in DayZ. He started his day without the intention of killing someone but the constant shooting and the paranoia about dying quickly changed that notion.

Also the pause that he mentioned when the other player entered the store. I think anyone who's played DayZ for a while has had that moment. Where two Survivors see each other at the same time and neither knows how to react. What will the other person do? Should I run, should I shoot, should I speak out?

I also loved the guilt that NFK felt when he'd killed this other person who wasn't really a threat to him. Because he'd survived a similar situation at Zub Castle where he was let free but instead of paying it forward he panicked and murdered thee other player. My first kill was like that, at Balota airfield where I killed a player out of panic, and for that reason I could relate to NFK's story and so did many others.

INTERVIEW WITH THE THINKTANKER
ABOUT HIS FIRST MURDER

It is night in the woods near Bor where The ThinkTanker and Cherno Journo have set up a campfire for their interview.

Cherno Journo
Thank you very much The ThinkTanker for taking the time and risking your life to give us the interview.

The ThinkTanker
Not a problem at all I actually think this is a super cool project first of all, and I'm glad that you're making a YouTube channel out of it. Because when I first heard about the idea that was the first thing that popped into my head. This would be a perfect YouTube channel, so I think it's a fantastic idea.

Cherno Journo
Thanks mate, thanks very much I appreciate that. Maybe you could just start by telling me how long you've being playing DayZ for, has it been a while?

The ThinkTanker
Well I've been playing DayZ for probably about a month and my first murder actually happened, I think day 3, something like that. And I wanted to play DayZ because I'd heard, mainly on Rock Paper Shotgun but also other places online,

about all of the amazing types of stories that people could tell. The idea of the open sandbox game in DayZ allows people to do some crazy cool stuff. You hang out with randoms, you find friendlies and do stuff with people you don't know, and that part appealed to me because I thought it would be a unique experience for a video game.

So I got on thinking that was actually the norm and of course you find that it is not the norm. At this point in the mod's development, pretty much everybody will shoot on sight. Like everybody that I'd met in the first few days would shoot on sight and I'm going to admit I was extremely, extremely bitter. I'd gone to churches and saluted, I'd talked to people on direct chat and told them I'm friendly, and every single person had gunned me down.

I was like "THIS IS NOT THE DAYZ EXPERIENCE I WAS PROMISED!" So it was really, really frustrating and so I think it was day three or four that I was playing and getting pretty bitter about the game. What happened was I decided I was going to run into Cherno, I would gear up and then get to the north. I thought there were probably nicer players up in the north. The people who want to shoot on sight and grief newbies on the beach, those guys are going to stay towards the coast. And people who want to survive out in the woods, do fun things, build civilizations, those people are going to be up in the north. And that was what I told myself.

So I figured that was what I was going to do, I would gear up and I would head out, out to the north. So I was right outside the grocery store in Cherno. I'd armed myself with a revolver and an axe, and I was just crawling along when I saw another player. The amazing thing was they did not see me, they were just crawling along, right out in the middle of the open there. Just crawling across the street, I think he was trying to keep the undead off him and everything.

It was just this magical moment where I thought, for once I saw a player, they had not seen me and in my head it just kinda clicked. I said I can get the drop on them. And all the bitterness kind of welled up inside me and told me go for it. Everybody that you've met has killed you on sight, everybody has betrayed you. This is the rule, this is the game, survival at any cost.

And so with kinda shaking hands I pulled out my revolver and took a few shots at him, and missed horribly. I missed completely, I think I was in third person, but it was terrible. I missed so bad, that the guy who was not ten feet away from me crawling towards this bush, I think that he thought someone else in the city was shooting because I shot so badly. So I realized I'm out of ammunition and he still has no idea that I'm here.

So I'm like, it's now or never. I pull out my hatchet, and I readied it on my shoulder, and I dashed forwards and started hacking away at him. I killed him with the hatchet but he'd turned around and he was able to fire off a few shots at me, and put me in shock, and I'd lost quite a bit of blood. And my hands were shaking, like literally shaking at my computer.

And I was thinking, holy crap! I just killed this person, I just totally did it. My first thought was I did it. And my second thought was holy crap that gun is loud there's going to be a lot of zombies. So I tried to loot his body real quick. He had blood bags, which at this point in the game I'd never seen. He had an AKM, which I was thinking that's great I need a real nice rifle now. I thought that I was set for life.

And I think two minutes later, because I'd never fired the AKM before, because I'd never done really anything with any higher level weaponry in the game. I was immediately killed by zombies not three minutes later. Between the hoard that he drew to his position and me just pretty much shooting anything and I tried to get out of Cherno, it was just an absolute disaster. And so all of the loot that I had just killed for was completely lost within just three minutes.

I stepped away from the game visibly shaking. It really, really affected me. That night I could not sleep. And that next day at work I could not focus on anything. All I could think about was the fact that, in a very real way that clicked in my head, I had committed a murder. That someone in the game, obviously it wasn't a real murder, but he had a really terrible day because he'd found some really nice stuff. And then some psycho with an axe came and chopped him in half. And I just sat there thinking, all day. And I'd never had a video game - well killing someone in a video game - ever affect me this profoundly.

I couldn't focus on anything. All I could think about was what it would feel like to be someone just crawling along, and then out of nowhere some madman with an axe just breaking you in half, severing your spine and crushing your skull. Then I realized what kind of psycho would do that. And the psycho was me. I felt this extreme, extreme amount of guilt over what I had done. That with no provocation and without trying to find out his intentions, based just on the loot he had on him and the fact that I had the drop on him, I killed another player.

It profoundly affected me to the point where I had decided after a day of literally agonizing over what I had done. Literally sitting there and unable to focus on anything else, it compelled me to get back into the game and find a way to atone for my actions. Now I didn't know the player's name so I couldn't find him on the forums, and honestly I wasn't a part of the forums so I didn't know anything. I know that I could never really atone for what I did to that one player, but it has affected my play style ever since. That murder, because I felt so conflicted, so just completely affected by the murder that I committed. I do not shoot on sight. Now

I'll defend myself, but I have decided in DayZ for the rest of the time that I play, I would never do that again. I would never kill a player that was helpless. A bandit... maybe, or maybe I'll just let him go. But I can never, I've been so affected by it that I can't – kill – another player.

(the camp fire goes out and is relit)

Yeah so that's my experience. It's just something that's interesting. DayZ is a very special game because it can evoke these kind of feelings. I killed millions of things in video games you know, but I've never felt like I've committed an actual crime. I've never felt like I've really done something wrong. And it wasn't until DayZ when I was a madman with an axe that killed some helpless person without saluting, without talking to them, without trying to find out anything. I killed someone on sight with an axe, which has got to be a terrible, terrible way to die.

It wasn't until that moment that I felt, really felt guilty and I think that's something very special. The game is very special in that it can evoke that emotion from any player at all, I just think that's absolutely fantastic.

Cherno's Final Thought

The great thing about the ThinkTanker's response to his first murder was the guilt that he felt. To him it was real and profound because he recognized that there was a person behind the character he just murdered. What I love about DayZ is how it reminds you of the people behind the avatars.

Also the other reason for choosing this story was due to The ThinkTanker's reaction to his first murder, how from that point on it colored his own playing style. I think for many players their first murder can really affect how they play the game from then onwards. In many ways I feel that the escalation in killing on sight is not just a response from the rampant hacking but also players trying to chase that first murder feel. Everything that The ThinkTanker talks about - the adrenaline, the rush - the stress is really a 'high'. And as you continue to play that 'high' becomes harder to find. You need to kill more players, get into more intense situations such as taking on squads, just to get back to that original feeling.

Of course if you have a negative reaction, such as The ThinkTanker's guilt, then the opposite happens. Now you're trying to atone for it, or prevent it happening to others. Then we get players who counter snipe Elektro, defend the unarmed, hunt for bandits. To me they are also trying to get back that initial 'high' of helping someone out. That feeling of getting someone out of a jam or saving their lives.

For me my first murder - as opposed to my first kill which was a fear misfire - affected me in the same manner. You can read it in my Survivor Journals or hear me tell it to the Donut Zombies Podcast – http://donutzombies.com/ - look for Bonus Episode 1. Also sub to CF Donuts and the gang, they put out some great content and will tell your DayZ story on the air if you like. I always imagine them as two Survivors camped out in Green Mountain sharing the stories – kind of like Three Dog in Fallout 3.

INTERVIEW WITH SLAYERIK AND SURLEYBOI ABOUT THEIR FIRST MURDERS

Cherno Journo rode through Elektro on his bike looking for a random interviewee. He found Slayerik and Surleyboi at the Elektro offices and interviewed them there as zombies continued to stream in. The first 10 minutes involved Zed management until finally it had calmed down enough to conduct the interview.

Cherno Journo
Okay let's do this quickly. I am the Cherno Journo, I travel the coast of Chernarus recording the stories of the Survivors. Would you like to be interviewed for my YouTube channel?

Slayerik
Sure thing.

Cherno Journo
Okay well what are your names?

Slayerik
Slayerik.

Cherno Journo
Tell me about your first murder.

Slayerik

Alright so I was in Balota, very new to the game. I happened to stumble upon another Survivor. We exchanged ammo, he gave me a clip for my empty AK. And we went to the top of the fire station building there, *(I assumed he meant ATC tower)*. And we heard a dirt bike approaching and we were like pretty scared, because if the guy has a dirt bike then he's probably an experienced player.

I pretty much freaked out and just opened up on the guy and killed him. I got a ghillie suit off him, silenced MP5 - all sorts of good stuff. The guy I was with ended up getting a broken leg from a zombie and neither of us had any morphine. So I kind of just left him there to die because I had to log out. It was pretty fun.

I was typing over the side chat that I was going to shoot him and I swear he must have been drunk. He was driving around in circles and figure eights on his motorcycle but whatever.

Cherno Journo

So it was almost death by cop in a sense. So how did you feel, you said it was fun, did you find it fun afterwards?

Slayerik

Yeah. Especially looting his Alice pack and other goodies.

Cherno Journo

So no remorse at all?

Slayerik

Some remorse I guess. Just because he was in the wrong place at the wrong time.

Cherno Journo

And how about you other Survivor?

SurleyBoi

My first actual, I guess firing in anger kill, were three guys that killed a Survivor, who was looking for help in Stary. I was on the outskirts of town with a sniper rifle. I saw what went down. Shot all three of them. I figured it was justice.

Cherno Journo

How did you feel when you killed the three bandits?

SurleyBoi

I felt like I had done the right thing but at the same time I still kinda felt bad but you know they killed somebody that really did deserve it. So I put them down, I did Chernarus a favor.

Cherno Journo

And have you taken on that role since? Do you now take on a police role and kill those bandits?

SurleyBoi

Sort of. That's what I kinda do. I try to hang out in places and take people out that are trying to take other people out. Sometimes it works. A lot of times I get shot. I've definitely died more to other players than I've probably killed, but still it's what I'm gonna do and I'm gonna keep doing it.

Cherno Journo

Before you kill these players do you let them know why? Do you explain to them that you're killing because of a moral reason, or do you just shoot them?

SurleyBoi

I used to but now I can't. Since there's no Global chat anymore it's kinda hard to do it. Which is why I tend to get shot a lot more. I don't generally tend to shoot people unless I catch them in the act.

Cherno Journo

Okay gentlemen thank you very much for what has been a fun and risky interview. This is the Cherno Journo, out.

Cherno's Final Thought

This was my fifth attempt to interview someone without having it preplanned and the first that was successful. Other times I'd been shot or found players who were still new to the game and therefore didn't have a lot to say. If you haven't seen the interview then watch it on YouTube, the set up on this one is great fun.

Slayerik's first murder was the first and so far only story of a player suicide that I'd heard of. From his description the player he killed wanted to die, probably to gear up again which many people find to be the best part of DayZ. I have interviewed people who do play like this but usually they just give away the gear and then suicide by zombies or falling. This was the first one I heard where they made the new spawn essentially work for the gear by killing them. And then the joy of finding loot and the callousness in abandoning the other player who gave him the AK ammo – was a very atypical DayZ experience.

Then there was Surleyboi's first murder, whose like many murders - was a revenge kill. What I liked about this was the Batman sense of being the arbitrator of justice, killing the other players for a supposed crime. Usually a revenge murder is because a close friend was killed, but for Surleyboi he didn't know who the person who was executed, but exacted revenge anyway. It showed part of that developing DayZ moral code, where a murder can be justified based solely on a player's actions. In this case the three were killed because they murdered an 'innocent' but there was no time or means to determine that innocence.

That murder shows what is inherently wrong with making a judgment of actions outside of context. Since he didn't speak with the other players he just had to assume their motivation was nefarious. But perhaps they had killed this one man because they had just witnessed him killing an unarmed player before. Or he'd murdered and betrayed them before. And how would someone have judged Surleyboi's actions if all they saw was him kill three other players from a distance. That cycle of violence could continue indefinitely. I'd like to believe that Surleyboi was justified in killing the three players, but we'll never actually know that.

INTERVIEW WITH ENDRID ABOUT THE TIME HIS LITTLE BROTHER WAS MURDERED

Picture Pobeda dam. The sun is setting, the night is clear and the sky is tinged with purple hue. Two strangers who've never met before run across the dam to share the story of murder. For this interview I couldn't have picked a better time or location to hear Endrid's story.

Cherno Journo
Ah Endrid there you are. Helllooo I am the Cherno Journo. Ah you are a hero?

Endrid
Nah I've got cammo clothing.

Cherno Journo
Oh close enough.
  (Cherno Journo disarms so no guns were in the shot)
Thank you very much for agreeing to the interview. We are here today to talk about the time your brother was murdered in front of you, your real life brother in game, is that correct?

Endrid
Yes. My brother lives in another state and we're several years apart so we don't get to hang out as much as we used to, so gaming is a good way for us to stay in touch. He was hearing

about DayZ, knew I was playing it, so he was tempted to buy it. He finally went ahead and bought it.

And so I decided to just go along with him and scour the towns, teach him, show him the ropes, how to basically survive in this wilderness. So we started off on the east coast and we started heading north west, going from town to town, going to different deer stands. I was showing him how to refill his water bottle, how to use the map.

At the same time I remembered we picked up some different weapons at the deer stands. He started out with an Enfield and then he finally got an AKM. At this time I had an M4A1 CCO SD. So I told him, listen don't fire your weapon unless you have to because I have the silenced gun. If we need to kill zombies then I'll do it so we don't aggro or alert other players. And he was really learning fast and I was proud of him.

Anyway since he was my little brother I was really concerned about keeping him safe. That was one thing I kept noticing was that I wanted to make sure he was good and that was the only thing I was thinking about. These guys in my team came into our channel and we told them we were about to go to Dolina. They said to be careful because we just had a skirmish there with some people. Now this was about half an hour ago so I thought alright it's going to be fine, I'm not really concerned about it, like who camps out in Dolina?

We start to cross the street and we're crouch-walking across the street in Dolina about 5 feet apart. And we hear shots fired, directly at us, sounded like a machine gun. It was just completely jarring and I yelled at my brother I said "Run! Run!" and we started running and I looked back and he's lying there on the street, and he's wounded. And there's zombies all over him.

And I'm running around like a chicken with my head cut off trying to figure out what to do. I wanted to find these guys but I couldn't stop moving because I had zombies on me as well. So I finally stop and I hide behind this building and I ask him "are you okay?" And he says "I can't stand up," and then I hear shots fired from his AKM. He says to me over the mic, "I'm sorry bro I had to." Remembering how I told him not to fire that AKM. I'm just like "No, no, you gotta do what you gotta do." So I was thinking Okay let me just kill these bastards but I couldn't find them.

Eventually the zombies just ended up killing him. So I'm hiding behind this building trying to find where these guys are. Eventually I get sniped in the head. We both died, right there.

Cherno Journo
Wow that's a really intense story. Can I ask how you felt, at the time or even just after, when you realized in a sense you'd failed your little brother and he died?

Endrid
I just felt absolutely terrible. I mean it's funny because it's a video game you know. To have intense feelings about a video game is a little bit ridiculous, especially to people who don't play games like this. But at the same time that guy in Cherno represented my little brother. I was supposed to protect him and I was showing him the ropes. What really disturbed me about the whole situation was that he was trusting me about it. When the zombies were all around him I didn't just go out and *try* to kill them. I should have just, that's what I kept thinking. I should have ran out there. I should have just killed the zombies so that at least he would have had a chance.

Instead I ran and I hid and that's what made me feel like shit. It's that if I can't risk myself to help my brother in a game, what would I do in real life? But at the same time I was so upset at those people. I was just trying to kill them and at least, you know, pay them back. I even sent him a text right after and called him and was like "I'm really sorry about that, I let you down. I should have tried to get the zombies off you." He was "it's okay, no big deal."

But yeah, that's kind of my story.

Cherno's Final Thought:

This was why I wanted to be the Cherno Journo. To hear and share stories like this. As the eldest of four siblings I knew exactly what Endrid was going through when he felt like he'd failed his little brother. Anyone who's had younger siblings knows the need to protect them and how awful it can be when you fail at it.

I always look back at this interview and feel like a real prick for saying that Endrid failed to protect his brother but it did evoke my most emotional interview to date. This interview shows the power that a bit of role playing can add to the DayZ experience, that just by virtue of having his little brother play with him, Endrid changed his game style.

He put his little brother before himself to show him the ropes. He felt pride when his little brother did something well and guilt when he let him down. The emotions were real and just another example of how DayZ is more than just a video game.

INTERVIEW WITH DEMYAN
ABOUT BETRAYAL

This was my first successful interview in a high risk location, this time at the docks of Cherno near the church. It was early morning when I rode my bike into Cherno following the red flare Demyan had left as a beacon. When I got close to the docks there was shooting but fortunately not at me. Waiting for me, hidden in the shadows, was Demyan, who walked out with his weapon lowered into the red flare light.

Demyan
Hello.

Cherno Journo
Helllooo. *(pause)* I was scared for a moment but I figured I wasn't losing blood so you weren't shooting at me.

Demyan
(shoots at a Zed as the flare extinguishes)
Perfect timing.

Cherno Journo
That flare was very good. I saw it from far away.

Demyan
So you're Cherno Journo, I'm surprised because I thought

this was going to be an ambush.

They both move into a nearby red building for the interview. Zeds keep coming in and Demyan shoots them.

Cherno Journo
Do you want me to start hatcheting some to save ammo?

Demyan
No it's fine if you want to start asking your questions I'll keep them off of us.

Cherno Journo
So we're here at the docks of Cherno to discuss your first betrayal. You said it occurred in this area, is that correct?

Demyan
That's correct, it was actually where I dropped the flares that you came to.

Cherno Journo
And what had happened? You said there were five people involved in this betrayal.

Demyan
That is correct. We met two unknowns who were friendly towards us and I was with two men of the Chernarus Quarantine Force. One of them was a Private named Snowspeckle, the other was a recruit whose name I don't remember. The two that we'd met, one of their names was Ghosty, it was a woman. And the other was actually wearing a head wrap, I should have known at that point what was going to happen.

Cherno Journo
And so where did you meet these two random players?

Demyan

I was running through Cherno actually trying to dodge Zeds, I had quite a bit of a trail on me. I saw a green Skoda on the road with somebody inside of it. They shouted in direct chat for me to come in so I hopped inside. It was the woman Ghosty that I had met. Then shortly after, in hopped her friend, the man with the head wrap.

I didn't say anything, initially, because she'd saved my life. After that we proceeded over to another vehicle, I asked them a few questions about what their plan was and where they were heading. They had found a V3S of all things, here in Cherno, about a hundred meters down the road east of where we are now. They needed parts and I offered to help because they'd saved me. In doing so they actually said that if I helped them find parts for this V3S they would give me their Skoda.

So of course I contacted my friends, who weren't with me at the time, but were meeting me to rendezvous. Said to them we could get a vehicle here. They both come quickly to help find all of the parts that they needed for the V3S. We got it fixed up and in doing so I'd broken my leg and lost quite a bit of blood. So this man in the head wrap gave me a transfusion and gave me morphine.

So we all get patched up and then we head back from the V3S to the Skoda. Split up, take both of the vehicles and were passing along here on the west side when the driver blacked out and clips a roadblock, which takes off the front wheel and damages the engine back to orange. We can't go anywhere and we're stuck. I don't know where our recruit is or where the man with the head wrap is.

But it's me and Ghosty and Snowspeckle and we decide that we have to make a quick decision because we've attracted a lot of attention and we're down at the docks. We hop to the other side right by those benches and sit down for a moment and talk about what we're going to do. We separate to get parts. I come back with a car wheel so we get the car back up and ready to roll.

I see my recruit friend's name roll up on the death list. I ask him how did he die and he said he was killed by a Bandit. Fortunately at that point I had connected the dots and realized it was the same person. We get set to load back in when the Bandit rolls around the corner by the church. He opens fire. Drops not only my friend Snow but myself with a broken leg. I'm bleeding out. The only reason that I'm still alive is that I managed to shoot him with a Lee Enfield and that was enough to bring him down.

Afterwards it was only me and Ghosty left so I asked her why he did it. And she said she didn't know. At that point I decided it was a very good idea to no longer travel with this group. I give her the extra ammunition that I have for my weapon, she gets into the car and drives off and I head back into the forest.

Cherno Journo
So Ghosty and the Bandit, had they been together for a while?

Demyan
They had been yes. She actually said that it was her friend.

Cherno Journo
But she had no idea why he suddenly decided to turn and kill you and your friends?

Demyan
No. No, apparently she didn't.

Cherno Journo
And so when the betrayal had occurred what were your feelings? What was going through your mind at those

moments?

Demyan
Honestly nothing was really going through my head except to kill him. I didn't realize until afterwards when I saw his name roll up afterwards that it was the very same person. I guess after that the only thing that I felt was guilt and stupidity. I was responsible for two of the men of my unit getting killed.

Cherno Journo
Betrayal. What are your thoughts in general? Why does the game have people help each other for a while and then suddenly someone turns? What do you think makes them do that?

Demyan
Any number of things. For one I think that when Dean made this game he made it as a social experiment if you will. People that betray other people, they can do it out of greed. They can do it out of convenience. They can do it out of mistrust or paranoia. They might do it simply because they find that the person that they're travelling with is either dangerous or unreliable, or perhaps they suspect they're not what they seem. But I think what it ultimately boils down to is somebody decides to betray another person because they care much more about themselves than they do any other person.

Cherno Journo
Great, thank you.

Demyan
I'd love to stay but with a rouge bandit on the server and a flare right in front of us we need to part ways.

Cherno Journo
No, no, let's go. Thank you for the interview.

Demyan

You're very welcome, have a good one.

And with that Demyan disappeared into the night.

Cherno's Final Thought

This interview covered a topic that I'm always curious about, the shattering of the fragile alliances that DayZ creates. Many people who came late to the game, and for me that's after October, found less DayZ and more Deathmatch Chernarus. Prior to this I recall that people did form alliances, they did work together and often these alliances would end with one of the players dead. It was something that always interested me, having been on the side of the betrayed too many times.

I could never understand why someone would just decide to turn on a player that they were working with. Many times when it happened to me, the people had seemed nice, there wasn't an indicator that darkness lay inside, but suddenly they'd turn and you'd find yourself dead. To me this always hurt more than just being killed on sight because it was an affront to the notion of survival. If I've shown that I'm not a threat to you then why betray me and kill me?

Although Demyan's story does not give any real insight into why this occurs - and I don't think anyone could - it does provide a very typical DayZ story, one I'd heard many times before but he was the first to articulate it so clearly. There is also the reaction of Ghosty who can't explain why her real life friend decided to suddenly betray them all. Perhaps we'll never understand it, perhaps it's just part of the disconnect that people have when playing online games, that allows them to act so far form their core selves.

INTERVIEW WITH TEACH AND SENTERS ABOUT THEIR BETRAYALS

For this interview we chose an out-of-the-way church in Pogorevka. When I spawned in I heard gunshots but ever faithful that I would be okay, I charged into the fray to find Teach and Senters, both with Bandit headscarves, in the church shooting Zeds.

Cherno Journo
I'm loving your headscarves. Okay gentlemen who do we have here? Who is Senters and who is Teach?

Teach
I am Teach, the one with the L85.

Cherno Journo
Alrighty Teach nice to see you.

Teach
And that is Senters with the AKM.

Cherno Journo
Senters. Okay gentlemen I'm here to record your first betrayal. Well a betrayal anyway. Let me hear the story. Who would like to start me off?

Teach

Well basically we had this huge firefight with another group. Then after a few hours of fighting they called a truce. Then in the disguise of a truce they shot us in the back in a barn near Elektro. Yeah, and they hid our bodies and all that shit.

So the next day I notice that one of our guys is playing with them. So I went and sniped them in Elektro. I killed a few of them quite a few times. And then we had this massive plan to put Zac into their group, the other guy, so Zac can take it from here.

Senters

Alright so at this time where he's killing them all in Elektro, he killed our guy and one of their guys a couple of times. And so we had the great idea to put me in the group. I started to talk to the guy that had left our group and joined theirs. I told him that they're really pissing me off and can I join your group. And he said sure we've one more spot come join our Vent.

So I did. I started talking to them, having fun, then they got a bus and picked me up in Komarovo. We drove through and hit Cherno. And in Cherno there was a firefight going on so I ran and grabbed bandages and blood bags and our wheel had been shot out. I'd been bandaging them and giving them blood so at this point they trusted me. And I killed another guy that was shooting at us.

I also got a tire and fixed up the bus. And when I did I got in to the driver's seat. When I hopped into the driver's seat, everybody followed. I told Teach, over here to my right, that we're coming to Elektro. He said he's got satchel charged planted on the Prigorodky bridge, the one just outside of Cherno, and to drive over it.

And so heading that way I was just shaking, with the

adrenaline just rushing. I got over to the bridge, I'd joined their Skype call before, told them "we're on our way, we're on our way." As soon as I crossed the bridge an AS-50 shot took out the wheel. Stopped right on the satchel charges and they blew them up. Yeah and killed about five or six of them. That was pretty intense.

Cherno Journo
And so obviously you died as well in that explosion?

Senters
Yeah I sacrificed myself in order to get them.

Cherno Journo
Wow that's awesome! So you were playing the double agent. So how did you feel when you exacted revenge and you blew up these betrayers?

Senters
I felt amazing, it was the best feeling.

Teach
It certainly was the best day in DayZ for us, I think.

Senters
Yeah I can easily agree with that.

Cherno Journo
Teach, at the first betrayal that you were a part of. How did you feel at that point? You obviously didn't know at that point that one of your squad members had betrayed you, so what was the feeling at that point?

Teach
Well let me put it this way - I had him in my sights, then I saw the name, so it took me about 5 seconds to hesitate and then I shot him down. I kinda felt bad about it because he had been playing with us for about three weeks maybe, I

don't know for sure.

Cherno Journo
Do you have any idea why he would have betrayed you, why after three weeks of playing together he'd turn?

Teach
I have no clue, no clue whatsoever. We have quite strict standards on using scripted in weapons and whatnot, we don't tolerate that one bit. He didn't quite agree with that so I think that's the main thing.

Cherno Journo
Thank you very much. This is Cherno Journo, out.

Cherno's Final Thoughts

This interview was a great example of DayZ meta-gaming at its finest, or lowest, depending on your point of view. The notion of sending in a double-agent into a group really opened my eyes to the possibilities that can exist outside of the ordinary game. Having never been a part of a group or clan I don't know what the general policies of membership screening are, but it seems that in DayZ one spy could cause great havoc, as Senters showed.

Also in this interview, both Teach and Senters did not understand why someone they played with for three weeks decided to betray them. The issue with betrayal is it's always going to be a one-time deal, you can't ever get away with it twice. Teach and Senters tried to explain a possible reason why they were betrayed but it seems that no one will ever know, people will do it for reasons they may not even understand themselves.

INTERVIEW WITH MANDALORE

THE ULTIMATE LONE WOLF

This was my second interview with Mandalore, the first being interrupted when we were ambushed. Mandalore was very concerned about his safety, not because of me, but from other players, as we spoke over direct chat. He had picked a random part of the woods and a low population server for the interview. We were far north with no towns or landmarks around us when I spawned in to find we had another player near us.

Cherno Journo
Heeelllloooo!
(runs down the hill)
I am the Cherno Journo.

There is a man running across the field and a Ghillied Survivor with an AS-50 between them.

Mandalore
Yep I figured as much.

Cherno Journo
Mandalore are you in the ghillie?

Mandalore

Yep do you see me?

Cherno Journo

I do but we have someone else running in front of us. Do you see him ahead?

Mandalore

That's not you?

Cherno Journo

No I'm behind you.

Mandalore

Is that you running South?

Cherno Journo

No I'm behind you. You see?

Mandalore

Oh!

Cherno Journo

That is hilarious. *(both laugh)*

Mandalore

That was kinda scary.

Cherno Journo

I thought oh no you'd lost your ghillie.

Mandalore

You said you'd be coming from the north and I saw that guy running.

Cherno Journo

I came from up here.

Mandalore
I thought that guy was you.

Cherno Journo
(Pulls up player list showing 8 players)
There's only like eight people on the server.

Mandalore
And is that a helicopter again? I think I heard a helicopter or maybe I'm just being paranoid.

Cherno Journo
Oh wow! Let's get up into this hill so we can at least see what's happening.

Mandalore
Yeah let's get up into these trees on the hill.

Cherno Journo
Okay Mandalore, thank you very much for interviewing with the Cherno Journo. We're up here in the woods of Chernarus, and you tell me you've been a lone wolf for a while here. You've got a beautiful sexy AS-50 there but you haven't had to fire it, is that correct?

Mandalore
Yeah I just prefer to avoid other players and not get into conflict. I've found out that way you survive more.

Cherno Journo
So you say that the role of the game is to survive. So how many days has your current character been surviving, with this particular play style?

Mandalore
I think it's like 26 days, I didn't really notice. But do bear in mind that I've been playing for a month and about 5 days I think, so that's pretty good – considering.

It's just that I have had some conflicts with other players and from my experience the best way to survive is to try and avoid them. You watch them, get some info, do they have a group, if they have a tent, and you can get some supplies – that sort of thing. But it's best not to get involved directly.

Cherno Journo
What is your usual tactic? Is it concealment?

Mandalore
Yes. Obviously, always concealment. When I see another player I don't think that I've ever been spotted – with this specific play style. Mostly because I take it very slow, I take my time, not moving through fields. I always use cover, I always use the tree line when it's there. I know how to conceal myself, the ghillie suit obviously helps.

In case I find another player I mostly stay still and I watch. Most people just spend a minute or so scanning an area and then they move on, and that's if they're being very careful. So if you stand still you can probably evade people, even if you don't have a ghillie suit.

Cherno Journo
And so ever since you've come north you haven't gone back to any of the coastal towns like Cherno, Elektro or Berezino?

Mandalore
Well there were a couple of times when I went and I regretted it after that. I do have a small story about that which made me not want to be with other people, because of what I've seen.

There was this time when I went to Elektro. I was about to go into the city but I always spend some time using my scope to see what's what. If there are zombies around, if there are any players. While I was scoping the area I saw a

Bandit holding up another Survivor, who had nothing on him. He just had the normal coyote pack. I thought he was going to kill him after the robbery but he didn't, I don't know, he was merciful or something.

The dude was pretty close to the office which is opposite the supermarket. And apparently he found a Lee Enfield there and went outside and killed the Bandit, who didn't run away after he robbed him. Obviously he shot with the Lee Enfield which is called the dinner bell for a reason. He was getting hit by zombies within a few seconds.

That was the time that I actually decided I'm going to help this guy. Because he did nothing wrong, he just defended himself, that guy just robbed him. It was possible that he was going to shoot him, he was a Bandit. Which means he obviously killed someone before. And I want to help the guy so I shot a couple of the zombies that were around him.

At first I think he thought that I was shooting at him, but then he calmed down because he stopped running. Unfortunately he broke his legs, one of the zombies gave him a hit and he went down. I think he went unconscious as well for a bit, but he got up again.

The sad part of the story is that while I was killing Zombies just when he was free to get out of there, he got shot by another sniper, who was also using a 50 cal. And it was at that moment that I zoomed out and I saw a guy on my left, I don't know how far away he was but he was right at the edge of what I could see. If I moved camera a bit he was gone, and I could only see him zoomed in.

I did not move, the guy had not seen me. I think he was trying to see where the shots were coming from. I did have on a ghillie suit and I was concealed behind a bush. He hadn't spotted me, I could see that he had a 50 cal, because it was a very long barrel obviously. Then he tried to change his gun, which made me nervous. With my luck the guy probably had an L85, which meant my cover was useless.

So at that point when I saw him changing his gun and started strafing around, I got the hell out of there and never looked back.

Cherno Journo
So what about helicopters? Have you ever had encounters with helicopters? Which is really what an AS-50 is for. It's for taking down vehicles rather than people. Have you ever been buzzed by a helicopter, anything like that?

Mandalore
Yeah there was one time when I was in a server which happened to have the thing where you can actually see people if you use your mouse. I don't know if we have it here. Where you use your mouse to switch weapons and you can see distance from an object. But you can actually see players that way. *(Mandalore is referring to a server with player tags activated)*

There was this chopper which spotted me right in the middle of the woods because the ghillie suit is useless there obviously. It did start raining death down on me, shot me once. But to my true spirit of not killing players, because I just don't want to do that. I just shot its engine down, it made a lot of smoke and went down.

Those guys got out and started shooting at me. But I just left - I didn't want to kill them. I think they had a pretty bad day, it wasn't a safe place to land. It was pretty close to the Northwest Airfield which is a PVP hot zone.

Cherno Journo
Yeah and if the helicopter's down, unless they have spare parts it's going to be pretty far from anywhere where you can get spare parts. So the whole time, once you took the

helicopter down, you didn't think about taking a shot? Because these guys shot at you. You had no inclination to take them down or shoot them? Because you would have had the advantage.

Mandalore

Yeah I definitely had the advantage. I mean they roughly know where I was while I knew exactly where they were. My weapon was very suited to taking them out. I think one guy had an M14 -I wasn't sure, but from the sound I think it was. I didn't want to get into a fight, I don't like killing people even if they are trying to kill me. I just avoid combat with people.

The game is about survival and I think it is a bit unfair if you get killed by another player. I don't see it exactly like that, I mean I'm okay with it. I know it's going to be my fault if I die from another player. But I don't want to do that to someone else because I know he's going to have a bad day, and I'm just not a bad person.

Cherno Journo

Wow that's very admirable Mandalore. So then have you ever had an encounter with another player where they've seen you first, or shot at you out here in the woods?

Mandalore

No, with the exception of that time with the helicopter. I don't think anyone has ever spotted me. Even that story I told you about with the sniper on Elektro. Even that guy didn't spot me. At least if he did he didn't even bother shooting at me because I was too far away. Or I had hidden before he could get a shot.

I take it very slow. I think patience is the key to not being spotted. Not moving. I mean when you hear a sound, when you feel that somebody is watching you or something like that. Your best bet is to stay still, don't move, and always,

always have a lot of patience.

I did have a pretty close call, I think it was yesterday. I was out in the fields I wanted to get some food. I did spot a cow so I said, okay that's going to be a nice day. But I always, always, before getting out of the tree line, scope the area out to see if there are other players. And what do you know, before I even take my range finder out, I hear a shot. The cow is dead and three bandits are going over there. So obviously I didn't want to get involved in that.

I probably could have taken them all out but I didn't want to even though I am better equipped than them. I just let them do their business and go away.

Cherno Journo

That's very admirable because you are very much against the typical cliché of the ghillied AS-50 sniper who's going around killing everyone. As you say those three guys had no idea about you. You could have taken them all out with three shots very easily. But you chose instead to walk away and let them have the spoils, of the cow in this case. But it could have been anything. So I think Mandalore you are definitely the true lone wolf.

Mandalore

Yeah thank you for that. It's not exactly what you'd think if you saw a guy with ghillie suit and a AS-50 you're probably going to shoot him on sight. But you know maybe give him a second chance or something because he might not actually be an asshole and he might not want to kill you.

Chances are he will though, I don't think many people do what I do.

Cherno's Final Thoughts

Of all my videos the interview with Mandalore has received the most controversy. Many people have called bullshit on him but I've seen him in action and when we were attacked he didn't kill anyone, even though he had two lives at stake. I think the reason why people attack this particular play style is it's hard to understand because it is so selfless, so against on-line FPS from the original Quake/Half Life death match days. I can understand that. If you don't kill other players and you also don't interact with them then why play DayZ?

In many ways if we all played like Mandalore then the game could be dull, we'd all be hiding in the woods waiting. This is probably an example of why Dean Hall said that DayZ is an anti-game, because if you play it as it was designed, to be a survival simulator in extreme circumstances, then we should all play like Mandalore. I know I don't play like this. Although we both don't kill other players if I see someone I run to them calling out over direct. That's not a good survival strategy but it makes for some crazy experiences.

I did interview a player who wanted to be on the top of the 'Days Alive' scoreboard back when the mod had a leaderboard. He had set himself up a tent and supplies well north near Pobeda Dam. He stayed away from towns, hunted and gathered what he needed, and would use the dam for water. He'd stay in the game for hours in the woods, playing a guitar while watching his screen. Avoiding all other players and any confrontations. The thing was he did this on a high pop server which was in the early days before the hacking became rampant. So every time he saw or heard a player, or needed to do a water or food run, his anxiety levels shot through the roof. He described it as hours of calm interspersed with moments of panic which is really how DayZ is for many players.

The actual interview was very dull and therefore didn't make it onto the channel but it was a play style that few would understand or enjoy. I always say that if someone is having fun playing the game then it's not up to anyone to judge or criticize that style. Mandalore's play style is unique, he really is the ultimate lone wolf.

As for the hermit player, unfortunately his story didn't have a happy ending. He was eventually killed. Not by hackers or by a bandit, but by mistakenly pressing respawn rather than log out at the end of a session.

INTERVIEW WITH EATFISH ABOUT HIS REDEMPTION FROM THE BANDIT LIFE

Cherno Journo

Okay so Eatfish we're out here at your lovely little home, in the middle of the woods at night.

Eatfish

Thank you.

Cherno Journo

Thank you very much for agreeing to an interview with the Cherno Journo. Why don't you tell me your story. You've got the hero skin on now but I hear that's not always been the case.

Eatfish

Ah no. I started my life out as a pretty bad guy. I definitely came into this experience thinking that every other player was meant to die by my hands. I would basically kill anything that moved. My first weapon was a Lee Enfield. At that point I didn't really understand that there were high end military weapons out there at all. I just thought the game consisted of getting a Lee Enfield and maybe a revolver and trying to kill anything that moved. Zombie, person, boar - it didn't matter.

I probably racked about a hundred and fifty murders before I realized there's got to be more to the game than just hunting players.

Cherno Journo

I was going to say was there a particular moment that made you change this style of play or did you just start getting bored of killing people?

Eatfish

Really I was just getting bored with hunting humans you know. Like I said when I started out it was a Lee Enfield and a revolver and I would make do with that. Then I figured out NWAF, Stary Sobor and chopper crashes and such had pretty good guns, that could do damage.

The first AS-50 that I got I probably went a little trigger happy. I think I killed thirty people in Elektro sniper hill. New spawns, people just trying to make do, trying to get by in crazy Chernarus.

Cherno Journo

When you were killing these people did you feel bad that they were fresh spawns and you were taking them out with high end gear?

Eatfish

At the time not really. But now that I look back I realize that, I see the error of my ways. It's basically a survival game and I was stopping people before they even had a chance. They didn't even have a hatchet sometimes.

Or take a DMR and sit up there on a night time server back then, when people actually ran around with their flash lights and chemlights and flares. Trying to make the experience more enjoyable for themselves. And use that as a beacon to rain down death upon them.

Basically like I said it got pretty old, I got tired of it and I started to wonder if there was more to the game than just killing people. The game is open to so many different types of play styles. You want to be a bandit and kill everyone, that fine. You want to be a taxi driver who just drives around the coast and picks up noobs, gives them weapons or whatever and drives them around, that's fine. Be a medic, totally fine. For example you, you want to be a journalist you can be a journalist. Just change it up and see what else the game has to offer beside just team deathmatch or deathmatch.

Around that time all of my real life friends had decided that scripter or hackers were ruining the game, which I agree with them on. It's not enough for me to quit for good. So I took up my rifle against banditry and the collective effort of scripters to ruin the game for everyone.

Cherno Journo
So what's your play style now?

Eatfish
Currently I'm killing bandits on the coast. Anyone who poses a threat to anyone in general.

Cherno Journo
So how do you determine if someone's a bandit? Do you just go off the skin or do you wait to see how they act?

Eatfish
I mean for example the other day, every time I spawn I pretty much just run around Cherno and Elektro having a good time. Just trying to find randoms, trying to kill people who kill other people. I give everyone the benefit of the doubt now, scarf or no scarf. I give everyone the benefit of the doubt. If you shoot at me I'll probably still not shoot back if you're not posing a threat. Like if you're a terrible shot I'll give you a few times to lower you're weapon or stop

and communicate. But if you're going to keep shooting I have to defend myself.

I was in Elektro when a female character was just chasing me through the town. We eventually cornered each other, she cornered me in the side rooms. She was trying to shoot me with a Makarov. I keep talking to her, talking over the chat to her. I'm like, I have a hero skin, I'm not going to kill you. You can leave here now and you will survive to go on and ruin somebody else's day.

She took it upon herself to lay down in the hallway and wait for me to come out the door. Unfortunately I came out and she started shooting. I ran out the door, backed around behind her, and she was still lying on the ground for some reason. She tried to turn and shoot me but she couldn't actually turn, she was laying against the wall. So I really had no choice but to unload my MP5 into her back. I did feel bad about it.

Cherno Journo
I'm surprised you actually waited so long as she chased you around town, to finally confront her.

Eatfish
Like I said I give anyone the benefit of the doubt under any circumstance now. I've leant that just because people are wearing headscarves doesn't actually mean that they're a bad person, in game or out of game. Maybe they've been killing people in self-defense and it's been making them look bad. I don't think that's necessarily a bad player.

After I killed that girl I met two people wearing headscarves, not even three minutes later, that were totally friendly and we actually ran around Elektro for about thirty to forty minutes before... the inevitable scripter death. Which is becoming way too common in this game.

You know it's still fun, thirty minutes at a time. Meeting randoms and having a great time. Laughing and in general playing against other bandits that are not so friendly.

Cherno Journo

So is this pretty much your new play style now? You walk around Elektro and Cherno and police it but also try to meet up with new players and try to have new experiences in DayZ?

Eatfish

That I've just started doing recently. Like I said to you before I was basically inspired by your video of when you met two random guys in the school house in Elektro. I thought if he could do it then it's not impossible. I won't say that I've got a 100% success rate when doing it. Probably 25% to 40% of the time I get killed with no weapon in my hand or whatever the case may be. It's the most gratifying play style that I've had in a long time, probably ever, playing this game.

Cherno Journo

What is it about that play style that makes it so gratifying for you?

Eatfish

I enjoy online communities, I enjoy really online gaming in general. So if I can meet random people that are going to play along with me and have a good time, that to me, is one of the more enjoyable experiences in gaming. I can go play a number of other games that are just straight killing each other. This is essence, it's a beautiful thing, I mean I think I said it earlier that everyone has the opportunity to choose their own path in Chernarus.

They're not tied down to just a bandit or a hero, there's so much grey area that it's just an amazing thing you know. I just love the freedom basically.

Cherno Journo

So it sounds like you've definitely made DayZ your own story. It's now your story, and your game, the way you play it.

Eatfish

Yeah I mean right now my group we've done the whole high end gear thing. We've done the whole low end gear thing of just running around with a hatchet trying to lumberjack people. The middle ground between those two is probably the most enjoyable. A lot of people they have an AS-50 and a L85 and to survive and preserve their precious gear they spend most of their time playing in the wood. Not doing anything really.

I still think the coast has a lot of fun to offer. A lot of people advise people to get off the coast right away. I don't think anyone starting this game or starting a fresh life should get off the coast. You never know what kind of interactions you'll have down there. Some good. Some bad. But they're always interesting.

Cherno's Final Thoughts

I'm always a sucker for a good redemption story and I thought Eatfish's was good because it's a common story I've heard from many players. After the initial rush of combat wears off, and the fear of the Zeds wanes, many players of the bandit lifestyle do become bored. I personally think this is because the Kill On Sight bandit gameplay is inherently the same as so many other FPS games.

I've been playing FPS games since the Quake days and I've been a big Battlefield fan since BF1942 and the Desert Combat mod. If I want my FPS fix I have a range of other games to play and I think DayZ is a pretty poor FPS. But as an open sandbox survivor game during a catastrophic apocalypse where there are no rules, it is the ultimate game.

This is why I can still enjoy the bug-ridden, scripter infested, mod after playing for over a year. To me it's not about the end game or the engine it's about the people you meet. Every time I play, the people I meet and the interactions are different. But if you kill on sight you'll only ever have three interactions - you kill them; they kill you; or someone escapes. That's it, there might be slight variations but that's it. You essentially take such a wide variety of possibilities and bring it back down to the same three that have existed since the start of FPS games.

I also liked how Eatfish's redemption hasn't been easy and he's now taken the polar opposite of his previous play style. When you read on in my Survivor diaries you'll read my own story of my first and only murder and how it affected me. In many ways my initial Cherno Journo stints were a way for me to atone and be redeemed from that sin. Although morally I could justify it as a video game, to me it struck a psychic chord. I still feel pretty shitty every time I pass the same spot when playing. I just hope that my videos and this book have somehow atoned for that sin.

THE SURVIVOR DIARIES

These journal entries are highlights from my first couple of weeks of playing DayZ including my first day and my first and only murder. At the time I wasn't the Cherno Journo, I was just a guy who washed up on the beach and was trying to survive. I had heard about DayZ from some friends and was told it was the game that I must play - they all knew how obsessed I was with zombie fiction and zombies games and told me DayZ was the game I should be playing.

I was lucky to have such good friends. These guys told me not to look up hints or tutorials, they wouldn't help me in any way with gear or rides from the shore. They said get out there, pick a server and just survive, work it out as you go. And that's what I did for the first month. I had no outside help. No maps of loot spawn locations. In fact I hadn't even watched any YouTube videos about the game then. It was gifted to me in Steam and off I went.

These diaries were written after every play session, sometimes multiple times during the day. I hadn't intended on publishing them - they were just a way for me to express what I felt at the time the only way I knew how, by writing. They haven't been edited, I've only gone through them once to fix the multitude of spelling and grammar mistakes. I wasn't really role-playing the game, I just took it very seriously, did what I would do in real life, and tried to survive.

These events all took place on the same public hive Australian/New Zealand server. This server had no tags so I did miss some of the player's names that I interacted with. I haven't edited any of the names that I did get so if you recognize yourself and you were playing around July 2012 - then it probably was you!

DAY ZERO

I woke up on the coast with no idea where I was. I brushed the sand off my face and looked around. There were just woods to my left and the sea to my right. The first thing I noticed was that it was quiet. All I heard were the waves and the sounds of the occasional bird flying around.

Then I realized I had a bag on my back. I looked inside but there was nothing in it. I also had a torch, a bandage and some painkillers. I look around again, waiting. *Will someone come by? Should I yell out?* I decided to yell out, "Heeelllooo," but there was no response.

Fuck it, I thought, and ran away from the water. Then I saw the road up ahead. Great this is a good thing, roads equal cars, which equals people. I figured if I followed the road I'd find something eventually. But which way should I go? I looked up and down it but there was nothing ahead in either direction. With no better plan I kept the coast to my right and ran down.

After running for a while I saw a group of buildings up ahead. This was good. This would help. I kept running and that was when I saw my first lot of zombies. They were scattered all around, some in the fields, some in the buildings, some on the road. I stopped near a tree and watched them. *Fuck.* I'd heard about these zombies. They were fast and they didn't stop chasing you, ever. I didn't know what to do. Should I go around the town or should I go in. The zombies were everywhere, so it didn't look like I could avoid them

I got down on my belly and began to crawl towards the houses. I went slowly, barely made a sound as I passed my first zombie. It was horrible, blood on its face and I swore it looked right at me but then let me pass. As I went down the road I crawled towards the first house. It was white and had a fence around it. I got up and lept over the fence and went to the door. I tried everything but it wouldn't open. I looked through the windows but I couldn't see anything inside. I guess that house wasn't enterable.

Back on my belly I crawled to the second one. Same thing, door wouldn't open and the windows were blocked. Fuck! I swore. The zombies were all around me so I decided to bug out. There was a road sign in front of me so I crawled towards it, at least I'd know where I was. As I got closer I realized it was in Russian and I had no idea what it said. Of course, I berated myself, this is Chernarus - why would they have English road signs? Fuck this was going to be hard.

And then up ahead, further down the road, I saw him. Another guy just like me, he was in blue and had a cap on too. But he also had a gun. Great I was saved. Without thinking about the zombies I got up and ran towards the guy.

"Urrgghhhh!" straight away the zombies started to groan and chased me. Oh shit, I thought as I ran, screaming out to the guy to help me. I looked back and there were three zombies behind me, chasing me. The guy up ahead turned around and saw me running towards him, with my three zombies in tow.

As I got closer I saw that he had a shotgun on him. "Help," I called out as I ran to him. He raised the shotgun, pointing it at me. I didn't think, I just ran. The screams of the zombies behind me were terrifying. As I passed him he fired and I turned to watch one drop down dead. He back-peddled and shot the second who also fell down. Then he re-loaded the gun. I didn't know what to do so I just stood there and watched him as the last zombie ran towards us. The zombie reached out and struck me before it was put down by a head shot.

The Survivor then turned the shotgun to me and I froze. Fuck he's going to shoot me. "Hello" I said but he just looked at me, his grey beard told me he'd been here for a while. "Thanks," I said meekly as though that might save my life. We just stared at each other, I wished I could tell what he was thinking. This was the first person I'd seen in Chernarus and now he was about to kill me.

Then I heard the sound of the shotgun reloading and he ran past me and down the way I'd just come. I turned and contemplated whether I should follow him but I had the feeling I'd just been given a second chance and I shouldn't push it. "Thank you," I called out again but he didn't turn or acknowledge that he'd heard me, he just ran off.

Since I couldn't go back, I decided to keep going forward along the coast. As I ran I could see a lighthouse in front of me; great, that'll have something inside. As I got closer I could see there was an opening at the back and a ladder up. I looked on the floor but there wasn't anything there so I decided to climb up. Up on the top I had a great view all around but there wasn't anything up there either. *Fuck*, I thought, *this is really going to be hard*. I looked further up to see if there were any landmarks when I saw a new figure running down towards me.

"Heeellloooo," I called out as he got closer to the lighthouse. "Hi," he said in the unmistakable twang of a Kiwi. *Hurrah*, I thought, *finally someone who I could work with*. He ran into the lighthouse and started climbing up the stairs. "There's nothing up here," I called down.

"Oh I know," he yelled back as he climbed up the top of the lighthouse.

Then I watched in horror and he tried to jump off the light house, fortunately he was unable to leap over the railing.

"What are you doing?" I asked confused.

"Fucking Kemenka," he said as he finally managed to leap off the light house and to his doom.

I just looked down at his dead body lying there at the base of the lighthouse. *Well that was weird*, I thought as I climbed down. At the bottom I contemplated looting his body but it didn't feel right, this guy had just killed himself. So instead I continued along the coast looking for someone or something to help me out there.

MY FIRST TIME IN BALOTA

As I ran along the coast I saw the airfield up ahead. I'd heard about Balota from other Survivors, that it was a good place to gear up on the coast. I scanned the airfield with my binoculars. There were a couple of hangers and the ATC tower. Figuring the tower was the best bet, I crawled my way over there first.

As I got closer I noticed that the Zeds started coming out of the hangers and the tower. Where were they before? I had no idea. Up ahead I saw a ladder that led up to the second level. Slowly, I crawled towards it, turning constantly to watch the Zeds. I couldn't get over them. They were relentless, once they see you they just don't stop. I'd never felt this before, the absolute fear that they evoke.

I grabbed on to the ladder and climbed up to the roof. From here I could see far off in every direction. There weren't any Zeds inside, which I was thankful for. I creeped in and looked around. There were some extra loot items but I saw the AK-74 just lying there on the ground with two clips. I scooped it up and reloaded the gun; fuck yeah, I was ready.

I was so enthralled in having a gun, a real gun, for the first time I didn't notice the Survivor running up the stairs with a trail of Zeds behind him. When he got to the top and saw me he just freaked out and ran back down. I'm guessing the Zeds had him blocked in because he called out from below.

"Don't shoot man, I'm friendly."

"I'm not going to shoot you," I yelled back. This was the first time someone had been scared of me. I wanted to help this Survivor, let him know I was friendly.

He tentatively came up the stairs, peeking over to me.

"You sure man?" he asked.

"Look, I'm not going to kill you," I asserted back.

"Okay I'm coming up, there's lots of zombies behind me,"

"Don't worry, I'll take care of them," I said feeling all powerful with my new AK. He stood behind me and I started to pick off the Zeds as they came up the stairs. It wasn't too hard as they walked slowly and I managed to pop many of them with headshots. After a while they stopped coming in and I turned to my new friend.

"You don't have a weapon?" I asked him

"Nah man I'm just a fresh spawn."

I looked in my pack remembering the axe I'd found earlier.

"Here take this," I said as I dropped it on the ground. He picked it up and armed it before turning towards me. *Oh shit I just fucked up,* I thought as we just looked at each other, *he's going to kill me.*

"So now what?" he asked.

"Dunno." I replied.

"The military tent's usually have good shit, lets raid them."

"I saw the tents before but they were barbed wired shut," I explained.

"You can still get in, I'll show you how," he said and then we were off. We went down the ladder and went we hit the ground I dropped down to start crawling.

"You can just crouch run, they won't see you."

"You sure?" I asked.

"How long you been playing?"

"Couple of days, still new to all this"

"Oh man I'll show you around. Just don't shoot the gun anymore, I'll kill any zombies with the axe."

"Sure thing"

We ran down the short road to the guard station near the exit. I was following my new friend when I heard the unmistakable sound of Zed aggro. I looked back along the runway and there were two running straight towards us.

"Oh fuck," I said as I started shooting. That did it, that brought down the entire airfield onto us.

"Fuck man why'd you shoot?" he asked.

"Sorry I just panicked."

"Okay, get into the little guard house and wait there. I'll clear them out."

I watched as he started chopping at the Zeds, walking backwards to avoid their hits. He was doing well, taking them out, and he really knew how to handle himself with the axe.

And then one hit him. I'd seen others hit him but this one was super strong and knocked him down. He lay on the ground as the Zeds came up and started eating him.

"Are you okay?" I stupidly called out. He didn't answer.

Oh fuck he's dying, I can't let that happen, I thought as I watched the Zeds eat him. I stepped out of the doorway and started shooting at them. Firing erratically, I hit some but my shooting sucked. They turned towards me and I just held down the trigger and unloaded in them

They hit me, and hit me, while I shot at them. The AK-74 started dry firing and I panicked and ran. My vision was now grey and it was extremely hazy, I could barely see.

"Oh fuck I'm going to die again," I yelled out as the Zeds chased after me. I ran into the closest hangar and inside a shipping container. The Zeds followed me in so I reloaded and shot at them, taking another one down.

Fuck this, I thought as I ran out and back onto the runway. I almost ran into another Survivor coming from the next hangar. He had a gun and that's all I saw when I unloaded my whole new clip into him, pure panic coursing through my veins. The poor bastard never had a chance and dropped down dead. The sound of flies instantly indicating that I'd killed him.

I didn't have time to think or feel guilty - I just kept running. The Zeds continued to chase after me as I ran down the runway away from the hangers. Away from the guy I'd just killed. There was some recriminations towards me blasted in the side chat text but I didn't have time to look at them. I just ran with still more Zeds behind me.

Then I heard the crack of the sniper rifle but didn't see where it came from. It hit me with the first shot and I fell down dead.

FATHER TOM

I was running along the coast once again when I saw the man on the bike. He rode towards me and so I hid in the bushes, by now I'd learnt to be wary of all others.

"Don't be afraid," the man said as he got off the bike. He was carrying an AKM.

I still stayed hidden in the trees, hoping that he hadn't seen me, that he was talking to someone else.

"If you're worried about my gun you can have it," he said.

That piqued my interest and so I stepped out from the bush to see what the deal was. The man stood there near his bike with his AKM lowered.

"What's your name?"

"CJ."

"I'm Padre Tom, good to meet you CJ," he said and saluted. I saluted back still wary that this might be a trap. I checked the player list and there was a Father Tom among them.

"You don't look like a priest."

Father Tom laughed at that, "I suppose not. I travel the coast helping out new spawns. If you want the gun you can have it."

"Really?"

"Yes really. It's a good gun, one hit for the zombies. All yours if you want it."

"Okay," I said still trying to figure out the angle. He dropped the gun but kept the ammunition. I picked it up but I hadn't realized there weren't any bullets.

Father Tom watched me, I didn't know how to lower the gun so I just kept it pointed away from him.

"Thanks," I said. It seemed a feeble thing to say to this guy who had just given me the best gun I'd seen so far.

"Do you need anything else. Blood, morphine, drink?"

I shook my head, "No I'm fine."

"How about bullets for the gun?" he said cheekily.

I looked down and realized I didn't have any ammunition.

"Oh yeah that would probably help."

"I'm going to ride off down the road a bit and then leave them there for you. I hope you won't try to shoot me once you have them."

"Why would I do that?" I asked horrified.

"You'd be surprised CJ, the things I've seen men do. Take care and stay safe."

"Thanks Father Tom, you too."

He didn't say anything else as he rode his bicycle down the road. I watched him stop a little way along, bend down and drop the AKM magazines. He then got on the bicycle and rode away. He gave a friendly ring of the bike's bell as he rode off into the distance.

THE GIFT

I crept slowly into the barn, once again I was on the coast with nothing on me. It was a small clump of farm buildings but I'd learnt that barns could yield some great loot.

As I got closer I saw a man walk out, carrying a crossbow. He turned and faced me.

"There's an axe in there if you want it."

"Errr sure," I said. This was the first person who hadn't shot at me immediately today. I went into the barn half expecting to find his friends inside with shotguns ready. But what I found was the axe lying on the ground just like he'd said.

I snatched it up and armed it as I walked back out. The other guy watched me as I exited, wary of what I'd do next.

"Want to team up?" he asked me.

"Sure. But I don't really have anything except this axe, thanks to you."

"No prob, the next town across is Cherno. It's fucking crazy there - you don't want to go in there. We could go North, find some good shit in the inland towns."

"I've never been inland," I admitted.

"You haven't?"

"No, keep getting killed trying to gear up on the coast."

"That's where you're going wrong. Forget the coast, inland's where it's at. I'll show you. What's your name?"

"CJ."

"CJ I'm Leroy. Let's go."

And just like that we started running up the hill. Leroy pointed out the power lines as we ran under them.

"See these power lines. If you ever get lost and see power lines just follow them one way or the other, they always lead to a town eventually.

"Got it." It felt strange to be going inland, I'd been told it was dangerous by other Survivors. That you needed to be kitted up to play with the big boy bandits up north.

But as we cleared the hill and ran down the other side it seemed peaceful. There were birds chirping and the woods were calm. I saw a boar running through the trees near us. The tree line ended as a vast open field spread out before us. Leroy stopped and quickly scanned around.

"We should be safe, there's nothing really here."

"Sure," I said jotting down all of Leroy's advice in my mental notebook.

"Now up ahead there's a town called Mog. It's not a great town but it has a supermarket so we'll get you kitted out in there. Remember stay low and keep quiet around the zombies."

I saw the town up ahead. Unlike the ones on the coast this seemed more spread out. Leroy pointed out the Supermarket and all the infected that were roaming round. We crouch walked slowly towards them, Leroy with the crossbow and myself with the axe.

One Zed saw us and ran towards us. Leroy lined it up with the crossbow and when he was sure of the shot he took it down. The Zed fell down dead but all of the others didn't pay us any mind as the kill was silent.

"Damn Leroy, that's an awesome weapon!"

"Yeah it's pretty bad-ass. It's hard to shoot but once you learn it's great for killing zombies. And you haven't seen the best part yet."

Leroy walked up to the Zed he just killed and pulled out the bolt from its body.

"Unlimited ammo. Well not unlimited because sometimes they're hard to find, but usually you can get your bolt back.

That was it, I was hooked. Silent and with unlimited ammo, I had to get me one of those. We crept closer to Mog and more infected started coming out from the buildings. We moved slowly towards them but for some reason we weren't cautious enough and three more ran towards us.

"I won't be able to get all three," Leroy called, "you're going to have to axe some."

"Sure," I replied, confident in my axing skills.

Leroy took the closest one down and reloaded his crossbow. I stepped forward and swiped my axe at the second and it dropped immediately.

"Step back CJ I'll get the last one."

"It's fine mate I got it," I said swinging my axe. I missed it and it hit me, there was a god awful cracking sound. I fell down on my belly and the Zed kept hitting me until Leroy took it down.

I tried to stand up but couldn't. Every time I moved forward I kept falling down.

"Don't bother, you've got broken legs." said Leroy standing over me, "do you have morphine?"

I'd never heard of morphine in game before so I told him no.

"You're lucky I've got one. But dude never leave the coast without getting some morphine. The shit's hard to find inland."

He pressed the injector down on my broken bones and I was suddenly able to stand up again.

"Thanks Leroy," I said and he looted the bodies.

"Don't sweat it," and he continued into town.

As we got closer a group of infected suddenly decided to chase after us. I don't know if we were just unlucky or we were making too much noise but now we had a bunch on us. Leroy ran off yelling that we should get inside a building. I tried following him but the Zeds were all around me and I'd lost him in the town.

Then I saw all the Zeds slowly walking into a building and heard that horrible sound again. The cracking of bones.

"Leroy are you alright?"

"Fuck man Mike Tyson here just broke my legs."

"Are you in that house, I'll help?"

"No I'm a goner, I gave you my last morphine, so I won't be able to walk. Get to the supermarket and save yourself."

"Fuck that man, you helped me, I'm not letting you die out here."

I ran up to the house where I could see the Zeds and just started hacking away at them. They were dropping to the ground and then I saw more coming up behind me. I could see Leroy lying on the ground inside. I let the Zeds behind me hit me as I focused on killing the ones between us.

"I'm out of ammo CJ."

"It's cool I'll axe these fuckers," I replied as I swung away at them. My vision started getting blurry and then I fell down, unconscious. The timer was slowly dropping as everything became more grey and blurry.

I could hear Leroy calling out but I wasn't able to say anything back. I heard him crawling closer to me and then the sounds of flies started, he was dead.

Fuck Leroy I'm sorry, I thought as I watched the Zeds chow down on me.

MY FIRST (AND ONLY) MURDER

I feel like absolute shit, I am a killer, I just murdered someone for no other reason than to murder someone. I look down at his body now and wonder what it was that possessed me. Why did I kill this man? No not man, survivor, just like me.

It started when I found myself in Kemenka. I knew by now that it wasn't worth staying on the coast anymore and the road north led to Zeleno. So that was my plan, I stopped along the way at the deer stands and was surprised to find they were empty.

At the first empty deer stand I just thought it was strange. At the second empty deer stand I was confused. By the time I found the third one empty, I was paranoid. There was definitely someone else nearby, but this time it was different. I had a map, I knew he'd be heading to Zeleno too. I decided to leave the next two deer stands for him and head to the barn just south of town.

I guess I was sick of it. Of all the bandits, of all the times I'd been killed. That frustration had welled up inside me and now I had a chance to take it out on someone. I would kill a man in cold blood, get my own taste of the bandit life. This thief, this person who was raiding *my* deer stands, he would feel my wrath.

I had a crossbow on me and although I'd never used it on another person I was formidable with it against Zeds. My plan was beautiful in both its simplicity and naivety. I would wait for him in the barn, he was sure to come here. It was an easy last stop before hitting town and allowed him to look down in Zeleno.

When he came in I would be ready, crossbow lined up at the entrance. As soon as I saw him I'd kill him. No calling out 'friendly', no hesitation, just straight-out murder. This would be my chance to dish out what had been handed to me constantly for the past couple of days. I kept the crossbow pointed at the entrance that faced away from Zeleno, certain this would be the one he would use.

My hands were sweating and I started to doubt myself. I started to hesitate about this so called plan. *What if he skips the barn? What if he isn't heading to Zeleno at all? What if there's more than one of them?* I didn't know if I was trying to talk myself out of it or I was just scared, but the minutes felt like an eternity.

Then I heard it, a cheery voice call out from outside. "Is there anyone in the barn?" I didn't reply, I just kept my crossbow trained on the doorway.

"Look if anyone's in there I'm coming in. I have an AK and I'm friendly." *Yeah sure,* I thought, *I'm not falling for that again.* I watched at the door fully intending on shooting him as soon as he came in. I was so focused on the door I didn't see or hear him walk in through the other door.

He took one look at me and trained the AK-74 on me.

"Hey man, what are you doing? I said I'm friendly. You won't be able to kill me with that crossbow."

I turned my head and saw him inside the barn pointing the AK-74 right at me. *Fuck! Now what?*

"Look man I'm sorry. I didn't know what was happening and I was just freaked out," I lied to him.

"Are you new?" he asked.

"Yeah I'm new, sorry," I replied.

"It cool. Everyone starts out new. Look we're close to Zeleno, I'll take you there and get you set up."

I looked him over. He was definitely a veteran of the apocalypse, his pack was green and large, his AK had a Kobra sight, and he was the right amount of wary and friendly towards me. This man had seen more shit than I ever would.

Then the thought creeped into my head. You can have that too, you can be kitted up like him. All you need to do is kill him. At first it was just a little idea, easy to repress. But every time I pushed it down it came back up for air with more ferocity, gnawing at me as we both walked along the concrete wall that surrounded the Zeleno market car park.

He was telling me all about the safest way to raid the town but I had tuned him out. All I was thinking about was killing him and taking his stuff. Then as he got to the end of the wall he dropped down on his belly and started to crawl.

Everything became slow motion at that point. There were a few Zeds in the area at the back of the store and he was more focused on them than me. He now trusted me and I was about to take advantage of that. I lined him up, this kind man who only wanted to help me, and with his head in my sights I squeezed the trigger.

The crossbow bolt embedded straight into his head and he died instantly. There was no marking of the moment, apart from the sounds of flies. No one was around to witness my betrayal, even the nearby Zeds were uninterested and kept roaming. I looked around and realized it was easy. Easy and selfish. Easy and stupid. Easy and wrong. I was the biggest douchebag in the world.

I didn't know what to do. His body lay there, his eyes accusing me. I couldn't stand it. Why did I feel so guilty when this was what I'd planned to do? I couldn't understand it but once the shock wore off the guilt hit me like a freight train. I left him there and ran off into the woods. I didn't even take the shit that I had earlier felt so entitled to that I murdered him for it. I just left him there and ran into the woods.

ABOUT THE AUTHOR

Cherno Journo is a writer who has braved the chaos and bandits of DayZ to record the stories of the players. More than just a game, DayZ has evoked real emotions from virtual actions: guilt from murder, anger at being betrayed, and the sense of camaraderie that can form when a group of strangers band together to achieve a common goal.

You can see him in action so to speak at
http://www.youtube.com/user/ChernoJourno